The Prostitute's Daughter

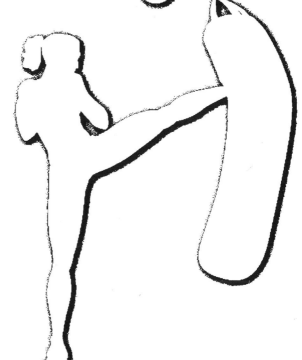

Adrienne D'nelle Ruvalcaba

THE PROSTITUTE'S DAUGHTER

Cover design by Heather Smith

ISBN: 978-0985467210

Printed in the United States of America.

Dedication

The Prostitute's Daughter is dedicated to all the amazing women who have experienced hardships in their lives and found the courage to love despite the pain.

Acknowledgements

Thanks to the following friends and family who gave encouragement and emotional support during the lengthy writing and editing process: Crystal Phillips, Vanessa Walker, Kelley Hessian, Megan Lara, Karla Blair, Mekisha Jones, Captain Maggie Barnes, Sergeant Cathirie Jones, and Marisa Winegar. You are *extraordinary* women, and I hope this story does credit to the inspiration and insights I received from you all.

*Trigger warning: This book contains detailed portrayals of the emotional aftermath survivors of sexual assault and physical abuse experience as they strive toward healing. There are *no* graphic descriptions of sexual assault.

Prologue

The poetic justice of the situation was not lost on him as he stared at her beautiful, serene face. The day he truly knew what it meant to love both completely and unconditionally happened to coincide with the day he truly knew what it meant to lose everything.

A silent tear escaped his eye as he looked down at her face again. She appeared to be sleeping, and at peace, but he knew that her soul was anything but peaceful right now. Yes, today was the first time in his life that he'd ever truly felt the all-consuming power of love, and of loss.

He reached out a trembling hand and touched her smooth cheek. Her eyes remained closed as he'd known they would, yet the absence of her warmth was still startling to his raw senses. The cold, waxy cheek, that just three days ago had been supple and warm, brought home the reality as almost nothing else could. Before he'd touched her, he could have gone on telling himself that she was just sleeping. Today, he truly knew what it meant to love... and to lose.

He wasn't ready to let her go, and a sudden, overwhelming need to climb into the casket with her and sleep for eternity threatened to overtake him. His life was over anyway, so why not join her? He contemplated it for a crazed moment that stretched into near infinity, but then the gentle whisper of his love for her brought him back to the edge of his sanity. She would want him to make it right somehow, and he couldn't make it right if he was dead.

A fellow mourner squeezed his shoulder in a show of support, and his single tear gave way to a torrent. Grief came up to smite him with a forceful blow that left him weak, breathless, in pain, and unable to speak coherently or stand without support. Violent sobs came from the nothingness within him and brought him down to his knees. He felt the side of her cool, silver casket against his forehead, and he heard his own strained voice, fraught with anguish, and somehow detached from his body and his control.

"They can't get away with what they did to you."

When he finally regained control of his voice, his tears transformed yet again. The torrential sobs slowly became gentle keening sounds as he clung to the casket. Someone was telling him that it was okay to let go, but they didn't know that it wasn't okay, that it would never be okay. Eventually numerous people surrounded him with their useless platitudes and their ubiquitous, overly helpful hands.

PART
I

Chapter 1

"It's kind of slow around here for a Friday night," Shane Gregory's longtime friend, Augustus, said to him. The two were on duty at the fire station, and there hadn't been one call all evening. Nashville, Tennessee, wasn't exactly a hotbed of fires and accidents, but usually they would have responded to at least one call by 8pm on a Friday night.

"Maybe people are finally taking all those public safety announcements seriously," quipped Shane, around a mouthful of his Kung Pau chicken.

"Yeah, right," Gus said. "Rush-hour wasn't so bad today, but just wait until all the drunks take the wheel later tonight."

Shane grunted in agreement as he continued shoveling food into his mouth. For the past five Fridays in a row, his dinner had been interrupted by an emergency call, and he was determined to finish tonight.

Gus eyed him with amusement in his bright green gaze.

"And for Pete sake, close your damn mouth when you eat, man! You need a woman to teach you some manners," Gus said as he watched Shane eat.

Gus was the only man Shane would take such admonishments from. The two had known each other since college, and Shane had been the best man at Gus's wedding ten years ago.

Shane swallowed and said, "Magda doesn't seem to mind the way I eat."

"That's because she's never seen you in your natural habitat," Gus laughed. Shane was a constant fixture at Gus and Magda's dinner table, and he did have impeccable manners when it counted. When there were no women around, however, Shane was very much a man's man.

Shane was too busy shoveling food to respond to Gus's comment. He really didn't want to have to leave his dinner again, so he continued eating at his insane pace.

"Animal," Gus muttered as he got up from the table.

Shane's spoon was laden with the last bite and poised halfway between his mouth and his plate when the alarm sounded.

Shane was suddenly all business as he and the other firefighters quickly donned their turnout gear and took their places on the screaming fire truck. There hadn't been an apartment fire in their area in some time, and the call that had just come in was for an address that Shane was already familiar with. It was an older, ten story building.

Gus and Shane were on the company's advanced search and rescue team. The two of them had been firefighters in New York City for a number of years before Gus decided to relocate to Nashville. Shane relocated years later, because he was originally from Tennessee, and life in New York had quickly grown stale for him without his good friend. Now, they were two of the best veteran fire fighters on the Nashville force. They were a perfect pair when it came to dragging people from burning buildings. Gus was big, burly, and built very much like an ox. He also had the tenacity to take on an enraged bull if the situation called for it. Shane was a slightly less bulky man, but at 6'6" he was just as solid and intimidating as his search and rescue partner. Other firefighters in the company often joked that the two of them could probably pack a herd of horses out of a burning barn if they had to.

"Looks like we got a doozie," Captain Shipman said as they arrived at the site and prepared to enter the building.

The first hose team had already hooked up and was advancing the line directly to the fire floor. Shane and Gus donned their masks and did a quick radio check before going in. Shane looked up at the building, and a strong sense of dread hit him when he saw the burned out windows of the apartments on the fourth and fifth floors. He and Gus would take the fifth floor, the floor directly above the fire, the floor with the greatest risk of death or injury.

It was something that they'd done many times before, in both New York and Nashville. They were the best in their company. With over 30 years of combined experience, and enough muscle to move mountains, they were expected to be the best and they loved living up to their reputation. This time, however, things were different. This was the first time Shane had ever run into a burning building where someone he knew was in the kill zone.

He charged up the stairs, taking them three at a time, until he reached the fifth floor. The first search and rescue team stopped at the fourth floor to search the apartments for people needing assistance. The hose team suppressed the fire on the fourth floor as the rescue teams began the meticulous search through all the apartments. They checked each apartment thoroughly, looking in cabinets and pantries, under beds, and in closets as they called out to people who might be trapped somewhere. Shane and Gus were the only two to advance into the uncertainty of the fifth floor.

Shane tried to tamp down his desperation to get to her. He had to do his job with a clear head. The smoke filled hallway was almost clear of people. Most had gotten out before the firefighters ever arrived, but they still had to quickly sweep the floor for trapped tenants. They carried out one elderly couple who were then whisked away to the hospital to be treated for serious smoke inhalation. The moments that it took to get back to the search were agonizing for Shane. His youngest brother would never forgive him if he let his wife's mother die in the fire. *Please just let her be alive*, Shane prayed as he approached her apartment.

She lived in the apartment at the end of the hall, the one farthest from the stairs. The apartment next to it had been completely blown out. Some sort of explosion had taken out the floor the ceiling and wall between the two apartments. There was one charred body in a twisted, grotesque position halfway through the wall of the two apartments. Shane approached, but it was apparent that the person was beyond help. He couldn't tell if it was a man or a woman.

"Shane!" Captain Shipman called on the radio. "What is your location?"

"I'm on the alpha side of floor five," Shane answered.

"Good. Dispatch has a victim on the phone. A woman trapped in the bathroom of 525."

Intense relief washed over Shane. He turned away from the unfortunate person in the wall and quickly entered her apartment. With the wall blasted out, and everything inside either flaming or charred black, it was hard to believe that she was in the bathroom on the phone. How could anyone be alive in here? The superheated air alone was enough to kill most people.

The evening of the fire started out on a peaceful note. Cece had just wrapped up one of the most important cake orders she'd ever received. The mayor's daughter, a young lady named Lynette Reid, was getting married in the middle of the summer, and Cece Graves had been honored with the task of making her wedding cake. It would be her first society wedding, and was certain to be a boon to her small bakery.

She was soaking in her tub, head back, eyes closed and lips curled up in a rare smile, when she felt the explosion. First disbelief, then dread assailed her. She froze and listened in expectant horror. When the second set of explosions shook her apartment and confirmed her fears, she got out of the tub and reached for her bathrobe. She opened the bathroom door, and looked down the hall to see the entire front half of her apartment on fire. Her living room wall was nearly completely blown out, and there appeared to be someone calling out for help.

She advanced toward the moans coming from the front room, and saw her neighbor sprawled half in her apartment and half in his. His clothes flamed, and as she looked, another explosion drove her back. She dashed back to her bathroom and grabbed her cell phone off the counter.

"911, what is your emergency?" a calm, female voice asked.

"There's an apartment fire, and some explosions coming from next door. Everything is on fire, and I can't get out. I'm in my bathroom." Cece then panted her address out in a rush of adrenaline.

"Ma'am, you need to find an exit. Is there a fire escape, or an alternate exit from your apartment?" the dispatcher asked.

"It's on fire!" Cece said in a shaking voice. "Something over there keeps exploding! What should I do?"

"The fire crew is on the way, ma'am. Are you still in the bathroom?"

"Yes!"

"Good. Can you open the window?"

"Oh God! Oh God, oh God, oh God."

"Ma'am, I'm going to need you to stay with me."

"There's no window," Cece choked out in a coarse, horrified whisper. "I'm going to die in here."

"Listen carefully, ma'am. Firefighters are on the way. You need to do exactly as I say until they get there."

"Okay," Cece said with a few deep breaths. She had to fight panic as smoke started seeping over the top of her door. Her power went out, and she could only see a limited area with the eerie, blue glow from her cell phone display.

"Turn on the water, and wet a towel. Do you have a towel?"

"Yes. I have a closet full of them."

"Good. Put one wet towel under the door and another one over the top. You want to keep as much smoke out as you can until they get to you. Use another wet towel to wrap around your face. Only breathe the air through the towel, and stay as low as you can. Do *not* breathe in the smoky air."

"Okay, I can do that," Cece panted. Terror had dried her throat and sapped her of her strength, but she still did as the dispatcher instructed.

"Good," the woman said in a falsely soothing voice. "Now leave the water running, and put as much water as you can on the walls around you, the door, and the floor. Use it to keep the fire out of the bathroom, and stay low."

The woman continued to talk to Cece and tell her that help was on the way, but Cece's hope of rescue deteriorated as the fire closed in on her tiny bathroom. Eventually, the water started making a hissing sound when it hit the hot walls and door. Smoke and flames licked at the top of the door and the ceiling, and the temperature in the bathroom steadily rose. Breathing through the wet towel was harder than it had first seemed, and Cece almost panicked several times while talking to the dispatcher. The tub was full to overflowing, and the water was still running onto the floor.

"I can't! I can't! Oh God help me!" Cece said into her phone as she looked up and saw the ceiling catching fire. The fire must be above her, and at any moment it would come crashing down to kill her. Smoke was filling the room, and the temperature still kept rising. In desperation, she flung water up at the ceiling, but all it did was hiss and pop and quickly become steam.

"I'm going to die," she whimpered into the phone with finality just before she plunged herself into the tub. The water coming from the tap was still cool enough to keep her from overheating. Every few seconds, she raised her head out of the water and took a breath through the soaked towel as the water continued to run. She wasn't sure why she wished to cling to life when it seemed that a ghastly death was certain. Perhaps it would be better if she just breathed in the water and let herself drown. Drowning had to be less painful than burning to death.

Just as she was about to take in a painful lungful of water, she felt a pair of rough, gloved hands yank her from her imaginary safe haven. Her eyes flew open, and the nightmarish sight before her caused the panic she'd fought so hard against to take over for a split second. She saw a huge, imposing masked shadow over the backdrop of a ceiling that was alive with undulating flames. It looked so much like what she'd imagined hell itself must be like. She was yanked into a world of intense heat, crackling wood and shattering glass, and slung roughly over the shoulder of the demon that seemed determined to carry her to the underworld.

"Don't breathe! And wrap that towel around your head!" the demon shouted above the roar of the fire and the rescue sirens. It had a deep, gravelly voice and a strong grip around her legs.

She quickly complied, and moments later it seemed like she was flying past all the smoke and flames and into a cooler environment. She couldn't see anything, because her face was shrouded in her wet towel, but she did realize that the demon was actually a fireman. She clung to him for her life.

"Shane, what's your status?" a voice on the radio asked.

The fireman answered, "525 is alive and on the way out."

"Listen, we got ladders to evac the seventh floor, and there are some rescue teams from another company helping out up there. Clear the fifth floor, and you and Gus get out of there," the captain commanded.

"It's clear. We did it before the call about 525," Gus answered, because Shane was busy trying to get to the stairwell with Cece.

The hose team fought the flames near the front of the hall as Gus and Shane approached the stairwell. It seemed as if the monster was to be contained soon... on this floor anyway.

Shane carried the soaking wet Cece down to the third floor before it finally occurred to him that she could probably walk on her own. He stopped in the middle of the stairwell, and gently set her down.

"You're lucky you didn't cook yourself in that tub of water back there," he chastised her immediately. He'd seen more than a few people who'd tried the same thing end up dead before the search and rescue team could reach them.

Cece didn't respond. She just pulled her sodden bathrobe tighter around her body.

When she finally did look up at him with red, tear-filled eyes, she still didn't say anything; she frowned, turned away, and walked the rest of the way down the stairs to the paramedics.

Shane watched her for a moment, and tried to dispel the uncomfortable memory of their first meeting a few years ago. She didn't remember that meeting, because she'd been busy trying to drag herself across the hospital floor to get away from some imaginary phantom from her past. Over the past few years, he hadn't been able to get that moment out of his mind. When she looked at him tonight, making eye contact through his mask, he'd been struck hard by the same sense of mystery that had gripped him during his visit to her hospital room. It was obvious that she didn't recognize him, but then again he hadn't expected her to. After all, they'd never actually been introduced. She probably didn't know he existed.

Gus caught up to him on the stairs while he was still standing there contemplating whether or not he should follow her and introduce himself properly. He had almost done so a number of times over the past three years, but in the end, the memory of his first sight of her lying broken and paralyzed in the hospital always stopped him. What excuse could he have for wanting to meet her? According to her daughter, she had an intense need to be left alone by everyone, especially men. He could respect that need.

"What the hell was that all about?" Gus demanded.

They walked down the stairs past the hose team, and Shane remained silent.

"Well?" Gus persisted.

"What?" Shane finally said.

"I've never seen you move like that. You could have been killed going in there to get her, and you didn't even slow down. You saw it was sagging and structurally unsound. Why did you go in there anyway? You're lucky it went down after you grabbed her instead of while you were grabbing her."

Shane looked at his good friend and said simply, "I know her. She's family." Gus was right; it had been a close call. A split second after he'd seen her in the tub, half of the ceiling had collapsed in front of the door and it took part of the floor with it on the way down. The weight of the tub full of water, Cece, and himself had all combined to cause the remainder of the floor to sag towards the gaping hole. It felt like his only option at the time had been to grab her and jump across the hole before the rest of the floor went down. If Gus hadn't been right there to give him a hand when he stumbled upon landing, he might very well be dead right now.

"We've got a major collapse on the alpha side of four, five and six. If you're still in that area get outta there!" Captain Shipman was saying over the radio. "I repeat, major collapse on the alpha side of four, five and six!"

The primary search and rescue on all the floors was now complete, and every rescue team, with the exception of Shane and Gus, had retreated from the burning building.

"We're heading out the front door of the building right now, Captain," Gus said into his radio.

Less than a minute later, they were standing near the commander, watching as multiple hose teams suppressed the raging fire.

"Helluva job, guys," he said to all the search and rescue teams. Shane and Gus had found a total of ten people on the fifth floor in need of rescue. Of those ten, only Cece had been in the kill zone. The other tenants on the opposite side of the floor had been far enough away from the fire to not have to worry about the flames, but there was heavy smoke damage to their units.

"Take a rest. Can't have my best guys overheating," Captain Shipman said to them.

"Take your mask off, man; you're scaring people," Gus said to Shane.

Shane had been so lost in thought he hadn't removed his mask. Maybe that's why Cece hadn't recognized him. He removed it, conscious of the fact that his face was probably dripping with sweat and beet red from the heat and exertion of running through a burning building. The night air on his face felt good. He closed his eyes for a moment, and wiped some of the sweat off with the back of his forearm.

"So, how do you know 525? She doesn't exactly look like she could be related to you," Gus asked.

"You remember my younger brother Norman? He's the one who got remarried about four years ago. 525 is his wife's mother," Shane answered.

"Are you kidding me?" Gus said in disbelief as he stared at someone off in the distance.

Shane followed his gaze, and caught sight of Cece standing near the paramedics watching the fire. She was still clutching her bathrobe and looking very much like a little deer in the headlights.

"No kidding," Shane said. They both stared at her as she stared at the fire.

"I have a mother-in-law, but she doesn't look anything like that," Gus said with a touch of awe in his voice.

"Hey, man, don't ogle her like that," Shane said.

"Why not? Everyone else is."

Shane looked around, and saw that Gus was right. Other guys from the primary search and rescue teams were getting an eyeful as well. Even some of the male fire victims were staring at her rather than at the destruction of their own property.

"She doesn't like to be stared at," Shane gritted out. He grabbed a gray blanket from one of the paramedics, and approached Cece with it.

"Cecilia, you look like you could use this," Shane said as he walked up to her and draped the blanket around her shoulders. Her hair was still damp, and her bathrobe clung to her in a very revealing way.

"How do you know my name?" she asked as she looked up at him.

Her brown eyes bored into his midnight blue ones, and he felt it again. Why did this woman have the power to tie his tongue in knots?

"My brother," Shane stammered out as she continued to stare up at him. She dropped her gaze, and suddenly he could think again. "I'm Norman's brother," he finally said.

"Oh. So, you're related to that Neanderthal my daughter married."

"Yeah," Shane said.

"That explains why I feel like I've seen you before."

"Yeah," Shane said again.

"Is everyone in your family so tall?" she asked.

"Yeah." *Why couldn't he think of another word?* "Have you been evaluated by the medics? Smoke inhalation is deadly if not treated."

"I have," she answered. "It's a good thing I had that wet towel, they said that everything looked good after they checked my nose and throat."

"Good. You sound fine, and you aren't coughing. Those are both very good signs," Shane said. She hadn't looked up at him again, but he saw her shoulders slump slightly when she looked back at the burning building.

"Do you have somewhere to go?" he asked gently.

She straightened her posture and looked up at him again. "I can stay with my daughter for the night," she said quietly, dismissively.

"Just let me know if you need anything." He was about to turn and walk back towards Gus, when her hand on his arm stopped him.

"Do you know which fireman is the one who got me out? I'd like to thank him properly. I was too rattled earlier to do so," she said with quiet vulnerability in her voice.

Shane felt a furious blush creeping up his neck as he said, "It was me."

She looked up at him again with tears in her eyes. They were the most subtle, unshed tears he'd ever seen, and she blinked them away so quickly he questioned whether they'd been there in the first place. "I thought I was going to die in there. Thank you so much," she said at last.

Chapter 2

Shane didn't wake up until almost two o'clock the next afternoon. The fire had smoldered on until almost dawn, and he had been so exhausted he'd gone to sleep on his couch almost as soon as he'd walked in his front door. The preliminary investigation into the cause of the fire had turned up a number of home oxygen tanks in the apartment next to Cecilia's. Her neighbor, an older gentleman with breathing problems, had been on oxygen for years now. How so many full tanks got into his apartment was under investigation, and the preliminary report indicated suspected arson. Oxygen fires were usually deadly, because they burned so hot and fast. Last night's fire had been no exception; ten people had died, and five had been hospitalized. Shane was still amazed that Cecilia had survived unscathed.

Once Cecilia entered his mind, he knew he was going to drive to his brother's house to check on her, but he needed to shower and shave first. When he'd talked to her last night, he'd been sooty, sweaty, and hairy. That wasn't exactly the impression he wanted to leave her with. Halfway through his grooming, he suddenly asked himself why it even mattered what Cecilia thought of him. He looked at his reflection, but his reflection didn't have the answer.

He probably knew a lot more about Cecilia than she would want, and none of it was firsthand knowledge. Rebecca had unwittingly been Shane's fount of information about her mother; the only thing he had learned from Cecilia herself was that she really didn't want to be hurt again. His first sight of her replayed in his head again as he dressed for dinner. She'd been lying in the hospital bed, temporarily paralyzed from the waist down from her injury. He'd just wanted to bring her some flowers, but she'd panicked and fell out of bed. He'd rushed forward to help her, and she'd whispered in a horrified voice, "Please don't hurt me." That moment had stayed with him for the past three years, leaving little trails of swirling mystery that he wanted to unlock.

He left his house around 4pm, and the drive to Norman and Rebecca's house took almost an hour. Shane enjoyed the unusually mild spring weather they'd been having lately. Typically, this time of year produced lots of strong thunderstorms in the region, but this month had been an exception to the norm. There was a cool breeze rustling through the new leaves and blossoms on all the trees as Shane drove up the long, windy private road that lead to his brother's house. From the front view, it wasn't apparent just how substantial the property actually was. One had to drive around to the garage entrance on the side to get the full effect of its massive size. Shane didn't drive around to the side; he just parked his Jeep in the front of the house and got out.

He rang the doorbell several times before Rebecca finally answered the door.

"Shane!" she greeted him with a bright smile.

"Hey, little sis. Am I too late for dinner?" he joked.

"Not at all," she said as she let him in. "Norman is grilling some steaks; I'll just tell him to throw one on for you."

Shane followed Rebecca through the kitchen and out to the patio to find Norman seated on one of the padded wicker sofas. When Rebecca approached, he opened his arms to her, and she sat down practically on his lap as she embraced him. After four years of marriage, they were still all over each other every chance they got, and it seemed to be a good thing. Some might consider them an odd couple, but Shane thought they looked good together. At 6'5", Norman towered over his 5'2" wife. They were complete opposites in looks as well. She was a very reserved and gentle African American woman, who worked as a therapist to troubled children, and Norman was the quintessential military man, all hard angles, stern features, and discipline.

Shane cleared his throat, but they ignored him for the most part. Cecilia wasn't anywhere in sight, but he didn't want to start the evening off by asking about her. He didn't want to be that obvious about why he came. He cleared his throat again.

"What brings you here on a Saturday night? Don't you usually have some hot date?" Norman asked.

"Do I need a reason to hang out with family?" Shane smiled.

"No one else does, but you do. It's been nearly a month since the last time I saw you. How have you been? Any big changes on the horizon?" Norman said. His arm was still wrapped around Rebecca as he spoke.

"I've decided to sell the florist shop. I don't really have the time for it anymore now that I'm working as a firefighter again," Shane answered.

"Speaking of fires," Rebecca said as she sat forward. "Did you hear about the one in Nashville last night? My mom's building almost burned down. She said she was trapped in her bathroom, and some fireman had to get her out. It was all over the news this morning."

"He's the fireman who got me out," Cece said from the doorway. Her low, quiet voice commanded their immediate attention.

"Why didn't you mention that when you got here last night?" Rebecca asked.

Cecilia merely shrugged and made her way to one of the many chairs strewn about the patio. "I don't know," she said after she sat down.

Cecilia felt the same uncomfortable silence that always descended on them as soon as she appeared. Maybe she should have stayed in her room. Norman looked uncomfortable, and Rebecca looked concerned. That's usually what happened when she was around.

"Have you thought anymore about staying here until you find another place?" Rebecca asked.

Cece shot an uncomfortable look at her daughter before answering, "I told you I can't. I'd have to get up at two a.m. every morning just to get to work on time. I'll be fine."

"We'd love to have you stay," Norman chimed in after his wife's subtle poke in the ribs. "You lost everything, and we're all family here. We want to help."

Cece cast Norman one of those looks that reminded him why he always felt so uncomfortable around her. He closed his mouth, gave Rebecca the "I told you so" look, and got up to check the steaks. The table was only set for three, so Rebecca went inside to get some dishes and silverware for Shane.

Shane looked at Cecilia as she sat distanced from everyone else. She'd chosen the chair that was farthest from him, and she didn't look like she wanted to be bothered. Her gaze was fixed on the wood line at the edge of the lawn, and she seemed to be a million miles away. She was wearing one of her daughter's dresses. The two women were almost the same size, but Cecilia was taller than Rebecca. That fact made it impractical for them to share the same pants, but the dress looked amazing on her.

An image of Cecilia standing in her bathrobe suddenly came to his mind as he watched her cross her legs and tug slightly at the dress. She looked down at her feet momentarily, and when she looked up again their eyes met. She then quickly looked back at her feet.

He was trying to think of something to say when Rebecca returned. They all gathered at the table for dinner, and Norman and Rebecca kept the conversation centered on politics and the weather. Cece remained silent for the most part. She was probably contemplating the loss of almost everything she'd work so hard for. Shane knew a thing or two about losing everything. He knew how she felt, and he also knew that it would get better.

Dinner was winding down when Shane blurted out on impulse, "You know, you could stay at my house."

Suddenly, he had three pairs of very surprised eyes staring him down.

"I'm hardly ever there. I spend so much time at the training academy and the fire station. You're welcome to use it until you find another place," he continued.

"That's a great idea!" Rebecca said enthusiastically.

"Yeah, it's even in the same part of town as the bakery. She wouldn't have to drive too far at all," Norman added.

"Well, I'm glad that's all settled," Rebecca smiled.

"Well, it's not settled yet..." Shane looked at Cecilia. "What do you think?" he asked quietly.

"You sure you don't mind me using your house?" Cece asked.

"I'm sure."

"I guess it's settled then. Thank you," Cece said as she stood up. "I'm sorry to leave you guys so soon, but I have a headache. Dinner was great."

Shane stood up too and said, "I'll walk you inside. I should give you the address and the key so you can let yourself in tomorrow. I probably won't be there."

Norman and Rebecca looked relieved to be left alone. Cece couldn't blame them; she knew that her presence made most people uncomfortable. She just smiled politely and made her way back to the guest room.

Shane followed her without saying a word until she got to her door.

"Here is the spare key," he said as he reached into his pocket.

Cece's words stopped him, "I'm not really going to stay with you. I just don't want my daughter to worry about me. She worries too much." She then stepped inside the room and closed the door. Conversation over.

Shane stared at the closed door for a few moments before making his way back outside to the patio to say goodnight to Norman and Rebecca.

 Chapter 3

Cece went back to work early Monday morning. She'd lost everything in the fire, and the only way she knew how to deal with loss was by working harder. That very work ethic was the reason she owned the bakery in the first place. When she'd first arrived in Nashville, pregnant, lost and broken, she'd had no skills and very little education. The only thing she'd had in her favor was an uncanny amount of determination to make something of herself.

She'd landed in a homeless shelter run by a local church. She could still vividly recall her first night there. She'd filled out lots of paperwork about who she was; all of it had been lies. She'd had no one and nothing at the time, and she knew the streets of the city were no place for a 13 year old girl.

Mrs. Lee had been on the board of directors for the homeless shelter at the time, and she'd been there the night Cece arrived. Her baby bump had been barely visible, but Mrs. Lee had noticed it. She had been the only one to notice.

Shortly after Cece was given a private room to sleep in, Mrs. Lee had come to her door. She'd given her a business card for a local bakery and said, "You be there four o'clock Monday."

When Monday rolled around, Cece spent the day worrying about the future, and getting ready for her four o'clock appointment with the miniscule Chinese lady who had slipped her the business card. Finding the bakery hadn't been a problem, because it was right up the road from the church where the homeless shelter was located. Cece was early, so she hung around outside until 3:45. Eventually, Mrs. Lee came to the door.

"I said four o'clock!" she yelled out at Cece.

Startled, Cece said back, "I'm sorry I'm early. I'll come back in fifteen minutes."

"No early! You late! I said four o'clock," Mrs. Lee shouted again.

"Did you mean four in the morning?" Cece asked, stunned. Who the hell started working at four in the morning?

"Yes! You want job, you be here. Four o'clock," Mrs. Lee said and then she harrumphed her way back inside.

Cece stood outside cursing herself for the missed opportunity and wondering if there was anything she could say or do for another chance. She crossed in front of the large front window, trying to work up the nerve to go in, when Mrs. Lee appeared at the door again.

"You gonna come in and get busy, or you gonna dance around out there all afternoon?" she shouted.

Cece immediately followed her in. It had been her first time in a bakery in her entire life. Nothing in her experience in the slums of Atlanta had prepared her for her first glimpse of the bake shop. The floor was covered in plain, pale gray tiles and there were a few tables and booths for people who wished to eat their sweets right away. The walls were a pretty, pastel pink with little murals of all kinds of sweets painted on them. There was one portrait of a wedding cake that caught Cece's eye right away. It looked like something straight out of a fairytale. The display cases in front were loaded with small decorated cakes, cookies, brownies, and other confections. The entire shop enchanted Cece so completely that she almost forgot for a moment that she was 13, pregnant, and alone in the world.

"I get to work here?" Cece breathed in wonder as Mrs. Lee watched her with the same ferocious frown.

"Yes! You want job, you be here four o'clock. Every day," she said. She turned toward the kitchen and motioned for Cece to follow her.

The back wasn't nearly as enchanting as the front had been; in fact, it wasn't enchanting at all. Mrs. Lee pointed to the many dishes that filled the sinks, and led Cece to a cleaning closet filled with supplies. Cece took the hint, and started cleaning. Thus began her two decade relationship with Mrs. Lee, a relationship that ended with Mrs. Lee's death and Cece's inheritance of everything Mrs. Lee owned, including the money she'd invested over the years, the bakery, and her old clunker of a car. These days, when Cece looked at her bank balance, she felt a slight sense of panic over the amount of money at her disposal. It was money that she often had no idea what to do with. She had every material possession she could imagine wanting or needing, but the one thing that she'd longed for since her childhood couldn't be bought for any amount of money.

Cece shook herself out of her reverie and got to work on several cake orders that were to be picked up that day. She may have started out knowing nothing but how to scrub the floors, but now she was one of the best cake decorators in town. It was a shame that nobody knew it yet, but with the mayor's daughter's wedding that would soon change.

She was behind the counter, working on the butter cream frosting for a little girl's princess cake, when the bell attached to the door jingled. She went to the front to help the customer, but there was nobody there. She thought nothing of it and went back to work.

The mayor's daughter was supposed to come by and approve Cece's sketch for her wedding cake. She'd been very vague in her description of what she wanted, and Cece thought she might have come up with something that she'd be happy with. The bride said she wanted something "traditional yet whimsical," whatever that meant. The two things together made up an oxymoron. Cece sketched a traditional cake, a whimsical cake, and one that she hoped was somewhere in between.

Half an hour past her scheduled appointment, the mayor's daughter finally walked in. She looked impossibly beautiful and polished. She had gleaming brown hair and a sleek, big city look from her designer bag right down to her stiletto heels. She looked more like she belonged in New York than Nashville, and she made no apologies for being late.

"Have you got those sketches, Miss Cece?" she asked with a surprisingly endearing Tennessee accent.

"Yes. I have three here that I prepared, and I also have a few pictures from the old cake catalogue that I thought you might like," Cece said in a professional tone.

"I just loved what you did with that cake for Shelby's baby shower, and when I heard that you were *the* Cece Graves I just had to hire you for my wedding. My father supports the foundation, by the way."

"Well, thank you, Miss Reid," Cece smiled. Every once in a while someone would recognize her name because her daughter, Rebecca, had started a foundation to help women who were victims of abuse, sexual violence, and sexual trafficking. She'd named it the Cece Graves Foundation, and it had been gaining lots of positive attention in the two years since Rebecca started it.

"No, thank *you*, Cece, and please call me Lynette."

"Thanks, Lynette. I'll just go get those pictures I mentioned, and we can get started."

By the end of the day, Lynette was happy with the design for her wedding cake, and Cece was glad to have met with the young woman. She was going to make a lovely bride.

She hung the closed sign on her little glass door and went upstairs to the tiny apartment that had served as her and Rebecca's first home. Mrs. Lee had let Cece use it until she'd saved enough to get her own apartment. Now that the entire building belonged to Cece, she used the little apartment as her own personal gym. She did most of her weight training and conditioning up there hidden away from the rest of the world.

There was a heavy bag in one corner of the studio apartment. The bag was where Cece spent the majority of her time that evening. The only useful thing she'd learned from the streets was that life would kick the crap out of you if you didn't fight back. She'd made the choice to fight back a long time ago, and she'd earned black belts in Muay Thai and Judo since then. Fighting was the only pastime she had; it was the only one she'd allowed herself for almost the last thirty years. She'd started when she was around ten years old, and martial arts had been one of the most consistent influences in her life. It had also been one of the only things keeping her sane.

She listened to music blaring from her stereo as she practiced her high kicks and elbow blows. The bag was really taking a beating tonight, because her usual sparring partner was out of town for a few weeks. Cece hadn't been to her best friend, Karen's, martial arts academy to train for almost two weeks, and her mounting frustrations had no other outlet at the moment.

She continued her practice drills until she was soaked with sweat and almost too exhausted to lift her legs up again. After a quick shower in her tiny bathroom, she reached into the bag of borrowed clothes from her daughter and pulled out a t-

23

shirt to sleep in. She hadn't had the chance to purchase a bed or a futon just yet, so she had to sleep on the floor that night. She had the mats that she frequently used for her workouts, so it wasn't too bad. The only things she lacked were a pillow and a blanket, but she'd been in worse situations.

She stared up at the shadows cast on the ceiling by the streetlight outside her shop and tried to sleep. Her body was completely exhausted, her eyes were heavy, and she had been up since three a.m., yet sleep still eluded her. Every time she closed her eyes, a mix of unwanted images flashed before her. The undulating flames on the ceiling as the fireman had yanked her from the tub came to mind over and over again as she tried to sleep. The feeling of being trapped and totally helpless lingered. She knew there was no fire now, and there was nothing tying her down now, but that feeling of being unable to escape stayed with her no matter how hard she tried to shake it off.

Even as she tried not to think about the fire, she felt her mind straying into another traumatic event from long ago, the event that had changed her life forever. She did her best to keep the memories from Rebecca's conception at bay, but she felt them crawling up out of the depths of her soul like icy fingers slowly moving up her spine. She willed herself to sleep and to think of nothing, but she just couldn't do it. Cece curled into a ball, with her back pressed firmly into the corner, and stared out at the apartment in front of her. Eventually, she resigned herself to the fact that she wasn't going to sleep, and she got up to start her day early.

Cece started every day that week early, and by Friday morning she had dark circles under her eyes. Her muscles were sore from her intensified training, and her hands were no longer as steady as they had been before the fire. She didn't want to admit it, but the past had come knocking at her door. She was once again having violent nightmares about the assault.

She was preparing to close early on Friday evening, when she heard the bell jingle. A customer; just what she needed right now. She looked up from behind the counter, and her eyes ran right into the eyes of the very man who had saved her life exactly one week ago. Her fake, professional smile froze in place.

"Can I help you?" she asked. Not, 'Hi, how are you?' or 'It's good to see you again, Shane,' all she had to say to the man who had risked his life to save hers was 'Can I help you?'

"I just came to see how you're doing, but since I'm here I'll take a dozen of those cream filled cupcakes," he said with a touch of amusement in his voice.

"I'm doing really well," Cece lied as she packed the cupcakes into a white box.

"Are you really okay, Cecilia?" Shane asked as he stared pointedly at her shaking hands.

"I was just about to close up, and go get something for dinner. I've already closed out the cash register, so you don't have to pay for those," Cecilia said. She ignored his question; it wasn't his business if she was okay or not. "I would have let you have them for free either way though," she added to soften the edge of her previous words.

She walked around to the front of the counter and handed him the box of cupcakes. "Did you see anything else you want?" she asked.

"Yes," he said as he looked into her tired eyes, "but the cupcakes are enough for now."

Cece shifted her gaze to the setting sun outside her window. He was making it clear that he planned on coming back, but why?

"Let me walk you to your car," he said. His voice was a deep baritone that vibrated soothingly in her ears.

She put up the closed sign and locked the door behind them after they stepped out. Her car was parked in the lot behind the building, and he walked slowly beside her as she approached it. He didn't seem to be in a hurry, so she slowed down to keep pace with him.

"How tall are you?" she asked out of curiosity. He towered over her, and at 5'7" she wasn't exactly a short person.

"Six and a half feet tall, and don't you dare ask me what I weigh. The answer might scare you," he joked.

Cece managed a small smile that he caught out of the corner of his eye.

When he went to open her car door for her, a slip of paper tucked under her windshield wiper caught his eye. It was one the brochures for the Cece Graves Foundation that her daughter had started, and on the back was a note to Cece herself. It said, "I'm sorry about everything."

He handed it to her and watched her reaction as she read it.

"Do you know who left it?" he asked.

"No," she said as she stared at it wide eyed.

"You know, that fire was set deliberately," Shane informed her. "Is there somebody who wants to harm you?" he asked. He'd gone from joking to serious in an instant.

"I don't think so."

"Cecilia, you can't stay here. I have a bad feeling about this."

"It's just a note," Cece said with more bravado than she actually felt. In truth, she was sick to her stomach. If she hadn't been sitting, she might very well have fallen over. The bell on her door had jingled several times that week while she was in the back, and when she'd gone to the front no one had been there. She'd been mildly unsettled about it until now; now she was very unsettled.

The funeral had taken place almost two months ago, and he still expected to see her walk through the door at any moment. He still expected her to show up for breakfast and dinner—to sit down across from him and tell him about her day. His heart was expecting something that his mind knew would never happen again.

He looked down at the crumpled brochure in his hand, and recalled the first time he'd seen it. He'd broken out in a cold sweat and almost passed out. It was as if the past was reaching out to take revenge on him. He'd thought it was over, he thought he'd atoned for it. Maybe there was no way to really atone for such a thing.

His head dropped into his hands as her face came to him again. He had to make it right, but the last thing he wanted to do was cause more pain and embarrassment. He'd seen firsthand what that kind of humiliation could do to a woman. If it hadn't been for the trial, she'd still be alive.

Sometimes in his dreams, her face became Cece's face, as if the two of them were interchangeable somehow. Maybe she was speaking to him from the grave, telling him what to do. Or maybe Cece had taken her away from him as punishment for what he'd done. After all these years, why get revenge now? And why take an innocent?

He crumpled the brochure for the Cece Graves Foundation and took another drink of his whiskey. He knew what he needed to do, but he needed more than liquid courage to help him confront Cece.

# Chapter 4

Shane sat at Gus's table for the third time that week, and wondered why he couldn't just go back to his own house. He was a grown man, it was his house, and he could tell he was getting on his friend's nerves. He'd been very high handed with Cece after finding the note on her car, and the result was that she was living in his house and he was avoiding it so she would feel comfortable enough to stay. It was one of the strangest situations he'd ever gotten himself into.

She'd been there more than a week, and they hadn't seen each other once. He stayed out every night until he was certain she'd gone to sleep, and she was gone every morning before he got out of bed. Her car in his garage every night was the only indication of her presence. She cleaned up after herself, left nothing out of place, and made almost no noise. It was kind of like living with a ghost.

Gus looked up from his plate of *eschabeche* and said, "You can't stay late tonight. We have plans that don't involve you."

Magda blushed furiously and kicked her husband under the table. "He's just kidding; you can stay as long as you need to, Shane."

"No, no. I've imposed enough. You two need some alone time to do what married people do," Shane laughed.

They all went back to eating.

"Why *have* you been over so much lately?" Magda asked.

"Long story," Shane mumbled.

"Maybe you should tell us. You look like something's been bothering you." Leave it to the only woman in the room to pick up on that.

"He looks fine to me," Gus muttered.

"That's because you haven't looked at him," Magda sighed in exasperation. "Ever since that fire a couple of weeks ago he hasn't looked like himself."

"I'm sitting right here. There's no need to talk about me like I'm a child," Shane said with a smile. "There's nothing wrong with me," he added when they both glanced at him.

"Maybe he's afraid to be alone after that fire," Gus muttered.

"Is that it, Shane? Are you afraid to be alone?" Magda asked.

Shane looked at his two good friends and shook his head. They were trying to provoke him into talking. Maybe he should stop trying to avoid his house.

"You remember the woman we got out of 525?" Shane asked Gus with a resigned sigh.

"Your auntie-in-law? What about her?" Gus laughed.

"Okay, that doesn't even make sense," Shane said.

"What about her?" Magda asked. She cast a chastising look in her husband's direction. "*Callaté!*" she hissed.

"She's staying at my house right now," Shane admitted.

Gus burst into laughter and nearly choked on his dinner. Magda had to reach over and pat his back for a few minutes. Shane looked on in amusement. The two of them made an odd looking pair, but they fit together somehow. They reminded him of Rebecca and Norman. Magdalena was a very slight Hispanic woman with lovely dark hair and brown eyes, and it was obvious to see how much she adored her husband. It was just as apparent that he adored her.

"Why is this so funny?" Magda asked Shane. Her eyes were wide with amusement and curiosity.

"Have you ever seen Shane avoid a woman before? Especially a hot one?" Gus laughed.

"No," she said.

"525 is quite a looker. Some of the guys down at the station are still talking about her legs," Gus said.

"Her name is Cecilia, but she goes by Cece. Cece Graves," Shane said.

"How did she end up at your place?" Gus asked.

"I managed to convince her that she'd be safe there after I found a suspicious note on her car last Friday. Someone left an apology for the fire, and since it was arson, I didn't think it was a good idea for her to stay alone where someone could get to her," Shane explained.

"That is so romantic," Magda breathed as she looked at Shane.

"I missed the part with the romance," Shane remarked.

"You saved her from the fire, and now you are protecting her from the bad guy," Magda said. Then she turned to Gus and said, "Why don't you ever do romantic things like that for me?"

Shane laughed because he knew she was just kidding. "You've got it all wrong. Cecilia isn't like other women," he said.

"Certainly not if she has you avoiding your own house for a week," Gus snickered.

Shane left after dinner, but he didn't go home. Instead, he drove to Cecilia's bakery and sat in a parking spot half a block away from the front of her building. He wasn't sure what he'd hoped to accomplish, maybe he wanted to catch a glimpse of whoever left the note on her car. He sat there until 11pm, and nothing suspicious happened. He made his way home, because he knew Cecilia would be sound asleep by now. There would be none of that awkward tension he felt when she looked at him. Every look she gave him seemed to scream that he should keep his distance, yet there was also something deeper and harder to detect in her eyes that reached out and beckoned him closer.

He parked his Jeep beside her car and entered the house through the utility room that connected the kitchen and garage. The kitchen was spotless, and not a thing was out of place. Just as it had been all week, the house was silent and dark, and the door to his guest room was closed. He paused outside the door for a moment and listened. No sound. It was almost like she wasn't even there. He went into the master bathroom and took a quick shower before getting in bed.

He had only been in bed for an hour when muffled screams coming from the guest room woke him. He jumped out of bed and ran towards Cecilia's room. Something crashed to the floor as he reached the locked door, and in desperation he kicked the door in instead of wasting time knocking. It sounded like she was being attacked, but when Shane bounded into the room, there was no one there but Cecilia. She was on the floor in a tangled heap of covers, seemingly fighting for her life. The lamp on the nightstand had crashed to the floor, and there were shards of glass all over the place. Shane gingerly stepped over the glass and approached Cecilia.

She was still in a fitful sleep, writhing on the floor, shaking and soaked with sweat. Shane knelt down and gently shook her.

"Cecilia, wake up," he said.

She immediately started clawing at his hands and trying to escape.

"No, please! No!" she whispered at him. "Please just let me go!"

"Cece, wake up," Shane said louder as he shook her more forcefully. "You're having a bad dream." He had to say it a few more times before her eyes finally opened. She looked around in confusion, and then at him. He immediately let her go.

"I think you fell out of bed. You were having a bad dream," he said quietly. She was still shaking, and there were tears all over her face. The same dark circles he remembered from last week were still under her eyes, only now they were more pronounced because her face was so pale. Her skin was normally a healthy golden brown, but tonight she looked very gray and sickly.

She turned away from him to hide her face. She frantically wiped the tears away before facing him again.

"Are you okay?" As soon as the question left his mouth he chastised himself for how stupid he must sound. She was obviously not okay.

She opened her mouth to say something, and a small sob escaped. She started to cry again as she jumped up and ran from the room. Shortly after she closed the bathroom door, Shane heard retching sounds. He listened at the door, despite knowing that Cecilia would see the act as a violation of her privacy rather than a show of concern.

A few minutes after she was done being sick, the shower started. Shane stepped away from the bathroom door and went to put on a shirt. She'd probably feel more comfortable if he weren't standing there bare-chested when she emerged from the bathroom. He quickly cleaned up the glass from the lamp and put the sheets back on the bed for her. She was still in the shower when he finished. It was Saturday night, and he didn't have to work in the morning. He didn't mind waiting for her to get out, but he could think of better things to be doing on a Saturday night.

When the bathroom door finally opened, Shane was standing there. There was no way Cecilia could avoid him. She had a little color in her cheeks now, but that same frightened, haunted look was still on her face. It was much less intense, but it was there. She stopped in the doorway, and the steam from her shower swirled around her as she watched him. There was no trace of her earlier tears. There was just a profound sadness that she hadn't yet managed to stuff beneath her tough exterior.

He knew there was nothing he could say to make her feel better. She'd been through some horrible things, and sometimes pretty words didn't help at all. He sensed that this was one of those times, so he cautiously approached her and gathered her up in his arms.

She was stiff and trembling for the first few minutes of the embrace, but he just continued to hold her and gently rub her back. She didn't say anything, and neither did he. The moment stretched on, and she eventually let her head fall against his chest as she took in a shuddering breath and began to cry again. She didn't make a sound, but he felt her warm tears wetting his t-shirt. He brought one of his hands up to caress the back of her head and held her closer.

"I'm so sorry about your lamp," she looked up at him and said.

"I really hope that's not why you're crying," he joked. His reward was a very small smile, more like a twitch of the lips really, but it was there. "You don't have to tell me," he added as he wiped a tear off her cheek.

Something in her face prompted him to take her hand and guide her into his bedroom. He made no pretense about the fact that he intended to share his bed with her that night. She glanced at him once before she lay down, and he smiled to set her at ease. He climbed in right after she lay down, and he wrapped his arms around her again. Her back was pressed fully against his front, with only their nightclothes between them.

"How long has it been since you've had a good night's sleep?" he whispered against her hair.

"Years," she whispered back. She curled her legs up into her chest and wrapped her arms around them. Shane wrapped his arms around hers and curled his body around her. She closed her eyes and fell asleep in a matter of moments, but Shane lay awake long into the night. He pondered the implications of sharing his home, and his bed, with her. To him, she was a fascinating person whom he felt an inexplicably strong connection to, but to her, he was nothing more than a near stranger. He kept that thought uppermost in his mind as he held her that night.

The next morning, Shane woke up to find Cecilia still asleep in his arms. It was past 7 am; as far as he knew she never slept past three thirty. She needed sleep more than she needed to open her bakery on time, so he didn't wake her. He carefully moved his arm from under her head and replaced it with his pillow. He dressed as quickly and quietly as he could, and left her alone so that she would have some privacy when she woke up.

All of Shane's consideration was for naught. Cece woke up the moment he took his arm from under her head. She was an extremely light sleeper, but she was also pretty good at pretending. She lay in the bed, concentrating on her deep breathing until she heard the quiet click of the door shutting behind Shane as he quit the room. She refused to let herself wonder what he thought of her now. Thoughts like that always proved to be useless in the long run.

She got up, made the bed, and left his room. Today was the first Sunday that her usual sparring partner was back in town. Karen and Cece had been sparring, training, and attending tournaments together for years now. Karen was the closest thing Cece had to a sister, and they were supposed to meet at the gym in less than half an hour. There was no sign of Shane anywhere in the house, so Cece threw on her clothes and drove to the gym.

Karen was waiting in one of the training rooms at her marital arts academy. She'd just finished teaching her early Tae Kwan Do class, and she was still wearing her *dobok*. Karen Christian Holly was a well-known fighter in the testosterone fueled world of mixed martial arts competitions. She held black belts in several styles including Tae Kwan Do, Judo, and Karate. Her fourth degree black belt in Tae Kwan Do gave her the title of Sa Dan, and it meant that she was qualified to teach students. To

Cece, Karen was an old friend and mentor, but to everyone else Karen was K.C. Holly the fighter who was a superstar in the world of women's MMA fighting. Five years ago, she'd lost a high profile match, and the loss had been heartbreaking to Karen on several levels. The company promoting the fight had failed shortly after all the hype was over, and Karen, the clear favorite, had lost in a stunning upset. Now that Karen was over forty, it was getting harder to schedule big matches.

"How was your vacation?" Cece asked as soon as she walked into the room.

"I'd hardly call it a vacation," Karen answered. She walked up to Cece and gave her a bear hug. "I heard about the fire. Glad to see you made it out all in one piece."

"Does everybody know about that?"

"Apparently. Where are you staying now?"

"With family," Cece hedged. Karen had been trying to fix her up for years, and if she knew about Shane she'd probably start asking the kind of questions Cece didn't want to answer.

Karen knew Cece better than almost anyone else on the planet, and she knew when Cece wasn't going to talk anymore. She didn't waste her breath asking who the 'family' was, instead she started stretching and doing warm up exercises. Cece did the same.

Despite the punishing stretches and drills, Cece couldn't clear her mind. Last night's events had shaken her to her core. The nightmare had been so real, she'd been convinced she was back in that dark part of town, alone and frightened. She'd seen his face hovering above her as he held the gun to her head, and promised to make her beg. His sickening voice had filled her ears, and now it replayed in little snippets as she defended against Karen's strikes and launched attacks of her own. Her blocks were lightning fast, but her punches lacked conviction today.

She and Karen danced around each other in the basic fighting stance and took turns striking and blocking. All the while, Cece was imagining a greater foe sneaking up behind her. She kept suppressing the urge to look over her shoulder. She kept telling herself that it was all in the past, but ever since the fire it seemed more like a present reality than a potent memory.

Cece looked over her shoulder once, and Karen landed a kick to the side of her padded helmet. She turned her attention back to the match, but it was all over at that point. Karen showed no mercy, and the sparring ended with Cece on her knees in complete submission. Both women eyed each other with surprise.

"Cece, are you okay?" Karen's unsure voice asked.

"Of course, I am. Why does everyone keep asking me that? It was just a fire."

"I asked because I've never seen you cry during a match before."

"I'm sorry, I should go now," Cece hurried from the building and headed straight for the sanctuary of her bakery.

On Sundays, she was only open from ten to three. Most of the Sunday customers were regulars who had known Mrs. Lee for years. The church Mrs. Lee had been a long time member of was just a few blocks from the bakery; it was the same church that Cece had gone to for shelter all those years ago.

Shortly after one o'clock, church ladies dressed in all their finery began to trickle into the shop. They greeted Cece, and asked all the usual questions.

"How are you?"

"How is your daughter?"

"Have they found out anything else about what caused that awful fire?

Cece gave only vague, noncommittal responses, and indicated that everything was just fine in her world. There was no reason to saddle these poor ladies with the truth; the truth was no way to reward their polite efforts to placate her.

After they'd taken their baked goods home for Sunday dinner, Cece was left alone again. Sunday was usually a busy day, so the respite didn't last long. The bell jingled continuously until closing time, and almost everything on display had been sold. She was about to close and clean up when she saw Shane approaching the door.

Cece had always confronted her problems head on, yet she wanted to dive behind the counter as soon as she saw Shane. She couldn't of course; it wouldn't accomplish anything other than making her look like a fool. She stood her ground and maintained eye contact as he opened the door and stepped inside. She barely heard the bell jingle in the back of her mind.

"Hi, Cecilia," his deep voice sounded too big for the small space between them. His presence seemed to overwhelm everything in the shop, including her.

"Shane," she said in acknowledgement. Maybe now he would leave her in peace.

"Looks like you're closing up for the day."

"I am. Do you want anything?"

"I just came by to talk to you about last night."

Cece didn't respond immediately; instead, she let his words hang between them for a moment. "What about it?" she asked at last.

"Cecilia, don't give me the game face, not after last night."

"Game face?"

"Yeah, that look you give everyone when you want them to know that you're okay; Rebecca told me about it while you were learning to walk again a couple of years ago. I know you don't need anyone—at least I know you *think* you don't need anyone. But, from what I saw last night, you need a friend more than anyone else I know right now. You keep a lot to yourself, and I think you should talk to *someone* about it. Why not try me?" He had walked around behind the counter as he talked, and now his hand was on her shoulder.

She looked up at him. His face was so open and so affable that it would have been easy to talk to him about anything...if she'd been anyone other than herself. Last night, he'd comforted her in a moment of extreme weakness, and it had felt good. For the first time in a long time, she'd slept, but that didn't mean she could suddenly start sharing things with this man. Some things should never be shared with anyone, especially not with a man, and most especially not with this man.

"There's nothing to talk about," she said with cold finality as she shook his hand off her shoulder and walked toward the door. He had no choice but to follow her.

"We'll talk tonight at my house. I'll be waiting," he said. His certainty grated on her nerves, and she could scarcely believe he'd had the temerity to issue a veiled command. They wouldn't talk if she wasn't there. But even as she thought about it, she knew she would go back. She felt safe with him.

When she reached his house that evening, he was in the kitchen cooking. It would be childish to continue avoiding him, so she went directly to him. He smiled when she walked into the kitchen. She couldn't manage to smile back, but at least she didn't frown at him. He had no right to show concern for her; she was nothing to him.

"Have you ever had paella?" he asked. His tone was conversational and his manner was very relaxed and easy.

"Never even heard of it," Cece admitted.

"You're in for a treat then. I'm making seafood paella. It happens to be my specialty."

"Do you need me to help with anything?"

"It'll be done in about five minutes, so you can relax. I've already set the table."

Cece did as he suggested and relaxed. She took a seat at the island where he was working, and he poured her a glass of wine. She sipped it slowly as she watched him. When the paella was done, he removed it from the heat and covered it. He cleaned and wiped the counters as she watched him. Every once in a while, he looked at her and smiled with such self-assurance she wondered if he'd ever had a moment of low self-esteem in his life. She raised her glass to take another sip, and realized it was empty.

When he finished cleaning, they took their seats at the dining table.

"It smells wonderful," Cece said as he served them and refilled their wine glasses.

"I hope you like it, but if you don't, I can whip up a peanut butter and jelly sandwich in no time."

Cece looked up at him and smiled with uncharacteristic warmth, "I'm sure I'll like it, Shane."

They ate in silence for a few minutes. Shane watched her as she continued to sip her wine. When her glass was empty, he refilled it for her.

"Tell me something about yourself, Cecilia."

"There's nothing to tell."

"Oh yes there is... What were you like before you had your daughter?"

Suddenly, Cece's eyes flashed up and clashed with his, "Why do you want to know? You think I don't know morbid curiosity when I see it? So you can do math, good for you. You know that I'm 40 and my daughter is 26, so I had her when I was 14... you want to know if I was one of those promiscuous teen mothers who allowed some stupid boy to get her pregnant and then treat her like shit!"

"Cecilia," his calm voice instantly diffused the tension. "I know about what happened to you back then. I only asked about you, because you're so guarded all the time. I understand why, but I just wanted to know what you were like before it happened."

"How do you know about that?" she breathed, horrified by his unauthorized knowledge about her past.

"Rebecca. The night of her first charity ball for the foundation, she gave a speech about you. I was there. It was a very moving speech."

"But that's nobody's business, especially not yours."

"I know."

She stared down at her empty wineglass before answering. "Even before I had her, I wasn't a nice person. I used to get into fights all the time. I thought I was such a bad-ass, because I knew a little Karate."

"Do you still practice Karate now?"

"No, now I do Judo and kick-boxing."

"What were your parents like?"

Cece didn't answer. "Why are you asking?" she demanded instead.

"Because it's hard to imagine parents who would throw out their own daughter just because she was pregnant. My parents wouldn't have done that to Shelly. Were you an only child?"

"I am an only child, and it wouldn't be so hard to imagine them throwing me out if you'd seen how I was back then." She swayed in her chair as she spoke. "Why do you want to know about *me*? Haven't you got better things to do with your time?"

"I've always been interested in learning more about you, Cecilia."

"Maybe you should just get *un*interested." As soon as the words left her mouth, she felt bad. Was that any way to talk to the man who had saved her life, opened his home to her, and even comforted her when she needed it last night? She straightened her shoulders, looked him in the eye, and said, "I'm sorry. That was rude, and you've been nothing but nice to me."

"If you really want to make it up to me, you can help me wash these dishes," he said as he stood up and started clearing the table.

Cece helped in silence. It didn't take long to clean the kitchen, and Shane didn't ask any more nosey questions during the process. Cece started to relax a little.

"You want to go for a walk?" Shane asked when they finished.

"Sure," Cece agreed right away, and Shane tried not to let his surprise show.

"There's a path that goes around the whole neighborhood and into a small park just up the street," he informed her on the way out the front door.

The neighborhood was a picturesque little piece of suburbia. There were children playing in almost every yard on the street that day. The evening was warm and breezy, and the sun was slowly sinking towards the horizon. Soon, the children's mothers would be calling them in for the night.

"This doesn't look like your type of neighborhood," Cece said as she took in the quaint, family atmosphere of the place.

"What makes you say that?"

"You're a confirmed bachelor, living in a little domestic paradise. It just doesn't seem like your kind of neighborhood."

"Confirmed bachelor, huh? Is that what you think of me?"

"I don't know," she shrugged.

"At least you didn't say confirmed, *old* bachelor."

"I don't even know how old you are. I'd guess late thirties at the most." She briefly studied his face as she spoke.

He laughed before replying, "And I would have guessed you were in your late twenties if you hadn't already told me otherwise."

"Stop trying to make me feel better about my age. I'm okay with being over the hill. It gives me character and authority."

Shane laughed again. "What kind of authority?" he asked between chuckles.

Cecilia cut her eyes at him and said, "The authority to tell you that you're a nice young man and that you should respect your elders."

"Elders? Meaning you, I suppose."

39

"Exactly," she said.

"Cecilia, I do respect you. I know you think it's not possible for a man to respect a woman, but not all of us are bad guys."

They walked on in silence until they reached the park. Cecilia looked up at him every once in a while as they walked the scenic little path. Once the path reached the park, it branched off into several smaller paths, each of which led to a separate area of the park and then met up again at the fountain in the center. No matter which path they chose, they would end up back at the center fountain. Cecilia led them down a path that wound its way toward the trees at the edge of the neighborhood. The setting sun was behind them as they walked the tree lined path.

"I know you're not all bad guys," Cecilia whispered as they reached the end of the trees and the path curved back toward the center of the park. The sun was now hovering just above the horizon, casting shadows all across the park. The fountain made a long shadow straight down the center of the path, and Cecilia stared down at it as they walked. The shadow was colorful, because the fountain had a multitude of bright glass panels in its design. It reminded Cece of a stained glass window in a cathedral, but it was much more whimsical than something one would see in a church. She marveled at the jewel tones that shone on the sidewalk as the sun went down.

"I thought you might like this fountain," Shane said as he studied her face; it was momentarily lit up by both a bemused expression and the colors from the fountain.

"It's incredible, actually," she said.

"I've always thought so," he agreed.

They walked around the fountain several times as Cece admired the design. She didn't tell Shane, but she was committing it to memory so she could sketch it later in her book. Some of her best inspirations for cake designs came from her surroundings, and she felt very inspired as she studied the fountain.

Shane looked on in silence and fought the urge to get too close to her. He hadn't expected to find that it was a pleasure to simply watch her. The wine she'd had with dinner had relaxed her, and now she moved with ease and a graceful elegance that indicated inner calm and self-assurance. She allowed her hands ie parts of the fountain that she liked the most, xture and feel of its more artistic elements. The e entire scene wasn't lost on Shane as he watched ʒ light.

ie sun went down, they walked back to the house air between them was heavy with all the things o say. He looked down at her several times, and er if she'd rather sleep in his bed tonight. That would nave been far too forward though. He wanted to tell her that he was there if she needed him, but he also knew the time wasn't right for such familiarity. He remained quiet.

Chapter 5

He sat only two rows behind Cece on the bus, and she never noticed him. Not that he did anything to call attention to himself. He'd always been the kind of man that women barely noticed and, now that he was older, he was practically invisible. The only time anyone took notice of him was when he was playing the piano. He'd made a name for himself over the past twenty five years, and there wasn't an orchestra in the world that wouldn't beg for the chance to perform with him. He'd worked hard to become a world-renowned concert pianist, and he relished the title. He'd made millions of dollars from performances and CD's, and earned the respect of just about every serious musician in the United States and Europe, and now he was reduced to following Cece Graves around on the bus.

He'd had no luck following her when she was in her car. He wasn't cut out for detective work, as he liked to think of it, and he lost her in traffic every time he tried it. Just the other day, a stroke of luck turned things in his favor. He'd been sitting at the bus stop near her bakery, waiting for her car to turn into the lot, when she'd stepped off the bus right in front of him. She hadn't noticed him of course, no woman ever did.

All he had to do after that was get on the bus with her at the end of the day, and take a seat behind her. He simply made the same transfers as she did, and then he paid attention to where she got off for the night. He'd been her shadow on the bus all week to make sure that at the same time every day she got off at the same stop. Now that he knew where she was staying, it would be easier to talk to her when he finally worked up the *courage to do so. She got off at the stop near the same park where she'd gotten off all week. He rose halfway out of his seat, with every intention of following her so they could talk in the park, but his heart slammed in his chest and he froze. The bus doors closed, and he sat back down.*

He reached into his pocket and pulled out the crumpled brochure again. He stared at it for endless moments as the bus continued on to who knows where. He would talk to Cece eventually, it just wouldn't be tonight. At least now he knew where to find her. Every time he'd tried to go into her bakery he'd backed out at the last second. It would be better to catch her in the park when there were less people around. He rode in the shadows and tried not to picture her face in the casket again. His therapist had told him that the grieving process could take years. It had been months, and he still didn't want to believe it was true. He floated helplessly, lost somewhere between anger and guilt. He had to make it right for her. His fist closed around the brochure again and he rode on as silent tears rolled down his shadowed face.

Cece practically skipped through the park on the way back to Shane's house that evening. After more than two months of living with him, she'd managed to find a nice place in her price range. Just three weeks from now she'd be free to move into her new house. Aside from the weekend she'd disturbed him with her nightmare, she'd stayed out of his way as much as possible. In the last couple of weeks, she'd seen very little of him. His new hours as an instructor at the training academy had kept him extra busy for the past few weeks.

She stopped when she reached the fountain in the center of the park and watched the sunset through the colorful glass and splashing water. No matter how many times she did it, she always noticed something new about how the light and water played off of each other to make a dazzling little display.

Cece pulled out her sketch pad and drew a picture of the fountain. For reasons better left unexamined, she added the silhouette of a man to the sketch. She added a fair amount of detail to the fountain, and even the shadow of the fountain. It was difficult to capture the full effect of the shadow without adding color to the lighter spots cast by the colored glass, but overall the sketch did catch the whimsy of the fountain. She left the male silhouette as simple as possible, and was actually on the verge of erasing it completely when she heard someone walk up behind her.

"Cecilia, I thought that was you," Shane greeted her.

She slammed her sketchpad closed and jumped up. "What are you doing in the park?"

"I could ask you the same question," he countered with a smile. She hadn't seen his smile in a few weeks, and this one affected her. She wondered briefly how many other women he'd used that smile on.

"I've been coming here every day after work," Cece admitted with a shrug.

"I see you were sketching something. Mind if I take a look?" He reached out his hand as if he had every reason to expect a positive answer.

Cece shook her head and said, "It's actually just some of my work. It would bore you."

"Will you at least show me one of them? I'll do anything you ask if you show me one."

Cece shook her head at him and laughed. "Anything?" she asked.

"Anything," was his fervent reply.

Cece flipped open the book, and turned to the first sketch she'd drawn of the fountain. She'd done it from memory after the first time they'd walked together in the park.

"This is very good. I like how you left out all the fussy details in this sketch. You captured the light and water very nicely in this one. It looks rather playful," he said in his best imitation of a stuffy art critic.

He handed the sketchpad back to her as she smiled and shook her head at him.

"Would you like to see some sketches of wedding cake designs?" Cece asked on impulse.

"Of course," Shane replied as he reached for the sketchpad again.

Cece held it out of his reach and said, "They aren't in this one. They're in another one that I have at home—I mean your house."

"Let's go see them then," he said as he offered her his arm. "You seem to be in a good mood today."

Cece looked up at him. She was in an unusually bright mood today. Perhaps it was the fact that she'd just found a new place to live, and she was no longer going to be a burden on him. It could also be the fact that Lynette's wedding was fast approaching, and she was excited about what it would do for her business.

"I am in a pretty good mood," she admitted with a grin. "I found a place, so I'll be out of your hair in just three weeks," she beamed up at him.

Shane looked down at her and was struck by several things all at once. First, she was absolutely radiant when she smiled. It was a genuine smile that lit up her face, brightened her eyes, and brought out a pair of killer dimples that he hadn't expected. The second thing that struck him was that he didn't want her to leave, and the third thing was that he enjoyed seeing her happy. She seemed to be expecting him to say something, but his tongue was tied in knots again.

Eventually, he found his voice and said, "I'm glad you were able to find a place, but do you think it's a good idea to be alone? They still haven't found the person who started the fire, and they aren't even sure who to look for."

"I've thought about that already. I think the chances of someone being after me are slim. That note was probably left by someone nice who was concerned. A lot of people in that neighborhood know all about my daughter's foundation. There is nothing to worry about."

The conviction and calm in her voice grated on his nerves, but he didn't let it show. They were already at his house again, so he held his tongue and unlocked the door. "I haven't forgotten about those sketches," he reminded her as she strolled towards the guest room. The fact that he'd been thinking of it as *her* room bothered him.

When she reappeared, she had three big sketchbooks and several photo albums in her arms. Shane rushed forward to help her with her burdens.

"I've got them," she said.

He plucked the biggest ones out of her hands anyway and said, "I know, but I want to help." When she looked up at him in consternation, he said, "Relax."

For once, she simply complied. He spread the books out on his coffee table and waited for her to say something. When she didn't, he picked up the photo album and asked, "How long have you been doing wedding cakes?"

"I started about fifteen years ago."

"How did you get into it?" Shane inquired. He thumbed through the photo album, admiring her work.

"It's a long story," she hedged.

"Cecilia, we have all night," Shane teased.

"Well," she began with a sigh. "When I first got to Nashville, this little old lady named Mrs. Lee gave me a job cleaning her bakery. After a few years of cleaning, she trusted me enough to let me make cookies, and over the next ten years I worked my way up to decorating cakes."

Shane waited a moment for her to continue before he smiled down at her and said, "Cecilia, that is the shortest long story I've ever heard in my life."

"I got into wedding cakes, because they're the only thing that ever made me feel even sort of happy. I'm never able to make people happy in person. I'll be the first to admit that I'm uncomfortable to be around, and I'm not the kind of woman who inspires people around her to be at ease and smile often... like my daughter. I can, however, make cakes that inspire happiness. That's better than nothing I guess."

"So, decorating cakes is not just a job to you?" Shane asked, although he already knew the answer to that question.

"Not at all. It's my contribution to the happiness of my customers. I've always wanted to make people smile, and this is the only way I can do it."

"You're not as bad as you think you are," Shane reassured her.

"Yes I am, just ask your brother," Cece returned.

Shane laughed outright at that comment. "Honey, you're his mother-in-law, and you're not just any mother-in-law. You've got a black belt in Judo and you practice kick-boxing. Of course he's going to be uncomfortable around you. If he does anything to hurt your daughter you'd probably kick his ass."

"Yeah, I would," Cece agreed pensively after thinking it over for a moment.

Shane momentarily forgot all about the photo album. "I'd pay good money to see that," he said as he studied her face.

"Did I mention that I'm doing the wedding cake for the mayor's daughter? She's getting married next month."

"No, you didn't mention that," Shane said. "Is it important?"

"Very. I've only done cakes for middle class weddings, never anything this big. If I can break into the society weddings I could easily get more business and double my income. Take a look at some of the pictures toward the back," she reached over and flipped to the end of the album.

Shane obliged her by looking at them. He was more interested in watching her, but once he did look at the pictures he was completely taken off guard by how exquisite they were. "You did these?" he asked in wonder.

"Yes," she beamed. Her dimples were out again, and he couldn't help smiling back at her.

"Cecilia, these are awesome. Definitely some of the best I've seen... and I've seen a lot of high society wedding cakes."

"You have?"

"I have. I own a florist shop, and I employ a guy who has designed the arrangements and floral decorations for a number of society weddings. You wouldn't believe how much money you can make if you attract the right clientele."

"The right clientele? Meaning rich people?" Cece asked with a laugh.

"Yeah," Shane shrugged. "If you want your business to grow, the mayor's daughter is your ticket. If you can wow that crowd, the word of mouth from that wedding alone can keep you set for a year or more."

"Would you like to see a sketch of her cake? It's a custom design."

"Sure," Shane agreed with enthusiasm.

As she flipped through one of her sketchbooks, Cece said, "This one took a while to finalize. Lynette said she wanted something traditional yet whimsical, and I'd always seen the two styles as mutually exclusive until I saw that fountain in the park with you last month. Certain elements from the fountain inspired the design for this cake." She then presented Shane with a colorful sketch of the cake. She had a real eye for artistry and color, and the cake reminded him very strongly of the fountain without being an actual copy of it.

"You are very talented, Cecilia," he complimented her. He continued to look through her sketches, and felt very much like she was giving him a rare glimpse into her soul. Every once in a while, he came across a sketch that seemed to have nothing to do with cakes, and then the next page contained a cake that featured elements from the previous sketch. The sketches alone could be considered fine art, because they were so beautifully done.

"I feel like all the hard work I've put into that little bakery over the past twenty-six years is finally about to be rewarded in a big way," she told him while he browsed her sketches and pictures.

"So, you've been there twenty-six years? You worked there while you were pregnant with your daughter?" Shane asked.

"Yes. Why?"

"It's just tough to imagine a young girl supporting herself by scrubbing floors while she's pregnant and alone in the world." His voice was uncharacteristically tender, and it set Cece on edge.

"Don't say it like that. Don't make me sound like a charity case. Mrs. Lee did me the biggest kindness of my entire life. She didn't just give me a temporary hand out and send me on my way to figure out life on my own. She taught me a valuable skill, she taught me the importance of hard work, and she gave me a chance when no one else noticed me. Those were the best years of my life."

"You must have meant a lot to her over the years for her to leave her bakery to you," Shane said in response to her impassioned speech.

"I think she left it to me because she had no one else. That's the only thing we ever had in common." Something in her voice changed the atmosphere in the room, and he could tell that her thoughts had taken a melancholy turn.

"Are you okay?" he asked without thinking.

Immediately, the vulnerability in her face disappeared and she said, "Of course I'm okay." Her game face was now firmly in place again.

"Cecilia, thank you for letting me see your sketches. They really are incredibly lovely."

"I'm glad you liked them, and if you're ever thinking about getting married, I hope you'll remember me," she said in the professional tone with the smile that didn't show her dimples.

That night, Shane fell asleep with a different image of Cecilia stuck in his mind. Tonight he envisioned her as she had been earlier, at ease and happy, with a pair of the cutest dimples he'd ever seen. It was a far cry from the haunting image of her lying on the hospital floor trying her best to escape some unknown demon.

"You need to re-chamber your leg before you bring your foot down and spin around to hook with your right," Karen instructed Cece as she lost her balance for the second time.

Cece was learning a new combination of moves; it was a combo that was pretty complex, and Cece was having trouble with the movement when it started from the left handed fighting stance. Her right hand was dominant, so she tended to struggle with any moves beginning from the left. She always made up for it by doing repeated drills until she could execute the move flawlessly.

Cece tried it again a few more times and was able to at least maintain her balance on the last try. "I'll be practicing that one at home later," Cece panted.

By the end of the session, both women were covered in sweat and smiling. Karen had given Cece quite a workout, but Cece would never admit how tired she was. If Karen was game to go one more round, then Cece was game too.

"You look like you're in a good mood today," Karen commented when she noticed Cece staring off into space with a smile hovering on her lips.

Cece snapped back to attention and said, "Yeah, I finally found a house. I move in in two weeks."

"Good for you! I guess it's nice when family is there to take you in, but it's even nicer when you can finally move on."

"Yeah," Cece agreed. She had been at Shane's house long enough. Staying with him brought out a side of her she hadn't seen in a long time. The other night, she'd showed him all of her work sketches and even some of her private ones. On some level, she knew she'd been showing off for him. She'd never cared what a man thought of her before, and she wasn't about to start caring now. The sooner she was on her own again, the better.

"Did you see the flyer on the bulletin board about the tournament next month?" Karen asked.

"No. Are you going to enter this one?" Cece asked. Karen won most of the tournaments she entered.

"Not this time, Sport, I actually thought *you* might want to enter this one. It's a kickboxing tournament. I recall you used to be quite a fierce competitor. Don't you want to see if you've still got it in you?" Karen was excellent at getting her students to challenge themselves, and she was just as excellent at pushing Cece's buttons. She knew her friend hardly ever backed down from a challenge or a chance to prove herself.

"I don't know if I'll have time to train. Next month is Lynette's wedding, and I'm doing the cake. I thought I told you about that already," Cece said.

"Stop making excuses," Karen admonished.

"Excuses?" Cece said. "Do you realize how long it takes to make all the decorations for a cake that serves over five hundred people? And do you know how long it takes to put it all together in the end? Do you know how stressful it is to know that so much hinges on this cake being a big success that if I fail it will bother me for years?"

"So, you're saying you can't spare one extra hour a day to train for this tournament?" Karen asked in disbelief.

"That's not what I'm saying. I'm saying that I can, but I don't think I should. Not now. This is too important to me to mess it up."

"Half an hour?"

"No," Cece snapped.

"Suit yourself," Karen shrugged. She slung her gym bag over her shoulder in a very nonchalant manner, but on her way out the door she left a flyer about the tournament next to Cece.

"You're so aggravating!" Cece shouted after her friend.

Her only reply was the sound of Karen's melodious laugh as she disappeared down the hallway. Even before she stuffed the flyer in her bag, Cece knew she would sign up for the tournament. How could she not?

Cece's mind worked furiously to come up with a tentative schedule for her extra training. She rode the bus from the gym to the bakery, and stared at the tournament flyer for more than half of the ride. Once her car was out of the shop, it would be easier for her to get from one place to another, but until then she was stuck riding the bus. The car situation was just one more thing that complicated her life, but she wouldn't let it stop her from entering the tournament.

She decided to start training that day. Instead of going straight back to Shane's house after work, she would stay late in her little personal training space upstairs. If she stayed an hour past closing every night until the tournament, she would be more than ready. Karen was definitely going to be happy about it.

Shane had just pulled into his garage when his cell phone rang.

"Shane, is my mother with you?" Rebecca's worried voice demanded as soon as he answered.

"I just got home, I'll see if she's in the house. What's up?"

"I've been trying to reach her for more than an hour. She didn't pick up at the bakery, and she's not answering her cell," Rebecca explained.

Shane went inside and briefly looked around for Cece. He called out, and got no answer.

"She's not here, but I'm on my way over to the bakery right now. I'll call you back when I get there," Shane said.

"Oh, you don't have to go all the way over there. I'd just wanted to invite you guys to dinner tonight. Norman and I have big news to share. Just tell her about dinner when she gets back to your house," she said and then disconnected.

Shane got back in his jeep and headed out. There was no way he was going to wait for her to show up; she hadn't answered her phone and he still had an uneasy feeling about the fire and the note. As he drove, he tried calling her number several times, but all he got was her voicemail. He left her a message asking her to call him back.

On the way to her shop, several scenarios played through his head. All of them featured an image of Cecilia in dire need of rescue. What if the person who'd left the note was holding her hostage at this very moment? What if she was lying dead in her shop with no help?

He pulled up to the curb in front of her shop a few minutes past four o'clock. The closed sign was up, and there was no sign of movement inside. He sprang out of his jeep and tried the door anyway. It was unlocked.

"Cecilia?" he called out as the door shut behind him. Everything seemed to be in order, but he didn't get an answer.

He walked to the back to check things out, and heard sounds coming from a small stairwell leading upstairs. He started walking up towards the door at the top, and the sounds grew clearer the closer he got. Music blared out of a stereo somewhere behind the door. He didn't even think to knock; he just turned the knob instead. The door opened, and he stepped inside with a sigh of relief. Cecilia was okay; she was more than okay, actually.

Shane stood in the open doorway and took in the scene as he waited for Cecilia to notice him. Her cell phone lay on the floor near the door, and the display showed more than ten missed calls. She was across the room on a padded mat doing some kind of stretch that Shane had never seen before in his life. She'd obviously just finished working out. She was wearing a pair of skin tight, black workout shorts that clung to her curves in a very provocative way. Every inch of exposed skin glistened with sweat, and Shane's mouth momentarily dropped open as he stared at her.

She held herself in a perfect handstand, giving him an unimpeded view of the beautiful athletic lines of her body. Every few seconds she brought her legs down into a full split as she maintained the handstand, and then she brought them back up again. He watched her do splits for almost a minute before she finally brought her legs together one final time and gracefully rolled out of the handstand and into another full split on the floor. Now she was facing him, and Shane saw that her eyes were closed. Her face was serenity itself—until she opened her eyes and saw him.

She leapt up and disappeared into the tiny bathroom without saying a word to him. He turned off her stereo and approached the bathroom door.

"Cecilia," he began, only to be interrupted.

"Go away," she gritted out.

"I can't," he sighed.

"Why not?" she demanded. "If you can find your way around a burning building, then surely you can find your way back out of my shop."

"Your daughter was worried about you. She'd been calling for more than an hour, and I came over to make sure everything was alright. If you'd answered your phone I wouldn't be here now," Shane informed her.

"I'm fine, so you can leave now."

52

"She wants us to come for dinner tonight. She said she has something big to tell you in person. Get dressed. I'll be waiting for you downstairs," and with those words he gave her the space she wanted.

He paced around in circles as he waited for her downstairs. Half of him wished he'd pounded on the door instead of walking right in; at least then she wouldn't have been so embarrassed. The other half of him wished he were still watching her now. Seeing her in her bathrobe the night of the fire had been bad enough, and now he also had the memory of those little black shorts to contend with. She had the most beautiful legs he'd ever seen in his life. He'd never been able to understand why some women thought skinny legs were attractive, and he was glad to see that Cecilia had such a healthy body. Apparently, kick-boxing did wonders for the female form—at least it had for Cecilia.

Half an hour later, Cecilia came down the stairs. She was fully dressed and had her game face firmly in place. The fact that she was dressed in pale pink caused him to do a double take. She wore one of Rebecca's dresses, and she looked stunning as always. Shane did his best not to stare at her, but he couldn't help noticing every little detail of her appearance, from the way her hair framed her face to the way the silk dress accentuated her tiny waist and fell around her calves in feminine folds that were so at odds with the tough persona she showed the world.

"That color looks good on you," Shane tried a modest compliment to see if she'd forgiven his intrusion on her privacy.

"Next time, knock," she tossed over her shoulder as she breezed past him and out the door.

The ride to Norman and Rebecca's might have been awkward if not for the fact that Shane was starting to get used to Cecilia's peculiar way of dealing with him. He'd noticed that she was more open if he showed interest in anything that had to do with her business. If he showed any personal interest, she'd give him the game face.

"When is the mayor's daughter's wedding again?" Shane asked.

"Her name is Lynette, and the wedding is in three weeks," Cece answered.

"That's coming up pretty quick. Right around the time you're moving out. You'll be pretty busy. Let me know if you need any help," he offered.

Cece let out a humorless chuckle. "All I have to move is myself and the clothes my daughter gave me. I lost everything else in the fire."

"Right," Shane winced. He hadn't thought of that. "I meant if you need any help with the cake. I'm pretty good with those pastry sacks."

"It's called a pastry *bag*, and Lynette's cake is going to be decorated with fondant and gum paste. So, unless you've worked with that before, you might actually just get in the way." The smile in her voice took the sting out of her words.

During the rest of the drive they discussed their jobs. Cece explained about all the different decorating techniques she'd learned over the years, and Shane told her about his new position as an instructor at the training academy for firefighters. The ride went by quickly, and before they knew it they were pulling into Norman and Rebecca's private drive.

"I'll never understand why the two of them live in a house this big," Cece said as she looked at it.

"I think Norman wants to have ten kids," Shane shrugged.

Cece's eyes widened and Shane cracked up at her comical surprised expression. Rebecca was standing in the open doorway when they got out of his Jeep.

"What's so funny?" she asked Shane.

Shane stole a glance at Cece before replying, "Inside joke."

Rebecca looked confused for a beat, and Cece stared at her as if she'd never noticed the fact that her daughter was a fully grown woman before that moment. Shane smiled again as he watched them.

They followed Rebecca across the foyer and into the formal dining room, to find that everyone else was already seated.

"What is this, a mini reunion?" Shane asked when he saw almost all of his siblings seated around the enormous table.

"I was in town for a conference at the tri-state orthopedic center, and everyone else lives around here. I don't know why you're acting so surprised to see us," George said. George was the doctor of the family. He'd gone into business with a dozen other orthopedic surgeons and opened up a very successful practice. He spent most of his time in the Chicago area, and Shane hadn't seen him since Rebecca and Norman's wedding four years ago.

"Forgive me, everybody," Rebecca interjected at that point. "Let me introduce you all to my mother, Cece Graves." She then went around the table and introduced each person one by one. "Mom this is George. He's a doctor and he lives in Chicago. You remember Shelly, their only sister, and Dylan my stepson. This is Edward. He's the oldest and he runs the horse ranch now. This is Brent. He lives in Nashville, but we hardly ever see him because, as the newly elected DA, he's the hardest working lawyer in town."

Shane watched as Cecilia greeted each of his siblings with a smile. He could tell she was uncomfortable, because she had her pleasant, professional smile plastered on her face. Her dimples were nowhere in sight. Once the introductions were finished, he and Cecilia took the only two empty seats at the table. Shane pulled out her chair for her before taking his own seat.

"Thank you," she said to him as she sat down.

Shane leaned forward to say, "You're welcome," and caught a whiff of her hair. She smelled like rose petals and baby powder, a combination which he found irresistible at that moment. Somehow he managed to tear himself away from Cecilia and take the seat beside her. Almost as soon as he sat down, everyone started talking all at once.

"So, what's the big announcement?" Shelly asked. "You said you'd tell us as soon as your mother got here."

Rebecca smiled a sweet sort of smile and looked over at her husband. "Do you want to tell? Or should I?" she asked.

Norman leaned towards her to plant a kiss on her forehead. Their hands were clasped under the table, and he gave hers a gentle squeeze. "You can tell them," he said in her ear.

Rebecca took a deep breath and squealed out, "I'm pregnant!"

Everyone at the table started blurting out words of congratulations, until Norman raised his hand to get their attention. "You didn't hear the rest. She's carrying twins," he added with obvious pride in his voice.

Another chorus of congratulations went up, but this one was spearheaded by Shelly's squeal of delight. "That is so awesome!" she said more than once. Shelly and Rebecca had grown very close during Norman's first deployment, and now they were best friends as well as sisters-in-law.

In all the excitement, Cece had uttered only one word. "Twins?" she'd whispered. Shane had been the only one to hear her, and he watched her carefully. She was an island of quietude in the sea of all their jubilant shouts and laughter. She smiled, and to the untrained eye she looked as completely happy as any mother should look. However, Shane could tell that Rebecca's announcement had triggered some kind of pain deep under the surface. This was a bittersweet moment for Cece, and very few people knew why. Shane caught the concerned look that Rebecca cast at her mother as Norman told everyone she was having twins, and he wanted to know what it was all about.

The rest of the meal happened in relative quiet. The conversation centered on all the things that expectant parents usually discussed. They discussed the gender of the babies, possible names, and the due date. Shane watched Cece very closely the rest of the evening, so closely he failed to notice that Rebecca watched him.

After dinner, everyone went into the living room to sit around and talk some more. Throughout the evening, Shane remained as close as he could to Cece without causing her any discomfort. She chatted with everyone, smiled often, and looked perfectly happy the rest of the evening, but Shane couldn't get her initial reaction out of his mind. Why had the fact that it was twins affected her so?

"Cece, do you want to get going soon? It's getting kind of late, and we both have to be up before dawn for work tomorrow," Shane asked her during a lull in the conversation.

"Yeah, just let me say goodbye to Rebecca in private," she answered.

When Cece took Rebecca off to a quiet corner of the room, Shane stood up and told everyone he was leaving shortly.

Cece didn't wait for Rebecca to hug her first. She wrapped her arms around her daughter and said, "I'm really happy for you, Honey."

"Thanks, Mom," Rebecca said in her quiet and endlessly patient voice. "I'm sorry about not telling you in private first. I didn't even think about it until after Norman told everyone I'm having twins. Are you okay?"

"Of course I'm okay," Cece said, but there was a catch in her voice and she was on the verge of tears. "Why wouldn't I be okay?"

"Because of Sarah, Mom. I'm not going to think less of you for thinking about her. She was the first thing I thought about when I found out it was twins. I should have told you in private."

"Rebecca, don't let that spoil even a little bit of your happiness. You deserve to be happy, and I'm happy for you. Yes, I did think about her, but not in a bad way. I just wondered what it would have been like to share this with her. I wondered what she would look like, and what her life would be like right now," Cece said. She hugged her daughter again before she continued. "You have everything I could have dreamed of for you; you have a great career, you're a good person, you have friends, you have a nice home, and even a husband who thinks you're the greatest thing since sliced bread. Just be happy about it, and stop worrying so much about me."

Rebecca hugged her mother one more time before telling her goodnight and watching her leave with Shane. The rest of Norman's family trickled out after Shane and Cece departed. By ten o'clock, Norman and Rebecca had the house to themselves again.

As soon as they were alone again, Rebecca said to Norman, "You need to tell your brother to stay away from my mother."

"Shane?" Norman demanded in surprise.

"Yes. Didn't you see the way he was acting at dinner tonight?"

"*No*," Norman said. He didn't want to talk about his brother. All he wanted to do was get in bed and cuddle with his wife, but she seemed intent on starting an argument. Maybe it was the pregnancy hormones. He hoped the fact that she was carrying twins didn't mean the hormones would be twice as bad.

"He was staring at her half the night, and following her around the other half. And when he pulled out her chair for her, I swear it looked like he was about to kiss the top of her head. Tell him she's unavailable, especially to him," Rebecca griped.

Norman ran an aggravated hand across his forehead. He looked down at his normally very sweet wife, and saw the seriousness in her expression. Her brows were furrowed together in obvious concern.

"All that stuff I've said about Shane being something of a playboy was mostly just jokes. He had a bit of a reputation when he lived in New York, but if you ask me, it was totally undeserved. My brother is a decent guy; he wouldn't do anything to hurt your mother, Honey," he tried to reassure her.

"You don't understand, Norman. You really should talk to him about this. I would, but I don't know him as well as you do. It will sound better coming from you," she argued back.

"I'm not going to interfere. They're both adults. If your mother isn't interested, she can just tell him so herself."

"That's exactly what I'm afraid of. You don't know my mother like I do. You need to talk to your brother, or he's going to get hurt."

"Honey, your mother couldn't possibly hurt my brother. He's been around the block more than a few times. Stop worrying so much about it," he said gently.

When she didn't immediately respond, he took advantage of her silence and kissed her. He was able to turn the direction of her thoughts to something much more pleasurable than arguing about her mother's love life. When he finally pulled her into his arms to sleep, she'd temporarily forgotten about her concerns. He loved her deeply, but he wasn't about to butt into his brother's personal life. Besides, he didn't think it was such a bad idea for Cece to have someone care about her. From what Rebecca had told him, and from what he'd seen, she led a very lonely life. Maybe Shane could be good for her.

That night, Shane found it hard to sleep. He paced the floor of his bedroom and fought the urge to ask Cecilia a bunch of personal questions. It was late, so she was probably sleep anyway. She'd stared out the passenger side window on the way back to his house, and he hadn't tried to strike up a conversation. He knew she wasn't very close to her daughter, but the two of them had been slowly building a real relationship over the past few years. Norman and Rebecca had actually talked of Cece quite a bit to Shane. He had been the one to ask all the questions, of course. He'd wanted to know more about her since the moment he first saw her, and now that she was here in his house he had a difficult time coming up with reasons why he should continue to give her space. She'd be gone in a few weeks anyway, so he had nothing to lose if he pressed the issue and tried to get to know her a little better.

Shane walked out into the hall and saw a sliver of light under Cece's door; she was still awake. He took a deep breath before knocking quietly. When she didn't answer, he tried turning the knob and found that the door wasn't locked. He walked in and saw Cecilia curled up on the floor in the far corner of the room. She had a sketchpad loosely clutched in her arms and a flashlight lay on the floor beside her.

Shane stared at her for a long time, debating whether or not he should just leave her alone. He watched the steady rise and fall of her chest. He noticed every little detail in the lines of her face, from the way her lips parted slightly to the way her eyelashes rested against her cheeks. When she reached up a hand to pull the blanket up over her bare shoulder, the sketchpad slipped out of her grasp, giving him a clear view of one of her personal sketches. It was a charcoal drawing of two little girls walking hand in hand down a sidewalk. He knelt down to pick it up, and Cecilia opened her eyes.

She blinked several times and said, "Shane?" with a wealth of uncertainty in her voice.

"I knocked," he blurted out before she got angry.

"But, did I say you could come in?" she countered. She sat up and pulled the blanket closer around her body.

"Why are you on the floor?"

She looked up at him in the dim light and shrugged. When she cast her eyes downward again, she saw her sketchpad lying in plain view.

"Who are the little girls in the picture?" Shane asked.

Cece reached out a hand and ran her fingers over the sketch. "I guess there are some things about my life that my daughter didn't blab about to everyone," she whispered.

Shane's ears burned at that comment, but he refused to feel guilty for wanting to know all about her. Someday she'd understand his motives, but now wasn't the time to explain.

Shane squatted down and leaned closer to Cece. He was close enough now to smell her rose petal soap again.

"Those are my daughters," she said with a shuddering breath. She turned her head so Shane wouldn't see that she was on the verge of crying. He'd already seen her cry once, and she didn't want to appear weak and needy. "Rebecca is a twin, but her sister Sarah was killed by a drunk driver who jumped the curb and ran up on the sidewalk one afternoon. They were five at the time. She died right there in my arms." Without another word she lay back down on the floor and closed her eyes as if she expected Shane to go away. He wasn't in the mood to take the hint tonight.

"Cecilia, you're *not* sleeping on the floor tonight," he said. He punctuated his words with action; he scooped her up, blanket and all, and started towards his room.

"Put me down, Shane," she whispered through her unshed tears, "I happen to like sleeping on the floor."

"Not tonight, not when I know that you can be comfortable right here with me." He used his foot to nudge the door to his room closed and deposited her on his bed.

She got up and started towards the door. He stepped in front of her to block her way. She looked up at him and said, "I'd move if I were you," in a deadly calm voice that would have made a lesser man step aside. Shane, however, straightened himself up to his full six and a half feet and crossed his arms over his chest.

"Just let me help you. You need a friend tonight." The concern in his voice made anger blossom in her chest.

"I don't *need* anybody," she gritted out. She then attempted to step around him and walk out of the room. When she got to his side, his arm snaked out and stopped her. When his other hand came up to take hold of her, she went into her fighting stance and blocked it with a swift, hard downward blow. He attempted to grab her again and she leapt back toward the bed.

"Leave me alone, Shane," she advised as she danced around him like she was in a boxing ring. She looked for a way around him without having to hurt him.

His legs were braced wide and his arms hovered ready to grab her again if she tried to get past him. "Cecilia, will you calm down? I just want to talk to you," he said in exasperation.

Cece made another sudden move for the door. She faked right and went left, but Shane still managed to get a good grip on both her arms. He pulled her closer as if he were about to hug her, and she panicked. She remembered what a powerful effect it had last time he'd held her, and she didn't want to be sucked into his orbit so easily tonight. She jumped up slightly and planted both feet squarely in his chest. He was incredibly strong, so she had to push hard with both legs for his grip to loosen. Once it did she pushed off and did a single back handspring before landing on her feet close to the bed. Shane looked down at her with a stunned expression on his face, and she took advantage of his shock. She advanced directly at him in a full frontal attack. She got in a few solid hits to his midsection, and then she brought one leg up to kick him in the chest. He stumbled back slightly, and she prepared to deliver the final blow, a spinning kick to the head with her right leg. She got good height in her initial leap off the floor, but when she brought her leg around to kick him, everything went wrong; he caught her foot before her shin made contact. She attempted to jerk her foot out of his grasp, but his grip was iron clad. All he had to do was hold her leg aloft and she lost her balance. He lifted his arms high over his head and held her dangling upside down. Her hands clawed at the floor as she tried to brace herself enough to kick him with her free leg, but he was too tall. As he held her, she couldn't touch the floor with anything but her fingertips. She struggled for a few more moments before admitting defeat.

"If I let you go, will you keep your hands and feet to yourself?" he asked.

"I'll try," she panted. Those words must have reassured him, because he immediately released his grip on her foot.

Cece didn't expect his abrupt release, and she fell to the floor with a loud thump to her head.

"Sorry, I thought you were going to catch yourself and attack me again," he apologized with a wince. "Is your head okay?"

"Just fine," she muttered. She slowly picked herself up off the hardwood floor and eyed Shane. He looked wary, and she almost smiled. At least now he knew she meant business.

"Are you sure your head is okay?" he asked after she swayed slightly.

"I'm *fine*," she said again. She flopped down on the bed, and felt the top of her head. She grimaced in pain, and Shane momentarily felt like the world's biggest jerk for dropping her.

"Let me see." Shane turned on the light and inspected her head. Upon finding a nice sized lump, he got her an icepack and instructed her to relax. He checked her for signs of a concussion, and once he was satisfied that she was mostly okay he crawled into bed beside her.

"I'm sorry about your head, Cecilia," he said into the silence.

"And I'm sorry for kicking you," she answered.

"No you aren't," Shane laughed.

"Well, I am a *little* bit sorry," she replied.

Shane smiled into the darkness. At least she was talking to him; it was more than he expected.

"How long have you been sleeping on the floor?" Shane asked.

"Years."

"Why?"

Cece simply shrugged and turned over on her side, presenting Shane with her back.

He scooted closer and wrapped his arms around her. "Why?" he asked again.

"I have more nightmares when I sleep in the bed. I like to press my back up against the wall at night, and the feeling of the hard floor and the hard walls surrounding me make me feel more secure," she explained.

"That wasn't so difficult, was it?" Shane whispered against her hair. He felt her tense muscles gradually begin to relax more the longer he held her. He skimmed one finger over the curve of her neck and shoulders, and then hugged her closer. His nose was buried in her hair, and the scent of her rose petal soap filled his nostrils and surrounded him with tenderness towards her.

"Why do you even care where I sleep?" she eventually got out with great effort.

"I just do. I want you to feel safe and comfortable," *with me* he added silently to himself. He didn't ask her any more questions, and she didn't volunteer any additional information. It was past eleven, so he lay quietly behind her and let her sleep.

Chapter 6

"This is your PASS device," Shane held up the small box-like object that was normally attached to a firefighter's Self Contained Breathing Apparatus, or SCBA. He taught a class at the fire academy, and was now informing a room full of new recruits about their turnout gear.

"The PASS device is automatically armed when the air circuit on your SCBA gear is activated. This is one of the most important pieces of equipment. Can anyone tell me why?" Shane asked the class.

Several hands went up, and he pointed to a tall young woman in the front row.

"The PASS device is important, because it sounds an alarm when the firefighter wearing it stops moving for ten to fifteen seconds," she answered.

"Very good," Shane said. He then continued talking about each piece of equipment and its function for the rest of the afternoon. Later in the cycle, the recruits would be required to finish their training in a field environment. Right now they talked about all the equipment, but soon they would use the equipment. Shane taught one of the basic classes dealing with search and rescue in a burning building, and his good friend Augustus participated in the part of the training where the recruits actually went into the burning building. The burning building the recruits would experience was a simulated fire set up specifically to train firefighters.

Shane had been through extensive search and rescue training during his years with the New York City Fire Department. All the training had been put to good use; he'd worked his way up to a first line supervisor position before he'd reached the age of twenty-five. Back then that had seemed like such a great accomplishment, and he'd been young and rash enough to let it go to his head and make him cocky. He'd experienced a world of things since then, and now he had a more humble attitude towards life. In the years since his departure from New York, he'd realized that he wasn't Superman.

As he stared out at all the fresh faces of the recruits, he thought back to his first year on the force. Firefighter positions in big cities were very difficult to attain. Competition was so fierce there were often hundreds of applicants for each job opening. Typically, only the top scorers in the written and physical exams were even considered for the position, but in New York even that hadn't been enough to gain notice. Shane had earned a bachelor's degree in mathematics from New York University by the time he was twenty, and he'd already held an Emergency Medical Technician certification from the state of New York before ever applying to be a firefighter. Those two things had pushed his application higher in the list of potentials, and his stellar performance on the strength and agility tests had been the tipping point. He'd been hired on his first try. However, it never would have happened if not for his friend Gus.

Gus had served on a small volunteer fire department in upstate New York, and despite training and an EMT certification, he hadn't been accepted with his first application. He'd enrolled in college so that his application would look better, and a young Shane had been his math tutor. There had been a firefighter in every generation of Gus's family for nearly a century, and he'd talked about it frequently. Eventually, Gus's fervor for the profession had rubbed off on Shane. They submitted their applications together and were both accepted to train at the academy within the same year.

"What are you still doing here?" Gus asked. Shane sat in the empty classroom staring out the window. He'd been thinking of his years in New York, and wondering where all the time went. It seemed like just yesterday he'd been a fresh faced twenty year old with his whole life ahead of him. Now he was older and wiser, and his life hadn't turned out nearly as he'd expected. Maybe he was only thinking such thoughts because his birthday was coming up soon. Friday he would turn forty-five; forty-five seemed like a millennium away from twenty.

"Nothing, man, I was just about to head home for the night," Shane answered.

"You still coming over this Friday?" Gus asked.

"I'm not sure," Shane hedged.

"You have to. Magda would kill me if the guest of honor didn't show up for his annual birthday dinner."

"You know, you two really don't have to do this for me every year," Shane said.

"She still feels bad about turning you down for me. She'll stop when you get married. Then she won't have a reason to feel sorry for you anymore," Gus laughed.

Normally Shane would have chuckled at that comment, and the fact that he didn't tonight was not lost on Gus.

"You still got a house guest?" Gus asked. He tried his best not to sound too concerned.

"Yeah, but not for much longer. She found a place. She's moving out next Saturday."

"Well, bring her along then. I'm sure Magda would love to meet her."

"I'll see if she wants to come," Shane said, although he knew she probably wouldn't.

"See you Friday," Gus said before he departed.

Shane remained seated and resumed his staring. It was almost dinner time, and he wondered what Cecilia was doing at the moment.

At that moment, Cecilia was closing her bakery so she could head upstairs to spar with Karen, who'd just arrived to train with her. She'd closed the bakery for a couple of hours in the middle of the day to go sign up for the regional kickboxing tournament. Karen had agreed to be her corner-man for the fight.

"You sure you wouldn't rather do this at my place?" Karen asked.

"Why? Is the floor not good enough for you?" Cece asked as she taped her hands for the match.

"I just thought it might be easier in the cage, but I guess there's enough space here since you don't have furniture," Karen commented. She took martial arts so seriously she had an entire gym in her house for training. It included a weight room and a cage in which she sparred with her multiple training partners.

Karen was a professional in the arts of Judo, Tae Kwon Do, and Muay Thai style kickboxing. She'd always taken it way too seriously in Cece's opinion. Karen lived and breathed martial arts every day of her life, whereas Cece just fed off of Karen's energy sometimes. This was one of those times.

Karen was way more excited about the tournament than Cece was. Cece was looking forward to the chance to prove to herself that she still had it in her to be a contender, but Karen tended to act like her life depended on the outcome of a match.

"Why do you care so much about this tournament?" Cece panted in the middle of the sparring. "I mean, you aren't even fighting in it."

"I know, but don't you want to come back strong after what happened to you? You haven't fought since you got shot. Don't you want to make a comeback?" Karen said as she danced around Cece, looking for an opening.

Cece landed a solid kick to Karen's right shoulder, and Karen staggered back a little. "I've changed a lot in the past few years," Cece said. She didn't want to tell Karen that she was more than a little nervous about the tournament. First of all, she hadn't fought in years. Second, she was entering the full contact women's professional division of the tournament. That meant that she would be in the ring in little more than a sports bra and some small shorts. The thought of people seeing her scars was positively nerve racking for her.

They were too busy striking and blocking for the next few minutes to talk much more. Karen seemed determined to put Cece through the workout of her life, but Cece managed to hang in until the end. When it was all over, Karen said, "Good job, Sport."

She'd seen how hard Cece had worked to recover after her brush with death, and she'd taken to calling Cece 'Sport' during their initial workouts after Cece had started walking again. At first, she'd done it just to annoy Cece enough to make her push herself, and then it had morphed into a sort of private joke meant to make her laugh. Lately though, she'd been using it more as an endearment.

Cece walked with Karen downstairs so they could grab some dinner before heading home for the night. She was floored to see Shane walking up to the door. What was he doing here?

If Karen hadn't been right there Cece would have dashed upstairs to avoid him. She hoped he hadn't come to discuss last night.

"You know him?" Karen asked after she caught the look on Cece's face.

"He's the family I've been staying with," Cece said.

Karen raised her eyebrows so high they almost touched her hairline, "There's no way you're related to him," she whispered.

"He's Rebecca's brother-in-law."

"Holy crap!" Karen said in a panicked whisper.

"What?" Cece demanded.

"The hottest guy I've ever seen in my *life* is about to see me looking like this!" Karen gestured to her casual clothes and disheveled hair.

"Will you stop? You look great, and he won't care anyway. I looked like a drowned rat when he got me out of that apartment fire," Cece reassured her friend.

"*He's* the fireman who saved you?!"

"Will you calm down? Jeez!" Cece snapped. She opened the door for Shane with a deliberate look of serious displeasure on her face.

"Hi," he said.

Cece stepped aside so he could come in, and as soon as he entered, he noticed Karen in the corner.

"Oh, I didn't realize you had company," he told Cece with an apologetic look.

"No problem, we were just finishing up, so you didn't interrupt anything. Karen, this is Shane Gregory, one of my daughter's in-laws. And Shane this is Karen Christian Holly, my best friend." Cece didn't miss the fact that Shane's face lit up like the Fourth of July as he looked at Karen. Cece knew her best friend had a striking appearance. Most men looked at her the way Shane was looking at her now. With her natural platinum blond locks and sky blue eyes, she had the face of an angel and the body of a goddess. She was also a few inches taller than Cece, giving her a leaner appearance when the two of them stood side by side.

"Karen Christian Holly?" he gushed, "you mean *the* K.C. Holly?"

"Guilty," Karen said with a cute little giggle.

"Wow... I remember that big MMA match you fought on *ESPN*... it was awesome," he said.

"Oh, you mean the one I lost?"

"I've always thought you should have won that one, but it was difficult to call," Shane said. He didn't know that it was the one thing he could have said to instantly endear himself to Karen forever.

"That one was heartbreaking, but I think I've had a few good comebacks over the years," she replied with a smile. She reached out her hand and said, "It's nice to meet you, Shane."

"Same here," he said, shaking her hand.

Almost as an afterthought, they both glanced at Cece.

"What were you two doing just now?" Shane asked Cece.

"Training for a Muay Thai tournament," Karen interjected before Cece could answer.

Shane turned back to her and asked, "You mean *Cecilia* helps you train for your fights?" in disbelief.

"Not this time, Big Guy," Karen chuckled. "She's the one fighting in the tournament; I'm just the sparring partner and her corner-man on fight night."

"Cecilia, you didn't tell me you're fighting in a tournament. When is it?" Shane asked.

Cece shrugged, and Karen said, "It's in about a week. Are you coming?"

"He's way too busy to watch me fight," Cece finally spoke up. "I don't know about you two, but I'm beat. I don't think I'll be joining you for dinner after all, Karen. Not tonight."

"But you promised," Karen pouted.

"Have you had dinner yet, Shane?" Cece demanded on impulse.

"No, but—"

"You should have dinner with Karen tonight. That way you two can get to know each other better. I'm sure you'll have lots to talk about," Cece interrupted. She handed Shane the key on her way out the door and said, "Just lock up and give me the key later."

The bus had just pulled up to the stop on her block, and she sprinted to it, pretending not to hear both Shane and Karen calling her name. Once the doors shut behind her, their voices were completely drowned out by the bus engine. She hadn't been lying about being tired. She was tired, but more importantly she didn't want to stand around and watch Shane fawn all over her best friend. Cece fiercely reigned in her emotions and told herself she was not jealous. So what if they were attracted to each other? Karen was a good person, and she deserved to be happy. If she found that happiness with Shane, then so be it. Even as she chastised herself for having any feelings at all, another part of her remembered how good it was to feel safe and finally get some sleep while in his arms. Safety had a powerful pull on Cecilia, and she'd never forget that, for two nights, Shane had given her the one thing she'd longed for most of her life—safety.

When she made it back to Shane's house, Cece took a quick shower and attempted to relax. She tried not to imagine Shane and Karen getting to know each other over dinner. It was none of her business what they did tonight, and she was determined not to think about Shane. The only problem with that plan was that Shane was all she *could* think about.

The sun settled a bit lower in the sky, and Cece went out so she could watch the sunset through the stained glass fountain again. Monday she would start making the decorations for Lynette's wedding cake. It usually took her a few days to prepare the decorations a wedding cake, but Lynette's would take a full week. The wedding was on the same Saturday she planned to move into her new house.

It was a nice, calm, clear evening, but the park was deserted. Besides Cece, no one else was there. She reclined on the hard, wrought iron bench and propped her feet up. She enjoyed the feel of the warm sun gently caressing her skin as it prepared to go down for the night. Every once in a while, a breeze would ruffle her hair and tickle her nose a bit. She cracked one eye open to look at her watch; it was now past eight. The sun sank lower in the sky, and would soon disappear over the horizon. Cece tried not to wonder what Shane and Karen were doing.

She closed her eyes again, and an unwanted image of Shane came to her. The admiration in his eyes and the way he'd smiled at her when he'd looked at her sketches had been nice, but she preferred not to think about it. She especially preferred not to think about how she felt when he held her close. She fell asleep on the park bench, trying not to think about him, but he was there. Just the remembrance of last night comforted her, and ensconced her in warmth that reminded her of the setting sun caressing her face. There one moment, and gone the next.

When Cece opened her eyes again, it was so dark she couldn't make out the fountain. It was so dark she couldn't make out anything around her. She attempted to sit up, but her arms and legs were too heavy to move. She blinked several times, thinking she was just groggy. She tried again to sit up, and felt the painful bite of a ragged cloth tied roughly around her wrists. She struggled, causing her deep abrasions to ooze blood that ran warm and sticky through her fingers. She opened her eyes, and then closed them against the darkness, the overwhelming darkness that wouldn't even allow her to see the way out. She cast her head about in frantic search for a door or a window. To her right was a large sliding glass door that lead to a balcony, but she had to get up to get to it. It seemed the harder she tried to get up the more firmly she was held in place. Cece struggled against her restraints until she panted and nearly lost consciousness in sweaty exhaustion.

Where were her clothes? She tried to scream out for help, but something in her mouth blocked her voice. It blocked her voice so completely she couldn't even hear herself scream inside her own head. She tried to bite down and spit the object out, but it went farther in and gagged her. The contents of her stomach churned and threatened to come out if she didn't calm down. She concentrated on her breathing until the wave of nausea passed over her.

She struggled again, but this time weakly, and with the resignation that she was likely going to die there. How long had she been tied down? Where were her clothes? Was Dot still alive? Even as she asked herself these questions, a voice deep inside whispered the answers that had always been there, the answers she wasn't ready to hear yet. There *was* still hope. Wasn't there? She *would* escape. Wouldn't she?

In desperation, she jerked her arms one final time and was rewarded with her freedom. She sprang up off the bed, and flew out the window. As she soared over the balcony railing, her clothes somehow reappeared on her body. The clothes made her heavy though, taking away her ability to fly and causing the ground to rush at her like a giant battering ram. When she landed, she looked up and saw him standing over her with the gun. He slammed the gun into her head, and she was once again lost in darkness.

When she opened her eyes again, she was right back where she'd started. The door to the balcony was still hovering to her right, just out of reach, and she was once again bound and gagged on the bed. Where were her clothes?

She struggled again, but this time she didn't get free. This time he came into the room to punish her. His cruel gray eyes observed her without emotion as he said, "You're gonna be begging me to kill you by the time I finish with you. Stupid little bitch! Do you know who I am?"

He grabbed her shoulders and shook her violently. He kept shaking until it seemed as if his fingers pierced through her flesh and dug into her bones. Her head slammed repeatedly against the bed, and screams and bile rose frantically up her throat, only to be stifled by the rag in her mouth. She tried with all her might to scream out for help, but his gray eyes hovered above her head and mocked her efforts. The gray eyes slowly faded back into blackness, and she was left alone, for a while anyway.

When she opened her eyes again, she saw the fountain before her. She sat up on the park bench, trembling and drenched in sweat. The nausea that had been churning in her stomach momentarily took over, and she vomited in the grass beside the bench. At least this time Shane hadn't been around to witness her nightmare. It was a small consolation, but there none the less. Cece washed her face with the cool water from the fountain and started back towards Shane's house. It was past ten o'clock, and he was probably still out with Karen.

Chapter 7

Shane didn't get a chance to talk to Cecilia again until Friday morning. She'd been avoiding him since she'd rudely shoved him and Karen off on each other for dinner earlier in the week. He'd gone by her bakery several times that week after work hoping to catch her, but she'd obviously found another spot to train. The past few nights she must've sneaked into the house after he'd already fallen asleep. She had to be one of the most aggravating women he'd ever met in his life.

By Friday morning, he was determined to talk to her. He was so determined he got up at the ungodly hour of three o'clock and waited outside her door. He didn't realize that he had a long wait ahead of him. When he finally did get tired of sitting there, he knocked on the door several times and got no answer. He unlocked it and went inside to find that Cece wasn't even there. Her few belongings had been cleared out, and the bed had been neatly made. She was gone.

Cece woke up to the sound of someone banging on her apartment door. A little spark of fear shot up her spine until she realized that it was probably just Shane. He still had the spare key to the main door of her shop, and she hadn't seen him since Monday night.

She squinted through the peephole and saw that it was Shane. She checked her watch; it was only four o'clock in the morning. Something drastic must have happened for him to be banging on her door so early. He was normally still in bed at this hour. She unlocked the deadbolt with shaking hands and threw open the door.

"What is it? What's happened?" she demanded. When Shane stared at her instead of answering, she almost panicked. "Has something happened to Rebecca?"

The distress in her voice got his attention and he said, "Nothing's happened. I just wanted to talk to you." He seemed caught somewhere between reassurance and vexation. He obviously hadn't meant to scare her.

She rubbed sleep out of her eyes and yawned, "You mean to tell me that you came over here at four in the morning to *talk*?"

"Yes," he said.

"*Mon Dieu, qu'est-ce qu'il y a?*" Cece muttered to herself as she let him in. She was starting to see that it was easier just to talk to him and get it over with rather than avoid him. If she didn't deal with him now, he'd be back. "Talk," she commanded after he shut the door behind himself.

"Have you been sleeping here all week?" he demanded. "Never mind, don't even answer that. I can see your bedding over there in the corner... Is the floor really that much better than spending the night with me?"

Cece looked up at him with tired eyes. She didn't have the energy to argue with him. He would never understand, so she shrugged.

"Cecilia, why are you so impossible?"

"I thought you'd be glad I moved out a few days early. Now you have your house back. You should be happy."

"You have no right to tell me how I should feel."

"Isn't that what you're doing to me right now? Telling me I should feel better in your house when *I* know perfectly well that I shouldn't," she countered.

"It's not the same, and you know it," Shane stated emphatically.

Cece shook her head and remained silent.

"Why did you leave?" he asked.

Cece shrugged and said nothing.

"Why did you ditch me with your friend, Karen, on Monday night?" he asked.

Cece shrugged again and said nothing.

Shane stared down at her in vexation and willed himself to just walk away from her and let it go. Her eyes flashed up at him, the centerpiece of a very mutinous expression which spread over her face. She backed up a little, and the light from the streetlamp outside her window struck her face so that she was no longer obscured in the predawn shadows of her apartment. He looked into her eyes again and did a double take. They were silver, not brown.

Her gaze faltered as he continued to stare into her eyes, and he got the powerful urge to pull her into his arms again. She clutched her robe tight around her neck with one hand and looked off to the side. A small sigh escaped her, and she looked back up at him. She opened her mouth to say something, and then closed it again with a forlorn look. Her face indicated just how mercurial her mood was this morning.

"Cecilia," Shane said her name as he inched closer to her. She ducked her head down a little farther. Why did he always seem to catch her when her guard was down? She'd spent the week fighting through her nightmares again, trying to come up with another coping mechanism, and she was exhausted in every way possible. In the past, she'd used alcohol to drown out the memories when they came on too strong, but alcohol was no longer an option for her. She'd promised her daughter she'd never drink herself into a stupor again. There was no way she could continue sleeping in Shane's house. The violence and frequency of her nightmares dictated that she must spend her nights alone. If he saw what a hollow shell of a person she really was, he'd be shocked and disappointed. She'd rather walk away with the memory of his admiration for her work than the knowledge that he felt sorry for her.

She refused to look up at him again while there was the chance that she could cry at any moment. She really wished he would just go away. Even as she wished he would leave, she wished even more that she were capable of asking him to stay. He had a lot to offer someone, anyone besides her.

"Did you have a good time with Karen? I think she really likes you," she finally said in a very small voice.

Shane didn't take the bait. He pulled Cecilia into his arms, cautiously at first, and then bolder when she didn't protest. He held her for long moments and breathed in the scent of her rose petal soap. It didn't take her as long to relax in his arms as it had the first time he'd hugged her. She even managed to release her death grip on her robe in order to briefly hug him back. He kissed the top of her head as he released his hold on her.

"I can't believe I didn't notice you were gone until this morning," he murmured.

"I was going to come back and tell you goodbye and thank you properly before I moved into my new place," Cece said.

"Goodbye?"

Cece nodded.

"Does that mean you don't ever want to see me again? I'd like to think that we've become friends over the past few months. We might not have spent a whole heck of a lot of time together, but you've got a friend for life right here," he said.

"Oh," Cece breathed.

"No goodbyes. We'll see each other again sooner and more often than you think," he smiled. "I didn't come over just to harass you; I actually want to invite you to dinner tonight. It's my birthday, and my best friend Gus and his wife Magda demanded that I bring you to their house tonight."

"Today's your birthday?"

"Yes. Now don't you feel bad for giving me such a hard time?" he teased. When she didn't respond right away, he took a deep breath and asked, "So, will you come? Please?"

"Wouldn't you rather invite Karen?"

"If I wanted to do that I wouldn't be standing here begging *you* to come... at four in the morning."

"I'll come."

"Good. I'll pick you up here after work," he said. "And, Cecilia, will you do me a huge favor?" he asked.

"What? You want me to make you a birthday cake? I can do that if you want."

"Not that," he laughed. "I was going to ask if you'd come back to my place, and stay for the week. I really don't like the idea of you staying here alone at night. Whoever left that note on your car obviously knows they can get to you here."

"I'll think about it." *Why couldn't she just say no?*

"I'll see you tonight then," Shane said. He leaned forward to plant a kiss on her forehead and whisper, "By the way, silver looks stunning on you."

He was gone before Cecilia realized he had been referring to her eyes. This was the first time he'd seen her without her brown contacts in. She silently cursed him for waking her up so early and catching her in such a vulnerable and natural state. And no one had ever called them silver before; she'd always thought of them as gray. The same shade of gray that had haunted her nightmares for most of her life.

The day was business as usual, except that every few seconds Cecilia's work was interrupted by thoughts of Shane. She was to have dinner with him and his friends, and not just any dinner; this one was his *birthday* dinner. *Why* had she said yes?

She closed an hour early for her training session with Karen. Since the day Shane had surprised them, Cece had been doing all of her training in Karen's personal gym. Karen had been right; it was way better to train in her private cage than in a cramped little apartment. Karen's décor never ceased to amaze Cece. She lived in a sprawling home almost the same size as Rebecca and Norman's, but there all similarities ended. Karen's house looked more like a sports bar and gym combined into one than someone's home.

She'd been raised by a single father whose main mission in life had been to train a world class athlete. Karen had never quite been able to make up for the fact that she'd been born a girl, but she'd been a dream-come-true for her father in almost every other way. She'd won the International Kickboxing Federation's amateur championship before she turned twenty and had earned quite a name for herself in the two decades since.

"Why are you so distracted today?" Karen demanded after Cece allowed her to land yet another easy hit to her midsection.

"That big wedding is coming up," Cece lied.

"It's something else," Karen grunted.

Cece remained silent for a few minutes, and tried harder to focus, but every other second she stressed about what she was going to wear to the dinner party. Karen had been recording all of their sparring sessions so that Cece could watch them and improve her technique; she knew this one would be embarrassing to watch later.

Karen's father rang the bell, signaling the end of the match. They had only gone six three-minute rounds. Cece had cut today's workout short so she'd have time to shower and change for dinner.

THE PROSTITUTE'S DAUGHTER

"Way to go, Sport! You've got this one in the bag!" Karen's dad yelled at her as she grabbed a towel to wipe the sweat from her face.

"It's Cece's fight this time, Dad!" Karen yelled back at her aging father.

"What?" he yelled back.

"I'm not fighting!" Karen carefully enunciated each word in a loud voice.

Her father stood up and shuffled off mumbling, "Then what am I ringing this darn bell for?" As he neared Cece's side of the ring he paused and looked up at her. "Hey, Cecilia! Haven't seen you in a while. Where you been lately?" he said.

"I've just been really busy at the bakery," she didn't bother reminding him that she'd been there every day that week; it wouldn't make him remember.

"Well, it's good to see you."

"Has he been getting worse lately?" Cece asked as soon as he was out of the room.

"Yeah, this morning he came down to breakfast naked," Karen said with a sad look. Her father had been diagnosed with dementia just two years ago, and rather than put him in a home she chose to take him in and hire a nurse to help out when she couldn't be there. "So, how's your friend, Shane?"

Karen's abrupt change of subject threw Cece off for a moment. "He's fine I guess," Cece hedged.

"He seems like a nice guy," Karen shrugged. She sent a sly glance in Cece's direction as she added, "He's not my type though."

"He's not?" Cece demanded in surprise. "You seemed to like him Monday night."

"All I said was that he was hot," Karen practically snorted.

"You never did tell me how dinner went," Cece said after a long pause.

"You want to know how dinner went? I'll tell you how dinner went. You're lucky I love you, or I would have kicked the crap out of you as soon as I saw you on Tuesday; *that's* how dinner went," Karen laughed.

"Sorry," Cece cringed. "I panicked and got all stupid when I saw him at the door," she admitted with a rueful expression.

"Have you ever considered maybe giving this guy a chance?" Karen said. "You aren't getting any younger, you know."

"What are you talking about?"

"He obviously likes *you* and not me. He was excited to meet K.C. Holly the fighter, but he couldn't have been less interested in Karen the woman. He spent half the night asking questions about you. Any man who has a thing for my best friend is definitely not my type."

"I think you're making it out to be more than it is. He's just been really nice to me lately because my daughter and his brother sort of forced him into it." Even as the words passed her lips, Cece knew she didn't believe they were true. She still wasn't ready to think of Shane in any other context than that of friend and helpful family member. Thinking of Shane as a man who was interested in her caused her heart to race and her palms to get all sweaty. It was easier to think of him as a friend.

"Why'd you need to go early today?" Karen asked.

"I'm having dinner with Shane and his friends," Cece shrugged.

"So you're going on a date?" Karen asked with a suggestively raised eyebrow.

"It's not like that," Cece said.

"It never is with you, Sport," Karen laughed on her way out the door.

Cece tried her best not to let Karen's good natured ribbing affect her too much as she showered and dressed for dinner. She had such a limited selection of clothes to choose from. Rebecca had given her a few dresses, two of which Shane had already seen her in. She was torn between a black dress that showed some cleavage and sage green dress that was more demure. She momentarily wished she had more time to shop for fashionable clothes. With a sigh, she decided on the more modest choice, because she didn't want to give Shane the wrong impression about tonight. Although she didn't go with the black dress, she couldn't stop herself from spending extra time on her hair. She tried not to analyze her motivation to impress him as she admired her reflection in the mirror.

When Shane showed up, he found Cece waiting for him downstairs in one of the booths. She stood up as soon as he walked in the door. Her eyes were brown again, and she had her game face firmly in place.

"Happy birthday," she said with a polite smile.

"Thanks," he smiled back at her. "I feel a little underdressed now. You look great."

"You don't look underdressed at all." The compliment may have been modest, but the look she gave him clearly said that she liked what she saw. She was aware of the fact that she was staring, but she couldn't help herself, and he was probably used to being stared at by women. He wore a pair of dark denim pants and a light blue button down shirt that complimented his midnight blue eyes very nicely. For such a big man he was very well proportioned. His shoulders were wide and his chest very muscular, but no part of him appeared bulky. Cece had to blink away the memory of those powerful arms around her.

"You ready to go?" he asked after what seemed like an eternity.

They stepped out into the warm evening air, and a breeze swept past them. The wind ruffled Cece's hair and messed up some of her carefully arranged curls. She reached up to smooth them back down and caught Shane staring at her. "What?" she asked.

"I just noticed that your hair looks a little different than normal," he answered as he opened the passenger door for her.

She waited until he got in and started the Jeep before she spoke again.

"What do you mean?" she asked.

"It looks a little lighter. Did you get it colored this week?" he asked.

"No. I normally use a color rinse to make it darker. I haven't used any since before the fire, so I guess it fades after a few months," she admitted.

"So your eyes aren't really brown, and your hair isn't really black? What is your natural color?"

"Reddish-brown with a few highlights. Trust me though, it looks better black."

"Why do you wear colored contacts? Why not just wear regular?"

Cece sighed. He was just full of questions tonight. "I think my eyes look better brown, and I have 20/20 vision, so regular contacts would be pointless. I only wear them to change the color," she explained.

"Why don't you like yourself the way God made you?"

"Are you kidding me?" Cece couldn't believe he'd had the nerve to ask her such a question.

"Not even a little bit," he answered her in a serious tone.

"How can you say such a thing to me? If I were a white woman it wouldn't matter how many different colors I dyed my hair. Why does the fact that I'm 'ethnic' make it worse for me to change my hair color?"

"Why do you get so defensive about simple questions?" Shane asked.

"I'm not getting defensive, I was making a point," Cece snapped.

"And what point would that be?" Shane prompted her.

"Never mind. You wouldn't understand anyway," she grumbled. What had been her point? She honestly didn't even know what had prompted her to attack him. She'd always been sensitive about the way she looked. Maybe if she didn't have the exact same hair and eyes as the man who'd taken away almost everything she'd ever cared about, maybe then she'd be able to look in the mirror with something other than loathing for her natural self. Shane could never understand, so she changed the subject.

"So, it's your birthday..." she said in a conversational tone.

"Nice try, Cecilia," Shane smiled. "You can't change the subject that easily. I don't know why you're so secretive and mysterious about everything. I just want to get to know you." When she didn't reply right away he continued, "When my little sister, Shelly, was in high school, she tried to dye her hair brown, and I wouldn't let her. Actually, I held her down while Brent threw out the hair dye. I've always thought that women are more beautiful when they love what they have naturally, rather than trying to conform to what beauty product companies want them to believe is beautiful. The only reason I'm asking about the hair and eyes is because I think you are beautiful the way you were born, and you should too. Everybody should."

By this time Shane had pulled into the driveway of a two story brick house in a middle class suburb north of Nashville. Cece was spared from having to reply, because he immediately got out and went around to open her door for her. He smiled the smile that made her feel things she didn't want to feel, and then he offered her his arm. She couldn't help smiling back. With his touch came the feeling of warmth and safety. She smiled again and tried not to enjoy his attention so much.

Right before he knocked on the door he bent down and whispered in her ear, "Remember it's my birthday. Be nice, and pretend like you actually like me."

Cece could tell he was teasing, and she was laughing at the pleading look he gave her by the time the door opened.

"Shane! Happy birthday," Magda greeted him. She had the warmth and familiarity in her voice that came from decades of friendship.

"Hi, Magda." Shane hugged the small woman, and then turned toward Cece. "This is my friend, Cecilia. She's the one who's been staying in my house since the fire."

Magda turned towards Cece and offered her a big smile and hand shake. "It's so nice to meet you, Cecilia," she said with a very thick Spanish accent. "Shane has talked about you so much!"

"He has?" Cece asked in disbelief.

"*Si*," Magda nodded. "Come in, come in. Make yourself at home."

"Thanks." Cece smiled. Magda was blessed with the kind of beauty that had the power to mesmerize both men and women. Her attitude was so open and inviting Cece couldn't help but like her.

"This is my husband, Augustus, but we call him Gus."

Gus reached out and shook Cece's hand, "It's good to see you again."

"Likewise," Cece returned. "You two have a beautiful home."

"*Gracias*," Magda smiled. "We hope you like Spanish food. We're having paella for dinner. It's Shane's favorite."

The four of them took their seats at the dining room table. Shane and Cece sat across from Magda and Gus. Cece couldn't help but stare at the two of them. Gus was almost as tall as Shane, and he was very bulky. He had massive arms and a chest like a barbarian body builder. His wife, on the other hand, was the picture of demure, petite beauty. Gus wasn't a handsome man by any stretch of the imagination, but his bright green eyes, freckles, and red-orange hair made for a striking and surprisingly attractive combination. The three of them talked about a variety of subjects and made several attempts to draw Cece into the conversation. She gave short answers, preferring to listen and learn rather than talk too much. She'd never been a great conversationalist anyway.

"So, what do you do, Cecilia?" Magda asked during a lull in the conversation.

"I own a small bakery on the north side of Nashville," Cece answered.

"Oh, that's interesting," Magda prompted, but Cece didn't take the hint.

She said no more about her business. Instead, she asked, "How long have you three known each other?"

Gus spoke up at that point. "Shane and I go back twenty-five years. Back in college he was my math tutor."

Cece glanced at Shane and saw a bright red blush creeping up his neck. "We actually both got hired onto the New York City Fire Department in the same year. We went through the training academy together," Shane said.

"How did you end up in New York? I thought your entire family was from Tennessee?" Cece asked.

"It's a long story. Let me tell it," Magda blurted out before anyone else could reply. "I can't believe you live with this man for almost three months and still you know so little about him, Cecilia."

"It's not like we're newlyweds; he offered me a place to stay out of kindness. Neither one of us knows much about the other," Cece tried not to sound too defensive in her reply.

Magda glanced at Shane before she continued. "He was raised in Tennessee, but his dear departed mama's last wish was for him to become a musician. He ended up in New York on a full scholarship to New York University. He was such a smart boy; he finished high school early and started college when he was just sixteen. Can you imagine doing something like that? He was a double major in music and mathematics." She paused for a moment while Cece looked at Shane. Her eyes were deeply assessing, and they practically picked him apart right there at the dinner table. He would have given anything to know what she was thinking as Magda went on, "He finished two degrees by the time he was twenty one, but instead of playing for the symphony, he signed up to be a firefighter."

"What instrument do you play?" Cecilia asked. For once she was the one burning with curiosity. Suddenly, she wanted to know a lot more about this man, everything in fact.

"I play the violin every Sunday in the church orchestra," Shane said.

"He plays the guitar too," Magda smiled at Cece. "Haven't you heard him practicing since you been in his house?"

"No."

"Okay. Enough about me," Shane interrupted. He could sense Cecilia's discomfort with Magda's probing questions. "Cecilia actually designs wedding cakes and cakes for other special occasions. I've seen some of her work, and she's really good," he said.

"How long have you been doing that?" Magda asked Cece.

"Almost thirty years."

"*Dios mio!*" Magda exclaimed. "You *look* like you're twenty-something. How can you have worked in a bakery for thirty years? Did you start when you were born?"

Cece smiled an ironic little smile. In many ways, she felt like her life had begun when she'd started working for Mrs. Lee. She had left the past behind and resolved never to think about it again, and with exception of nightmares she'd been able to keep that resolution. "I started working there the day I was born actually," she said to the table at large.

Magda and Gus looked at her as if they thought she might be a little crazy, but Shane chuckled and patted her hand. She turned to look up at him, and their eyes met. She'd looked into his eyes plenty of other times, and she'd known he was an extremely handsome man from the moment she'd met him. There was no reason for her insides to suddenly feel like they were vibrating with new life when he smiled at her tonight. Magda and Gus didn't exist anymore as Shane stared deeply into her eyes. There seemed to be some secret message imbedded in their midnight depths, and Cecilia wanted nothing more than to know what it was.

Gus cleared his throat loudly and Cece dropped her gaze to the table; Shane's hand was still resting lightly on top of hers.

"Time for cake!" Magda stood up so fast her chair scraped the floor. "I'll be right back. Gus, you want to help me with the cake?"

"You know I'm no good at lighting candles," Gus groused as he kept his seat.

Magda gave him a look that obviously meant something to him, because in the next instant he trudged behind his little wife to the kitchen.

"Well, *that* wasn't awkward at all," Shane smiled at Cece.

"Your friends are nice, but Magda is kind of pushy," Cece whispered. "I feel like I've offended her by not knowing every little thing about you. She's probably going to quiz me later."

Shane smiled and brought her hand up to his lips. "Thanks for being such a good sport. They like you."

Cece's lips parted slightly, and she was about to say something when Gus and Magda returned with the cake. She smiled when she saw that it was just an oversized chocolate cupcake with one candle on top.

"So, how old are you?" she asked Shane after he made his birthday wish and blew out the candle.

"Too old to still be making birthday wishes," Gus cut in.

"Forty-five," Shane sighed, "I'm getting old." Cece looked at him in surprise, and he winked at her. "But I'll still remember to respect my elders."

Chapter 8

Shane's birthday dinner went so well, he smiled about it all weekend and halfway into the next week. Cece had been relaxed and almost normal with him all evening, and he'd even managed to convince her to spend the week in his house. They'd reached a truce of sorts regarding the sleeping arrangements. He'd promised not to enter the guestroom uninvited, even if he heard her having a nightmare. As long as he didn't intrude on her privacy at night, she would remain in his house for the week.

It was Wednesday afternoon, and Cecilia had been putting in extra hours at the bakery in order to complete the decorations for Lynette's wedding cake. He'd stopped by the bakery a couple of times that week to watch her work. It had been nice to see a different side of Cecilia. While she'd concentrated on making all the marzipan and gum paste details for the cake, Shane had assisted her with the cleaning and other mundane tasks. He also got to spend much more time watching her and getting to know her. She was more relaxed and willing to talk while she worked; in fact, she turned out to be quite a chatterbox while decorating cakes.

He parked in her small lot and walked up to her door with a smile on his face. He looked forward to seeing her progress on all the tiny flowers she'd been crafting all week.

"Hey there, Big Guy," Karen said from behind the counter as soon as Shane walked in the door.

"Hi, Karen. It's nice to see you again," Shane smiled.

"You looking for Cece?"

"Yeah. Is she in the back?"

"No. She won't be back until closing time. She took the day off."

"Day off?" Shane asked. He thought Cece never took a day off. "Is everything alright? Did something happen?"

"That depends on your definition of alright," Karen said with traces of sadness in her normally peppy voice.

"What's going on?" Shane asked.

Karen looked up at him. "I'm thinking that if Cece wanted you to know why she took the day off she would have told you herself."

Shane shook his head in vexation. "What is with you women and being so mysterious? I ask a simple question, and I get the run around every time." He turned around to walk out, and Karen's voice stopped him.

"Wait," she said. He turned back around and gave her a look that would have intimidated most men. She raised her chin up a notch and said, "If you tell me why you're so interested in Cece, I'll tell you anything you want to know. She's a very private person, but she doesn't always know what's best for her."

"What are you, her father now?" Shane snapped.

"Yeah, something like that," Karen snapped back with added venom. "I'll withdraw that offer if you give me anymore attitude."

"You'll tell me *anything* I want to know?" he wanted crystal clarity before he told her anything about his feelings for Cecilia.

"Anything that I know," she said.

"You swear?" he asked.

"What are we, in grade school now?" she said. "Just tell me why you've been pestering my friend, and I'll decide if you need to know more about her."

Shane guessed that was all the assurance he would get out of her. She was even more of a hard nose than Cecilia was at times. He sighed and said, "I care about her... a lot. And I haven't been pestering her."

"There are some things that she'll never talk to anyone about, not even me. It might be easier for you to pick another woman to care about. In the past twenty years Cece has dated very few men, and the last one ended up in the hospital after he hurt her. Rebecca can tell you all about it."

"Why are you telling me about that? Does it have anything to do with where she is now?" Shane interrupted.

Karen shrugged. "Just thought you should know. Anyway, about why Cece took today off..."

"Well?" Shane prompted when she didn't go on.

"Do you know that Rebecca hasn't always been an only child?" Karen asked. The tone of her voice had taken a melancholy turn.

"I know. She told me about Rebecca's twin, Sarah. She said she died when she was five."

"Today is the anniversary of her death. Cece takes the day off every year to put flowers on the building where it happened and on her grave," Karen said.

"That wasn't so bad, was it?" Shane asked. "I don't think Cecilia will kill you for telling me that." He tried his best to sound reassuring, because Karen now had tears streaming down her cheeks.

"You can't ever mention it to her. She never talks about it, but I know that's where she goes," Karen sobbed.

"How would you know that's where she goes if she's never talked about it?" Shane asked in confusion.

"I just know, because I was there when it happened. That's how we met."

Shane waited a few minutes while Karen fought to bring her crying under control. "Are you okay?" he asked.

"No!" Karen screeched at him. "She won't talk to me about it, but I just know she still hates me for it. I just know she does."

"Why would she hate you?" Shane asked gently. Karen wasn't making any sense right now, but he wanted to get to the bottom of what was bothering her.

Karen dried her face and looked up at him. "It all seems like just yesterday sometimes," she sniffed. She walked over to one of the booths and sat down. He sat across from her and waited for her to continue.

"I'd just won my first big championship, but I was still considered an amateur kick boxer at the time. I thought I was invincible, and I thought I didn't have to listen to my father anymore. I was almost twenty at the time, and I'd started dating this *nothing* guy. He was a loser, and my father hated him. The only reason I continued seeing him was to get on Dad's nerves. I just wish I'd figured that out sooner. He came by to pick me up from the gym around four o'clock that afternoon, but he'd been drinking. I got into the car with him anyway. That was the single biggest mistake of my life. I should have taken the keys or called the cops...anything but let him drive. He started swerving all over the road, and when I told him to pull over and let me drive he did pull over, but he didn't let me drive. He punched me in the face and told me to get the fuck out of his car. I was standing there in the street with my nose bleeding all over the place when he took off again. He accelerated too quickly, didn't have control of the car..." By this time Karen's words had devolved into unintelligible sobs.

Shane reached across the small table and squeezed her hand. "You can't blame yourself for something that idiot did," he said.

She looked up at him with red, swollen eyes and went on, "It was the worst thing I ever saw in my life. There was almost no traffic that day. His car skidded straight across the street, up onto the curb and right over Sarah. She was standing there with Cece and Rebecca when it happened. None of them ever saw it coming. Cece and Rebecca were on the sidewalk near the bus stop, and Sarah was back a little farther from the curb. She was close to the window of the building so she could see her reflection as she posed. You know how kids like to play in the windows...

"His car went straight at her. She never had a chance. She was there one second, and gone the next. She disappeared under the car, and Cece screamed. I'll never forget that scream as long as I live. I ran across the street, and looked at the front end of the car, but she wasn't there. Cece and I both looked around for Sarah, thinking, hoping, that she had been spared somehow, but we were wrong. Cece was the one who finally noticed her legs under the car. She crawled under there while people gathered to gawk at us. She pulled at Sarah's legs, but she wouldn't budge and she didn't make a sound. There was no crying, just Cece screaming her name over and over again. We all knew she was dead before the fire truck and ambulance even got there, but Cece stayed under the car and clung to Sarah's little legs. I'm not even sure if she noticed all the blood on the sidewalk around her.

"I didn't know what else to do, so I held onto Rebecca. I didn't want her to see what was going on, and Cece wouldn't let go of Sarah... The paramedics knew she was dead as soon as they

88

got a good look at her. They told Cece she should let go, because Sarah was gone, but Cece just kept screaming at them that she wasn't gone. They knew she was dead, and they didn't want Cece to see when they took the car off of her. They had a hard time making her let go. Cece kept insisting that she had to be with her daughter. She kept saying she couldn't abandon her. They put up those white sheets they use to keep the public from seeing everything while they removed the car. Two big EMT guys grabbed Cece and kept her back while they moved the car. She waited until they got it up on the tow truck before she twisted free and ran over to look at her daughter. No one expected it, and I'm not entirely sure they could have stopped her if they had. She threw the sheet back, and all I could do was cover Rebecca's eyes before she saw too."

Shane stared at Karen as he let the entire story sink in. Cece's version of her daughter's death had been much more succinct and less emotionally connected than Karen's. He was actually fighting back tears right now.

Karen looked down at the floor and allowed the tears to flow unchecked down her cheeks. "She threw the sheet back, and we all saw Sarah. The car had come at her from an angle and smashed her upper body into the brick corner by the window. Her head and shoulders had been pinned by the bumper. Before they removed the car they discovered that there wasn't much left that was recognizable. They didn't want Cece to see that, but she saw anyway. I turned away and took Rebecca into the coffee shop next door, but Cece passed out cold right next to Sarah. They had to sedate her after she woke up again.

"I stayed with her, and called my father to come help. Cece didn't have enough money for a funeral and burial, so my father paid for everything. At this point, Cece still didn't know that my ex-boyfriend had been driving the car. She just thought that I was some nice by-stander."

"Does she know now?" Shane asked.

"Yes. A few weeks after the funeral, I went to talk to her. I felt so guilty; I had to apologize. She didn't take it so well."

"What happened? You two are pretty good friends now..." Shane said.

"She went a little crazy and beat the crap out of me. She didn't know any Judo at that time, just some Karate and whatever she had picked up on her own. When she came at me, I tried my best to defend myself without hurting her. I put her in an arm bar, and that should have ended it. Judo is all about submission holds and using your opponent's weight and momentum against them. I had her in a hold that should have ended it, but she chose to let me break her arm rather than submit. And then she still managed to break my nose and crack one of my ribs even with one of her arms broken," Karen explained.

"How did you two end up as best friends after all of that?" Shane asked in amazement.

Karen smiled a very small and sad sort of smile. "I was a very good fighter. I'd never been beaten by another woman, especially not one smaller than me. I was really impressed that she could do that with a broken arm. I'm still not sure why Cece accepted my friendship. It took her a while to warm up to me, but I can tell you that our fight started it. She said that she wanted me to teach her the technique I used to break her arm so she could defend herself better. She's been getting free Judo and kick boxing lessons from my father's martial arts academy ever since. She did tell me once that if I ever brought up what happened to Sarah she'd never talk to me again. Since then, I've kept my word about that. You're the only person I've ever talked to about it, besides my dad."

"Why *did* you tell me?" Shane asked.

"Two reasons. One, that's a hell of a burden to carry around for twenty years, and two, Cece never talks about anything that bothers her. I suspect you might end up being the best thing that ever happened to her. She hasn't scared you off yet, and that's a good sign. I'm hoping that you'll be able to offer her some type of comfort today when she gets back to your house. Just don't be obvious about why. If you act too concerned about her feelings it tends to piss her off."

"I've noticed," Shane sighed. He reached across the table to squeeze her hand again. "You can't keep carrying around this guilt. You eventually did the right thing by telling him to pull over. Sarah's death isn't your fault, and if Cece thought it was there's no way she'd be your friend right now."

"Thank you, Shane," Karen whispered. She felt lighter in spirit after talking to him, and she breathed a sigh of relief. He had a very warm and comforting air about him.

"1 promise not to tell Cecilia about our talk." He squeezed her hand one more time before he left.

Shane drove to his house to change out of his work clothes, and then he went for a walk in the park. Karen's story had unsettled him in several ways. He had responded to hundreds of automobile accidents during his career as a firefighter. He'd seen more catastrophic accidents caused by drunk drivers than fires over the years, and he knew how the families of the dead usually reacted. He imagined that it must have been an excruciating scene for everyone involved, especially Karen and Cecilia. Karen was carrying around guilt that would probably never completely go away, and Shane was one of the few people who could understand that type of guilt.

He thought back to the time when he had been a firefighter in New York City. He'd been on the force for fifteen years, and was something of a golden boy in the department. He'd gotten every promotion at the earliest possible time in his career. He'd taken every class he could, and he'd done everything flawlessly. At thirty-five he'd been in charge of a rescue company in the city, and he'd thought he might have a real shot at being fire chief someday. It would have been the pinnacle of his career as a firefighter.

Things had gone so perfectly for him during those first fifteen years he'd been invincible in his own mind. All the terrible things that happened to other firefighters had always just missed him and the ones he cared about. He'd heard of plenty of deaths, but it was always some other city, some other company, some other firefighter involved. And then one day it was his company, his firefighters.

A call had come in about a burning building in a dilapidated industrial park in the middle of winter. Although the building had been abandoned for years, standard procedure was to send the search and rescue teams into the building to search for victims. In the winter, abandoned buildings were usually filled with homeless and indigent people. Shane's company had been the first on the scene, and he had been in charge of the initial search and rescue operation. He'd been the one in charge when tragedy struck. His mind shied away from the memories as he neared the fountain in his neighborhood park. It all seemed like a lifetime ago, yet the memory was so vivid in his mind that it could have happened yesterday.

He sat on the bench and watched water spurt out of the fountain. Half of his mind was on Cecilia the entire time. He'd had a good time with her the day she first saw the fountain, and now it reminded him of her. He sat staring at this particular fountain, and allowed his mind to wander into musings about fountains in general.

When water came out of a fountain it made such a delicate display. The patterns of the water could be disturbed by inserting a single finger into the streams. The water could then trickle harmlessly between one's fingers and disappear. For someone who wasn't familiar with water, a fountain could give the impression that water was a substance that was easily manipulated or contained. The fountain showed the aesthetic value of the water and the gentle qualities that could serve as a comfort to those who encountered it.

Shane watched as the water went up in a delicate arch and continuously splashed down into the small pool at the bottom of the fountain. He watched until a sudden deluge of rain from a thunderstorm poured over the fountain, obscuring the once delicate arches of water with a powerful downpour that overwhelmed and soaked everything in the park, including Shane.

He hid behind an old cherry bark oak tree and watched as Cece strolled somberly through the little cemetery. She carried a small bouquet of flowers in her arms; she'd stopped at a flower shop up the road to buy them. He'd followed her on the bus this time. He'd been surprised when she left the bakery shortly after the doors opened this morning. She'd left her car in the lot and boarded the bus. He'd stepped on right behind her, and she hadn't noticed him. Women never noticed him.

He crept from tree to tree as he followed her across the cemetery. He stayed in the shadows so she wouldn't be scared away. The last thing he wanted to do was scare her before he figured out exactly what he should say to her. After all these years, what could he possibly say?

Eventually, she came to a stop at one of the graves and knelt down. She stayed there for so long he sat down and leaned against a tree trunk as he watched her. He took the flask of whiskey out of his breast pocket and drank some while he watched her. He didn't know how much longer he could stand being in the cemetery. The last time he'd been in a cemetery had been to bury her. *She'd only been gone for a few months, not nearly long enough for him to face the cemetery again without some liquid courage. He took another swig from his flask. He had to make it right for her.*

Tears sprang to his eyes again as soon as he thought of her lying in her casket. The cold cheek that should have been warm, the peaceful expression that didn't truly reflect the turmoil she'd been through in the months prior to her death. Death. There was that word again. He took another swig and watched Cece.

Cece looked up at the sky after an angry flash of lightening startled her. She said a few words to the headstone, kissed her hand and rubbed her fingers over the name engraved on the stone, and then she turned to leave the cemetery. Almost as soon as she turned away from the grave, the sky opened up and the rain came crashing down on them. He sat under the tree and watched her sprint through the cemetery and back up the sidewalk toward the bus stop. This time he didn't follow her. He knew where he could find her tomorrow, and he was more interested in finding out who this grave belonged to. Whose grave did Cece Graves just visit?

He got up, and closed his flask with surprisingly steady hands. His heart slammed painfully in his chest, and his legs could barely hold him up as he approached the grave Cece had just abandoned. His approach was slow and steady; the rain and thunder were no inducement to hurry. Every step he took seemed to transport him more firmly back to the past. It was not her *grave. He had to keep telling himself that it was not her grave with each additional step, and yet each step seemed like an eerie echo of the same steps he'd taken to get to her grave site the day they'd buried her.*

He half expected to see her name on the stone, and he fell down to his knees in relief when he saw the name Sarah Graves instead. He wasn't crazy after all. He wasn't reliving that day again. That knowledge didn't bring her back, but it did calm his heart some. He took another drink of his whiskey and looked at the birth and death dates. He didn't know for sure, but it was reasonable for him to guess that Sarah had been Cece's daughter. It was also reasonable for him to guess that Cece had no idea who Sarah's father was. It really was too bad about her daughter's death. Death. There was that word again.

Chapter 9

Cece was completely soaked by the time the bus pulled up, and she didn't feel like going back to the bakery. She hated seeing the concern and sadness in Karen's eyes every year when she returned from her day of remembrance. She'd wanted to tell Karen for the longest time that she was over it, but that would've been a lie. The death of a child is something a mother never truly gets over; she just learns to live with it if she's lucky. Today, she'd thought all day about Rebecca's pregnancy. She was due in January, and Cece was looking forward to the birth more than she could say. Even as she looked forward to the new life that Rebecca carried inside her, Cece still couldn't shake her pessimistic thoughts about death. Things could change in an instant, and she'd seen it happen more than a few times in her life. She couldn't wait to see her grandchildren, but at the same time she was terrified of having more loved ones to lose. In the past, she'd always emotionally distanced herself from everyone as a way to prevent being hurt again, but recently it had been increasingly difficult to create that distance. She found she simply didn't want to anymore.

While on the bus, Cece called Karen to tell her she wouldn't be back to the bakery that day. Karen didn't ask any questions; she simply assured Cece that she would lock up before she went home for the night.

Rain was still pouring down when Cece got off the bus near the park in Shane's neighborhood. Normally, she would have strolled through the park and admired the fountain for a minute or two, but today she sprinted the short distance to his house. She was soaked when she got there, so she stood next to the garage door and tried to squeeze as much water as she could out of her clothes before she entered. His Jeep was in the garage, and she crept inside trying not to make a sound. She was in a glum mood today, and she didn't want to face him and all his questions about her life.

The house was so quiet, Cece thought Shane must have gone out again, either that or he was in the shower. All the lights were off, and the television set wasn't even on. She walked down the hall towards the bedrooms, and paused when she heard music coming from his room. He was playing scales to warm up, as Rebecca often did before she played something on her piano. Even the scales he played sounded like a beautiful little prelude to something superb. The notes stopped her in her tracks and draw her closer to his partially open bedroom door. Her shoes squished as she shuffled closer, but she didn't stop until she was right on the verge of entering his room.

Eventually, he started playing an actual song. Cece was certain she'd never heard it before, and she was also certain that she could happily listen to Shane play his violin forever. The same feeling that had come over her the first time she'd entered Mrs. Lee's bakery came over her now. She felt as if everything inside of her was vibrating with new life. The music flowing from his room had such a depth and richness, Cece felt herself responding involuntarily. The music elicited an emotional response that she hadn't known she was capable of on such a sad day. She felt it move up her spine and give her chills, the same chills she got when her daughter Rebecca played the piano. Cece didn't have a gift that touched people in such a way, but she was certainly capable of being touched by those who did have that gift.

The first song ended, and Shane immediately launched into a second one. Cece continued to listen in fascination while still inching closer to his door. She poked her head around the door and caught a glimpse of him as he played. She knew she was invading his privacy, but she couldn't help herself. Maybe she'd feel guilty later, but right now all she felt was... she wasn't sure what she felt, but she liked it.

His hair fell over his brow as his fingers moved over the strings. Cece watched how his muscles flexed as he glided the bow over the strings. She marveled at how he could appear so strong yet so sensitive at the same time. Her eyes were riveted to every part of him as he played. When he finished with the second piece, he set his violin down on the bed and looked at the sheets on his music stand. A pensive frown crossed his face, and he wrote something on the music sheets with a pencil.

He seemed to be done playing for the evening, so Cece decided to retreat to her room before he noticed her. She took one step back, and her wet sneakers squeaked loudly on the hardwood floor. Now that he wasn't playing anymore, Shane easily heard her. He looked up, and saw her shadow in his doorway.

"Cecilia," he called out before she could get farther away from his door. She didn't want her eavesdropping to be so obvious.

"Yep, it's me," she said.

"I know it's you," he laughed. He opened his door all the way and took in her soggy appearance. The rain was still beating down on his roof, and Cece fought the urge to tell him that it was raining. She had to think of something to say, something conversational.

"How was your day?" she finally asked.

"It was good. How was yours?" Even as he asked, Shane cursed the circumstances that forced him into these mundane conversations with her. He didn't want to stand there and make polite inquiries about her day. He wanted to hold her and comfort her, because he knew today had been hard for her. Would she ever be able to talk to him without him having to pry or catch her at just the right time?

For a moment, she looked like she was about to say something substantial, but then she sighed and said, "It was pretty busy."

"Have you had dinner yet?"

"I have," Cece lied, despite the fact that she hadn't eaten anything all day. "I need to go change out of these wet clothes."

She rushed down the hall before he could think of a single statement that might make her stay with him. He had three more nights with her, and then she would be gone. He imagined it would be much harder to spend time with her when she was no longer living with him; it was already hard enough while she was right in front of him.

Shane kept his door open and picked up his violin. His mother had given it to him when he was in the second grade.

She'd taught him how to play, and when he'd showed real promise, she'd hired an expensive private tutor. He was the only one of his siblings to have benefitted from such a privilege. Shane's mother had been a lifelong patron of the arts, and she'd influenced all of her children very strongly, Shane especially. She'd played the piano, the viola, the violin, and sang like an angel. The violin had been her first instrument, the one she'd had the most emotional connection to, and the first one she'd taught to all her children. Shane's older brothers hadn't liked music as much as he did, so they never went beyond a basic ability to play. Shelly had showed more promise as a singer, so their mother hadn't pushed the violin on her, and Norman had just reached the right age to learn when their mother had died.

Her death hadn't been sudden; everybody had been expecting it towards the end. During the last year of her life, she'd spent most of her time in bed, and she hadn't been able to play the violin much at all. She'd been able to sit at the piano bench for a little while every day and play for Norman before he'd started school, but eventually the day came when she couldn't get out of bed at all. Shane remembered those days with crystal clarity. Every day after school, he'd gone up to his parent's bedroom to check on her. She'd looked very haggard sometimes, and others she'd looked like an angel with her bright red hair spread out all around her.

Shane's violin teacher had constantly berated him about being more emotionally connected to the music he played. He'd said Shane was murdering his ears with an overabundance of technical proficiency and a lack of soul. Shane hadn't liked the man much after that. He'd still participated in his daily lessons, but he'd done so without any enthusiasm.

Immediately before his lessons, he'd played in his parents' room for his ailing mother; he'd considered that to be the best part of his day. When he played through a difficult piece correctly, his mother would smile and her hazel eyes would brighten just a bit. That was all the encouragement he'd needed to practice even harder. Somewhere deep in his twelve year old heart, he'd felt that if he played well enough he could heal her with music.

One day, his violin teacher had showed up for the lesson a few minutes early, and since Shane always left the door open while he played; the teacher had heard the end of his private performance. Shane had emerged from his parents' room to find the man waiting for him at the bottom of the stairs. He hadn't said a word about Shane's performance until the middle of the lesson. Shane recalled the scene vividly.

"Stop," Mr. Hsiao commanded right in the middle of Shane's playing.

Shane stopped and looked down at the little man. "What did I do wrong this time?" he asked.

"Was that *you* playing upstairs when I arrived?" Mr. Hsiao asked.

"Yeah," Shane mumbled.

"Why aren't you playing like that now?"

"What do you mean?" Shane asked in confusion. He'd played every note flawlessly.

"I mean, I could feel the musicality and emotion coming from your performance earlier, and now I feel nothing," Mr. Hsiao explained. "The way you're playing now leaves me cold."

"Sorry. I'll try it again." Shane raised his bow and played through the piece again. "How was that?" he asked at the end.

Mr. Hsiao shook his head and pushed his glasses farther up his nose. "What were you thinking about when you played earlier?" he asked.

"That's not your business," Shane said defensively.

"It's not my business, except that emotion can be the difference between brilliance and talent. And as your teacher, I must tell you this. What you played upstairs shows me that you can be *brilliant*; what you're playing *now* tells me that you are a nice boy with a lot of talent."

The old man had managed to bring tears to Shane's eyes with that comment. Shane turned away, and pretended to examine a particularly interesting spot on the wallpaper. Eventually, Shane composed himself enough to whisper in his awkward, preteen voice, "I wasn't thinking. I was just playing for my mother so she'll feel better. I play for her every day after school."

Mr. Hsiao nodded at Shane, and then went to open the door of the den. "Play for your mother now. I'm sure she can hear you with the door open wide. Play whatever you think she'll most like to hear," he smiled.

Shane played a very short bit from the violin part in Brahms's second piano concerto. His mother loved to listen to it as she fell asleep, and he closed his eyes and imagined her smiling that gentle smile that she often had when she told them goodnight. When he finished, he opened his eyes and looked at Mr. Hsiao.

"Lesson over for today," Mr. Hsiao said.

Shane didn't reply; he carefully placed his violin back in the case as Mr. Hsiao packed up his instruction books. Shane could barely make eye contact with him, because he was so embarrassed about the tears that had trickled out while he'd played.

On his way out the door, Mr. Hsiao placed a hand on Shane's bony shoulder and said, "From now on when you play, imagine an open door. Imagine your mother in the next room listening, and play for her."

Shane heard Cecilia in the hall again, and he let go of his musings about the past to go to her. She had changed into a plain white t-shirt and a pair of gray sweats, her hair was up in a ponytail, her feet were bare, and for once she wasn't wearing her brown contacts. Her face looked sad, tired, and relaxed all at the same time. She was hanging around right outside his door as if she were waiting for an invitation to enter.

"Come in," he said to her.

"I heard you playing earlier when I came in. Sorry about lurking around like that; I just didn't want to disturb you." She curled her toes against the floor in obvious nervousness while she talked.

"It's okay," Shane smiled. She glanced up at him, and turned to exit his room. He reached out a hand to stop her, and then immediately retracted it. He still recalled what happened the last time he'd tried to detain her against her will.

"You're not afraid of me now, are you?" she laughed at him.

"If I were completely honest about that, Gus would revoke my man-card," Shane joked. "I was just going to tell you that you can stay and relax on the bed if you want. I was actually going to play for a while longer." When she hesitated, he added, "I take requests."

"I don't know," she hedged. "I don't want to disturb you while you concentrate."

"There's no way you could disturb me. I'm a total exhibitionist, and I play best with an audience. Here, sit right here on the bed. You can lie back and close your eyes, and just listen to the music. I'll play something seasonal for you. Have you ever heard Vivaldi's *Four Seasons*?"

"No," Cecilia answered quietly.

"*Winter* is the most popular movement, but I'm going to play some of the soloist part from *Summer* for you now...my favorite has always been *Summer*. I think you'll like it, and since it's summer right now, it's fitting."

Cecilia smiled slightly as she sat down on the bed. She didn't know whether or not he'd been serious about being an exhibitionist, but she did know that she wanted to hear him play some more. He picked up his violin and his bow and he made beautiful music as she reclined on his bed. She listened very intently, but she didn't close her eyes for a moment.

Shane was very aware of Cecilia's eyes on him while he played. Her silver gaze roamed all over his face and body, studying every nuance of his performance. He'd never been stared at for so long by a woman before, and he found the experience to be equally titillating and nerve racking. He thought of himself as a confident guy, but he wasn't used to Cecilia's direct, scintillating gaze. If she'd been any other woman, he wouldn't have felt unsure, but the fact that it was Cecilia staring at him really affected his insides. He played as she lay on the bed watching him. The entire time he played, he also fought off feelings of desire. Her silver eyes caressing him and following his every move had managed to turn his mind in a more sensual direction. He wondered what it would be like to feel her hands caressing his body as her eyes had just done for the last few minutes. When he got to the end of the piece, he didn't know which emotion was stronger, relief or disappointment.

"Shane, that was beautiful," Cecilia breathed.

"Thank you, my dear. You know you're the only woman I've ever done a private performance for, besides my mother," Shane admitted.

Cecilia pulled her legs up to her chest and hugged herself tight. Her toes curled into the comforter and she rested her forehead against her knees. "Why are you being so nice to me? I've never done anything for you," she said.

Shane sat next to her on the bed and put a hand on her shoulder. "Believe it or not, some guys can be nice without an ulterior motive, and without expecting something in return," he answered. She didn't tense or move to shake his hand off, so he pressed his luck and put his arm all the way around her. To his surprise, she scooted closer and leaned her head against his shoulder.

"I'm almost finished with Lynette's cake. Are you going to come by and see the entire thing tomorrow? I'd really like to show it to you," she said.

"Of course I will. I get done with class around three. What time can I come?"

"You can come whenever you want. I'm putting it all together tomorrow, well everything except the clear gel icing. I'll have to do that on Saturday morning right before I deliver it," Cecilia answered.

"Why can't you do that on Friday?" Shane asked.

"Friday, I'll be fighting rounds in that tournament most of the day," she reminded him.

"Oh... right. I noticed you didn't invite me to that one," he said. When she didn't respond he added, "I'd love to see at least one of your matches."

"I'll think about it," was her grudging reply.

She kept her head against his shoulder and remained quiet for so long Shane wondered if she were falling asleep. He was content to hold her, but he could feel her sadness. He wanted her to talk to him about it.

"Cecilia," he whispered against her hair. "I know you're hurting right now. Just tell me what I can do for you, and I'll do it." His arm tightened around her as he spoke.

It took almost a full minute of nerve racking silence, but eventually she drew in a shuddering breath and spoke. "There's nothing you or anyone else can do," Cecilia replied sadly. "I went to Sarah's grave today. She died exactly twenty-one years ago today. She would have been twenty-six years old. Maybe married like Rebecca, or maybe doing something great with her life. I wonder what kind of person she would be if she were here now. I've wondered that every day since she died. Every time Rebecca hit some important milestone in her life, I pictured Sarah doing the same thing. They were identical twins you know."

"No. You never mentioned that," Shane answered. "How often do you visit her grave?"

"I went every day for the longest time, and then I went only once a month when Rebecca was in junior high and high school. Now I go once a year. Today when I went, I was so sad. It's never a happy occasion to visit my daughter's grave, but today it was so hard to see that little headstone. She was only five years old, only five. And now Rebecca is having twins."

"How do you feel about Rebecca having twins?"

"I think it's wonderful for her. She completely changed after Sarah died. They were both really outgoing together, but once it was just Rebecca, she got all quiet and shy. She was like a totally different kid, but now she's more like her old self. When she told everyone she was pregnant, I could feel how excited she was. I think it's wonderful for her."

Cecilia didn't say anything else for a long time. She was content to let her head rest against Shane's shoulder. She didn't know what it was about Shane that inspired her to feel such ease around him. She'd never had a real intimate relationship with a man, had never even wanted to, and now she found herself wanting, more than anything, to be friends with this man. The two nights when he'd shared his bed with her had been the most restful nights of her entire life. She'd do almost anything for that feeling of safety to be a permanent part of her life. She imagined what Shane would say if she asked him to sleep with her tonight. What would he say if she asked him to hold her close and never let go? He'd probably think she was crazy.

They sat listening to the rain as the light in the room completely faded away with the day. Shane didn't talk again, but he kept his arm firmly around Cecilia. He didn't want to ask any questions that would ruin the relaxed and trusting atmosphere that surrounded them that evening. She obviously didn't want to push him away completely, but he still sensed a great hesitation within her. His physical attraction to her was strong, but he knew he would have to win her over as a friend if there was ever going to be more between them. He'd ached to kiss her for the longest time, but he knew in his heart that now wasn't the right time for that step. Tonight she needed a friend.

Cecilia spent most of the next day putting Lynette's wedding cake together. The entire cake was almost as tall as she was. It consisted of seven tiers, all covered with a layer of marzipan and a layer of rolled fondant to give it a smooth, flawless finish under all the handmade decorations she'd worked on all week. The top layer had been the hardest to complete; it included a miniature replica of the fountain from the park, complete with colored sugar as the stained glass panels. The rest of the cake featured clear gel icing that cascaded down all the tiers and pooled at the bottom tier as the water did in the bottom of a fountain. Cecilia had molded two marzipan birds to sit on the top of the miniature fountain as the cake topper. The entire cake featured a multitude of floral details made to look like a whimsical, overgrown garden surrounding a romantic and traditional fountain. She'd even made some little marzipan lily pads that would float in the clear gel icing after she'd piped it onto the top of each tier. Cecilia had to admit that this was one of the most exquisite cakes she'd ever designed. Her favorite part of the design was something she'd saved as a surprise, and she was certain Lynette would love it.

She took a step back to admire her handiwork, and Karen said, "That looks stunning, Cece, but how are you going to deliver it?"

"The top three layers can go on at the last minute. See how the tiers aren't sitting right on top of each other once you get to the bottom of the third one? Basically the entire thing can easily be separated in half for delivery. You still up to helping me with this one? It's the heaviest cake I've ever done."

"Of course, but do you think you put enough roses on this one?" Karen laughed. "I still can't believe you actually made all of those. They look so real."

"I've been making them for fifteen years now. If they didn't look real after all that practice, I'd feel ashamed. Do you really think it looks stunning?"

"Yes," Karen practically shouted.

"This is the one that's going to do it. I feel it," Cece breathed. It had turned out better than she'd hoped, and she still hadn't added the finishing touches.

"You still want me to take the pictures, or would you rather hire a professional for this one?" Karen asked.

"Are you serious? You take great pictures. You have for years."

Karen looked back at the cake again, and circled the counter several times to study all the details. "You're going to be the world's most famous cake designer after this wedding. I just know it," she smiled encouragingly at Cece.

"I just want to get enough business from this to focus most of my time on special occasion cakes; I've never wanted to be famous. It's not that I don't like baking the daily cookies and brownies and all that stuff, but I just feel so good when I complete a big project like this. I think Mrs. Lee always wanted the bakery to go in this direction, but towards the end she just didn't have the energy," Cece said.

"She would be proud," Karen assured her. "So, Sport, you ready for tomorrow?"

"Ugh. What is with you right now? Can we just focus on the cake and not that stupid tournament?" Cece said in frustration.

"I'll just take that as a no," Karen said sarcastically. "It'll be fine."

"I know it will, but I don't want to talk about it. Especially not right now," Cece sighed.

"Okay. You want to meet at my place or at the academy?" Karen asked.

"I'll come by your house in the morning, that way I can do my warm up in private," Cece said. "Can we drop it now?"

"Whatever you say, Sport. Thanks for lunch. I'll see you tomorrow. Don't stay up too late with this cake. Get some sleep," Karen said, and seconds later she bounced out the door. If her father hadn't been so adamant about turning her into a fighter, she could have been the world's perkiest cheerleader.

Cece turned back to Lynette's wedding cake. She still needed to attach a few more roses to the bottom tier of the cake and make more lily pads to rest in the fountain on top. She was working on the remaining lily pads when Lynette walked through the door.

"Hey, Lynette!" Cece greeted her. "Did you come by to get a last minute look at the cake?"

"Is that it?" Lynette asked as she eyed the cake.

"Yes. This is it. I still have to add the clear gel icing that is supposed to be the water in the fountain, but other than that it's pretty much finished. Come take a look at it," Cece said.

Lynette circled slowly around the cake several times, just as Karen had done earlier. When she looked at Cece again there were tears in her blue eyes. She looked upset.

"What's wrong? Isn't this what you wanted?" Cece asked. She tried not to let her near desperation show in her voice. If

Lynette was unhappy enough to cry about the cake, it could spell disaster for Cece's business.

Lynette burst into tears and sobbed, "It's perfect!"

"Then why are you crying?" Cece asked in confusion.

"Because the wedding is off! I caught him in bed with my best friend last night," Lynette wailed. She then rushed at Cece and clung to her much like a daughter needing comfort.

At first Cece stiffened up, but then she patted the young woman's back and tried to soothe her with words. "I'm sure you'll find someone else. You're a very beautiful young woman." Even as she said the words, Cece knew her heart wasn't in them. She couldn't say what she was really thinking; she couldn't say that he was obviously a piece of shit that wasn't worth her tears. She almost wanted to tell Lynette to stop crying and go upstairs to use her punching bag to vent.

"I can't believe this happened... and two days before our wedding! He promised me he'd love me forever."

"I'm really sorry about what happened, Lynette."

"I'm sorry too. I've already cancelled everything else, but I feel bad about the cake. It looks like you worked so hard, and now I can't even use it. I'll still pay you for it, of course." She had managed to compose herself enough to stop clinging to Cece and dry her eyes on her hand kerchief.

"Don't worry about paying the full price. The deposit will cover all the materials I used," Cece told the still sniffling young woman.

"But what about all your hard work?" Lynette sniffed.

"If you wanted to deck your ex-fiancé and give him a black eye or two, I'd consider the debt settled," Cece said in a serious tone.

Lynette glanced down at her feet and started crying again. "I broke my lamp over his head last night."

"Good girl," Cece smiled at her. "That's the least he deserves."

"I should go now. I still have to go talk to the catering company. Thanks for listening, Cece."

After Lynette departed, Cece sat down hard in a chair and stared at the massive cake for almost half an hour. All her hard work had amounted to nothing. She decided to put the entire thing together anyway. That way she could at least get the picture of the finished product. She piped the gel icing into the special spots she'd made on each tier with gum paste and cake boards. She then carefully placed the remaining roses and lily pads. It only took her another couple of hours to finish the entire thing, and when she was done, she pulled out her digital camera and took pictures from every angle. It was a shame that the entire cake would go to waste unless someone who needed a wedding cake at the last minute just happened to drop by. It could happen, but it was highly unlikely.

The last minute surprise she'd been saving for the bride was something so simple, yet it gave the cake a whole new dimension. She added a small battery powered light that had been made to look like a flickering candle to the little replica of the fountain at the top of the cake. She'd left a hollowed out space in the little sugar fountain just for the light. Once she turned it on and put it in, she stood back and admired the cake again. The light flickered through the colored sugar panels and looked almost like the sunset glaring through the fountain in the park. Little spots of color flickered down on the pristine white fondant that covered the cake. Cece dimmed the lights in the bakery, and the glowing little fountain looked even more magical. From every angle, the cake looked amazing. It was everything the bride had asked for; it was traditional, it was whimsical, and it was hopelessly and unapologetically romantic. It was too bad that she was the only one who would ever see it.

With a deep sigh, Cece went to the back to put away all her tools. She banged the pans and decorating tips in her frustration. She slammed the drawers and the cabinets and made such a racket she didn't hear the bell jingle when Shane walked in.

His eyes went straight to the cake as soon as he walked in the door. He honestly hadn't expected to be so impressed by Cecilia's work, but the cake on the counter left him nearly speechless. He circled around it several times as Karen and Lynette had done earlier. The sheer size of the thing was enough to give anyone pause, but then there were the unique design and flawless execution. The real thing in front of him was far better than any of the pictures and sketches he'd seen, and the pictures had been exquisite.

Cecilia appeared in the doorway leading to the back and said nothing. She watched as Shane continued to study the cake.

"I thought you said you weren't going to put in the clear icing until Saturday morning," he said.

"Well, things changed," Cecilia shrugged. She walked over to him and stared up at the softly glowing little fountain on top. "What do you think?" she asked.

"I think you're going to have so many new orders you'll be turning business away after this wedding. I can't believe you did all this by yourself; it's huge," he answered.

"But do you *like* it?" she asked with a hint of vulnerability in her normally strong voice.

"Of course I like it. I love the way the fountain glows and casts the colorful shadows down on the rest of the cake. What's in there?"

"It's just one of those little battery lights that looks like a flickering candle."

"So, why did you put it all together tonight? I thought you said that the gel icing would make the lily pads soggy if you put it on there too early..."

"Lynette's wedding is off. She found her fiancé in bed with her best friend last night. She came by and told me earlier this afternoon, and I decided to go ahead and finish up the cake. I always take photos of my finished cakes; actually Karen usually does the photos. Normally she would have taken a few once I'd set up the cake in the reception venue, but this time there isn't going to be a reception. I finished it so I can have a picture to put in my album."

"Jeez, that's terrible," Shane said.

"I know."

"What are you going to do with all that cake?" he asked.

"Try to sell it for a fraction of the cost. If no one buys it by Sunday I'll have to throw it out or give it away."

"How much was Lynette going to pay you for it?"

"Five thousand dollars. This one was so expensive because it's so large," Cecilia answered.

"That's not expensive for a cake like this. I've seen wedding cakes that weren't nearly as impressive for twice that price," Shane said.

"It's not like it matters much now. The money wasn't the issue with this cake anyway; I already have more money than I know what to do with. I just really wanted to be taken seriously as a cake designer. I'd like to be one of those bakers who has their work featured in bridal magazines. I've even thought about publishing a cake decorating book someday. It feels like I've been wanting these things for such a long time, and I've slowly been working my way up there, building my credibility as a serious cake designer, and I thought my big break had finally come. I doubt another opportunity like this one will fall in my lap." Cecilia knew she sounded pessimistic, but this was her life. Besides an ability to create exquisite cakes, there was almost nothing else she could do.

"How did Lynette end up hiring you? She had to have heard about you from someone she knew," Shane said.

"I donated a cake to a surprise baby shower for a teenager who got pregnant. Lynette is involved in this program that helps teen mothers finish high school, and every once in a while she takes a more personal interest in one of the girls. The girl's name is Shelby, and Lynette attended her shower. I have no idea why she did; she'd never met the girl before. She happened to love the cake I made, and she'd just gotten engaged the month before. Her personal assistant called and asked me if I did wedding cakes, and she hired me," Cecilia explained.

"That must have been some cake you made for the shower," Shane commented.

"I can show you a picture of it," Cecilia said as she reached into one of the drawers under the counter. She flipped through a few pages and then handed the album to Shane. "The inspiration for this one came from one of those Anne Geddes calendars. I've always loved how she photographs babies in ways you wouldn't expect."

Shane studied the pictures of the cake with a thoughtful expression. At first glance it appeared to be a cake covered in many different types of flowers, but on closer inspection he saw that each flower also contained a unique miniature baby delicately nestled inside. The amount of work and detail that went into the cake was impressive. "You made all those flowers and babies?" he asked in disbelief.

"No. I ordered them from the marzipan baby depot," she quipped.

Shane looked at her and smiled, "Sorry, obviously you worked hard on this cake, and that one," he pointed to the massive wedding cake atop the counter.

Cecilia shrugged. "I work hard on every cake. This is my business, my life," she said quietly.

"What are you going to do now?"

"Get some sleep for that tournament tomorrow and start working on all the orders for next week. I have two more wedding cakes, an order of cupcakes for a bridal shower, and a bunch of birthday cakes. I think June and July are the most popular months for having babies."

During the entire conversation, an idea had been bubbling in the back of Shane's mind. He'd do anything to make her happy, and her disappointment about Lynette's wedding was getting to him. She wasn't crying or behaving in a dramatic fashion, but he knew that this wedding had been important to her. It would have been her big break, and there was no guarantee that she'd ever be hired by another client like Lynette.

"If you had another chance at a big wedding, would you take it?" Shane asked all of a sudden. He leaned forward, all eagerness and impulsiveness, and awaited her response.

"Of course I would. Why? Do you know someone who's shopping around for a wedding cake?" she asked.

"Not exactly, but I have an idea that might work for you. Just hear me out before you say no," he answered.

She stared at him for a long moment before she said, "Go on. I'm listening."

"You could design the cake for *my* wedding. The guest list would be just as impressive as Lynette's, if not more so—"

"You're getting married?" she interrupted before he could finish.

"Not exactly... it would be a fake wedding. That way you can still get your big chance to show off what you can do," he explained. "I may not have nearly as much money as you do, but what I do have could mean a lot in this situation."

"What do you have?" she asked.

"Think about it Cece; I'm Edgar Howard's grandson. Everybody in the world knows who he is, and I've had people interested in my life for years now. Years ago, some magazine named me as a potential heir to his fortune, and since then I've had a lot of requests for interviews and statements and such. When I lived in New York, I couldn't even go out with a woman without seeing something about it in the gossip column the next day. All that speculation about my personal life used to bother me. That's one of the reasons I left New York, and it's also why I don't do a lot of casual dating. If I announce that I'm getting married, people will pay attention—the right kind of people to help your business. The chance to do a wedding cake for the notorious grandson of one of the world's richest men could be just what you need if you want people to know what you can do as a cake designer. Nobody has to know that Granddaddy Warbucks would rather leave his fortune to the New York Zoo than to any of the grandchildren he's never once acknowledged."

She didn't say anything for a few minutes. She looked up at Lynette's wedding cake and thought about all the work she'd put into this bakery over the past twenty-six years. Since Mrs. Lee's death, she'd looked inside her heart and really examined what she wanted in her professional life. Beyond any doubts, she knew what she wanted most was to be a respected cake designer. The next logical step towards that goal was to attract bigger clients and hire an assistant.

"How are you going to get some woman to agree to a fake wedding?" Cecilia asked after thinking it over. "And what if she tells everyone it's fake? Then we'll end up looking like idiots," she added.

"Not if *you* are the woman."

"Me?" Cecilia practically squeaked. The blood supply to her head suddenly disappeared, and her heart slammed inside her chest. She grabbed the counter for support and looked at Shane. He stared right back at her, and she couldn't detect any amusement in his expression. He'd been serious. His midnight blue eyes blazed into hers, and for one crazy instant she felt as if she were falling off the earth. Why had he suggested such a thing? It wasn't like she was desperate; her bakery was already successful, and she had the means to be financially independent for the rest of her life. And no one would believe a sudden engagement between the two of them.

"It *will* work, Cecilia," he said as if reading her thoughts.

She opened her mouth to tell him how preposterous his idea was and said, "I'll do it," instead.

Chapter 10

He visited little Sarah's grave again early the next morning; he couldn't stay away. This time when he went, he decided to leave his flask behind. Cece hadn't showed up at her bakery that morning, and he didn't know how to begin tracking her down. The only things he knew about her were where she worked, where she got off the bus after work, and where her daughter, Sarah, was buried. He still had no clue where she lived; not that he would go knocking on her door if he did know. He still needed time. The last thing he'd expected to find was that Cece had lost a daughter.

The funeral replayed in his mind again. His last sight of her had been absolutely heart rending. The knowledge that he'd never see her or touch her again had irrefutably destroyed what little was left of his soul. He still couldn't even think her name without tears coming to his eyes.

"Sita," he whispered as he stood over Sarah's grave.

Someone had once told him that death was the most natural part of life, and he'd always disagreed with that statement. If anyone were to ask him what the most natural part of life was, he'd answer "birth."

Sita had been a beautiful woman; everybody had told him so. Any time they were together, he'd received plenty of compliments about her gorgeous hair, which was as black and silky as ink. He touched a hand to his old balding head and felt another pang of loss. She'd often joked that he could borrow some of her hair if he ever wanted it. He'd always politely declined, and she'd always playfully patted the top of his head. She'd been wonderful—until everything changed for the worst.

Death was not the most natural part of life. There had been nothing natural about the way his dear Sita had died. Her birth, however, had been natural. He remembered her birth well. She'd come into the world with a head full of hair and a pair of the most magnificent brown eyes he'd ever seen. He'd loved her from the first moment he saw her, but now she was gone. His dear Sita was gone. His daughter was gone. He looked down at Sarah's grave again. The last thing he'd expected to have in common with Cece Graves was a beloved daughter's death. Death. There was that word again.

Shane unexpectedly got the chance to attend Cecilia's final match after work. Karen had called him on his cell phone to let him know when and where it was. He knew he'd had a good reason to like Karen when he first met her. The conversation had been short and to the point.

"Hey, Big Guy," Karen had said.

"Karen?"

"Yes, it's Karen. You still want to see your girl fight tonight?" she asked.

"Yeah. Of course," he answered quickly.

"Good. Be at my martial arts academy at eight. Give them your name at the door, and they'll take it from there. I'm Cece's corner-man, or I'd sit and cheer with you. If you ever tell Cece I helped you get in, you're dead," and with that warning she disconnected.

Shane smiled to himself. He imagined Karen might actually be able to follow through on that threat, but he knew she wouldn't, because she was such a nice person. He wasn't afraid of Cecilia's reaction to him seeing her fight; he'd learned that he could handle her with simple kindness. His only concern was that if she noticed him before or during the match she might get distracted and make a mistake. He definitely didn't want that on his conscience.

Cecilia had been on his mind all day. He hadn't really expected her to agree to his impulsive proposal last night, but he was glad she did. It meant that she would have to spend a lot more time with him in the near future. He knew a fake engagement wasn't the best way to pursue a woman, but Cecilia wasn't just any woman. She seemed to have very guarded interest in him as a man, but she was willing to accept him as a friend. It was better than nothing; it was definitely something he could work with.

Last night hadn't been all about the cake for him. He was honest with himself about that, even if he hadn't been honest with her. He never would have suggested such a scheme if he hadn't already had strong feelings for her. He'd been half in love with what he knew about her since before he ever met her, and he was not the type of man who fell for every pretty face he came across. All the time he'd spent listening to Rebecca talk about her mother had solidified his respect and admiration for her. Only a truly strong person could survive some of the things she'd been through; but Cecilia hadn't just survived, she'd thrived.

While she'd spent months learning to walk again after her near fatal injury a few years ago, Shane had learned all he could about her behind the scenes. It had been easy to get his sister, Shelly, to talk about the shooting, because she'd been so traumatized by the events leading up to it. Shelly had given such a glowing report of Cecilia's actions, it was impossible for Shane not to be impressed and even more curious about her. Up until the night of the fire, he'd never seen her up close. He'd had only the one glimpse of her lying on the hospital floor. In that moment, she'd looked like a truly tortured soul with pain deeply engrained in her entire being. It had been impossible not to want to reach out to her, impossible not to care. She had somehow reached the limits of human endurance and come out stronger and better. Now, Shane saw her as a shooting star who had the potential to light up his entire life if he could catch her somehow.

He'd been fascinated by her for some time, and now that he'd gotten close enough to see just how beautiful she really was, inside and out, there was no way he could fade meekly into the background again. She had given him enough encouragement to hope for a future with her, but he was determined not to rush. He wanted her more than he'd ever wanted anything else in his life, so he had to constantly remind himself to let her set the pace of their budding friendship.

After work, he dressed in jeans and a t-shirt for the fight. He did his best to blend in, but at his height blending in wasn't always possible. Karen had wisely given him a seat far enough back so he wouldn't be noticed by Cece and become a distraction. The fight was to take place in a midsized arena that could seat a few thousand spectators. Most of the seats were filled tonight.

Cecilia's match was to take place right before the male championship match. Shane knew that most of the people in the seats were there to see the men fight; that's just the way it was with sports. Women always drew less of a crowd. He sipped his water and waited for the match to start.

Shane was busy scanning the crowd when the announcer came on over the loud speakers and introduced the fighters. In the blue corner, there was a ruddy faced auburn haired woman named Danny Fico. She was clearly revved up and ready to go. She entered the ring to raucous applause, and she lifted her gloved hands up several times to encourage even more cheering from the crowd. She danced around the ring a little, and seemed to really revel in her moment in the spotlight.

When the announcer introduced Cecilia, Shane's eyes went immediately to the aisle leading up to the red corner. Cecilia jogged quickly down the aisle and entered the ring without much fanfare. The announcer introduced her as Coco Green, and Shane laughed at the silly pseudonym she'd picked. Cecilia hadn't tried to hype up the crowd as her opponent Danny had; she appeared to be all business tonight. From this far back, it was hard to tell what she was thinking, but Shane guessed that she was probably somewhat nervous. There were a lot of people watching, because this tournament was a regional qualifier for the International Kickboxing Federation's annual championship tournament.

Cecilia and Danny stood at the center of the ring with the referee. The crowd cheered as the bell rang, signaling the start of the fight. In the first round, Cecilia was very careful. She blocked nearly all of Danny's attacks, and got in a few hits. She didn't appear to be as aggressive a fighter as Karen was. Shane had seen a few of Karen's matches, and she tended to come out with both guns blazing. She'd won more than a few fights by knock out. During the first three rounds of this fight, Cecilia showed herself to be more of a defensive fighter.

By the fifth round, Cecilia still hadn't taken any punches or kicks to the face, but she had taken a nasty one to her side. Shane had cringed right along with her. She was sweaty, and her hair was slightly disheveled, but she didn't look tired yet. By round six, Danny's over eagerness had begun to wear on her. She was starting to look tired, but Cecilia still danced around the ring like she'd just stepped in. Shane smiled as a sense of pride welled up inside him. She was exceptional at everything she did, and he couldn't help admiring her even more.

At the end of the sixth round, Karen hugged Cecilia and said something in her ear that made her laugh, and Shane wondered what it was. Karen wiped Cecilia's face with the towel, and gave her a squirt of water from her bottle before the next round started. The next three rounds went by pretty much as the first three had. Cecilia appeared overly cautious at times. She'd had several opportunities to land a big kick or punch, and hadn't taken them. Shane wondered why she was holding back as he watched the fight. On the tenth round, the scores were almost even. Cecilia was up by a couple of points, because she was lightning fast at blocking and made it difficult for Danny to land any hits.

At the very end of the tenth round, Danny faked a right hook, and when Cecilia went to block it Danny's left foot came up to strike the side of her face. The hit caught her completely off guard, and she staggered back. Everyone in the arena was on their feet cheering until Cecilia righted herself. For a moment, it had looked like she was going to go down. Shane gritted his teeth, because the kick looked like it hurt. He had to fight the urge to run up there and ask her if she was alright. When the bell rang again, Cece went back to her corner with a look that couldn't have been described as happy by any stretch of the imagination. Karen offered her a bucket and some water, so she could rinse and spit. Her mouth was bleeding from the brutal kick to the head. She didn't look like she was in much pain as the doctor briefly examined her; for some reason she looked irritated now. She and Karen exchanged a few words before the fight resumed.

Round eleven started, and Cecilia came out with a look that Shane had never seen before. It was somewhere between what he called her game face and the look his mother used to give him when he'd really messed up as a child. Her look of razor sharp focus seemed to electrify the crowd, and everyone around him sat forward in anticipation. He was literally on the edge of his seat watching her as she advanced towards Danny.

Danny's one good hit must have given her a confidence boost, because she came out swinging. She tried to do another fake out combo, but Cecilia was ready this time. When Danny faked right, Cecilia stepped in with a couple of quick jabs that snapped Danny's head back. Danny backed up and attempted to deliver a kick, but Cecilia blocked it and got in another jab to Danny's head, followed by an elbow. Danny's guard came down briefly, and Cecilia finished the fight with a kick so swift and hard it seemed to come out of nowhere. Her right leg flashed up, and her shin caught Danny squarely in the face. Danny's head snapped back, and she fell down with a thud in the middle of the ring. The referee ran to Danny, but it was clear to everyone that Danny wasn't getting up to continue the fight. It had been a sudden and exciting end to the match. Shane watched as they announced Cecilia, or Coco, as the winner. She barely smiled. Karen, on the other hand, was absolutely jubilant. Once they'd cleared the ring, Shane decided to leave. He enjoyed sports, but he didn't want to stay for the male championship fight. He'd much rather go check on Cecilia.

Since he didn't know his way around the arena and attached martial arts academy, he called Karen's cell phone. She didn't answer, so he left a voicemail. Eventually he got a text instructing him to meet her near the one of the back exits. When he got there, Karen was already waiting for him.

"Where's Cecilia?"

"She's in the back lying down with some ice," Karen answered. "What did you think of the fight?" she smiled.

"It was a good fight, especially the end. I've never seen Cecilia do anything like that," he said.

"You should see a match between me and Cece; she can do a lot more than what you saw tonight."

"Really?"

"Of course! I've been trying to get her to fight full time since we first started training together, but she didn't want to leave the bakery. At first, it was because she didn't want to give up a steady job, but eventually it was because Mrs. Lee got too old to keep up with it on her own, and Cece was way to loyal to abandon her. When you can go ten rounds or more like Cece can, there's a ton of money to be made—even if you don't win every fight. Cece could have been *huge*, but she chose to stay smalltime and decorate cakes. I'll never understand it. I mean, she trains with me and my crew, and we're *the best* at what we do. For Cece to fight only part time was one of the biggest wastes of talent I've ever seen in my life."

"What makes you say that?"

"Think about it, Shane. Cece training with me all the time yet fighting part time is kind of the same as if some talented, unknown boxer had been training with *Mike Tyson* his entire career and just never wanted to step into the big leagues. It's a waste of potential."

"Maybe she would think abandoning her bakery is the bigger waste of potential," Shane said thoughtfully.

"Right," Karen snorted. "Her take-home for tonight's fight is a cool six thousand dollars; let's see her make *half* that in a few hours at the bakery."

Karen flared up so fast Shane thought it prudent to change the subject. "Why didn't she use her real name?" he asked.

"She always uses an alias when she fights. It's usually Coco Something-or-other, Coco Green, Coco Black. She's reasonably well known as Coco, but not at all as Cecilia. One thing I learned about your girl early on is that she values her privacy more than most. I like that people know my name, but Cece hates that kind of thing when it comes to fighting."

"Who usually wins between you two?" Shane asked.

"We're about even on everything. I'm more aggressive overall and willing to take risks to land a good hit, but Cece can really capitalize on her opponents' mistakes. Poor Danny didn't even know what hit her in that last round."

"I didn't see Danny make a mistake," Shane remarked with a small frown. "It looked to me like Cecilia managed to stun her with a few good hits, and when she dropped her guard that last kick ended it."

"Oh, she made a mistake alright; she kicked your girl in the face. Cece hates getting kicked in the face. She was playing nice before Danny made that move. Didn't you notice how quickly it all ended once Cece decided she'd had enough?" Karen laughed.

"Where is she? I want to talk to her," Shane said with a smile.

"Follow me. I already let her know you watched the fight. Now that it's over, she's cool with it."

Shane followed her down a long corridor, through a few sets of double doors and into another hall. She stopped at the first door on the right and knocked before barging in. Cecilia sat doubled over on a wooden bench. She held an icepack to the side of her head, and she didn't bother looking up when they entered.

"Hey, Sport, you've got a visitor," Karen said in her endlessly chipper voice.

Cecilia looked up, and her eyes widened in surprise when she saw Shane taking up the entire doorway. "I thought you were kidding! You mean you really invited *him* to my fight?" she grouched at Karen. When Karen shrugged, Cecilia threw the icepack at her. Karen dodged the makeshift missile and giggled at her friend.

"He sat way in the back, and you didn't even notice him," Karen said in her own defense. "Anyway, he watched the fight, it's over now, and there's nothing you can do about it. I'm going to watch the other fight now," and with that Karen bounced out of the room.

Cecilia got up to retrieve her icepack and avoided looking in Shane's direction. She was no longer wearing the short shorts and sports bra she'd fought in. Now she was wearing baggy sweats that covered everything.

"How's your head?" he asked.

"It'll be fine. That's not the worst kick I've ever taken," she sighed.

She stood in the middle of the room, and Shane came to stand right in front of her. They were now toe to toe, and he was looking down at her with a small smile lurking about his lips. She would have looked him in the eyes, but for some reason she couldn't look beyond his lips. A brief memory of those lips kissing her forehead flashed in her head; they had been warm and gentle against her skin. He was such a large man, yet she'd never once felt threatened while in his presence. Before she realized what she was doing, one of her hands had come up to his face. She brushed her fingers over his bottom lip and let them linger against his cheek. His hand came up to grasp hers. He held it against his cheek and closed his eyes for a moment, savoring her gentle touch. He then kissed her hand and smiled down at her.

"You had something on your face," she lied as she pulled her hand back and took a step away from him. Her heart felt like it was somewhere in her throat, and her entire body felt warm and flushed. Why had she touched him so intimately? She'd never done anything that forward before.

He cleared his throat and said, "I noticed your car in my garage. Do you need a ride?"

Cecilia hadn't even thought about how she'd get back to Shane's house. She'd left her car in his garage and taken the bus to Karen's house that morning. She didn't feel like waiting around for Karen, so she went with Shane.

"You know, we're going to have to talk about our wedding sometime soon," Shane said as soon as they walked into his house.

"What about it?" Cecilia asked.

"Have you given it any thought since last night?"

"Not really," she answered. She hadn't really thought of anything beyond the tournament all day. "Have you?"

"I have. I think it's important for us to agree that the truth stays between us. As far as anyone else knows we really are in love and engaged to be married," he said.

"I wasn't planning on telling anyone about it. I thought we could just have a wedding with that impressive guest list you promised me, and leave out all our friends."

Shane shook his head. "Cecilia, that won't work. If you really want to get the kind of business you're seeking, it can't all be about how the cake looks. Guests always remember a special wedding. If we can make it authentic and magical all the details will seem even better, and they'll be more likely to talk about the details like the cake and the flowers. If it seems fake, it won't work, and it will *definitely* seem fake if our family and friends aren't there."

"There's no way I can let my daughter think I'm actually getting married," Cecilia stated emphatically. "And what about your family? What are you going to tell them?" Cecilia demanded.

"I'm going to tell them that I've found the woman of my dreams and that I'd do anything for her. They'll be happy for me," he said. They both sat at his kitchen table, and he handed her a glass of water as they talked.

"It's one thing to deceive strangers, but our *families*?" Cecilia took a sip of her water and waited for Shane's reply. He gazed at her as he thought about it.

"We can let them think we broke up soon after the wedding. By that time it won't really matter what they think. All that matters is that everyone thinks the wedding is real while it's happening."

Shane's idea seemed so simple, yet Cecilia knew it could lead to all kinds of complications in both of their lives. She should have said no when he first suggested it, but she'd been sitting right next to Lynette's wedding cake. All her hard work had been staring her in the face, reminding her that her opportunity to expand had been dangled in front of her only to be snatched away by the circumstances. Circumstances had been taking things away from her for as long as she could remember.

"Didn't you say that you wanted all your years of hard work to finally pay off? You came here with nothing, and now you own a successful bakery. You can take it in any direction you want; you said you just need the right wedding to get you started. You can have that wedding with me. This is the opportunity of a lifetime for your business, and all you have to do is accept it," he said. He was leaning halfway across the table, looking at her closely and waiting for her response.

She looked across the table and allowed her eyes to roam all over his face. When she finally looked into his eyes, she found that same secret message that had been there a few times before. This time she didn't look away; she maintained eye contact as she asked, "Why Shane? Why are you willing to do this for me? It makes no sense. You barely know me, and I'm not even a nice person... it makes no sense."

Shane reached across the table and grasped both of her hands inside his. Cecilia curled her fingers into his warmth and looked down at his hands as he spoke. "Because I..." he began, only to hesitate for a long moment. He looked down at their hands. Her small hands were nestled inside his, and it felt so right. He cleared his throat and started again, "Because I think you're a great cake designer, and I want people to see that. Plus, I've always wanted to have a wedding. I think this will be kind of fun."

"Let's do it then."

Shane released a sigh. He hadn't even realized he'd been holding his breath. They were actually going to do it.

"I'll leave the other details to you, but the cake is all mine," Cecilia said with a small smile. "How do you want to tell everyone?" she asked as an afterthought.

"First, we have to get engaged. I think I can create some good buzz with a public proposal, as long as you're okay with that," Shane answered.

"I am," Cecilia yawned. "Sorry. I guess I'm getting old," she joked.

Shane looked at the swollen side of her face and said, "You've had a long day. Go get some sleep, and we'll talk more about all the details tomorrow."

"I'm moving into my new place first thing tomorrow," she reminded him. "Anyway, we don't really need to discuss every little detail. I'll take care of the cake, and the rest can just be a surprise." She yawned again and rose from the table with a small smile. "Good night, Shane," she said quietly.

"Night, Coco," he smiled back.

# Chapter 11

Cecilia hadn't seen Shane since she moved into her new house a few days ago. He'd been out of sight most of the week, but definitely not out of her mind. The morning she'd left his house, he'd insisted on helping her move her things. Cecilia laughed now as she thought back to Saturday morning. She'd tossed her bag at him and said, "Here are my things."

"This is all?" he asked in disbelief.

"Yeah. Why?"

"It's not much. I thought you would have bought more clothes by now," he said.

"I wear the same thing to work every day," she said, pointing to her white uniform. "And I've never had a bunch of clothes," she shrugged.

Shane followed her out the door, and watched in puzzlement as she walked right past the garage and started down the sidewalk towards the park.

"What are you doing? I thought you were going to your new place today," he said.

"I am," she answered. "It's on the other side of the park, so I thought it would be nice to walk."

"You're renting a place in my neighborhood?" he asked with barely contained delight.

"No," she looked back at him and smiled. She'd been in such a playful mood that morning. She let him look confused for a beat before she clarified, "I bought it."

Now she was in her new house painting the walls pink. It had been her favorite color ever since she first saw it in Mrs. Lee's little bakery. Something about it inspired confidence and comfort. She wanted to surround herself with as much comfort as possible. She knew she would need it in the nights to come.

She didn't realize just how influential Shane's presence had been until she spent her first night alone in her new house. She'd begun to feel safe with him, and now that feeling was gone. She couldn't ask Shane to come stay the night with her just so she wouldn't be afraid. There was no way she could ask such a thing, but a small part of her knew he would come if she asked.

She'd mentioned the fact that she didn't like sleeping in beds, but she couldn't bring herself to explain just how pervasive fear was in her life. Every night she struggled with her deep and abiding fear of darkness as well. She either slept with a light on, or she didn't sleep at all; that's the way it had been for the past twenty-six years. The only exception had been the time she spent in Shane's house. Even with her nightmares, she'd had more peace of mind knowing he was in the next room than she'd ever had at any other time in her life. And the nights she'd spent actually in his arms had been heavenly, although she would never admit that to him.

The apartment that had burned down a few months ago had never really felt like home. She'd moved into it after recovering from her injury a few years ago. She'd stayed in Rebecca and Norman's house for almost a year, and as soon as she was strong enough to live on her own again, she'd taken the first apartment that came along. The rent had been cheap, but other than that she'd never really liked the place.

She looked around her new house with a sigh of satisfaction. One of her accounts was now two hundred and fifty thousand dollars lighter, but the security of owning her home more than made up for the expenditure. She wished she'd taken the plunge sooner. All of the walls had been stark white when she moved in, and now the living room, kitchen and dining room were a pale pastel pink. It was such a light, soft pink it actually looked off-white in some lighting. She'd spent the past four days painting after work, and she was happy with the results of her labor. She looked around at the pink walls and white crown molding and wondered what Shane would think of her paint job. He'd come in briefly to tour the empty house on Saturday morning, but he hadn't said much about it.

He had made it clear that they needed to spend a lot of time together in public before the wedding. She was going to attend church with him on Sunday, and they were going to have dinner together this Friday. She was looking forward to Friday for reasons better left unexamined at the moment.

Shane had a way of looking at her that made her feel she could trust him with everything, and she'd never felt she could trust a man before. Her experiences early in life had taught her that most men wanted only one thing from women. For this reason, she'd never thought a man could be a good friend, at least not until Shane showed her otherwise. The night he'd first hugged her and shared his bed with her had done more to dispel her prejudice than anything he could have said. He could have said he didn't have any ulterior, sexual motivation for sharing his bed with her, but he didn't have to. She had felt the purity of his intentions through every pore in her body. He'd radiated warmth and safety and compassion, everything she'd needed that night. Everything she'd ever needed.

Cecilia had lied to everyone about where she came from. Sometimes she wished she'd never had the drunken conversation with Rebecca in which she'd confessed that she'd been raped. She'd actually blasted her poor daughter with the ugly truth as a way to punish her and push her away. At that time in her life, it had been easier to push everyone away than admit the truth. Even when she had finally let it out, she still hadn't been able to tell the whole truth. She'd let Rebecca think that her parents had kicked her out over the pregnancy, but that had been an outright lie. She'd actually been in and out of foster care and group homes most of her childhood.

It had been easier to make up a lie about unsympathetic parents than to tell the truth. The truth was rarely ever as satisfying as a lie. Cecilia's mother had been a prostitute, and she'd never been sure of whom her father was. She had very few memories of her mother, all of them powerful, but none of them good. They'd lived in a hotel in a part of Atlanta that was infamous for sex trafficking. Cecilia's mother, Cora, had been a young woman, yet she'd looked old and worn by the time she'd died. Perhaps Cora could have been a beautiful, successful woman if circumstances had been different for her. Cecilia often imagined that her mother could have been something more than a prostitute if she'd had a chance.

Many of the johns who had visited Cora hadn't cared that she'd had a child. Cecilia had witnessed more adult acts before the age of six than most people saw in a lifetime. She'd seen Cora's pimp punish her if one of the johns had been bothered by her presence. Cecilia had tried her best to stay quiet and out of the way while her mother was working, but it had been hard. Her loathing for her mother's profession had spilled over into a loathing for anything remotely sexual. At times she didn't know which she hated more, seeing her mother sell her body to men, or seeing her mother beaten by the cruel pimp who'd owned all the girls living in the hotel.

Cecilia had always feared her mother's pimp. He was a large, light skinned Creole man who'd gone by the street name Red Bone. He'd had red hair and gray eyes that had often seemed like malevolent chips of ice. Red Bone had been a very angry person, but his temper hadn't been the hot kind that boiled over in obvious ways. He'd been a quiet man, prone to great cruelty if pushed too far. Cecilia had witnessed more than a few of his acts, including the one that had killed her mother. She'd never forget that day. It was the day she'd gone from being the insignificant daughter of a prostitute to being an insignificant orphan in the foster care system. What would Rebecca think if she knew where her mother had really come from? Cecilia often pondered that very question, and she'd never been able to find an answer that satisfied her. Why tell her the truth anyway? After all these years, what could it accomplish?

A knock at the door interrupted Cecilia's thoughts. It was nearly nine at night, and she wasn't expecting any company. Her heart skipped a beat at the thought that it could be Shane at her door. She looked through the peephole with sweaty palms and a racing pulse only to find Karen at her door.

"Hey, Sport," Karen smiled as Cecilia threw open the door.

"Karen!" Cecilia greeted her friend. "I thought you said you couldn't come over until next week."

"Change of plans," Karen shrugged as she stepped inside.

"Nice of you to show up *after* I'm done painting," Cecilia remarked.

"What can I say? My timing has always been impeccable. Listen, Sport, I've got your check from the fight. You forgot it when you left Friday night."

"Thanks. You want to have a look around while you're here?" Cecilia offered.

"I still can't believe you bought a house." Karen looked around at the pink walls and then back at Cecilia. "Pink, huh?" she said with a raised eyebrow.

Cecilia shrugged. "Come on, so I can show you the house. I don't have any furniture yet."

She gave Karen a quick tour of the house. It was an ordinary family house, except for the one feature that Cecilia had fallen in love with. The kitchen was sensational. The previous owners had obviously been into entertaining. They'd had a deluxe custom kitchen built to suit their needs. It included everything from a large walk in pantry for food to a butler's pantry for serving dishes and linens.

"Wow," Karen said as she looked around the kitchen. "You wouldn't expect this kitchen to be in such an ordinary house."

"I know, and that's exactly why I bought it. The bathrooms are just as nice, especially the master bath," Cecilia smiled.

"Everything looks great, especially the paint job. I actually came over to talk to you about your next fight," Karen said in a rush.

Cecilia shook her head. "There isn't going to be a next fight," she said.

Karen immediately went on the offensive. "Why not?" she demanded. "You can't just quit after making your big comeback. I talked to my promoter, and he thinks he can book at least one fight a month for you. As long as you are willing to put in a little extra work in training. I told him that you'll be training with me though, so that won't be a problem." Karen looked as if she expected Cecilia to agree with her, and she actually looked a little hurt when Cecilia put up a hand to stop her.

"I'm done. No more public fights. I won't be going to the kickboxing championship either."

"But why? You made six thousand dollars in one night, and Mitch thinks you can make even more. He thinks people will watch your fights because they'll recognize your name. You could easily make as much as I used to," Karen went on.

"Karen, no." Cecilia stuck to her resolve. She'd never told Karen no before. In the past she'd always went along with whatever Karen had wanted. Every sparring match, every training session, every lesson, and every sanctioned fight in the past twenty years had all been Karen's doing. This was the first time Cecilia had ever put her foot down and said no. It was the first time she'd ever *wanted* to say no.

"You've changed so much in the past few months," Karen whispered. She had tears in her eyes, and Cecilia momentarily felt badly for her.

"Why don't you just fight like you always do? The only difference is that I won't be doing it with you anymore" Cecilia said in a gentle, patient voice.

"That's *not* the only difference," Karen said forcefully. She suddenly looked very angry. "I'll let you think about it, Cece. You used to make quite a bit just doing it part time. Imagine what you could do if you focused all your energy on this for a while. Hire an assistant at the bakery so you don't have to be there all the time. I know you can afford it."

"What is with you? I'm not fighting anymore, and that's final," Cecilia practically shouted at her friend.

"Fine," Karen gritted out. She turned and walked out the front door, leaving a stunned Cece behind. In the twenty years they'd known each other, Karen had never once acted like that. Cece searched her mind for a reason for Karen's strange behavior and found nothing. Karen hadn't fought in the last tournament, and given her strange behavior just now, Cece wondered why.

By Friday, Shane had made reservations at one of the nicest restaurants in town and purchased an engagement ring. He knew it was all a ruse, but every time he rehearsed the scene in his head, he got nervous. She thought they were only going out for dinner; she had no idea that he was going to issue his fake proposal tonight. He kept telling himself that it wasn't a big deal because it was fake, but it *was* a big deal because his feelings for her were genuine.

He'd always been the type of guy who wore his heart on his sleeve. He'd never given any woman he was involved with reasons to doubt his feelings, so having to hide so much from Cecilia was a new experience for him. He stood on her front porch and took a deep breath before ringing her doorbell. He was dressed in a suit and tie, and he hoped she'd taken his suggestion and bought herself something nice to wear. It was a special night after all.

Shane wasn't sure what he was expecting while he waited for her to open the door. He'd seen Cecilia in a variety of outfits, and he always thought she looked beautiful. When she opened the door tonight, however, he was completely taken aback. Not only had she taken his suggestion, but she'd also taken it up a notch. She was wearing a flowing silver dress that ended just above her knees. It was made of some kind of sheer, gray material over a shimmery silver lining. It was one of those asymmetrical designs that featured only one full sleeve. Her other arm was bare from the shoulder down. She'd paired the dress with strappy silver heels that made her legs seem a mile long. Her hair fell around her shoulders in soft cinnamon colored curls and coils that framed her face just right. She tucked a stray coil behind her ear and looked up at him. She looked absolutely stunning. His favorite thing about her appearance tonight was the fact that she wasn't wearing her brown contacts. Tonight he could stare into her beautiful eyes as much as he wanted.

He didn't realize how long he'd been staring at her until she spoke. "Nice tie," she smiled.

Shane looked down at his tie and smiled back at her. He was wearing a silver tie that matched her dress. "People are going to think we're one of those cheesy couples who always coordinate our clothes," he laughed.

"I can go back inside and change. I have a black dress that will go just fine with these shoes," she offered.

"*No*," Shane said quickly. "You look perfect just the way you are."

She locked her door, and he offered her his arm. They looked just like a genuine couple as they walked the length of the sidewalk to his Jeep. He opened the door for her, and had to fight the urge to stare at her legs as she settled in.

The restaurant he'd selected was one of the nicest Cecilia had ever seen. She hadn't been to all that many restaurants in her life; she'd always been too busy with more pressing things like running the bakery and training for fights. This was the type of place that had a dress code, but Cecilia and Shane had no problem when they walked through the door. The maître'd seemed to be familiar with Shane, and more than a few people around the bar turned in recognition as they walked by.

One of the men at the bar stood up and approached them. "Shane Gregory," he said. "It's been a long time."

"Yes it has," Shane responded.

"I never did get the chance to thank you in person for that campaign contribution you made," the man went on.

"Now isn't the best time. I'm with someone." Shane grasped Cecilia's arm and gently pulled her to his side. She'd been hiding behind him like a shy child when the man stepped in front of them. The move was so out of character for her, he almost laughed.

"I see," the man said as he looked at Cecilia. "Well I'm coming up on an election year, and my campaign could use your support again. You enjoy your evening," and, with a polite smile in Cecilia's direction, he turned back to his companions at the bar.

"Who was that?" Cecilia whispered as soon as they were seated.

"That was the mayor's cousin, Senator Reid. He ran for a first term in the state senate a few years ago, and I was one of his major contributors when they were fundraising for the campaign. I didn't expect to see him here tonight. Sorry about that," he said.

"I had no idea you were into politics," Cecilia said.

"I'm not, and that's exactly why I didn't want to listen to him talk my ear off about his campaign," Shane returned with a frown.

"Why did you contribute then?" she asked him. He looked uncomfortable, but she didn't change the subject. She'd answered some tough questions for him over the past few months, and now it was his turn.

"It's a long story, Cecilia," he sighed. "But I'll tell you now. My grandparents and I had a disagreement about ten years ago. I'm sure Rebecca has told you by now that none of us get along with our mother's parents."

"All I know about your family is that your mother ran away from her millionaire parents to be with your father who had nothing at the time," Cecilia told him.

"Her parents were billionaires. They still are. It's actually kind of funny from an outsider's perspective. After my mother ran off with my father, they never spoke to her again—they actually legally disowned her—and neither of them ever had any more children. They didn't even know she'd died until my oldest brother was all grown up, and by then my grandmother felt bad enough to want to make it up to us. They've been divorced almost since my mother ran away. The entire fortune was split down the middle in the divorce settlement, and since then they've been trying to out-do each other financially. My grandmother lives in California. As part of the divorce settlement, she gained control of the *IBN* network. It wasn't worth much back then, but she used almost all of the cash from the settlement to turn it around. Over the years, she's made it into one of the highest rated networks in the nation. My grandfather, on the other hand, lives clear across the country in New York City. If it were possible for them to have settled farther apart without moving to separate countries, I'm sure they would have done so."

"What does your grandfather do?"

"He owns *Howard Oil*, which is the fastest growing oil company in the world right now, and he also owns the *H&M Financial Group*. He started out as an investment banker, and he made his first billion managing *H&M*. He lives in New York, because that's where his financial headquarters is, but the headquarters for *Howard Oil* is actually in Texas. His oil business makes a ton of money, but he gets a lot of bad press from environmental groups because of it. Every year, either my grandmother or my grandfather is at, or near, the top of that stupid Forbes list. Money is all they care about, and my brothers and sister and I might as well be some slime they picked up on the bottom of their shoes."

"I don't get it. Where do politics fit in?" Cecilia asked.

"Politics came in when they went too far trying to one up each other. I think my grandmother felt it most severely when my mother died, because she was the first one to reach out to us. Once my brothers started getting married, my grandmother set up a trust fund in each of our names. She'd decided that each one of us would gain access to our trust fund on our tenth wedding anniversary; the only stipulation was that she had to approve of our spouse. How ludicrous is that? She thinks she can control our lives with money, just like they tried to control my mother. George, Ronald, Norman, and Oliver all have access to their trust funds. They have for a while now. But I decided to go and confront the old lady instead of going by her terms. I flew out to California to tell her to her face that I'd never get married for money. I told her she could take all her money and stick it where the sun don't shine. I thought she was going to have me thrown out or at least yell at me, but all she had to say was, 'You're just like your father.' Imagine that; it was her first sight of one of the children of her only daughter, her *late* daughter, and all she could muster up was a mean comment. I haven't seen or heard from her since that day, but she did make it clear to me that I'll never see a penny from her whether I get married or not."

Cecilia waited in silence for him to go on. The waiter came by and took their orders before he continued.

"So, after that fun little visit, I went back to New York, and less than a week later I received a letter from my grandfather. He'd heard about the confrontation between me and my grandmother, and he thought the whole thing was funny. He thought it was so funny he decided to reward me for standing up to her. By the end of the week, he'd given me more money than I knew what to do with. At first, I was irresponsible with it. I spent it on all kinds of things that would make my poor mother sick to think about, and today I have very little to show for it. At first, it seemed like a good thing, but then all that money became a burden.

"Between the tabloids making me out to be some notorious playboy, and the women who pursued me because they wanted access to my bank account, things got pretty miserable for me. My upbringing in Tennessee, with a father who placed a man's value on how he treated his loved ones, didn't prepare me for what I went through in New York after everyone found out Edgar Howard was my grandfather. Suddenly, I was more than just Shane Gregory, the country boy turned firefighter. Suddenly, I was *somebody*, somebody people wanted as their friend, somebody women wanted to fall in love with. It didn't take me long to realize that those kind of friends and women couldn't possibly make me happy, because all they cared about was cash and a potential connection to my grandfather. One day I decided to just give it all away, and as soon as the money was gone, so were all the new friends. When I first moved back to Nashville, most of what was left went towards helping a friend out of some serious debt. Over the past few years, I've donated it all to charities and political campaigns. I only donated to politicians who are more liberal minded and aren't already in the pocket of some big businessman like my grandfather or my grandmother. Senator Reid just happened to be one of them. It's actually kind of funny that he thinks I'm loaded. I make good money as a firefighter, and the flower business does okay these days, but I don't have nearly as much as he seems to think. Actually, I don't have as much as anyone seems to think. Compared to you, I'm a pauper."

"Wow," Cecilia sat back and said when he finished. "That is quite a story. I guess your father really must have been something special to get your mother to walk away from all of that money and power."

"They loved each other, and he made a good life for her. She wasn't destitute by any means. He bred and trained thoroughbreds, and after he established a name for himself, he made good money doing that. He built her the house she wanted, and together we made every stick of furniture in it over the years. My oldest brother, Edward, took over the family business, and it still does very well. The rest of my brothers and my sister turned out just fine, and I'm not too bad myself. My mother would be proud of all of us, despite what her parents think about the choices she made. She had a better life on a horse ranch with my father than her parents could have given her in that mausoleum they lived in," he said fervently.

"How did they meet in the first place?" Cecilia asked.

"He was in charge of the stables out at one of their estates. Have you ever heard of the Howard Hills Estate? It's near here, and it's the one where my father worked. They only used it occasionally, but when they were there, they threw some legendary parties for all their fancy friends. My grandmother owns it now, but rumor has it that she let it fall apart over the last fifty years. If you look it up on the internet, you can find pictures of what it used to look like. It used to be famous for its ballroom. When they first had it built, people all over the world were talking about the stained glass dome they had custom made to go over the center of the ballroom. My father met my mother while he worked there. He was only twenty four at the time, but he knew what he was doing."

"He must have if he ended up married to your mother," Cecilia remarked with a twinkle in her eye. "What made you decide that you're never going to marry? It can't have been all because of your grandmother."

Cecilia didn't know it, but she'd struck a nerve with that question. Shane had been an idealistic pre-teen when his mother passed away. At such an impressionable age, he'd witnessed his father's grief, and that had tainted the way he felt about love ever since. That grief had affected him as almost nothing else in his young life had. He'd missed his mother too, but after a while he'd started to get used to living without her. His father, on the other hand, had never healed. The loss of his wife had sapped everything from him. He'd gone on, but his love of life and fun spirit had been permanently dampened.

All of his adult life, Shane had been terrified of having the same thing happen to him. He didn't want to find the love of his life only to lose her and never be able to move on. In the flash of a moment, all these thoughts went through his head, but to Cecilia he simply said, "I just didn't think I'd ever come across the right woman." He looked down at her hands. She was subconsciously fingering the fine table cloth as they talked. He reached across the table to grasp her hands. "And what about you Cecilia?" he asked as he looked into her eyes. "Why haven't you ever married?"

She looked down at their clasped hands before she spoke. "I don't think I could, even if I wanted to, at this point."

His hands were so big and strong they dwarfed hers and made them appear small and delicate. He ran his fingers over her neatly manicured fingernails. He liked that she kept them neat and trimmed rather than using elaborate colors and designs. She had a simple and unassuming style that he found very attractive. "Why not?" he asked.

"I'm forty years old. I have a better chance of being struck by lightning than finding a man who will put up with me. I haven't even dated anyone in more than five years," she admitted with a regretful little smile.

"Five years, huh? What made you decide to quit trying?" he asked.

"Every time I tried dating someone things just shut down when the relationship got to a certain point. Men don't like to wait too long for things to get physical... It's easier on everyone if I just accept my life as it is and live with it," she answered.

"Cecilia, look at me," Shane commanded gently. Once she'd made eye contact, he went on, "Any man would be lucky to have you in his life. If you've come across jerks who can't understand that you need a little more time, then they aren't worth your consideration."

To any outside observer, they looked like a happy couple. He maintained his hold on her hands, and continued to gaze at her like a man in love. She smiled up at him throughout dinner, and the conversation flowed easily. The few people who had recognized Shane were already keeping tabs on the couple. They wanted to know who the mystery woman was, and people loved nothing more than a little mystery combined with a little romance.

Shortly after they'd shared dessert, Shane reached into his pocket and felt the small jewelry box that had been there all evening. He looked into her eyes again, and she smiled at him. He liked that she was enjoying herself.

He moved his chair closer to her, so he could whisper in her ear, "Cecilia, have you noticed that couple who's been watching us all evening?"

"Not really. Was I supposed to?" she whispered back.

"They're just some acquaintances of mine, but it's a good thing they're being so nosey right now."

"Why?"

"So they can see me give you this," he said. He pulled out the jewelry box and opened it in front of her.

She inhaled sharply and asked, "Why didn't you tell me you wanted to do this tonight?"

"Because I wanted you to look surprised—like you do now," he answered. He gave her a tender smile and cupped her cheek with one of his hands. "All you have to do now is look happy, say yes, and let me kiss you," he whispered for her ears only, but for the couple watching he said clearly, "Will you marry me?"

Although Cecilia's "yes" came out in a mere whisper, her smile and nod made her acceptance of the fake proposal obvious to the couple watching. Shane took her left hand and made a big show of raising it to his lips and kissing it before sliding the ring onto her finger.

Cecilia's heart was pounding, drowning out almost every other sound around them. She could no longer hear the gentle clinking of wine glasses and fine silver. The dull roar of conversations across the restaurant disappeared beneath the overwhelming roar of her own pulse. The only thing she was aware of at that moment was the fact that Shane was about to kiss her.

They sat close together with their bodies angled toward each other. Shane put one arm around her back as he leaned in close again. "Just relax. You look absolutely gorgeous tonight," he said in her ear. His deep voice caressed her, and made her want to lose herself in him. Every time he got close to her, she was reminded of the first night he'd held her. She felt so safe and warm in his embrace that it was the most natural thing in the world for her to allow her eyes to drift shut and enjoy his warmth surrounding her tonight.

He pushed her hair to the side and planted a single kiss at the top of her neck near her jaw line. From that single kiss, Cecilia felt a longing blossom deep within her. It touched on not only the physical side of love, but on all the things she'd denied herself for most of her life. It was easy to pretend she didn't need the same things other women needed, to pretend she didn't want them even, but Shane's kiss shattered that pretense in the blink of an eye. In the infinitesimal instant that it took for him to kiss her neck, she was forced to acknowledge that after years of pushing, she finally wanted to reach out and pull someone closer to her. She wanted Shane's kiss more than she'd ever thought it possible for her to want any man's kiss.

His hand stayed entangled in her hair, and he massaged the back of her scalp as his lips traversed a path from her neck to her face. Once he reached her lips, he paused for an agonizing second before kissing them. It began with such gentle pressure she wasn't entirely sure he was kissing her at first. He encouraged her participation with teasing little nibbles along her bottom lip that left her wanting more. He slid his tongue along the edges of her lips, and they readily parted in anticipation of more. Cecilia's entire face was flush with longing by the time his tongue finally swooped inside to claim hers.

That was the only time in her life she'd ever been so completely caught up in the moment her surroundings fell away into nothingness. The only thing she was aware of was Shane's kiss. Every secretly worn down part of her soul suddenly hummed with renewed energy as his tongue caressed hers for that endless sliver of time. When the kiss ended, she opened her eyes to find him staring down at her with an expression she'd never seen on any man's face before. He hugged her close one more time, and then released his hold on her.

When Cecilia was finally able to shift her focus away from Shane, she realized that an older couple was standing over their table.

The woman spoke first. "We couldn't help but notice you just popped the question, Shane. Congratulations," she smiled.

"Thank you, Mrs. Bakersfield," Shane smiled at the matronly older woman.

"So, who's the young lady?" she asked.

"My name is Cece Graves," Cecilia spoke up at that point.

Mrs. Bakersfield looked at her in surprise and said, "I'm Sibylle Bakersfield. Shane and my husband used to be partners until my husband decided to retire from the flower business a few years ago. It's nice to meet you."

"Nice to meet you too," Cecilia smiled.

"Shane," Mr. Bakersfield nodded with a touch of embarrassment in his voice. "Congratulations. Hopefully we didn't intrude too much," he added with a pointed look at his wife. After a few more smiles and waves, the couple exited the restaurant, leaving Shane and Cecilia alone again.

Cecilia couldn't tell if he'd enjoyed the kiss even half as much as she did. She wanted to know, but she wasn't about to ask.

"What are you thinking right now?" he asked her before she could think of anything to say.

"I was just wondering what Rebecca is going to say about this," she sighed as she looked down at the ring twinkling on her finger.

"Cecilia, it'll be fine. Anyway, it's too late to back out now. Sibylle Bakersfield has the biggest mouth in the city. She'll call her brother who works for the state attorney's office with my brother Brent. Your daughter will probably hear about this before you make it back to your house tonight," he told her.

Chapter 12

Karen was pounding away on the heavy bag when Cece showed up for their weekly sparring session at the gym. She had a look of intense anger on her face; obviously something was bothering her.

"Hey, Karen," Cece greeted her.

When Karen didn't respond, Cece walked across the room and stood behind the bag. She wrapped her arms around it to stop it from swaying back and forth.

Karen finally acknowledged her presence with a frown. "What are you doing here?" she asked.

"It's Sunday. We do this every Sunday... What's with you lately?" Cece returned.

"Last time we talked you said no more fights. I didn't expect you to spar with me any more after that," Karen grouched.

"I said no more public fights," Cece reminded her.

"Same thing," Karen grunted as she went back to ignoring Cece and punching the bag.

Cece let her vent for a few more minutes before speaking again. "Karen, are you okay? I can tell there's something bothering you and I don't think it has much to do with whether or not I fight anymore."

"Well aren't you perceptive?" Karen snapped.

"Well? What is it?" Cece asked as she caught Karen's gaze. "What's going on?"

"You aren't the only one who can keep secrets," Karen said with a mocking little smile. "I don't want to talk about it."

"You know you can talk to me about anything."

Karen punched the bag a few more times before replying. "Yeah, just like you talk to me about everything..."

"Come on, Karen. That's not fair," Cece said.

"What's not fair about it? We've been friends for twenty years now, and you've never once talked to me about anything important. So why should I talk to you about my life?" Karen demanded.

"Because I care," Cece reminded her.

Karen stopped punching the bag and pinned Cece with a look that seared straight through her and said, "Well, I've cared about you for twenty years, since the day we met, and I can't tell that it's ever made a difference."

Karen's direct reference to the day Sarah died instantly inflamed Cece's emotions. "The day we met..." Cece whispered in a breathless echo, feeling like she'd just been punched in the stomach. In the next breath, she exploded, "What was I supposed to talk to you about? Was I supposed to tell you every day about how hard it is to pick up and move on after I saw my own daughter killed? Is that what you wanted to hear? Did you want me to tell you about all the nights Rebecca cried herself to sleep in my arms after that day? Or was I supposed to go on about how guilty I've felt for not turning around when I heard the tires screeching that day? Is that what you want to hear?"

"I'm sorry! I've always been sorry, but you made me swear never to bring it up," Karen whispered with tears in her eyes.

"It wasn't *your* fault. *I'm* her mother. I should have looked when I heard the tires. You don't know how many times I've replayed that sound in my head... All I had to do was turn around, and Sarah would be alive today. I *know* you've always felt guilty about it, but I just couldn't talk about it. I still can't." Cece was now fighting back her own tears. "Please don't ask me to talk about Sarah. I want to know what's going on with you, but please don't ask me to talk about her. It still hurts too much."

"Have you ever considered the fact that talking about it might make it less painful for you? When you keep everything bottled up it seems worse than it is," Karen said.

"What could possibly be worse than seeing my own daughter killed?!" Cece screamed at her. "Talking about it isn't ever going to make it any better!"

ADRIENNE D'NELLE RUVALCABA

Karen recoiled in the face of Cece's raw anguish. It was difficult to imagine living with the memory of that day from a mother's perspective. Karen didn't have any children of her own. "Okay," she said with a shaking voice. "Just calm down."

"No, *you* calm down," Cece returned. "You started it. First you get all on my case, because I don't want to fight anymore. Then you jump down my throat when I try to find out what's bothering you. Why are you acting like this?"

Karen took a moment to wipe more tears out of her eyes before replying. "Because you don't *want* to fight anymore, and I *can't* fight anymore," she admitted with a defeated look.

"Can't?" Cece asked. "Why can't you?"

"Because I can't get medical clearance anymore. My doctor referred me to a neurologist, and it turns out I've had a few too many concussions during my career. He recommended that I retire unless I want to end up like Dad."

"Karen, I had no idea..." Cece said sadly. "What did Mitch say when you told him?"

"You're the first person I've told. Mitch is still trying to line up an MMA match for me... There's no way I can tell him he's about to lose his star client," Karen sighed.

"You have to tell him soon. He's your promoter."

"I know. I just don't know how to say it. When he mentioned the next fight, I told him I thought you should fight in my place, but he looked at me like he thought I was crazy," Karen admitted.

"Me? I've never fought in a mixed martial arts tournament in my life. All I do is Judo and Muay Thai."

"Yeah, but a lot of good MMA fighters come from those backgrounds," Karen said.

Cece sighed. "Karen, I'm not changing my mind about this. I'm *forty* years old. There's no way I'm going to suddenly start a career as an MMA fighter. I couldn't, even if I wanted to. You're the one who's always had your name in lights. I never wanted any of that. I'm sorry it's come to an end, but trying to use me as a replacement just won't work."

"You're right," Karen sighed with a remorseful look. "Besides, you have your cake business to worry about," she added.

"That too," Cece agreed.

140

"You know, I've always been a little jealous of you. All I've ever had is fighting. Dad started training me in martial arts before I was even potty-trained. Martial arts are all I've ever done with my life, but you have something else to fall back on. You can design some of the best cakes I've ever seen. Do you know what I'd give right now for another shot at life? The chance to do something else with my life, besides just fight all the time, passed me by years ago."

"Karen, you can do whatever you want now. It's not like you don't have money. Besides that, you run the academy, you own the gym, and you own half of the arena. You do plenty of other things besides fighting."

"But all those things center on fighting. Sometimes I wonder what I would have been if I'd had a mother instead of a father," Karen sighed.

Cece didn't say anything for a moment, instead she thought of her own mother, the defeated prostitute who'd never really seemed like a mother at all. In all her years in foster care and group homes, she'd barely allowed herself to dream of a life with parents. Normalcy had seemed like some untouchable, foolish dream. Why waste time thinking about it when it could never happen?

"But you have a wonderful father," Cece said eventually.

"I know." Karen slapped at the tears covering her cheeks. "It's not that I don't love him, because I do, even now that he's not always himself anymore. Actually, that makes me love him more, because I feel like I have to take care of him like he took care of me. I'll always be thankful for Dad, always, but I'll always wonder if I could have been a better woman if I hadn't been raised like I was a boy. I mean, I don't even know how to put on make-up. I'm forty-one years old and I can't wear make-up. What kind of woman am I?"

"I thought you liked yourself the way you are," Cece said.

"I do," Karen insisted, but her gaze faltered before she continued. "I just wish I could be more than just K.C. Holly the fighter. Hell, I can't even be *that* anymore."

Cece watched as another tear escaped Karen's eye and made its way down her cheek. She sniffed and looked so forlorn Cece reached out and patted her shoulder. "I could always teach you how to decorate cakes," she smiled.

"I might actually take you up on that," Karen chuckled.

"Good. It might be kind of fun teaching you something for a change," Cece said. "Just remember that I start baking at four every morning," she reminded Karen with a smile.

"I'll never understand why you don't just hire an assistant so you don't have to go in so early every day," Karen grumbled.

"I save an extra twenty-five thousand dollars a year by doing everything myself. When I get tired of saving money, I'll hire some help," Cece answered.

"Suit yourself," Karen shrugged. "So, you want to get started now? We've wasted enough time with the chitchat."

Cece glanced at the clock and bit her lip. "I don't have time now," she said.

"Why not? You don't open 'til ten on Sundays, and—Oh my God! What is that?!" Karen demanded as she stared at the engagement ring on Cece's finger.

Cece swallowed. "I've been going to church with Shane. It starts at ten, but I need extra time to shower and change into something nice. We can spar next week."

"I just love how you didn't even attempt to answer my question," Karen said as she continued to stare pointedly at the ring. "It looks like an engagement ring."

"That's because it is," Cece admitted.

The look of delight that came over Karen's face was priceless. "You're engaged?" she asked.

"Yes."

"To be married?" she went on in disbelief, her blue eyes still wide with surprise.

"Yes."

"I knew this would happen, but I didn't expect it to be this fast. Congratulations." Karen grabbed Cece's hand and studied the ring for a moment. "It's a gorgeous ring," she said.

"Thanks, Karen." The air in the room suddenly felt too thick for Cece to breathe properly. Karen was genuinely happy for her, and she had the urge to blurt out the truth. She wanted to, but she didn't. It was one thing to hide her past and make up a more palatable story about where she'd come from, but it was an entirely different matter to make up a lie about her future. Karen was going to be so disappointed when she and Shane split after the wedding.

Cece tried to put those thoughts out of her mind as Karen grabbed her up in a big bear hug. "I'm so happy for you," Karen said, and Cece felt the guilt grind into her even more.

At church, Cece had to get through another round of congratulations, but it wasn't so difficult because she barely knew any of the people there. For the most part, they all seemed like very nice people, many of them pillars of the community who served on various boards and committees and owned various businesses in town. On the surface, she seemed to be one of them, but Cece thought they were probably the sort of people who would look down on her if they knew where she'd really come from.

After the service, Shane took her around and introduced her to everyone as his fiancée, and she'd simpered like a mindless idiot as she'd repeated her name over and over again for all the smiling couples in their finery. Everyone seemed to love Shane, and as his fiancée, she was an immediate favorite among them. By the time they got clear of the sanctuary, they'd been invited to lunch by five different couples, and Cece had been referred to several wedding planners in the area. She'd refused all the invitations of course; she still had to get to work.

She'd been behind the counter for several hours when Rebecca showed up.

"Hi, Mom," Rebecca greeted Cece as she stepped inside. The bakery had been like home for Rebecca for most of her life, yet today she seemed very uncertain as she looked at her mother.

"Rebecca! I didn't expect to see you today. What's going on?" Cece smiled at her daughter.

"What's going on? I could ask you the same thing," Rebecca responded.

"What do you mean?"

Rebecca held up the newspaper she'd been clutching behind her back. "Check out page six," she said.

Cece wasn't sure what to expect, but she was completely taken aback when she opened the newspaper. In the top half of the engagement announcements, there was a relatively large photo of her and Shane kissing. Her left hand rested against his cheek almost as if she'd been purposely showing the ring off to the photographer. The caption under the photo read, "Heir to world's largest fortune proposes to founder of local women's charity."

"They didn't even get the basic details right. He's not the heir to anything, and you started the foundation, not me," Cece grumbled as she stared at the paper in dismay. She should be happy that the fake proposal gained so much attention; it could only mean good things for her business. However, she was far from happy. She was deeply affronted that one of the best and most personal moments of her life had been broadcast to others, to strangers. Shane's kiss had been the first and only kiss she'd ever fully enjoyed and taken part in. It had been special to her, and now it was frozen in time forever in the newspaper.

"Mom?" Rebecca's soft voice interrupted her turbulent thoughts. "Why did I have to read about this in the paper? You could have called me; you're my mother," she sighed.

"I was going to tell you today. Actually, Shane and I were going to make the announcement together," Cece grouched. "I had no idea someone was there taking pictures."

"Well, I guess it doesn't really matter how I found out. The important thing is that you're happy," Rebecca said as she came around the counter to hug her.

Cece felt the gentle swell of her daughter's growing belly as she returned the hug. A little thrill shot through her as she thought again about the fact that she was going to be a grandmother before next spring. "I am happy, so you can stop worrying about me so much."

"How's your new house coming along? Have you bought any furniture yet?" Rebecca asked.

Cece hadn't, but she was spared from having to reply when a few customers came into the shop. Rebecca rung up their purchases as Cece continued to work on a birthday cake that was to be picked up that day shortly before closing.

After the customers left, Rebecca joined her by the cake and said, "That looks really pretty."

"Thanks, Honey," Cece smiled. Rebecca continued to watch as she piped out a multitude of butter-cream flowers across the top of the cake.

"I can't believe you can do that so fast, Mom."

"I can show you how if you still want to learn," Cece offered.

"Sure," Rebecca said in surprise. She'd often begged her mother to teach her how to make flowers when she was younger, but Cece had been forceful in her refusal. She'd told Rebecca that

144

she needed to concentrate her time on more productive things instead of learning how to decorate cakes.

"Here, take the bag," Cece instructed.

"What if I mess it up? Doesn't this one get picked up today?" Rebecca asked.

"Don't worry about that. You can fill in the middle with some flowers, and if you don't like the way they look, I have time to take them off and then you can try again," Cece reassured her daughter.

At first, Cece gently guided Rebecca's hands, but when she held the bag with more confidence Cece stepped back to watch. The flowers she made weren't nearly as good as the ones Cece did earlier, but they still looked okay.

"So, this thing with you and Shane... how did it start?" Rebecca asked as she continued to work on the flowers.

Cece didn't know what to say. She hadn't practiced any lies about the fake engagement, so she decided to go with the literal truth. "A couple of months ago I had a nightmare, and he... he um..."

"He what, Mom?"

"He stayed with me, and just held me all night."

"Oh?" Rebecca's hands paused over the cake as she studied her mother.

"I feel really safe with him."

"Well, that's good, but how did you two go from that to being engaged? It just doesn't make much sense when you've never even seriously dated anyone in the past. I mean, remember what happened with Mr. Holt? I thought you hated men."

"Things just happened," Cece hedged. She really wished Rebecca hadn't brought up Mr. Holt. She still felt badly about how things had ended with him. He'd been a coach and a history teacher at Rebecca's high school, and he'd had a massive crush on her from the first time he'd met her. Cece had known of course; he'd made his feelings painfully obvious with his multiple trips to her bakery just to flirt with her. He'd been an incredibly charismatic and handsome man, but the only reason she'd finally consented to go out with him had been to please both Karen and Rebecca. He'd been Rebecca's favorite teacher, and Karen had been hounding her about going out for years.

Cece had gone out on five dates with him before he'd tried to kiss her. Looking back on the incident it was easy to see that she just wasn't ready for a relationship at that time. She could still barely admit to herself that she needed counseling. At that time it had been easier to categorize all men into the same group and secretly despise them all. As much as she'd wanted to believe she'd gotten over the attack on her own, there had still been bitterness, mistrust, fear, and hatred lurking just below the surface. Those things had tainted all of her encounters with Mr. Holt.

On the night of their fifth date, she'd invited him inside after he'd taken her home. Cece had wanted to talk more, and maybe even hold hands to explore her burgeoning attraction to him, but he'd taken her invitation as a green light to make a move. Cece's memory of the entire event was a little fuzzy these days, but she did remember clearly that he'd kissed her passionately. She'd tried to tell him to let her go, but he'd pulled her closer, and his tongue in her mouth had made it difficult for her to breathe, much less talk. She'd felt threatened, and then she'd panicked.

Instinctively, she'd brought her knee up into his groin with enough force to make him let her go and double over in pain right as she stepped back and delivered a powerful kick to his chin. Perhaps if his mouth hadn't been hanging open at the time it wouldn't have been so bad, but as it was his teeth had slammed together and fractured his jaw—a fact Cece had learned later from Karen. Rebecca had run into the living room to find Cece standing over him as he lay unconscious on the floor.

"What did you do, Mom?" Rebecca had demanded with rising panic in her voice. "Mr. Holt! Are you okay?"

He'd regained consciousness quickly, but he hadn't been able to talk. When he started spitting out blood, Rebecca had called Karen to help get him to the hospital. Cece had stood stoic and silent as he lay on the floor, and she'd offered not one word of apology. Her last memory of Mr. Holt had been the look of confusion he'd given her as Karen helped him into her car that night.

After they left, Rebecca had approached her mother and asked, "Why did you hurt him?"

"He's a man," Cece had snapped in a voice devoid of all human kindness. "Men only want one thing from women; even if they get all in your face and pretend to be nice it *always* boils down to sex. They're all the same. They're all worthless dogs, even your precious Mr. Holt."

Nowadays she tried not to remember how she'd acted that night. She knew it took months for the poor man to completely recover, yet he hadn't told the truth about what happened to him that night. According to Karen, he'd told the emergency room physician that he'd been mugged by a masked assailant. Cece had been too relieved not to be in jail to analyze his benevolence too much. Over the years, she'd thought about finding him so she could apologize, but she knew she was probably the last person on Earth he wanted to see.

Rebecca was still holding the pastry bag, waiting for Cece to elaborate on what kind of "things" had happened between her and Shane.

"How long did you and Norman date before you got married? Wasn't it something like three or four months?" Cece asked pointedly at her daughter's prying look.

"Yeah. I'm sorry to be so nosey; it's just that I'm so surprised by this. I mean, it was obvious that Shane had it bad for you that night I told everyone I was pregnant, but I didn't realize you felt the same about him."

"Well, I do. So you can stop worrying about it."

"You've changed so much since that fire," Rebecca said in a near whisper.

"I guess love does that to people," Cece said just as softly. Rebecca didn't pick up the pastry bag again, so she went over and finished the cake as Rebecca watched.

They spent the rest of the afternoon working together, and Cece pulled out her practice set and taught Rebecca how to pipe butter-cream frosting like a pro. Cece chattered most of the time about all the different techniques she could show her someday, and Rebecca didn't ask any more questions about Shane. As closing time drew near, Rebecca turned to her mother and gave her a hug.

They held each other for a long time before Rebecca finally said, "Whatever happened between you two, I'm glad it happened. I know I've been pushing you to get therapy, but this thing with Shane seems to have made more of a difference than I would have thought possible. You seem like you have a little more peace now. Do you know what I mean? It's like, for the first time ever you're not pushing everyone away; you're not pushing *me* away."

As her daughter spoke, Cece felt her earlier guilt grinding into her again. What had she been thinking to agree to such a scheme? The wheels were in motion, and it was too late to back out now, but Cece was still concerned about the potential aftermath. Rebecca was going to be so disappointed when she and Shane went their separate ways in the end. When it was all over, so many people would be disappointed—Karen, Rebecca, Shane's family, and although she could barely admit it to herself, even Cece would be disappointed.

Chapter 13

After leaving little Sarah's grave, he couldn't bear the thought of following Cece around for much longer, but instead of getting on with the confrontation, he went home and took a mind numbing, month long drink. During that month, a lifetime of memories crowded every moment of his thoughts, and the only way to slow the memories to a bearable pace was to slow down all his thoughts with drink. There were still two thoughts he could never get rid of; no matter how much he drank, Cece and Sita dominated his tired mind.

His daughter, Sita, had been months away from her twentieth birthday when she'd taken her own life. He'd never forget the night he'd come home from a performance to find her lying, still warm, in her bed. Even as his mind shied away from that night for the millionth time, he knew that he must face it. He would have to face much more in the coming weeks.

It had all started so suddenly. One day Sita had been a normal, happy college student, and the next she'd been an angry, fragmented shell of her former self. He'd come home to find her sitting at the breakfast table with swollen eyes and a completely blank expression plastered on her face. She'd been living in the dormitories on campus for two years, and she'd visited often. It was clear from the moment he saw her that this visit wasn't like the others.

"Sita?" he'd called out as he rushed across the room.

She'd immediately cast her eyes downward. This downward glance wasn't the shy glance she had a habit of giving people she didn't know well. This glance was an obvious indication that something was seriously wrong in her world. She'd glanced down in shame.

"What's wrong?"

She couldn't look up at him again. She'd raised her face several times only to hide it again with both hands as she'd started to cry.

"Sita? What is it?" he'd asked her repeatedly. She couldn't speak; she'd just continued to shake her head back and forth. Every once in a while, he'd caught a glimpse of her face through her curled fingers. Her mouth had been open in an ugly grimace as if she'd been crying out in extreme pain, but it was silent pain. She'd made not a sound.

He'd implored her to talk to him that night, but all she'd done was cry her silent, soul racking tears; even his own tears of concern hadn't been able to loosen her tongue. She'd finally gone to bed late that night in the bedroom that was still decorated in the pale pink and white tones of her girlhood. He hadn't changed anything during the two years she'd been living at the university.

He'd sat in the chair beside her bed and stroked her hair as she'd cried herself to sleep that night. She'd clutched her pillow and curled her small body into the fetal position, and he'd watched her long into the early morning hours. She hadn't spoken a single intelligible word all night, and he'd never seen her so upset before. At first he'd thought some young man must have broken her heart, but he quickly dismissed that notion. She'd never even had a boyfriend. He couldn't get past the shame in her eyes as she'd tried to look at him. He'd thought about it all night as he watched her fitful sleeping.

When she'd opened her eyes in the morning, they'd been swollen and red, and as soon as she'd seen him looking at her she'd looked away in shame again. The shame in her eyes had made him ask the question he feared he already knew the answer to.

"Sita, did something happen to you?" he'd whispered tearfully.

Her little shoulders had started shaking as she took in a shuddering breath and started crying again. She'd nodded and hid her face in her hands.

"What?" he'd asked. "What happened?"

She'd opened her mouth to say something, but no words had come. All she could do was shake her head and cry.

"Did somebody do something to you?" he'd whispered.

She'd nodded again.

He'd known she couldn't bring herself to say it out loud, so he'd said the ugly words for her, "Sita, were you attacked by a man?"

She'd nodded again and turned her back to him. He'd wanted to reach out to her, but she'd hugged her knees to her chest and started sobbing when he'd squeezed her shoulder.

He'd left her alone after that. She'd needed something that he couldn't give her at that moment. She'd needed a gentle mother's touch, but Sita's mother had died when she was small. He couldn't be a mother to her, but he could be a father. And as her father, he'd been angry. As soon as he'd left her room, he'd called the local police to report the crime. At the time, it had seemed like the right thing to do, the only thing to do.

He took another drink from his flask and reclined back in his office chair. He hadn't seen any of his friends since all their initial house calls immediately following Sita's funeral. A mirthless smile crossed his lips as he imagined their reaction to how much he'd changed since then. He'd never been a large man, but he'd lost enough weight to resemble an old bag of bones, and he hadn't been completely sober in months. His piano sat in the middle of the great-room, gathering dust along with everything else in his mansion and in his life.

The police had taken Sita's statement and instructed her to go to the emergency room. A woman at the front desk had checked them in; her manner had been very succinct and businesslike as she'd instructed them on which forms needed to be filled out and where they were to wait. He'd filled out Sita's medical history, his insurance information, and their reason for being there in the midst of a waiting room filled with people suffering from various ailments. Once the paperwork was done, he'd assumed they would be escorted directly to an examination room, but they'd waited at least another three hours before a triage nurse called Sita's name.

The nurse had been much like the lady in charge of the front desk. She treated Sita with politeness, but other than that her manner was as cold and sterile as the hospital walls and equipment surrounding them.

He'd waited on the other side of the large curtain drawn to give Sita's bay a false sense of privacy. He saw the shadows cast by the nurse and Sita as she lay back on the bed to give strangers intimate access to her body. He understood that they needed to collect evidence, but it was still hard to see. He turned away from the shadows on the curtain and tried not to listen to the small sounds of distress made by his daughter.

When they'd finished, he'd peeped around the curtain. Sita was sitting on the edge of the exam table and hiding her face in her hands. She hadn't cried in front of the strangers; she only allowed herself that luxury when he was the only one in the room with her.

Once all of the initial statement taking and evidence collection had transpired, Sita had been referred to a local women's center for counseling. She'd wanted to go alone, but he'd insisted on accompanying her to her intake session. Even if all he did was sit in the waiting room for two hours he wanted to be there with her. He *needed* to be there with her.

Just like at the hospital, they'd checked in at the front desk, but this time they'd waited only moments before Sita was called to the back. The therapist had been a very gentle looking lady with a small, matronly stature and a shock of white hair cut in a pixie style. She'd smiled one of those smiles meant to set patients at ease. Her smile had seemed to say, "You're in good hands with me." He had trusted her instantly.

At first, he'd sat in the waiting room and concentrated heavily on the details in the tops of his shoes, the patterns on the wallpaper, and even the number of fibers in the carpet—anything but the melancholy faces of the other women in the waiting room. One lady in particular still had fading bruises on her face, no doubt left there by some insignificant brute.

It wasn't until near the end of the session that he'd noticed the brochure. Tucked away among many other brochures and magazines as it was, it was a wonder he noticed it at all. "*The Cece Graves Foundation: For Survivors of Abuse and Sexual Assault*" had been printed across the top in bold, black letters against a vivid, red background. He'd gone very still. He hadn't thought of the name Cece Graves in twenty-five years. What were the chances that it was the same girl from all those years ago?

With shaking hands and sweaty palms, he'd gotten up and plucked one of the brochures from the stack. What were the chances?

His only daughter was in the back with a counselor because she'd been raped, and he was suddenly beset with long buried images from his own murky past. Was Cece in this very building? Would she come out at any moment to point the finger at him? No... she'd never seen his face... she didn't even know who he was. His heart still hadn't calmed down. It had alternately raced and skipped beats until Sita had reappeared from the session and they'd left the building. He'd been so consumed with getting out of there; he'd failed to ask her how her session had gone.

That night, he'd fallen asleep with the sound of Cece's voice repeating in his head.

"I'm Cece. Please stop. My name is Cece, Cece Graves. My name is Cece Graves and I'm 13 years old. My name is Cece, Cece Graves..."

In his dreams, he'd seen Cece's face, and then he'd recoiled in guilt, shame, and even horror as Cece's face had somehow become Sita's.

"My name is Cece, Cece Graves..."

He'd thought he would never have to see or hear that name again after what he'd done for her, but he'd been wrong.

Guilt had settled deep within his chest like a hot, heavy stone. He'd longed to tear at his chest with his bare hands to purge himself of it.

Shortly after she'd started counseling, Sita had stopped going to school. She hadn't withdrawn from the university; she'd simply quit going to all of her classes. And she hadn't told him; of course she hadn't told him. He'd found out the hard way. He'd looked at her grades for the semester, and she'd failed every course. He'd been shocked. She'd been in counseling for more than two months before her grades came in and she'd seemed to be making progress.

"Sita, what is this?" he'd tried to ask as gently as possible. "Don't you care about your grades anymore?"

She'd looked down at the floor and remained silent. She'd said very little to him in those days.

"You were on the Dean's List every semester. You could still do it if you want to," he'd gone on in the face of her silence. "Sita...?"

Still she remained steadfastly silent. She hadn't talked to him about anything. All he'd known at that time was what he'd learned from the police and the prosecutor.

"Come on," he'd said brusquely. "You cannot sit and do nothing with yourself. You are too bright for that. We will go together to register for next semester." He'd grabbed her hand to pull her out of the chair, and she'd snatched it back.

"I'm not going back to school," she'd said quietly, her voice shaking with many emotional undertones.

"But, Sita, you *must*! Doing nothing is making this harder for you. You need something positive to focus on, especially right now," he'd insisted.

"I'm not going," she said, and this time anger gave out the strongest signal in her voice.

"Going back to school will be better for you than sitting around here doing nothing all day!" His frustration with not being able to help her made him lash out more harshly than he'd intended, but when tears sprang to her eyes he regretted both his tone and his words. He opened his mouth to apologize, only to be interrupted.

"School will *not* be better!" she'd suddenly erupted. "Do you know what it's like to sit in class and know that half of the students are whispering about *me*? Behind my back! To my face! Those guys who raped me were on the football team! They were *seniors*! Now all I am is the campus *slut*! Do you *really* think going back to that school is better than being here?" She was panting and looking at him in such tumult he had to look away. "At least here, I am *safe*," she ended in a tragic, broken little whisper.

He hadn't known what else to do, so he'd attempted to hug her. She had pushed him away and run back to her room. She'd spent most of her time in her room those days. Even as he'd tried to be there for her, in the months leading up to the trial, he'd still been immersed in his own inner turmoil.

Before the trial, the prosecutor had talked to him and Sita together. There had been a total of four defendants, and the prosecutor had advised them to try them all as co-defendants in the same trial rather than subject Sita to the ordeal four separate trials. The downside was that they would all be found either guilty or innocent on the same body of evidence. He hadn't really understood all of the legal ramifications, but he'd thought justice would be better served with one trial.

It had been a short trial which lasted only one month, but it was a month that had changed his life forever.

The judge had been a tall, pale, austere man. The bailiff had called for everyone to rise as the judge approached the bench. He'd kept his right hand over Sita's for support from the moment the judge had taken his seat. Throughout most of the trial he'd gripped her little hand. It had grown tense at times during the testimony from the doctor who had examined her, and lax at others.

The prosecution had laid out a case that seemed like a decisive win, but the details had been difficult to hear. As her father, he'd ached for her and he'd angered for her as the prosecution had laid out the details of that night for all to envision: The shy, young pre-med student attended her first college frat party, only to be plied with alcohol despite being underage. In her drunken state she'd been vulnerable, and those strong athletic boys had wasted no time in taking advantage of her in the most vile way possible—taking turns forcing her to submit to their will.

Once the defense had the chance to present its case, everything took a very bad turn. The defense attorney had been a relatively young woman with a very sleek and powerful look. From the way she'd commanded immediate attention, it was clear that she'd been born to be a trial lawyer. She began with the confidence of a winner, and that very confidence had caused dread to settle deep inside him. She glanced at Sita once, with a somewhat regretful look in her eyes, before she attacked.

She'd launched immediately into an all-out assault on Sita's character and credibility. She never denied that all four of her clients had slept with Sita; instead, she claimed that it had been consensual on all counts. At that statement, he'd felt Sita's little hand tremble, and his own anger had started to rise. How could that arrogant woman suggest such a thing? His daughter had never even had a boyfriend.

The woman had gone on in her powerful, authoritarian voice, "Your Honor, I'd like to present the court with Exhibit F, a digital video taken by a fellow party goer."

Sita had stiffened in surprise, and so had he. Neither of them knew anything about this video. The prosecutor glanced at them once before jumping up and saying, "I object! Permission to approach the bench, Your Honor."

Both the prosecutor and the defense attorney approached the bench. Tense minutes ticked by as they engaged in a furiously whispered conversation with the austere judge. When both sides stepped away from the bench, the bailiff was asked to play the video on the big projector screen for everyone to see.

The courtroom fell silent, and then that silence was replaced by the sound of the party music on the video. He'd never been more shocked in his life than he was at that moment. Was that his daughter on the screen? Was that his Sita up there dancing on a counter and asking for more alcohol? The video went on to show her remove her shirt and flash her bra to the cameraperson. When she sat down on the lap of one of the defendants and allowed him to touch her as she writhed on top of him, he had to close his eyes. He didn't want to believe that *his* Sita had done all of those things.

Although his eyes were closed, he couldn't block out the sounds of the blaring music, the chatter, and the sound of a cocky, young voice saying, "You want it bad, don't you?" and then the worst sound of all...his own daughter, his Sita's voice saying, "Yes."

The defense had wrapped up their case quickly after the video, and the prosecution's rebuttal went by in a blur. He was so engrossed in trying to banish the unwelcome images of his daughter on that young man's lap; he registered very little of what was said. He'd managed to calm down some by the time the prosecution presented its closing argument. Even now, in his whiskey induced stupor, he could recall almost every word they'd said. The words from both the prosecutor and the defense attorney frequently peppered his dreams as he flopped helplessly between haunting images of Sita mingled with memories of Cece.

He took another drink from the bottle cradled in his lap and closed his eyes. The prosecutor's face floated somewhere in his brain, and slowly dissolved into the scene from the courtroom. The prosecutor had stood, looking very much like a skinny American Santa Claus, and launched gently into his closing statement.

"Ladies and gentlemen of the jury, please do not allow the defense's smoke screen to distract you from the evidence and the facts of this case. The victim's behavior that night in no way gave those four men the right to rape her. Evidence collected from the rape kit shows that she fought hard to defend herself. You don't sustain bruises, skin and blood under your fingernails, and vaginal tears from a consensual act!

"All that tape proves is that the victim was attracted to one of the men who raped her. Whether or not that attraction would have led to something is pure speculation. From that video, we certainly cannot conclude that this young woman *willingly* had sex with all four of these men, but from the hard evidence we *can* conclude that they, in fact, raped her. Remember the definition of rape. If at any time the victim asks the aggressor to stop, and the aggressor does not stop, it is rape. Even if it started out as a little bit of mutual attraction and consensual kissing, it most definitely didn't end that way. You *must* find these men *guilty*."

The courtroom sat in silence as the prosecutor walked back to his seat.

He glanced at Sita to find her staring at her feet. Her little hand was still clutched loosely inside his.

When it was the defense attorney's turn to speak, he felt Sita's hand grow tense again.

"Let us not forget," she began loudly and then took a dramatic pause as she looked at each of the jurors, "the beauty of the American justice system. A defendant is innocent until proven guilty by an *absolute* preponderance of the evidence. A guilty verdict in a criminal trial can only be delivered if there is *no reasonable doubt*. Ladies and gentlemen of the jury, in this case you have a reasonable doubt. In the video, you saw one of the defendants *clearly* ask permission, and the *alleged* victim clearly said '*yes*.' She was even taking off her own clothes and sitting on his lap *voluntarily*! People, if that's not reasonable doubt then I don't know what is. There is no way you can convict these men for taking her up on something she clearly offered. There *is* a reasonable doubt in this case, and it would be a gross miscarriage of justice if you don't find these young men innocent."

The jury had deliberated for almost two hours, and during deliberations they had asked to see the video again. He and Sita had stayed together, but not a word had been spoken between them. She wouldn't lift her head long enough for him to see her face. He didn't know what he should say, if anything, so he remained silent.

Eventually, word came that the jury had reached a verdict. The bailiff called the court to order for the second time that day, and everybody rose again as the austere judge approached his bench. Everyone then sat and waited for the jury to return from the deliberation room. As they filed into the courtroom, not one of them looked in Sita's direction. He knew then that the outcome wasn't good. His palms grew sweaty and his heart hammered relentlessly at his old chest.

"Madam Foreman, has the jury reached a verdict?" the judge had asked.

"We have, Your Honor," the woman's voice rang out in the silent courtroom, but he barely heard her over his thundering heart.

"And what say you?" the judge asked, sounding almost bored with the proceedings.

"As to the count of aggravated rape, we find defendant one, Chad Wilson, not guilty. As to the count of aggravated rape, we find defendant two, not guilty..." she'd droned on, and all the words leaving her mouth had run together in an unintelligible stream, incomprehensible to him. The only words that had penetrated the fog in his brain at that moment had been the words, "not guilty." They had sounded over and over again like a death knell. *Not* guilty...*not* guilty...*not guilty*?

In the weeks after the trial, he hadn't been able to bring the verdict up in conversation with Sita. She'd sat frozen in the courtroom through the rest of the proceedings, and had spoken less than ten words the rest of the day. He'd left her in peace during those first few weeks as he'd tried to make sense of his own feelings. At first, the video had shocked him, but eventually that shock had turned to horror and humiliation laced dangerously with anger. How could *his* daughter have acted like that?

The months leading up to the trial and the trial itself had been very public affairs, played out in the local media like some sort of macabre circus for the morbid curiosity of the masses. He'd taken an extended vacation from his music, due in part to his daughter's need for him and in part to his own need to hide from all the prying eyes.

About a month after the trial, he'd gone back to work. He was scheduled to perform one of Beethoven's piano concertos with a nearby symphony orchestra soon, and he could no longer delay going to rehearsals. The day he went back he'd stood outside the door to the room, trying to find the nerve to go inside. Bright chatter interspersed with laughter had filtered through the door as he'd placed his sweaty palm on the doorknob. However, as soon as he stepped inside the room he was met with awkward silence. Almost every single musician in the room avoided looking directly at his face as they greeted him. Every rehearsal thereafter had been just as uncomfortable.

When the final rehearsal before the performance ended, he couldn't take the tension and silence anymore, and, in spite of his private nature, he addressed it.

"I know what you are all thinking, and cannot say," he'd lashed out. No one had responded, and he'd stalked out of the room in silence.

Later that same night, he'd made the mistake of getting on the internet and browsing the video sharing site for that offensive video of his daughter the night of the party. The video had been removed from the page, but the title and the comments still remained. As he'd scanned through a multitude of expletives, calling his daughter everything from a whore to an evil bitch, he was suddenly beset with rage. This time, however, not all of it was on Sita's behalf. How could she have behaved so scandalously? He wondered how many other men she'd been with. He'd always thought of her as sweet and innocent, and he didn't want to face the fact that she'd done the things he saw on the video in court that day.

"Why are you looking at that?" her quiet voice had materialized out of nowhere and startled him so badly he'd almost lost his seat. He'd clicked the close button, and the offensive page had disappeared from sight.

"Why were you looking at that?" she'd asked again.

He'd felt his rage at her grow stronger, but somehow he couldn't think of a single thing to say to her.

"Why were you looking at that garbage?!!" she'd screamed at him. "You think I don't know what everyone says about me?" Her fists had been balled up, and he'd seen her heart pounding through her shirt. His own heart had probably been doing the same thing.

"How could you have behaved like that?" he'd demanded with quiet fury.

"Like *what*?!" she'd screamed back at him.

"The video, Sita! The video!" he'd yelled back at her. "Do you have any idea what it was like for me to see you *dancing on that table...taking off your shirt...all over that boy*? How could you behave like that in front of everybody?"

"How could I behave like *WHAT*, Father?" she'd screamed at him again. "Why not just say it? 'Sita, how could you behave like such a *WHORE*?!'" she'd shouted in his face, her voice dripping with mockery.

By then, his anger had gotten the best of him, and he'd slapped her hard across the face. "Yes," he'd panted. "How could you behave like such a whore?"

She'd held her cheek for a long moment in stunned silence, and when she'd finally looked up at him again he almost hadn't recognized her. "I hear that from people at school who know nothing about me, and people who see the news and just don't understand," she'd paused to take in a shuddering breath before continuing, "...but *you*, Father? What's *your* excuse?" With that final statement, she'd run from the room, still holding her stricken cheek.

How those words of hers still haunted him. Even now, as he lay with his bottle cradled in his arms, he wept. If only he hadn't been so hard on her that night. If only he hadn't read those comments and gotten so angry with her. If only he'd known that those would be the last words he'd ever say to her. The next night he'd come home, from a performance so brilliant it was a career high for him, to find his only daughter's lifeless body, lying still warm in her bed.

PART
II

Chapter 14

Soon after their picture was printed in the paper, Cece and Shane's lives took a dramatic turn. Shane's grandfather, Edgar Howard, had been rushed to a New York hospital, and speculation that he'd suffered a massive stroke ran rampant. Old rumors that Shane was a potential heir to his fortune circulated with redoubled vigor. When news of their engagement was added to the mix, Cece and Shane were suddenly thrust into a spotlight they weren't prepared for. Financial and political pundits on the news networks discussed the rumors and debated the impact Shane could have on the oil and financial industries if he did inherit his grandfather's powerful fortune. The likelihood of him inheriting was presented as a remote, yet disastrous, possibility.

Night after night, Cece watched snippets of news updates, and Shane repeatedly assured her that nothing would come of the speculation. He was certain his grandfather wanted nothing further to do with him, and Cece believed him. He was so steady and constant as a friend, believing him and having faith in him was beginning to become second nature to her.

Most times, Cece didn't know what to discuss with Shane when he was around, so she kept their talks centered on work related topics. He told her about his early days running the flower business. According to him, he'd come in at a time when the Bakersfield's were deep in debt and on the brink of losing everything. It had been hard for her to hide her admiration for him as he'd described the work he'd done to turn everything around. When he talked of making the flower business profitable again, he also spoke in detail about the typical profit margins for other business in the wedding industry. He seemed to have a better grasp of the ins and outs of the industry than Cece did, so she was grateful for his input. This gratitude usually led Cece to start discussions about her profits, a subject which she had never introduced with anybody else—not even Karen and Rebecca.

One day, about a month after the proposal, Shane showed up as Cece was closing for the day. He walked in with a rueful little smile on his face and a magazine tucked under his arm.

"Hi there," she smiled as he approached the counter.

"Hi, Cecilia," he said as he plunked the magazine down on the counter. "Have you seen the latest story about you? Apparently, you used to work as a government assassin. That explains why these reporters can't dig up anything about your past. You're part of some elaborate, liberal scheme to bring down my grandfather's oil company after I inherit it," he chuckled.

"Let me see that," Cece said as she snatched the magazine from the counter. The story included an old photo of her from one of the many Muay Thai tournaments she'd competed in. It was at least ten years old, and it showed her delivering an aggressive kick to her opponent's head. "Where do they keep digging this stuff up?" she groused.

Shane chuckled again and reached for the magazine. "I'd like to frame this picture and hang it on my wall. One of the guys at the firehouse brought this in, and everyone razzed me pretty good about it today," he said.

As Cece's eyes met his, she couldn't help but smile back at him. For a moment, she felt almost like part of a happy couple, but then she reminded herself that they were barely even friends. The moment passed, and Cece said, "Do you still want to look over my accounts with me?"

"Absolutely," Shane replied.

Cece locked the door, led the way to her small office and sat down at her computer. As Shane pulled up a chair and sat beside her, she had to resist the urge to roll her chair closer to him. She opened the spreadsheets for the past few years and tried her best not to notice how good he smelled. They hadn't been this close in weeks, and his proximity caused her mind to skip back to the night he'd proposed.

After about an hour of looking over her financial records, Shane commented, "It looks like you could probably afford to hire a few assistants. Your profits have been consistent for years, so you don't even need a boost in sales to support more staff.

Plus, you pull in a ton of income from leasing space to other businesses in this building."

"I know," she sighed.

"Then why haven't you considered hiring before now?"

"Because, I save so much money doing everything myself. That's the same way Mrs. Lee was. She told me once that the only reason she hired me was because she knew I needed her, not the other way around. She never once felt like she needed anyone's help. Even towards the end, I was the only person she allowed close to her. If she hadn't noticed I was pregnant and felt so sorry for me when she first met me, she never would have hired me. She was very miserly when it came to spending money on upgrades or hiring more help, but she always treated me well."

"You don't have to run the bakery *exactly* as she would have run it, you know."

"I know, and that's why I'm going to hire some help. I never really had a reason to plan more personal time into my schedule, but now that Rebecca is pregnant, I'm starting to rethink my entire life."

"I see," Shane said with a thoughtful look in his eyes. "One of the first things I noticed about you is that you work all the time. Once you become a granny, you'll probably be more than happy to have some assistants to delegate to. If I were in your exact position, I'd seriously consider hiring three to five workers," he said. When she didn't reply right away, he added, "The initial expenditure of capital will be worth it when your business increases after our wedding. You'll also have more personal time to spend with your daughter."

At the mention of their wedding, Cece's mind traveled back to their kiss again and stayed firmly fixated on that subject for a few pulse pounding minutes. She cleared her throat and said, "I'll put an ad for those positions in the paper tomorrow. I've also been thinking of making some renovations, so I'll just take care of everything at once. If I get started right away, I can have a grand reopening soon after the wedding."

"Wow," Shane said as he smiled. "You are a very decisive woman."

Cece smiled back and said, "Thanks," as she shut down her computer.

They were on their way out the front door of the building when Shane said, "I almost forgot to tell you; I just found out today that I'm going to be out of town for a month. I leave first thing Monday. I would have had to go on Friday morning, but the boss gave me an exception since our engagement party is scheduled for Friday night. He can be nice when he wants."

"Where are you going?" Cece asked, feeling surprised by the shard of disappointment that sliced through her.

"I'll be in Colorado at a water rescue training facility. If any reporters hassle you, you're going to have to deal with them on your own."

Cece locked the door and turned to face him. "I can handle them," she shrugged.

"Are you going to be okay? Really?" he asked.

"Of course," she insisted. "And I promise not to hurt any of them if they chase me for a statement. I wouldn't want to make you look bad," she joked with a daring little smile.

"Speaking of reporters bothering you; I had to drive around for almost an hour to lose someone who was taking pictures of me from the parking lot at work. Now that my grandfather has been released from the hospital, things should settle down. If they no longer think he's on his deathbed, there's no reason to follow me around just to be the first to catch my reaction to his death. I really hate having to leave you alone to deal with this."

"I'll keep that in mind, and I'll be careful," Cece replied with a smile. Instead of irritating her, this time the concern in his voice warmed her. She made the mistake of looking into his eyes just then, and what she saw sucked her into a moment she wasn't fully prepared for. It was impossible to tell what he was thinking, but something in his expression grabbed her and held her attention. She wanted him to kiss her like he had a month ago in the restaurant, but she couldn't think of an excuse to make it happen. No one was around to witness it. In the next breath, Cece was even more honest with herself; she wanted him to reach out and kiss her, not because someone else was expecting it, but because he *wanted* to.

"What's on your mind?" he asked with a gentle hand on her shoulder.

"I was just wondering how many people are going to be at the engagement party," she lied.

Was that disappointment she detected in his expression? He cleared his throat and said, "Maybe fifty. Only close friends and family were invited. It won't be too bad."

She wasn't sure if she moved closer to him or if he moved closer to her, but they were somehow within a hairsbreadth of each other. He leaned towards her as she tipped her head back to look up at him. His hand slid down her arm in a light caress, and her lips involuntarily parted with a sigh.

"Maybe we should practice before the engagement party," he said as his heavy lidded gaze fell to her lips.

"Practice what?" she asked in a whisper.

"Acting like a happily engaged couple...kissing."

He barely got the word 'kissing' out before she wrapped her arms around his neck and pulled him toward her. In the next instant, his lips were on hers, and the experience was everything she remembered from their previous kiss—everything and more.

The subtle hint of his cologne and deodorant filled her nostrils and sparked a flame somewhere deep within her. In the heat of the moment, she forgot all about the fact that they were standing on a public sidewalk, and she wrapped her arms around Shane's neck. He made a small sound of surprise somewhere deep in his throat as she kissed him back in a sudden explosion of passion. Their tongues played an intimate little duel, each flicking and retreating, caressing and evoking sensations that Cece had never felt before. It robbed her of her breath and her ability to think of anything beyond the circle of his embrace. As his hands went around her waist to haul her closer, she leapt up and wrapped her legs around him. From her new position it was easier to reach his lips without him having to bend down too far. She took advantage of it by kissing him all over his face with an almost feverish intensity. The sound of passing cars was drowned out by their ragged breathing, and Cece forgot they weren't alone as Shane started kissing her neck. He was working his way back to her lips when someone in a passing car shouted, "Get a room!" at them.

The spell was broken, and embarrassment set in as Shane slowly lowered her to the ground. She had never been so assertive with a man before, and she wasn't entirely sure where all those emotions sprang from. Her legs trembled as she brushed her ardent thoughts away and tried to be reasonable. He was doing her business a huge favor by opening himself up to public scrutiny; the least she could do was go along with it without letting her emotions get in the way.

He opened his mouth to say something, and she cut him off. "I was pretty convincing as a fiancée just then, wasn't I?" she asked, trying to keep an expressionless face.

"Yes...you really were," he agreed after carefully searching her face for a moment.

That night, Cece sat in her window seat long into the early morning hours and drew detailed sketches of her ideas for the new bake shop. The space next to the bakery was once an ice cream shop, but for the past two years it had been vacant with no one wanting to lease it. Cece hadn't advertised the space, because she'd planned on using it as an extension of her existing space. She hadn't gotten around to it because she didn't feel an expansion was warranted when she didn't have the extra business to support such a move. Now, however, those feelings had changed. In her entire life, she'd never had any faith in anything a man said, yet here she was now, on the brink of making serious changes to her bakery and her life based on Shane's promise. He was certain that their wedding would dramatically increase her business, and she believed him.

The next morning, she put up a help wanted sign and paid for an ad in the newspaper. She also set up several appointments with contractors to get started on the remodeling and expansion of her space. Cece had never been one to procrastinate once she'd made a decision.

By the end of the day, she'd accepted more than ten job applications from young women who'd seen the sign in her window. All of them had seemed like excellent candidates for the job, so she knew she was going to have a hard time making a decision. She'd also met with several contractors. The last meeting took place shortly before closing.

"Young lady, I'm here to talk to the owner about an estimate for a remodeling job. If you could just fetch him, I'd be much obliged."

Cece raised her eyebrows and said, "I'm the owner."

"Oh... right. Of course... so, what was it you was wantin' done?" He looked so contrite, Cece felt bad for her initial urge to make him leave. "My secretary wrote 'Cecil' on the appointment slip, and this building used to be owned by a little lady named Jiang. I heard she'd passed on a few years ago, and I assumed she must have sold it before she retired. I haven't seen her around for a number of years."

"You knew Mrs. Lee?" Cece asked.

"I wouldn't exactly say I *knew* her. I haven't seen her in more than two decades. I'm just the guy who helped her get the place set up when she first opened," the man explained.

Something in his demeanor made Cece take a closer look at him. He looked to be in his mid-seventies—about the same age Mrs. Lee would have been if she were still alive. "I worked for her for twenty-five years. When she died, she left everything to me, because neither of us had any family. She hired you to...?"

"Paint, lay tiles, install the display cases. That sort of thing. Actually, she never even hired me. I met her at a salvage yard, and she asked me for advice on which tiles would work best. When she told me she meant to do everything herself, I offered to help out when I could. I never charged that little lady a dime."

Cece looked around at the floor and the walls. She'd always liked the hand painted murals and plain gray tiles, but it was time for a change. "You painted the murals?" she asked.

She could have sworn she saw a blush creep across the old man's face as he said, "We painted those together. I'm no artist, but I like to think we did a pretty good job."

"I've always loved them," Cece admitted. "I can't believe I worked for her for so long and she never told me she painted those murals herself—with your help, or course."

The man looked at the walls and cleared his throat. "Well, there's no telling why people keep some of the secrets they do," he said.

He started to look uncomfortable, so Cece dropped the subject. She spent the next half hour explaining the changes she wanted to make and watching as he wrote everything down on an estimate sheet.

"That's quite a bit of work you want done," he commented. "You know it's going to take months."

"That's the same thing all the other contractors I talked to told me."

"Well, my name is Leonard Peterson, and I've been doing this for more than thirty years. I'm sure you won't find a better contractor around here, especially not for this price." Leonard handed Cece a carbon copy of the estimate sheet and smiled at her.

She quickly scanned over it, and then she almost laughed when she saw the estimated total cost for the work she wanted done. It was the lowest estimate of the day.

"Thanks, Mr. Peterson," she said.

"Call me Lenny. Just give me a holler when you decide what you're going to do."

Cece watched him depart with a smile hovering on her lips.

Shane didn't get to see Cece again until the night of the engagement party. She'd really caught him off guard the other night with her overwhelming response to his kiss. Just when he thought he knew what to expect from her, she managed to throw him off kilter. The last thing he'd expected to find was that she had so much pent up passion ready to burst forth at any moment. He wondered what would have happened if they hadn't been standing in the street at the time.

The biggest question in his mind was whether or not she had been all over him just to show she could handle pretending to be engaged in front of his family. If it had been all to prove a point, then she was one heck of an actress. And if it hadn't, they would have a lot to discuss before he left town on Monday. He smiled as he locked his door and made his way over to her house to pick her up for dinner. He had no idea what to expect.

He tried to keep a cool face as he knocked on her door.

"You look great," he said when she answered.

"You're early," she smiled up at him. She was wearing her bathrobe, and nothing else. It was the same robe she'd been wearing the night of the deadly fire.

"I know. I wanted to talk to you before the party."

She clutched her robe tighter about her body and looked up at him. "What's up? Have you changed your mind?"

"Not at all. I wanted to talk to you about the other night."

Her expression immediately went from open to completely closed. "What is it with you and wanting to talk about everything?" she asked as she turned and started walking towards the back of the house. When she stepped into her bedroom, she left the door open, so he took a chance and followed her in.

"It's good to talk, Cecilia," he said as she turned to face him.

"Well? What about it?" She didn't meet his gaze. She tossed the question out as she turned and marched toward the closet.

Shane watched as she pulled out three dresses—the silver one from the night he'd proposed, a black halter top with a flowing mid-thigh length skirt, and a long red spaghetti strap dress. He wondered which one she planned on wearing tonight.

"What about the other night?" she repeated when he didn't answer.

"When we were kissing, were you trying to shut me up about the party by proving that you can pretend to like me? Or, did you *want* to kiss me like that?"

"What do you think?"

"I don't know. That's why I'm here asking you."

"I could ask you the same thing," she countered with a mutinous look.

Shane answered her challenge the only way he knew how. He strode across the room and wrapped his arms around her. He maintained eye contact as he lowered his face toward hers with such slow deliberation she had plenty of opportunity to push him away. The fact that she didn't push spoke volumes and gave him a reason to hope. "*This* kiss is just between you and me," he said as he kissed her.

The same magic that happened the other night in the bakery happened again. Her legs went around his waist and she clung to him as she kissed him back with an intensity that rivaled his own. He suddenly felt lost as the scent of her rose petal soap surrounded him. He ran his hands along her bare legs and caressed her silky skin as their lips melded together. Tonight there was no hesitation; tonight she was warm, passionate and inviting; tonight she was all woman.

Despite their frenzy of kissing and touching, he somehow managed to make it to the bed and lie her down. "I guess that answers my question," he said as he stood up and started to remove his clothes. He didn't get any further than taking off his shirt and tie before they were kissing again. He knew he was acting like an overeager young boy with no self-control, but he was completely powerless to the way she made him feel just then.

"What about the party?" Cece whispered as Shane bent down to kiss her neck.

"What party?" he grinned down at her. He saw an answering smile in her eyes and had to catch his breath. He smiled again, and then he hugged her close and playfully rolled across the bed with her. When they came to a rest on the other side of the bed, she was the one on top. Her curly hair hung down in his face, and he brought his hand up to move it out of his eyes.

His hand was shaking as he touched her face, prompting her to ask, "Are you okay?"

"Sorry. It's been a long time since I've been with a woman," he whispered. "The last woman who touched me was the phlebotomist who drew blood for my annual check-up about six months ago. I got a completely clean bill of health, by the way."

"How long has it been since your last relationship?" she whispered back.

"More than a year," he admitted.

Cece giggled at his embarrassed look and ran her fingers through his hair. "It's been a long time for me too."

"How long?" he asked. When she cast her eyes downward and refused to meet his gaze, he repeated the question.

"Almost twenty-seven years."

The quiet vulnerability in her voice pulled at his heart and he hugged her close to his chest. "So, that was the only time?"

"Yes."

"Then you've never been with a man, because that doesn't count."

"I had two babies and my entire life changed. I think it *does* count."

"But being forced isn't the same as doing it willingly; it isn't the same as making love."

"I know." She lifted her head off his chest and looked into his eyes. "I'm sorry," she said as she got off of him and pulled her robe tight around her body.

"Why?" he asked as he sat up beside her and put his arm around her.

"We were having fun, and I just killed the mood."

"No you didn't," he whispered, and then he kissed her again. "But we do have to get ready for the party."

She turned her face away from him and said, "I still don't even know which dress to wear.

He thought he detected unshed tears in her voice, so he moved around to her other side to see her face. She was crying. "What's wrong?" he asked.

"I don't know. I'm sorry. I don't know why this happens to me when you're around. You're doing something nice for me, and you shouldn't have to worry about me being all over you like that. It won't happen again."

"Cecilia, I started it, and in case you can't tell, I *love* having you all over me."

"You do?"

"Yes! And if we didn't have to get ready for this party and I wasn't going out of town in a couple of days, I'd show you exactly how I feel about being close to you. You deserve better than some rushed encounter, and I don't want to take that step with you right now when I won't be able to see you for a month. I care about you, Cecilia, and I want to do things right with you."

"I care about you too," she said as she reached out for his hand. His heart lifted as he reached back. He looked into her eyes again and breathed in the moment. For once she wasn't looking like she expected the worst, and there was something like trust in her expression. He squeezed her hand, and she smiled and then dropped her gaze in an uncharacteristically timid expression of her feelings.

"What were you saying about your dress?" he asked.

"Which one do you think I should wear? You know everyone who's going to be there tonight, and I want to look right for the part," she said.

Shane stood up and examined the three dresses. "Well, there are already pictures of you wearing the silver one, so I think that one is definitely out. You looked gorgeous in it by the way. The red one is probably stunning on you, but it's long and you've got the most perfect legs I've ever seen, so there's no way I'm letting you wear a long dress tonight."

"*Let* me? How would you stop me?" Cece laughed.

"I think I could find a way."

Cece gave him a playful smirk as she picked up both the black dress and the red one and walked into her closet. When she emerged, she was wearing the long red dress, and she looked amazing—just as he'd expected. She was holding a pair of heels in her hand, and when she sat on the edge of the bed to put them on, Shane took them from her and kneeled down at her feet.

"I think I like this red dress better. It's giving me all kinds of ideas," he said as he slowly ran his hand up the entire length of her leg. He caressed her leg as he guided her foot into the first heel, and then he did the same thing to the other leg.

By the time both of her heels were on, Cece's entire body was a mass of tingling nerves, and Shane still wasn't done touching her. He pushed the slinky dress up until most of her legs were bared, and then he started kissing them. He started at her ankle and worked his way up with tantalizingly slow little nibbles.

"Shane," Cece breathed his name in a plaintive little whisper. "If we're late, it's going to be all your fault."

"Sorry, Sweetheart, but it's hard for me to keep my hands off your legs, especially with the split up the side of this dress. Did I ever tell you red is my favorite color?"

"No, you never mentioned it."

He kissed the inside of her thigh just above her knee, and then he looked up at her. She placed a hand on his cheek and smiled down at him. "You're going to torture me all night in this dress, but I promise I'll try my best to keep my hands to myself. I just want you to know that every time I look at you, I'm going to be thinking about how great it feels to kiss your legs. You smell so good."

"So much for not letting me wear the long dress," Cece said with a little grin.

Shane laughed as he stood up and offered her a hand. "I didn't realize it had a split down the side until after you put it on. As long as I get to see your legs, I don't care which dress you wear tonight."

Cecilia placed her hand in Shane's and stood up. He leaned down and kissed her one more time and then picked up his shirt and tie. He was too busy staring at her to button his shirt properly, and when he had one extra button at the end of the row, he briefly looked down in confusion. When he looked up again, Cecilia was smiling at him.

"Let me give you a hand," she said as she reached out to undo the buttons. She took a moment to appreciate the lean, hard maleness of his chest before buttoning his shirt properly. She'd never seen a completely naked man before, and she admitted to herself recently that she wanted to see more of Shane. Her attraction to him hadn't started out as a physical thing, but their first kiss had changed that in the blink of an eye. She didn't know how to make the big leap and tell him that she wanted something more. At this point, she wasn't even sure how much more she wanted, and she wasn't sure how to tell what was on his mind.

"I'll go grab my keys while you finish dressing," she said as soon as all his buttons were done. She went into the kitchen for a glass of water and a bit of emotional space to think clearly. She waited at her island until he appeared in her doorway.

"If we leave now, we'll only be about fifteen minutes late," he said.

Cece took a deep breath and asked him a question for a change. "Shane, what are we doing here? I mean what are we *really* doing? This was supposed to be all about a cake, but now I feel like it's about something more."

Shane looked at her as she stood there in her beautiful red dress. He couldn't seem to think with a level head when she was around, and this time was no different. He didn't know how she would react to the truth, but he couldn't think of anything better to say at the moment, especially not with his emotions still running high from all the kissing they'd just done.

"That's because it is about something more," he admitted.

"What?" she asked. "What could you possibly have to gain by letting everyone think we're getting married?"

"I wanted to get to know you better, to get closer to you."

"Why go to all this trouble just for that? We could have been friends either way."

"Cecilia, I think you and I both know by now that I want to be more than just your friend."

"Then why not just ask me out? Isn't that the normal way to go about it?"

"With your background? You walk around with the biggest 'unavailable' sign I've ever seen in my life on your forehead. If I had made my interest in you obvious from the beginning you wouldn't have given me a chance. I want to be your friend, and I want you to trust me, but that's not all I want.

You were moving out soon, and you were so disappointed about the Reid wedding. I was just grasping at straws with this whole pretend wedding thing."

Cece was silent for a long time. She stared up at him with a blank expression on her face. She didn't look angry, or did she? When she finally did speak, her eyes were shimmery with unshed tears. "So all that talk about how you loved my work—the time you spent in my bakery pretending to admire my cakes—all of that was just so you could get me to sleep with you?" she asked in a deceptively calm voice.

Shane felt the tide of emotions that she was barely holding back, and he reached out to her. "No," he insisted, his calm voice stemming the tide. "I meant every word I ever said about your work. You really are one of the best cake designers I've ever seen; if I didn't believe that I wouldn't want to help you show off your talent to everyone else. Even if we only end up as friends after all of this, I'll still want you to see your business grow."

She stared at his outstretched hand and said, "I really trusted you. I thought you cared about my business, but now I don't know what to think."

"Cecilia, I do care about your business. I just care about *you* more."

Cece looked down at her feet and completely covered her face with her hands for a moment, and when she looked up at him again, he didn't know what to think. She still had tears in her eyes, but she was smiling. She sniffed and then wiped her eyes. "That's the sweetest thing anyone's ever said to me," she finally said.

At her words, Shane released the pent up breath he hadn't realized he was holding.

"What are we going to do now?" she asked as she took his hand and looked up at him.

"I think we should still go with the original plan. The only difference is that now you know my ulterior motive," he smiled. "Will you go out with me tonight?"

"I kind of have to if we want to keep up the charade," she answered.

Suddenly his smile was gone, and he was all seriousness as he said, "No, you don't have to. All that stuff I said about us needing to be seen together all the time was just so I could have an excuse to spend time with you. From now on, when I ask you out, it won't have a damn thing to do with the wedding plans. Let's get through the engagement party, but after tonight, if we go out, I want to know it's because you want to spend time with me and not because you feel like you have to."

Cece stared out the window as Shane pulled up to the front of the engagement party venue. She hadn't expected the party to happen in a place where lots of couples held their wedding receptions. She'd delivered several cakes to this hotel over the years, and she knew how nice it was on the inside. Shane got out and opened her door, and then he handed his keys to the valet parking attendant.

"This place is really expensive, Shane. I don't want you spending money you don't have on this," she whispered.

"Will you relax," he whispered back as he put his hand on her waist and walked inside with her. "We have to keep up a certain appearance for this to work, so just look at it as an investment in our future."

Cece didn't miss the fact that he'd said *our future*, but she didn't bother correcting him. She tried to calm her fluttering pulse as they crossed the opulent marble lobby and walked into a banquet room filled with people. As soon as they walked in, the sea of people converged on them. Cece wasn't a math genius, but there were obviously more than fifty people—a lot more.

She looked up at Shane to chastise him for lying and saw that he was just as surprised as she was. She opened her mouth to ask him if they were in the right room when his only sister walked up to them.

"Nice of you guys to show up," Shane's sister, Shelly, said over the noise of the crowd.

When Shane cleared his throat and glanced down at Cece, she noticed an embarrassed flush creeping up his neck. She smiled at Shelly and said, "It took me so long to decide what to wear, I made us late."

Shane gave her waist a gentle squeeze to show his appreciation, but he spoke up with the truth anyway. "It's my fault we're late, and don't ask why, because it's personal."

"I've been swamped trying to explain to everyone where you were. Why did you have to invite so many people? I mean, you *do* know that the idea of an engagement party is to introduce yourselves as a couple to close friends and family," Shelly admonished him.

Shane all but rolled his eyes as he told her, "I didn't invite all these people; hell, I don't even recognize some of them."

Shelly cast her brother an exasperated look before sashaying over to a small podium with a microphone near the front of the room. She held up her hands and got everyone's attention.

"The happy couple has finally arrived," she announced with a big smile, and the room immediately filled with applause. Cece couldn't help but feel a warm glow at so much acceptance. She looked around to see everyone smiling at them. Shelly went on to say, "It's customary to give a short toast to the couple, but tonight we have a little surprise presentation planned. Anyone who knows my brother can understand how shocked we were at this sudden engagement. About ten years ago, Shane swore he'd never marry."

As Shelly spoke, the lights dimmed and a slide show started playing on a projector screen beside her. She discretely left the podium, but no one noticed; everyone's eyes were now riveted to the slide show.

Even Cece couldn't tear her eyes away from the first image that appeared on the screen. There was more applause and outright catcalls from some of the many women in the room as a picture of Shane without his shirt on appeared on the screen. His face was covered in grime and sweat, and he wore only the bottom half of his turnout gear. He held his mask in one hand, and there was a charred, burned out building in the background of the photo. The caption on the photo indicated that he had been January in the firefighter calendar that year.

"You were in one of those hot fireman calendars?" Cece demanded in shock. He really didn't strike her as the type of man who liked to flaunt his body just because he had a nice one. If anything, he'd always seemed a bit on the shy and modest side. That was one of the things she liked about him.

"It was for a good cause. All the profits that year went to widows of firefighters killed in the line of duty," he explained. By the time the next photo appeared, some of the redness had left his face. "I'm kind of afraid to look now," he muttered.

"If it's any consolation, you're the best looking fireman I've ever seen in my life," Cece said, partly because it was true and partly because she wanted to see his face change colors again.

When she looked up at the screen again, there was a picture of her up there. It was so totally unexpected she actually started. She remembered the picture on the screen very well. It was taken during an exhibition round she'd done against Karen years ago. The point of the match had been to show off rather than to win, and the two of them had really entertained the crowd that day. It had been the biggest match Cece had ever fought in. The photo on the screen showed her midair, executing a back flip to get out of Karen's range. The next few photos that popped up were all in sequence and they all came from that one exhibition fight. She looked up at Shane again, but his eyes were still on the screen.

For the next five minutes, they watched the slide show along with everyone else. There was much cringing on both their parts, but they got through it without revealing that they'd just learned a great deal about each other. Everyone in the room thought that the slide show held no secrets for the two of them. The last picture to appear was the one that had been printed in the newspaper the weekend Shane proposed. Everyone oohed and aahed over it as if it was the most adorable thing, and then Shelly took the microphone again and raised her glass in a toast. "To my most difficult brother, Shane, and his kickass fiancée," she said. Everyone else laughed and raised their glasses, and then it was over.

"That wasn't awkward at all," Shane said in her ear as the quiet background music started back up.

Cece smiled and said, "What do we do now?"

"Now all we have to do is go around and talk to everyone. Just mingle together for about an hour, maybe dance a little, enjoy some of the cocktails and refreshments, and then we can leave."

Cece glanced over at the refreshment table with longing. She hadn't had anything to eat since lunch, and it was well into the evening. She'd always had a healthy appetite to go along with her athletic lifestyle. "You can get started on the mingling without me, I'll find you after I've had something to eat," she said.

Shane was about to protest and tell her he'd come along with her when the Bakersfield's showed up next to him. He turned around to greet them.

"It's nice to see you again, Shane," Sibylle said.

"Likewise," Shane smiled. He turned back to where Cece had been standing a moment ago, but she was gone. He looked back at Sibylle and smiled again.

"You remember my daughter Nicolette, right?" Sibylle smiled as a stunning young woman stepped forward.

Shane vaguely remembered her as the young twenty something that his business partner had introduced him to about five years ago. Mr. Bakersfield had tried to get Shane to take his daughter out on a date, and Shane had declined because of the age difference. He didn't think he could have much in common with a woman who was nearly twenty years younger than he was.

"It's a pleasure to see you again. You're so grown up now; I guess you'll be catching some lucky young man's attention and getting married soon yourself." At his words, Nicolette shot an uneasy glance at her mother, but Sibylle didn't want to take the hint. She'd always been a grasping, and somewhat devious social climber in Shane's opinion. He didn't know how a man as nice as Mr. Bakersfield had ended up with a wife like her. She wasn't ugly by any standards, but the hard attitude she had scared the hell out of him. What kind of woman would try to gain the attention of a man his age for her young daughter?

"We don't know how soon it will happen for Nicolette," Sibylle cut in before her daughter could answer. "It's difficult to find a real man her age."

"Sibylle, would you like to go grab a punch? My throat is parched," Mr. Bakersfield interjected with a pained look at his wife.

"No, but I think I might like a brandy," Sibylle answered.

"My dear, don't you think you've had one too many?"

Shane pretended not to hear and smiled a sympathetic smile at Nicolette. She was a beautiful young woman with her sleek chestnut colored hair and vivid green eyes. She would have no problem finding a man when she was ready for one.

She must have sensed Shane and her father's discomfort, because she gently took her mother's hand and said, "I'll come with you to get a brandy, Mother. I could use one myself."

After Nicolette led Sibylle away, Mr. Bakersfield looked up at Shane and said, "I'm sorry, Shane. I don't know what's gotten into her lately. After what you did for us, taking over the business and paying off my debts, you don't deserve that type of behavior at your own engagement party."

"Don't worry about it. I was under the impression that Nicolette was living abroad."

"She is, but Sibylle told her to fly home for an emergency almost as soon as we got the invitation to your party. She hasn't given up on the idea she had years ago, and I didn't know Nicolette was going to be here until right before we arrived."

"Don't worry about it. I'm sure she won't cause a scene."

"I hope not," Mr. Bakersfield sighed. "Congratulations again, Shane. I'm going to find Sibylle and Nicolette so we can head home for the night."

As soon as he walked off, Shane started looking around for Cece. The pictures of her doing her acrobatic moves in the ring had surprised him. He wondered how she could continue to amaze him with her abilities. Was there anything she couldn't do?

He smiled and chatted with everyone he passed during his search for Cece. Once he remembered she'd been hungry, he turned towards the refreshment tables set up along the perimeter of the room. He caught sight of her long red dress, and the leg showing through the slit up the side was unmistakable. He was so busy staring at her leg that he literally ran into a friend who was trying to get his attention.

"Shane! Congratulations man," Jake Holt said as he clapped a hand down on Shane's back.

"Jake," Shane smiled. "I didn't think you were in town, I haven't heard from you in so long."

"I've been really busy lately. Last year, the girls' varsity made it to state. This year we want to win. I've been busy with the summer training camp for the girls. I can't believe you're getting married, man. Who's the lucky lady?"

"Didn't you see the slide show?" Shane laughed.

"No, I just walked in the door a couple of minutes ago," Jake admitted with a sheepish look.

Shane and Jake had been friends since college. Like Gus, Jake had also been one of the many people Shane had tutored. Jake had been a student athlete on the basketball team, and he and Shane had clicked because they were from the same region of the country. They had both felt out of place in the big city, and they'd kept in touch since their college years. They usually managed to get together to play a game of basketball once a month with several other friends, but since the fire they hadn't seen each other.

"Come on. I'll introduce you. She's so awesome you won't believe she was still available," Shane smiled as he caught sight of Cece's leg again. He remembered the scent of that rose petal soap she favored and the way her silky legs had felt against his lips earlier that evening.

Jake followed Shane's intense gaze and said, "Is that her in the red dress over there? If it isn't, then you better hope she didn't notice all that drooling you're doing."

"It's that obvious, huh?"

"Yeah, but I'm happy for you, man." Jake patted Shane's back again as they made their way toward Cece. She was facing away from him and appeared to be in deep conversation with Sibylle and Nicolette Bakersfield.

Shortly after Cece made it to the food, she sensed someone's eyes on her. Normally, she would have met the person's stare head on, and maybe even demanded to know why they were staring, but tonight she was on her best behavior. When she finally got a good look out of the corner of her eye, she saw that the person staring was the nosey old woman from the night Shane had proposed. She couldn't recall her first name, but she remembered the last name. She offered Mrs. Bakersfield a small, tight smile and continued to enjoy the fresh fruit she'd piled onto her little plate. She would have offered a more genuine smile, and even made an effort to converse with the woman, if she hadn't been glaring at her.

As she moved off to the side, she heard Mrs. Bakersfield's voice start up on a bitter and plaintive note. "It's not too late, Nikki. Just because they're engaged doesn't mean he can't be persuaded in another direction. I saw the way he looked at you just then."

"But, Mother," the young woman with her hissed in a furious whisper. "Haven't you ever thought that if he were remotely interested in me he would have sought me out? He's known where I live for nearly five years now, and in case you didn't notice, the two of them seem to be in love."

"But all that money! Nikki, Edgar Howard is practically on his deathbed, and I heard from a reliable source that Shane will inherit everything—*everything*."

"I don't care about the money. Don't you have enough already? Do you really have to use me to get more?"

"More? Is that what you call one of the biggest fortunes in the world? It isn't just more; it's everything."

"Not to me. I guess now would be a good time to tell you that I'm seeing someone, and it's serious. I never would have come here if I'd known this was what you wanted," Nicolette sniffed.

No one else near the table seemed to have understood the conversation, because Sibylle and Nicolette had been speaking French. Cece had understood every word, because French had been the only language her mother had used with her. The dialect the Bakersfields were using was different from the one her mother had used, but Cece understood enough to follow the entire conversation.

She approached Nicolette and said, "I couldn't help but overhear your conversation," in the dialect she'd learned from her mother.

Nicolette looked up at her in humiliated shock. The tears in her eyes only added to Cece's ire. "I'm so sorry," the young woman said. "My mother has these crazy ideas regarding me and your fiancé, but I don't share them."

Cece turned her stare on the mother and got directly to the point. "Madam Bakersfield, don't you think it would be best to let your daughter live her own life? If she wanted to go after my fiancé she should do it because *she* wants him, and not because her money hungry mother told her to."

"How dare you—" Sibylle began, only to be interrupted.

"No, how dare *you*!" Cece snapped. "I don't care that you want more money, but it's disgusting to try and use your daughter to get it, especially when she obviously doesn't want to go along with your crazy scheme."

Sibylle looked as if she were about to say more, but something directly behind Cece caught her eye. Cece turned around to see who had walked up, and she fully expected to see

Shane. She wasn't at all prepared to see Jake Holt, the man she had last dated before giving up completely.

He obviously hadn't expected to see her either. As soon as their eyes met, he started as if he'd seen a ghost.

"Cece?" he said in shock. "You're marrying Cece Graves?" he said to Shane.

Shane barely heard him as he was too busy demanding, "Since when do you speak French, Cecilia?"

Sibylle and Nicolette quietly slinked off as Cece's eyes darted uncomfortably from Jake to Shane. How in the world did those two know each other? And of all the times for her to run into him, why now? Her guard was so far down from the unexpectedness of the encounter that she answered Shane's question without thinking about it. "I've always spoken French. I actually had a hard time learning English when I started school here." That was something she'd never told a soul before, not even Rebecca.

It took Shane another moment to realize that Cece and Jake already knew each other. He'd barely registered their reaction to each other because he was still reeling from the fact that she spoke perfect French. She'd also implied that she came from another country. He was suddenly hit with renewed curiosity so strong he almost dragged her out of there so he could pepper her with questions.

"How do you two know each other?" Shane asked.

Neither of them would meet his gaze, but Jake finally spoke when it became obvious that Cece wasn't going to. "We dated each other for a while, but that was years ago," he said. He subconsciously fingered his jaw as he looked down at Cece.

"I'm really sorry, Jake. I would have apologized years ago, but I didn't think you ever wanted to see me again."

Jake hadn't expected her to come right out and address the fact that she'd broken his jaw, and he stared down at her in disbelief.

"What are you sorry for?" Shane asked her.

Cece shot Jake an apologetic look before she explained. "I overreacted the first time we kissed and accidentally broke his jaw."

"With what?" Shane demanded in shock. He and Jake were roughly the same height, and Cece didn't look like she was big enough to do serious damage to such a large man.

"Her foot," Jake bit out.

"I'm really sorry about hurting you, Jake. Rebecca mentioned that night just a few weeks ago, and I've been feeling bad ever since. I don't expect you to forgive me, but I just want you to know that it wasn't you. You are one of the sweetest guys I ever went out with. I just couldn't handle more than friendship at that time in my life." She walked off abruptly after finishing her impromptu statement.

Shane and Jake watched her walk away, each lost in his own private thoughts. The chatter in the room masked the awkward silence between the two of them for a few moments, but eventually Shane spoke.

"So that story you told me about being robbed at gunpoint..."

"Was a lie," Jake admitted. "She invited me into her apartment that night, and I kissed her. I guess I got a little excited because we'd been going out for a few months and it was the first time she'd ever invited me in. I'm sure she's probably mentioned it to you since the two of you are getting married."

"She's never talked about you," Shane said.

"Figures," Jake muttered. He'd been thinking about Cece quite a bit lately. He'd always known there must have been some logical explanation for her panic that night, and after he'd heard of her daughter's foundation he'd put two and two together. If she had simply told him that she'd needed extra time and space he would have totally understood. "Well, we knew each other way back when her daughter Rebecca was in high school. That was a long time ago. She probably barely remembers me. How did you two meet?"

"Her daughter married my younger brother, Norman, a few years ago. I don't think you've ever met him. He's the one who is in the military. He's stationed at Fort Campbell right now."

"So, you two have been together for a few years? I could have sworn you were seeing someone else just last year."

"Well, we didn't officially meet until just this spring. Before this year, I knew who she was, but hadn't ever seen her in person. You remember that big apartment fire that was all over the news in early April?"

"Yeah. A lot of people died in that fire. What about it?"

"She was living in the apartment next to the one where the fire started, and my company was the first search and rescue to respond to the call. We met when I got her out of her apartment. She's lucky to be alive," Shane said. He didn't know why he felt the need to give out so many details about his association with Cecilia, but he did know that the way she and Jake had looked at each other a few minutes ago didn't sit well with him.

Jake was looking across the room at someone when he spoke again, "I'm happy for the two of you. You used to say that you were never going to get married after all that business with your grandparents, but I guess it was only a matter of time until you came across someone who could change your mind about that. She could change a man's mind about anything."

Shane followed Jake's gaze, and just as he'd suspected, it led straight to Cecilia. She was chatting with Shelly and Rebecca about something that had the three of them laughing. He wondered what Jake would say if he knew the truth.

Chapter 15

The day after the party, Saturday, Cece met with Leonard Peterson again to finalize a contract for the improvements to her building. She'd have to close down for the demolition phase of the work, and that phase was to start first thing Monday morning. She spent all day Saturday selling and giving away any goods left in the display cases and in the freezer. She also interviewed several applicants, and hired someone to help her with the cleaning in the future. By the time she closed for the day she felt like she'd made important progress in her life. She reflected on that progress as she walked through the neighborhood park towards her house. It was still late summer, but within the last few days the weather had taken a decidedly fall-like turn.

A breeze blew past her, sweeping her hair over her shoulder and into her face as she approached the colorful fountain. She'd never get tired of looking at it. She sat for several minutes on the bench and tried to clear her mind of all the clamoring and cacophony of her own thoughts. On the one hand, she was screaming at herself not to take Shane's assurances that he cared about her too seriously, but on the other, she almost didn't know how to feel about him. She smiled to herself as she remembered the special time they'd shared prior to last night's engagement party. She hadn't seen him since he'd left her at her house late last night. He'd asked her out on a date, and she'd accepted. This time she knew exactly what she was getting herself into, and she was excited about it.

Someone walking up the path toward the trees caught her eye, and she subconsciously followed their movements as they drew nearer. It was a slender, balding man with glasses and a dark complexion. Something about him seemed familiar. Maybe he'd been to her bakery before. She stood up and started walking toward her house, and when she passed him, she smiled at him. His eyes darted quickly away from hers and he put his head down and hurried on. He looked like a sad, lonely old man who didn't want to be bothered.

When she got to her front porch, Cece found a small box sitting beside one of her wicker chairs. She sat down next to it and briefly examined it before picking it up. Attached to the box was a card with a handwritten note from Shane. She fingered the bold, sweeping letters for a moment before reading it. "Cecilia, I wasn't sure if you had anything appropriate to wear for tomorrow. Hopefully, the things I picked out for you find your favor. I will be there to pick you up at four thirty tomorrow; p.s. Karen gave me your measurements, so everything should fit."

Cece opened the box to find a pair of rugged and sturdy looking shoes, some lightweight pants, a shirt, and a hat. It wasn't exactly her idea of a first date outfit, but she would go with it. She went inside and tried on the new clothes just to be sure everything fit properly. She wouldn't put it past Karen to give Shane sizes that were too small just so the clothes would fit tight. In Karen's world, tight equaled sexy. Cece sighed in relief when everything fit just as it should. The shoes were much more comfortable than they looked, and the clothes reminded her of something that an outdoorsman would wear.

She usually spent her Sundays working, but tomorrow would mark the first day of the bakery being closed for remodeling, and Cece was actually looking forward to the chance to sleep in for a change. She turned off her alarm, curled up in her window seat, and fell asleep that night thinking of all the positive things that were about to happen in her life. For the first time in weeks, she actually slept through the night without a nightmare.

The next day, she awoke to the sound of Shane knocking on her door. She got up and checked the clock on her way to answer the door.

"What are you doing here so early?" she asked as she rubbed sleep out of her eyes.

"Early? Didn't you get the package and the note I left for you?"

"Yeah, but..." Cece's voice trailed off as she remembered her first day of work with Mrs. Lee. She'd made the exact same mistake. "I thought you meant four thirty in the afternoon."

"Oh." At least he had the grace to look embarrassed at his faux pas. "I should have put a.m. on there, but I assumed that you'd know since you get up at three every day."

"Not if I don't have to," she clarified. "Come in and have a seat. It will only take me a few minutes to get dressed and brush my teeth, and then you can explain to me where in the world we can possibly be going this early in the morning."

"Take your time, Cecilia," Shane said as he followed her inside and took a seat in her living room. Most of her house was still unfurnished, and the only area available for seating was the bay window that faced the east side of the house. When he sat down, he noticed that the window seat was still warm and there was a pillow bunched up in one corner and a small blanket in the other.

Cece returned a short time later to find Shane pacing circles around her living room. It was funny how the room always seemed to shrink when he was in it. He was a larger than life force, and when he looked down at her and smiled she couldn't help but smile back.

"You look even cuter than I thought you would," he said as he paused his pacing to stare down at her in appreciation. "Do you feel comfortable in those shoes?"

"They're different from the ones I normally wear, but I like them."

"Good. Let's get going now; we have lots to do today."

"Where are we going so early in the morning?" Cece yawned as soon as they were in his Jeep and on their way.

"For someone who gets up at three every morning, I would have thought five would seem a little late."

"It does for work, but it's still early for being social."

"True, but we aren't going somewhere very social."

"Where are we going then?"

"It's a surprise, so I can't give you too many details. We had to leave early because the drive to Southern Illinois takes a few hours. I'm taking you somewhere special to me," Shane smiled.

Cece didn't see the point in questioning him anymore after that, so she quieted down and let him concentrate on the driving. Once they were outside the city, Cece stared out the window and watched as the countryside flew by. The gentle rolling hills that were characteristic of middle Tennessee eventually gave way to an area where rocky bluffs and large trees dominated the sides of the road. She didn't often get the chance to sit back and enjoy the ride, so she soaked in the changing landscapes as the sun came up for the day.

Eventually, they turned off the main highway onto a smaller road. Cece, having almost no experience with country roads, would have described this one as treacherous. It was winding, narrow, and way too steep for her peace of mind. Looking out the window was no longer an option, because the steep drop down the side of the road was too close for her. Every time a car appeared in the opposite lane, it seemed that they were within an inch of death on such a narrow road.

"Don't be nervous. I've been down this road hundreds of times."

Cece glanced down and realized she was clutching the seatbelt across her chest with both hands. "Sorry," she said as she released her grip.

"We're almost there," he reassured her as he turned off the paved road and onto a tiny gravel road.

"Will you tell me where we're going now?"

"Hiking." He pulled into a parking spot and turned toward her with a smile. "That road can be a little nerve racking, but it's a good short cut to get to this trail. We can take the bigger road when we leave." He brushed his hand over her fingers and smiled at her again. "I guess it's a little late to ask if you like hiking."

"Would you believe that I've never been hiking before?"

"Really? That's surprising," Shane said.

"Why?"

"Because you're in such great shape, and you seem to like being outside. Why haven't you ever been hiking?"

"It's just something that never came up until now."

"That's how it is for a lot of people who come from the city," Shane remarked. He handed her a canteen of water, and they started up the trail. By now the sun was up, but the temperature was still very mild.

"You say that like you haven't lived most of your life in cities."

"I was born and raised on a horse ranch. That's about as un-citified as it gets," he grinned as they walked. "I love the outdoors."

"So where exactly are we right now?" Cece asked as she looked around. There was nothing but trees as far as she could see.

"We're in the Shawnee National Forest. This trail is actually a horse trail that my dad used to go riding on a lot before he passed. I've always preferred hiking it on foot though. It leads to an awesome sandstone cliff. It's called the *Indian Kitchen Trail*."

"So, we're hiking to a cliff?"

"Yeah. This time of day it will be a nice hike. The weather has been cooler than normal this week, so this is a perfect day for something like this."

"How long does it take to get there?"

"Maybe a couple of hours at the most. There's a special spot I want to show you. Not a whole lot of people know how to get to it, so we should have some privacy."

"More privacy than this?" Cece asked as she looked around again. As far as she was concerned, they were smack in the middle of nowhere.

Shane was right about the day being mild by summer standards. They hiked in relative comfort, and Cece was thankful for the fact that there didn't seem to be too many bugs, critters, and spiders. Shane pointed out various trees and side trails branching off the main trail as they came across them. Every once in a while he glanced down at her and smiled in that way that sent her insides into flutter mode.

"How's your first hiking experience going?" Shane asked after they'd been on the trail for about an hour. The temperature had gone up with the sun, and they both wiped at the sweat accumulating on their brows before Cece answered.

"I have to admit; it's pretty fun. It's just not something I would have thought to do on my own. I'm glad this was the surprise; it's definitely a good one." They both took another drink before continuing.

"You wouldn't believe how muddy this trail can stay even for a week after it rains."

191

"Why does it stay so muddy?"

"The horses."

Just then, Cece heard the slow, steady clip-clop of approaching hooves, and she turned just in time to see an older couple on horseback coming around a bend in the trail.

"Morning," they smiled at Cece and Shane as they passed.

Once the older couple had moved on, Shane decided to try and steer the conversation away from more general topics and into personal things. The number one thing on his mind was finding out where Cecilia had really come from, but he tried to tamp down his overwhelming curiosity. He didn't want to seem pushy.

"So, Cecilia," he said, striving for a relaxed tone. "After seeing those pictures of you the other night at the engagement party, I must admit I'm curious about how you got into martial arts in the first place. You mentioned knowing some Karate as a child, but what made you want to learn?"

When she looked up at him, she still wore the same relaxed expression she'd had all morning. She didn't appear defensive or offended when she replied, "One of my foster par—I mean friends—was a Karate instructor. I got into way too many fights when I was a kid, and he tried to help me learn some self-control. He thought if he taught me Karate that I would learn how to master the battle within myself, conquer my anger, and not want to fight all the time."

Shane didn't miss her slip, and he took a chance and called her on it. "You were about to say foster parents weren't you? Did you have foster parents growing up?" he asked carefully, half expecting her to clam up.

"Yes," she sighed. "One of my foster parents taught Karate. That's what got me started."

"So when you ran away..."

"I ran away from a group home. I lied about my parents kicking me out. I didn't have any at that time."

"Did you ever have any? I mean, other than foster parents?"

"I had a mother once."

"What happened with your mother? Why did you end up in foster care?"

"I'd rather not talk about what happened to my mother."

Shane fought the urge to pull her into his arms and hold her. The quiet strength in her voice almost completely masked the underlying vulnerability that still lingered. "Okay. I understand," he said.

They walked on in silence until they reached the end of the horse trail. There was a circle of wooden hitching posts and no obvious rock formations, prompting Cece to ask, "Is this *Indian Kitchen*?"

"No," Shane answered as he followed her gaze to the circle of posts. "I think a lot of people stop here though. You can only get to the spot I want to show you on foot, and not too many people know about it."

They took another drink and stood around resting for a few minutes before Shane lead them down a smaller, less obvious path. This new path was significantly more rugged and rocky. Cece had to clamber over several large rocks and small boulders obstructing the way as she followed behind Shane. When she slipped on a slick, mossy spot on the side of one rock, Shane rushed over to give her a hand.

"You okay?" he asked.

"Yeah, it was just a little slippery right there." She smiled up at him, embarrassed that she nearly fell in front of him.

He picked her up and lifted her over the next big rock in one seemingly effortless, fluid movement. When she looked up at him again, she was struck by how capable he was as a man. He maintained his hold on her hand and assisted her over the rest of the big rocks on that section of the trail as if he were her own personal Superman. He stayed close until they reached an easier part of the trail.

Eventually, Shane turned off the trail for a narrow path that cut through an area thick with small trees and shrubbery. When they came through the little thicket, the path seemed to end abruptly. Cece hesitated, and Shane took the lead saying, "This part is pretty narrow, so it's safer to go single file. I'll take the lead since I know the way."

Cece followed behind him and tried her best to ignore the fact that death was inches away. The path skirted around the face of the cliff; on the left side was a rock wall and on the right was a sheer drop of about a hundred feet into the water below. The entire path was less than two feet wide, and Shane strode forward as if nothing out of the ordinary was surrounding them.

Cece inched forward with an overabundance of caution, making Shane glance back at her and ask if she needed help several times. Each time, she smiled and said she was fine.

"Are you okay with heights?" he asked when she slowed down again.

"Sure," Cece swallowed. She hoped her trepidation didn't look as obvious as it felt at the moment. Until today, she'd never had an occasion to test how comfortable she was with heights.

He seemed satisfied by her answer. When he turned back around to continue the treacherous section of the trail, Cece followed close behind. This time she tried to concentrate on Shane's back rather than the steep drop just to her right. A few hundred yards later, the rock wall curved slightly to the left, and the path widened into a small clearing. It ended in a large crevice where two adjacent sides of the rock wall came together at an angle. There was an area of flat rock big enough for the two of them to stand comfortably. Closer to the edge, the rock sloped downward into a small cliff just over the water. Nestled in the little corner as they were, Cece quickly got more comfortable with being up so high. Shane sat down on the rock, and Cece sat beside him to look down at the water below. After everything they'd traversed to get there, she was grateful she took the risks. The view was nothing short of spectacular.

"Wow," she breathed. "I've never been to a place that was so peaceful yet so exhilarating at the same time... it's beautiful up here. I see why not many people know how to get to this spot though."

"Most of the people who use this trail are horse riders, and there's no way you can get a horse to this little spot."

They sat and stared at the creek below. The water didn't look crystal clear or deep blue as water often did in pictures. This water looked murky and brown; it definitely wasn't the kind of water she would want to take a swim in. As Cece stared down at the water, her thoughts strayed into the murky realm of her own childhood—something else she didn't want to submerge herself in. During her years in foster care, she'd developed only one friendship. After the shock of losing her mother, her first night in the group home had been extremely difficult for her. She'd been about six at the time, and she'd never forget how hard she tried to hide the fact that she was crying her heart out. Once the lights went out and all the girls settled down, Cece didn't want to disturb them. She hadn't understood a word of what anyone said to her all day, and she was terrified of the consequences of making too much noise. In the hotel, the consequences had always been frightening and severe at best. She tried her best to cry silently, but there had still been the occasional sniffle that night.

At some point in the night, Cece had felt a gentle hand on her back, and she'd looked up to see one of the older girls hovering over her bed. The girl had said simply, "I'm Dorothy." That night, Dorothy had stayed with her and comforted her, but most importantly, Dorothy hadn't seemed to care that Cece didn't speak any English. The two of them found ways to communicate anyway, and by the time Cece learned English she and Dorothy were inseparable. They were so inseparable everyone referred to them as sisters, even though they didn't look a thing alike. They both tended to go by the shortened forms of their names; Cece and Dot. Best friends for eternity.

"Penny for your thoughts?" Shane said quietly beside her.

"I was just thinking about a childhood friend."

Shane reached out his hand and ran a finger across her knuckles in a light caress. She glanced over at him, and she detected a calm willingness to listen in the midnight depths of his eyes. His relaxed look encouraged her to elaborate.

"When I was in foster care, a girl named Dot befriended me. She completely changed my life, and every once in a while I think about her."

Shane's fingers continued to quietly caress her knuckles. She looked at the swirling water below and went on, "She's the only person in the world who ever truly loved me without having any obligation to do so."

"Have you spoken to her recently?"

Suddenly, Cece's face was a mask of feigned indifference as she said, "No. I haven't seen or heard from her since the day I ran away." She stood up and brushed the dirt off of her clothes.

Shane stood up beside her and said, "It's a good time for us to start heading back."

The hike back to his Jeep passed mostly in silence, but there was a companionable quality to their silence that hadn't been there before. Somewhere in the middle of the trail, Cece paused to admire the scenery. They were completely surrounded by the lush, green summer forest, and Cece tipped her head back to look up at the tall trees. The clear blue sky was only visible in small snippets between the multitudes of tree tops, and there was something indescribably magical about being outside yet feeling so sheltered by all the trees. She looked back at Shane, and was about to move on when she heard a soft rustling sound that seemed far off. It grew louder as it got closer, and after about ten seconds of wondering what it was, she finally just asked Shane.

He quirked his lips and said, "The wind," in almost the same instant the breeze actually reached them. Cece smiled, partly because the strong gust of wind felt good against her sweat dampened skin and partly because she'd never heard a breeze coming from that far off before.

"When you're in the middle of the forest like this, you can hear the big gusts coming from pretty far off before they get to you. It is neat now that I think about it." Cece felt silly for only the briefest second for not being able to figure out something so obvious. Shane's eyes were laughing, but not at her. She chuckled at herself, and when they continued down the trail, their hands were somehow clasped together. Cece wasn't sure who initiated the contact, but she didn't attempt to let go. They held hands until they got back to his Jeep.

When Shane let go of her hand to open the passenger side door for her, Cece smiled up at him and said, "This was a really awesome first date, Shane."

A slow smile spread across his lips as he leaned down closer to her face. For one intensely exciting moment she thought he was about to kiss her, but he whispered in her ear instead. "This date's not over yet, Cecilia."

Later that night, as the two of them sat across from each other eating dinner at steak restaurant, Cece reflected on all she'd shared with him throughout the day. First the early morning hike, then a relaxing afternoon at a spa, and now a romantic dinner for two. She tried her best not to imagine him doing all these things on first dates with other women, and she had to try even harder not to ask him if he had.

Eventually, she lost the epic battle with her curiosity. He was in the middle of chewing a mouthful of steak when she asked, "So, is this typical first date behavior for you?"

He took a moment to swallow before asking, "What do you mean?"

"The hiking, the spa, and now this..." She gave a dramatic sweep of her arm to indicate the direction of her thoughts. Shane had arranged to have a private dinner with her, sans curious onlookers, by buying out the entire restaurant for the evening. The two of them had the staff all to themselves, and there was even a bluegrass band to play music while they talked and ate. "I mean, how in the world can you afford to pay for the entire restaurant just for us?" she asked.

"I've never done anything like this in my life, and the truth is that this isn't nearly as pretentious as it looks," he grinned. "I just thought you'd enjoy a nice quiet evening with just the two of us. After all the hype over the engagement party, it was obvious that taking you out to dinner in Nashville might have been a problem, so I called in a favor from some old friends," he admitted.

"Oh, really?" Cece said skeptically.

Just then, the server returned and said with a grin, "He called in a few favors—*big* favors—Ma'am."

"Dammit, Charlie! Can't you ever just mind your business?" Shane groused as Charlie refilled their water glasses and walked away.

"What was that all about?" Cecilia asked.

"Charlie is actually the owner of this establishment. He's usually closed on Sundays, but I twisted his arm to get him to open with limited staff just for us."

"You must have owed Charlie a pretty big favor, like he said," Cece teased as she watched the redness creep into Shane's cheeks. She kept her eyes on him as the quiet music continued in the background. "This is the first time I've ever listened to bluegrass," she remarked with a smile. "I like how instrumental it is."

"I'm glad you like it. A lot of people don't realize the level of difficulty involved in playing some of the bluegrass that's out there. These musicians playing for us tonight are some of the most talented I've ever known."

Something in his demeanor piqued her curiosity, and she asked, "Have *you* ever played any bluegrass?" just as Charlie returned with another basket of bread.

"Has *he* ever played any bluegrass music?" Charlie exclaimed. "Little lady, you're on a date with the best fiddler our group ever had."

"Jeez, Charlie! Can you lay off and give us some space?" Shane said with a good natured chuckle.

"No probelmo," Charlie laughed as he raised his hands in surrender and walked away.

"You and Charlie were in a band together?" Cece asked.

"Yes. I played the fiddle, as he already mentioned. Charlie did vocals, and the rest of the band is playing for us right now. That's Otis on the bass, Henry and Ron on the banjos, and Bill on the fiddle tonight. I've known these guys for most of my life, otherwise they probably wouldn't have dropped what they were doing to help me tonight," Shane admitted. "I thought you'd appreciate a nice quiet evening with just the two of us. I wasn't trying to come across as Don Juan, but I did want this date to be special."

Cece looked down at the candle between them, and then around at all the red roses surrounding them and adding to the cozy atmosphere. "Why? It's not like I'm some spoiled princess who is used to having men fall at my feet. You didn't have to go to this much trouble to impress me," she whispered after a long silence.

Shane didn't answer immediately. Instead, he picked up his fork and continued eating. He sensed the tension in her, but he didn't attempt to dispel it. He let her finish her dinner under the mistaken conclusion that he was just trying to impress her. Sometimes he just didn't know what to say to her, and this was one of those times. He wanted her to relax, enjoy the evening, and stop questioning his motives, but at the same time he understood why she was so leery.

Charlie appeared again and asked if they wanted dessert. When Cece politely refused, Shane stood up and walked to the small bandstand to talk to his friends. After his quiet conversation with them, he approached her with a barely suppressed smile. His eyes locked onto hers and she felt almost insanely happy for a moment. An involuntary giggle escaped her, and she suddenly understood why her daughter seemed to glow every time her husband, Norman, smiled at her. In the back of her mind, she was aware of Charlie taking the stage and adjusting the microphone stand. Shane offered her his hand and said, "Would you care to dance? I asked them to play a special waltz for us."

Cece stood up on her toes to whisper in his ear, "I don't know how to waltz," just as Bill played through the first few bars of a beautiful introduction.

Shane smiled down at her panicked expression and said, "You're going to have to learn before our wedding reception, and now's as good a time as any."

"But your friends are looking at us."

"Since when has that ever stopped you from accomplishing something?"

"Okay, show me what I need to do," she said as she placed her hand in his and squared off her shoulders.

"First of all, just relax and follow my lead. Waltzing is simple as long as you can count to three, and this particular waltz has always been my favorite. It's a bluegrass classic called *Kentucky Waltz*. When I was younger, I used to be the one up there playing the fiddle solos as I watched all the couples dance, and now I get to be the one waltzing with the pretty girl," he whispered in her ear.

She looked up at him, and he smiled just as Charlie started to sing with a voice that was surprisingly deep and rich. The melody washed over them, and Cece relaxed and followed Shane's lead. Shane wasn't that effective as a teacher, but Cece was an excellent student. She'd always had the uncanny ability to learn physical things very quickly, even when she didn't have the best instruction. After about half an hour, she was gliding across the floor as if she'd been waltzing for years.

"Wow, you're a natural at this," Shane said.

"So are you. Did your mother teach you how to dance when you were younger?"

"No. She died before I reached the age where I cared about dancing. She taught me how to play the violin and how to sing, but that was it in the arts department. I actually learned how to dance while chasing this girl who wanted nothing to do with me back in college."

Cece looked up at him in disbelief. "How did you really learn to dance?" she chuckled.

Shane laughed with her. "I really did learn to impress a girl. Her name is Viridiana, and you might actually meet her someday, because she's Magda's older sister," he said.

When it became apparent that he wasn't going to expound, Cece smiled at him and asked, "Magda's sister, huh? You had a thing for her?"

"Something like that," Shane admitted.

"I just realized how little I know about you," she said thoughtfully. "Tell me about this thing with you and Viridiana. How long ago was it? Last year? Were you in love with her?"

"It's actually ancient history," Shane began. "She taught dance classes at the university while I was a student there. At first, I signed up because I was tired of feeling so insecure about asking girls out on dates. I was enamored with her from the moment I laid eyes on her, but when she looked at me, all she saw was a tall, skinny kid who could count music pretty good. The first time I ever asked her out, she actually laughed in my face. She honestly thought I was joking, and I was too embarrassed to explain that I had been perfectly serious.

"That was the same year I started tutoring Gus. Once he figured out that I was having trouble getting girls to go out with me, he suggested I start lifting weights with him to work on my physique. I was already pretty strong from doing chores on my father's ranch, but I'd never lifted weights with the specific intention of bulking up to look better. It took almost two years, but eventually I started looking less like the male version of Popeye's wife, Olive Oil. The entire time I worked out with Gus, I still took dance lessons from Viri.

"Eventually, I asked her out again. By this time, I was twenty and she was thirty-four. I could tell she was attracted to me, because she didn't laugh in my face that time. She actually considered it, but she still said no. A few months later, I caught a break when her regular partner had to drop out of this big swing dance competition due to a serious injury. She had less than three days to find a new partner and teach him the routine, and she gave me a shot. I'd been taking lessons with her long enough for her to realize that I was her best choice, because I could execute the routine. I'd practiced it with her a ton of times when her regular partner wasn't around, and she knew that our physical chemistry on the dance floor was great.

"I did okay as a last minute replacement; we got second place in the competition. That night, she invited me out to have a drink with her. We went back to her apartment, and one thing lead to another. The next morning, I woke up feeling like it was

200

the best night of my life, but she was horrified and demanded that I leave. She was the first woman I'd ever slept with, and I loved her very much at the time. My feelings were hurt pretty badly when she asked me to leave... actually, I was devastated. I thought that she was going to give us a shot, but she was too caught up in what other people might think of us. It took me a while to give up trying to convince her that I was the man for her, but I'm glad I did."

"Why?"

"Because we weren't meant to be together; we're better as friends. More importantly, if I hadn't come to my senses, I never would have met you. Viri was very spoiled and privileged and beautiful; she was a challenge, and I was an inexperienced young man who was fascinated by her looks and the way she danced. If I came across a woman like Viri tomorrow, I wouldn't feel the least bit of inclination to pursue her. But you, on the other hand, are exceptional. You make me want to spend the rest of my days proving that I deserve you."

Cece's steps faltered at Shane's words, but he steadied her and continued leading their slow, sensual waltz. As the music ended, Shane twirled her into the most private corner of the room and held her close for a moment. "What are you thinking right now?" he asked her.

"You didn't have to go to so much trouble to impress me. I already care about you, Shane."

He placed a finger under her chin and tilted her head so he could look directly into her eyes. "I wasn't trying to impress you, Honey. Haven't you ever had someone do something because they want you to feel special, and know they care about you? I'm not some young twenty something whose self-worth is all tied up in whether or not I can be the most impressive first date a woman has ever had. Tonight was all about you feeling appreciated and special. If *I* weren't so impressed by *you*, I wouldn't have felt inspired to do something this out of the ordinary for you."

Cece attempted to look away from his intense gaze, but his eyes wouldn't let her. "Why would you be so impressed by a cake decorator?" she asked. There was a challenge in her voice, as if she were daring him to disagree with her overly simplified assessment of herself.

"Because you are more than just a cake decorator. Do you remember me telling you that I've been a fan of yours for a while now?"

"Yes, but—"

"No buts. You probably don't remember the first time you ever saw me, but I've been captivated with you since that day."

"I remember the fire, Shane."

"I'm not talking about the fire. I'm talking about the day you fell out of the hospital bed. You had to be rushed to surgery right after it happened, but I was there right before the nurses and doctors came running in."

"You?" Cece breathed. "That was you?" For the last few years she'd thought she must have imagined the man standing in her hospital room. She'd been lying in the hospital bed, unable to move from the waist down, and in unimaginable pain both physically and emotionally. Her skin had started to crawl as a sudden memory of what Red Bone had done to her broke free from the vault she'd kept it in for so many years. In that moment, she'd been thirteen again, and lying tied to the bed fearful of what she knew was going to walk through the door at any moment. She'd been so firmly in the grip of her terrifying flashback; she'd managed to yank herself out of the hospital bed in an attempt to escape. She always thought she'd imagined the blurry figure of the man she'd been so terrified of, until now.

Shane ran his hands down the length of her bare arms and pulled her closer. "Yes, that was me. I wasn't trying to scare you. I just wanted to bring you some flowers and talk to you, even if it was just for five minutes."

"Why?"

"Because Shelly came to my house after it happened. I hadn't seen her so broken up about anything since her husband was killed in action over in Afghanistan. She told me all about that night. She told me about how you kept that crazy man from doing whatever he was about to do to the little girl, and about how he had a gun when you went after him. Everyone there was scared, but you were the one who took action and ended it. And the whole time Shelly sat there crying about the fact that you were probably going to die; I knew you were going to survive, and I was right. You are one of those people who can come through anything stronger and better than before. That moment in the hospital when you saw me, I didn't know what you were so afraid of, but I did know that you aren't one of those people who gets immobilized with fear and ceases to take action. Think about it Cecilia... you were lying in a hospital bed critically injured and paralyzed, literally paralyzed, from the waist down, but you didn't let that stop you from trying to defend yourself as best you could. And the night of the fire... when I got to your apartment I thought there was no way you could still be alive in there, but you were. You didn't panic, you did what you could to stay alive, and thank God you did. I've never met a woman like you before in my life."

He raised her hands to his lips and looked into her eyes before continuing in the same soulful manner. "Since that day in the hospital, I couldn't get you off my mind. Something about you touched me deep inside that day, and I wanted to get to know you. I would have introduced myself sooner, but Rebecca made it clear that you needed some time to heal both physically and emotionally. I kept my distance, but you were always there in the back of my mind. Before the fire, I already felt like I knew you because I'd learned so much about you from your daughter and my sister. So, tonight I thought I'd let you know how special you are to me; actually I don't think I can keep it to myself anymore. This isn't just some passing fancy, Cecilia. I've been impressed by everything about you for years now, and I've been smitten with you since the night we met. I hope that doesn't scare you."

He kissed her hands and never broke eye contact as he spoke about his feelings for her. It was difficult to tell what she was thinking from her facial expression, but he did detect a quickening in her breathing, and her pupils dilated slightly as he leaned closer to her face. Her feelings might not be as advanced as his were at the moment, but she was definitely not completely immune to him. He brushed his lips over her cheek, and whispered in her ear, "You can trust me, Cecilia. I know you haven't ever felt safe enough to really trust a man before, but I'd never hurt you. You've been afraid with good reason, but you don't have to be afraid anymore... you can trust me."

She pressed her face into his chest and wrapped her arms around him. They stood holding each other, and swaying slightly to the music as the band continued playing. Eventually,

Cecilia raised her head off his chest and looked up at him. "I do trust you."

Shane smiled and pulled her back out onto the makeshift dance floor. "How about one more dance before we call it a night," he smiled.

Cece soaked in everything Shane said to her, and let his words swirl around in her brain as they danced. How could he have harbored feelings for her for so long? Suddenly, his eagerness to have her stay in his house took on a different tone, and she smiled to herself as she remembered how often she had worried about being a burden to him. Of course, he'd been prudent to hide his feelings from her. Had she known from the beginning, she never would have grown to trust him as much as she did right now. She would have thought he wanted nothing more than sex, and then she would have hated him for it.

The music ended, and he held her close for a long time before they left the restaurant. On the drive home, he didn't say much, but he did look over at her and smile every once in a while. Cece hardly knew what to say, if anything. When Shane had confessed to having strong feelings for her since the night of the fire she'd felt pure elation. He was a man, and he'd expressed a romantic and sexual interest in her, and for once in her life she wasn't mistrustful and suspicious of his motives. Actually, she looked forward to the next step in their relationship, and she found herself fantasizing about being intimate with Shane.

"Just sit tight," he said as he pulled up to the curb in front of her house. He jogged around and opened her door for her. His hand always managed to situate itself either on her waist or at the small of her back when they walked side by side, and tonight was no different. As they walked up the sidewalk towards her porch, his hand stayed firmly planted on her waist, and she felt a warm glow radiate outward from that point of contact and encompass her entire body.

"I had such a great time today," she said when they reached the front door.

"Good," he smiled. "Today has definitely been one of those days that you never want to end."

She looked up at him, and the light caught her face at an angle that made the depth in her eyes appear fathomless for an instant. As he stared into them, he felt an inexplicable force pulling him towards her, and then he realized she was the one applying the force. She'd grasped the front of his shirt with both hands, and she slowly pulled him closer until the tips of their noses were touching. She took in a deep breath and then planted a single kiss on his lips before she let him go.

"I still don't want it to end," she whispered.

Chapter 16

"I'm sorry, Ms. Cece, but this is a support column. We can't just go knocking it down just so the room will be more 'open,'" Leonard said to Cece.

"Well, we have to do something about it. I thought this was just a wall when I designed the new space; I didn't know there was going to be some giant pole inside the wall that had to stay," she grouched.

"I would suggest working around it. You can still have your open floor space; it will just have a column in the middle of it. We can add a façade of some kind to make it look more like an architectural element than a structural support. Right now it looks unfinished, but we can make it look a whole lot better."

"Is it going to change the estimate?"

"Not by much. Honestly, ma'am, there's no way you can remove this column unless you want your building to be structurally unsound and fall down at some point. If you want to hire an architect to help you plan the rest of the space we can halt our work right now until you decide what you want to do. I would suggest that you let us continue the demolition phase though."

It was almost quitting time for the day anyway. Cece looked at her watch and then back at the ugly column that had been hiding in the wall. "It's almost time to go anyway. Why don't you guys just go home early, and I'll think about what I want to do. It's hard to think with all the noise going on in here right now."

Leonard looked so relieved Cece almost laughed. She'd been hanging around harassing him and his crew all day. She knew she was being a nuisance, but she needed something to do with her time. She couldn't start training her new assistants until the demolition phase of her renovation was over, she wasn't currently training for any more fights, and Shane was out of town. She was bored out of her mind.

Leonard called out for his crew to wrap up for the day, and they all left an hour early. Once the last crew member was out the door, Cece looked around the bakery. It was amazing what a difference eight hours had made. The front was now twice the size it had been before tearing down the wall. She looked at the pole again and decided it wasn't as bad as she'd been making it out to be. She could definitely work with it; she had to. She made a few notes and left them on the counter for tomorrow, and then she locked up and headed home for the night.

When she pulled into her driveway, she saw Rebecca waiting for her on the porch. She wasn't sitting in one of the wicker chairs like she should have been. Her pregnant belly was even more obvious than it had been last time Cece saw her.

"Why are you sitting out here on the step?" Cece asked as she got out of the car.

Rebecca raised her head up off her knees, and Cece saw that she'd been crying—a lot.

"What's wrong?" Cece asked.

"Norman's having an affair!" Rebecca sniffed.

Cece took a breath, and plopped down next to Rebecca. Shocked didn't even being to describe how she felt. "A what?"

Rebecca dropped her head back down to her knees and mumbled past the tears in her voice, "An affair... with his ex-wife. I saw them together today."

Cece looked down at her daughter's rounded belly protruding out from both sides. It seemed way too big for Rebecca's small frame, and made her appear smaller and more delicate. Her little shoulders shook as she sobbed into her shirtsleeve, and Cece reached out a hand to touch her.

"You should have called me instead of sitting out here on the porch. How long have you been here?"

"Just a couple of hours," Rebecca sniffed.

"Why didn't you call me?"

"I thought you were busy, and I didn't want to bother you."

"You aren't bothering me. I'm your mother."

Rebecca picked her head up to look at Cece, and then dropped it back down in dejection.

"Come on, let's go inside."

Cece unlocked the door and watched Rebecca struggle to stand up. At five months pregnant, she looked like she was already in her third trimester. She waddled past Cece and went directly to the kitchen to sit at the table. Cece still didn't have any furniture other than a kitchen table and a bed that she'd put in her room just so it wouldn't be so empty. She also didn't have much extra food in the fridge.

"Are you hungry?"

"Not really."

You want to talk about it?"

"Not really."

"What happened?" Cece persisted.

Rebecca wrapped her arms around her belly and sighed, "I stopped by the gym where Norman goes to play basketball in the evenings and I saw him playing a game on the outside court with Juliana. At first I wasn't upset, but then I sat there and watched them for a while. They seemed to be having such a great time. I thought about getting out of the car and confronting him about it, but then I thought I might be overreacting. I mean, they were just playing a game of basketball... but then, right after the game was over, they started kissing. They were all ever each other! I'm glad I didn't get out and confront him. I would have looked like the world's biggest idiot, so I just drove off. I didn't really think about where I was going until I was halfway to Nashville. They're probably still together!"

Tears streamed down Rebecca's face as she recounted the incident, and with each passing moment Cece felt a murderous rage growing stronger within her. When Cece reached out to embrace her, Rebecca lost what little control she had over her emotions. Her entire body shook with the force of her emotions and she sobbed, "He doesn't love me anymore! He probably never did! And I'm having his babies. What am I going to do, Mom?"

"I'll tell you what we're going to do. First of all, you don't ever have to see that rotten bastard again. You can stay here with me."

"But I love him so much! How could he do this to me? Everything was so perfect until this happened."

Cece pulled back and looked at Rebecca; she had never seen her this emotional before. She gave her a little shake and said, "You need to calm down and eat something. It's not good for you to be this upset while you're carrying twins."

Rebecca looked at Cece with red, tear-filled eyes and broke into sobs again. "I'm not hungry," she sniffed, and then in the next breath she moaned, "How could this happen? Things were so perfect until today."

Cece grabbed a box of tissues. She took one out and approached Rebecca with it. She wiped all the tears off her face with slow deliberation, and then she grasped her daughter's chin and said, "He's a man, Rebecca. Apparently they're all the same—even your precious Norman."

Later than night, Cece lay in her window seat and reflected on all that had happened that day. She didn't have a clue how to deal with Rebecca and give her what she needed. She'd taken her over to Karen's house for the night, because she didn't have much food or comfort to offer her. Tomorrow she would go grocery shopping and buy a comfortable chair for Rebecca to sit in before bringing her back.

On the way to Karen's house, Rebecca had cried until she threw up the little bit of food that Cece had convinced her to eat. Cece had never seen her daughter so miserable before, and she had never felt so angry before. From the moment she met Norman, she'd wondered why he'd married Rebecca. The two of them were so different, and Norman was so much older, but Cece had kept her mouth shut about it. The only reason she'd accepted their marriage was because Norman seemed to make her happy. Now that he wasn't making her happy anymore, Cece was going to do something about it. She already had a list of divorce lawyers to call in the morning, but she wouldn't bother Rebecca about those details until she'd had a few days to process the new turn her life had taken.

Cece closed her eyes and tried to relax, but every few seconds she saw another image of her daughter's dejected little face looking up at her. First, the six year old Rebecca who wanted to know where her sister Sarah was, and then the twenty six year old Rebecca who wanted to know why her husband would cheat on her. Cece pressed her fingers to her temples in an attempt to stave off the headache she felt coming on.

The house was silent, and Cece wished her thoughts could be as quiet as the room was at the moment. She turned over and raised the shades just a crack so she could stare out the window for a while. Almost every house on the street was completely dark. A few people left their porch lights on at night, but Cece never did. She used motion sensors that came on when someone got about halfway up the sidewalk. While she was busy gazing out the window, a truck pulled to a stop at the curb in front of her house. The truck seemed familiar, and Cece fixed her angry gaze on the man who got out and started up her sidewalk. When the light came on, Cece's suspicions were confirmed. There was Norman standing in the middle of her sidewalk. He looked up at the house as if he weren't sure whether or not he should continue, and then he noticed Rebecca's car parked just outside the garage. When his moment of hesitation was over, he took another step forward, and Cece shot out of the window seat.

By the time she reached the door and unlocked it, he was at the top step. She threw open the door and charged across the wide porch at him, delivering a vicious front kick to his chest. It happened so fast his face barely had enough time to register shock before she leapt at him. Both of her feet hit him squarely in the chest, and he tumbled back, rolling over once on his way down the steps. He came to a rest sprawled on his back with one of his legs still extended up the steps. Cece had grabbed onto the post next to the steps with both hands as she kicked him, and she used the momentum from the kick to swing one full circle around the post and land back on her feet at the top of the steps as he fell back.

He lay there in stunned silence. Cece padded down the steps and kicked his leg off of them with her bare feet. She stood directly over his head, and looked down at his blank expression. She could tell he was in pain, but it was nothing compared to the pain he'd inflicted on her daughter. She waited for his eyes to focus on her before she spoke in a soulless voice lacking any compassion for the pain she'd just caused him. "I guess you didn't get my message; you're not welcome here."

She didn't wait for his response. She gave him one more kick to the leg, marched back up the steps, closed the door, and went back to her window seat.

When Cece left the house the next morning, she noticed Rebecca's cell phone lying on the porch in the shadows. She picked it up and checked the display. It still worked, and it said that she had almost fifty missed calls. Cece skimmed through the call log and saw that all of them had come from Norman. The voicemail box was also full, and Cece knew Norman was the culprit.

She was on her way to Karen's to check on her daughter. For a moment she considered taking the phone with her so she could return it, but then she recalled how Rebecca had cried most of the evening. It was probably best if Rebecca weren't bothered by him right now. Cece shoved the phone in her pocket and made a detour to the cell phone carrier Rebecca used.

Once she found a customer service representative, it was simple for her to purchase a new phone for her daughter. All she had to do was pretend she was Rebecca, and pay cash for one of the most expensive phones they had. She had the same number and phone service transferred to the new phone, but with one notable exception. She'd blocked all the numbers Norman used to call Rebecca.

The people at the store had used a device to help her transfer all of the contact information to the new phone, and by the time she walked out there was almost no difference between the new phone and the old one. Cece hoped Rebecca didn't notice, but it wouldn't really matter if she did. Rebecca was too upset to realize what was best for her. She stopped back by her house and left Rebecca's old phone there before continuing on to Karen's.

She found Karen in the cage, sparing with her trainer. She gave a quick wave and went off in search of Rebecca. Eventually, she found her in the kitchen hunched over a cup of milk. She was staring down into the cup as if its contents reflected more than just her own face. Her eyes were still swollen and red, and she looked morose.

"Have you eaten anything today?"

"Yeah. Karen threatened to sit on me if I didn't."

Cece patted Rebecca's shoulder and said, "Things will get better."

Rebecca was quiet for a long time before she finally said, "No they won't."

Cece resisted the urge to argue with her. Norman was just a man, but her daughter wouldn't see it that way.

"What makes you think that?"

"I trusted him, Mom. You probably wouldn't know what that's like since you've never trusted anyone in your life. But I trusted him with everything."

"Then that should tell you something."

"What should it tell me? That trusting people is a bad thing? That's what you were going to say isn't it?"

"No," Cece lied. "But it should tell you that trusting *men* is a bad thing—especially when you trust them with everything. Look where you are right now. Do you think you'd be here pregnant and alone if men were worth trusting?"

Rebecca looked back at the warm cup of milk. She hunched her shoulders again and turned her face away. Cece turned away from her daughter to stare out the window. Heaviness had settled in her chest sometime yesterday night after she'd left Rebecca with Karen. The feeling only intensified as she spent more time in Rebecca's presence today.

"Can you give me a ride back to your house so I can pick up my car and go home?" Rebecca asked.

"Why would you want to do that?" Cece demanded. She sprang out of her seat and crouched down in front of Rebecca.

"Because, Mom! Do you think sitting here listening to you tell me how wrong I was to trust my own husband is helping?" she said with tears falling freely down her cheeks.

"But—"

"Besides, I need to get some clothes for work tomorrow."

"Rebecca, I'm sorry I was giving you a hard time. Why don't you just stay here and let me take care of the clothes for you. I don't think you should go back yet. Just stay here at Karen's house. At least she has furniture and food."

"I also need to find my phone. I didn't tell Norman where I was going, and he might have tried to call me."

"*Fuck* Norman!" Cece exploded. "So what if he did call? He doesn't deserve the chance to absolve his guilt with some bullshit apology and excuses."

"But what if he really is sorry?"

"He's not! He might be sorry he got caught, but he's not sorry he did it. Men never are," Cece spat in disgust. The disgust wasn't aimed at Rebecca, but she seemed to take it personally.

She recoiled and crossed her arms in front of her chest as if protecting herself from Cece's rage. Seeing this reaction reminded Cece that her daughter was a gentle and sweet type of person, so she made a conscious effort to change her tone. "Look, Rebecca, you just need some time to think before you try to confront him. Stay here at Karen's. I'll buy you some new clothes and bring them later today," she said in what she hoped was a gentle tone.

"Have you seen my phone? I lost it somewhere yesterday, and I need to call in to let the center know I might be a little late tomorrow. I think I left my key card at home before I came here, and I need to stop by and get it before work tomorrow, or I won't be able to get into the building."

"I'll take care of it for you. Just relax for the rest of the day." Cece reached into her pocket to pull out Rebecca's new phone, and the list of divorce lawyers fell onto the floor. Rebecca noticed it before Cece had a chance to stuff it back into her pocket.

"What's that?"

"We can talk about it later."

"It looked like it said divorce lawyers."

"That's because it does," Cece sighed. At Rebecca's hurt look she added, "It's best to be prepared."

"Oh God, this is too much," Rebecca moaned as her head fell onto the counter in dejection. She cried quietly for a few minutes before speaking again. "This time yesterday he was telling me how excited he is about the babies, and now this. I don't even want a divorce."

Cece couldn't think of anything to say that wouldn't make Rebecca more upset, so she placed the phone on the counter beside Rebecca's head. "I found it on my porch," she said as she got up to leave the kitchen. On her way out, she turned to tell Rebecca that it would get better, that she would make sure of it, and she caught her looking through the call log. There wasn't a single missed call from Norman in there, and her shoulders slumped again as she laid the phone down and stared back into her cup of milk.

After a day full of shopping and taking care of things for Rebecca, Cece went home to her empty house. Luckily, she didn't have to go to Rebecca's house to look for her electronic key card; it had been in her car the entire time. She found it when she drove Rebecca's car to Karen's for the evening. Dinner with Karen and Rebecca had been a tense and mostly silent affair. Rebecca had a hard time not crying every few minutes, and Cece's simmering rage made it nearly impossible for her to keep a cool face. Karen constantly looked from Rebecca to Cece and back again with a frown on her face. Cece took it all in, and concluded that everyone was better off if she left early. After dinner, she said good night to Rebecca and called a cab. While she waited outside for the cab, Karen tried to give her a pep talk, but she wasn't the least bit interested in listening.

"You look like you could use a bout with my trainer," Karen remarked.

"I could actually use a bout with my sorry ass son-in-law."

"I know, Sport, but it isn't your place to kick his ass. I'm guessing that his pregnant wife taking off is the best punishment. I'm surprised he hasn't called her yet. She's been looking at her phone every ten seconds since you left earlier."

"He did call, but I didn't see the point in telling her. I got her a new phone and blocked his number."

"Why?"

"Because she's my daughter, and he hurt her. You think I'm going to give him the chance to do it again?"

"But Cece, it's her life, not yours. I think the two of them can work through this. Maybe you should let them try."

"It's her life, but she's my daughter," Cece said fiercely. "She's the only daughter I have left."

"I get that," Karen replied, "but even if you have the best intentions you aren't doing the right thing by being deceitful. You should at least tell her he called. She's miserable."

"She doesn't need to know. She's too soft and forgiving, and he doesn't deserve her—not anymore."

"Cece—"

"Don't *Cece* me, and you better not say anything about him calling to Rebecca. All it will do is make things worse."

"I'll keep my mouth shut for now, but I don't think it's right."

"She's the only daughter I have left. I'm not going to give him the chance to hurt her again."

"I'll see you tomorrow, Sport," Karen said. The cab had arrived to take Cece home.

Now, she sat in her window seat and thought about that conversation with Karen. What if she was making a mistake that Rebecca would never forgive her for? Being so deceptive about the phone hadn't felt right, but at the same time she'd felt compelled to do it. She had a feeling that Shane would probably disapprove of her actions, and the fact that she cared at all what he thought started to bother her.

When she'd stayed with Norman and Rebecca a few years ago, she'd witnessed a few of their intimate moments. He'd been so good to Rebecca that Cece had actually believed he was a good guy. She had even started to open herself up to the possibility that there were more good guys out there somewhere. Now she sat in her living room thinking that if someone as lovesick as Norman could cheat, then any man could cheat.

While she sat in her silent living room thinking her clamorous thoughts, she heard Norman's truck pull up to her curb. She thought she'd managed to calm down some, but as soon as she saw him step out of the truck her blood pressure spiked. Blood hummed in her ears and her heart galloped as she got up and opened her door. The motion light came on when he was about halfway up the sidewalk. She stepped out onto the porch in full view and flexed her fingers as she stared at him. Her eyes dared him to take another step towards her. When he took that step, she vaulted over the porch railing and landed in the yard, cutting him off.

"I could have sworn you wouldn't come back," she sneered up at him.

"Look, Cece, I don't want any trouble. I just want to see my wife."

"Go home, Norman," Cece commanded.

He ran an aggravated hand through his hair and said, "Not until I see my wife."

"So, it's going to be like that then?" Cece asked as she took up her favorite fighting stance.

"Like what?" Norman asked as he backed up a few steps.

"You're not getting in that house unless you can get past me, so you might as well just leave now and save yourself the humiliation."

"I'm not going to fight you."

"I'm glad you came to your senses. Goodbye, Norman."

"I'm not going to fight you, but I'm not leaving either. Not until I see my wife," he clarified.

Cece flexed her hands again and said, "I've got all night."

Norman shook his head. "I don't have to deal with this," he said. He started walking toward the porch, but as he tried to pass Cece, she swept her foot out, kicking his legs out from under him and sending him sprawling into the grass. He got back to his feet quickly and said, "What is wrong with you?"

Cece maintained her stance and ignored his words. She only reacted to his attempts to get past her. His size intimidated her a little, but only because she knew that brute strength could be an advantage if she allowed him to get too close or catch her off guard. On his last attempt to get past her, she managed to send him flying over her shoulder with a perfectly executed hip toss. He landed with a thud and all the air whooshed out of his lungs. He lay on the ground grimacing, and Cece sauntered over to him. When he didn't attempt to get up again, she said, "Go home, Norman. There's no way I'm letting you talk to my daughter after you cheated on her."

"I did not cheat on my wife," Norman huffed out. He was still rubbing his chest and writhing on the ground as if he were in a great deal of pain.

"Liar," Cece spat out. Rage was evident in every line in her body.

Norman got up slowly, and kept his hands up in a gesture of surrender. "Please, just let me see Rebecca. If she wants me to leave, I'll go immediately, but please just let me see her."

If Cece hadn't seen her daughter's tears yesterday and then again today, she might have been able to muster up some sympathy for Norman. "I already told you, if you want to get in that house you have to get through me. I've got all night, Norman. I suggest you save yourself the trouble and just go home."

He looked like he was done trying for the night, so Cece turned her back on him to go inside. While her back was turned, he made one last attempt to get past her. Although she wasn't exactly expecting it, she hadn't let her guard down. When he rushed past her, she lunged at him, but he didn't go down right away as she'd hoped. He was big and strong enough to stay on his feet and continue walking toward the steps with her on his back. She had to wrap her arms around his head and viciously yank him back to get him to go down, and when he did lose his balance, they went down together. Cece took no notice of the pain as she landed on her back. She used the only advantage she had left at that point and wrapped her legs around his neck. His face turned red as she cut off his circulation by squeezing as hard as she could. He made several attempts to free himself, but Cece hung on as if her life depended on it. When he stopped resisting, she let him go.

They both struggled to their feet, still panting from exertion and glaring at each other. Cece took up her fighting stance again and pinned Norman with a look that dared him to keep trying. He stared back at her for a few tense minutes, and then eventually shook his head in disgust. "I just want to talk to my wife," he tried one last appeal to Cece's soft side.

He didn't know that her softer side had disappeared with her daughter's tears yesterday. "She's not going to be your wife much longer, but she'll always be *my daughter*. I suggest you get yourself a damn good lawyer. If you come near my house again you'll be sorry."

Cece turned away from him and walked back towards the house. Part of her welcomed another excuse to hurt him, but he didn't make another attempt to get through her. Her hand was on the door knob, holding the door half open, when his quiet, almost inaudible words stopped her.

"She wants a divorce?"

Cece glanced back at him. Misery was evident in every nuance of his being, from his arms hanging in limp dejection down at his sides to the almost comical lugubrious look on his face. She might as well have just stabbed him in the heart with a knife. But there was still a tiny bit of hope in his eyes, as if he were praying that he'd misunderstood her. "Yes. She's already hired a lawyer," Cece said, twisting the knife and dashing his hopes. She slammed the door in his face and went to take a shower.

She lingered in the shower long after all the hot water ran cold. No matter how much she scrubbed, she just couldn't wash away the feeling that she was doing something wrong. Every time she considered taking Karen's advice about stepping aside, a deeper and more primitive instinct to protect her daughter would take over. On three other occasions she'd failed to protect someone she loved in a crucial moment, and on those three occasions she'd lost them permanently.

As the cold water fell down on her head, she allowed her mind to wander back to places she hadn't visited for years. Back in Atlanta, before she'd become a foster child, she'd had one small opportunity to save her mother, but she'd been too afraid to take it. The day it all came to an end was etched permanently in her memory. She remembered every detail of Cora's near escape from Red Bone. She remembered the frantic visit to Miss Georgia, an older lady from down the street who had a secret reputation for helping prostitutes escape abusive pimps. She remembered the money Miss Georgia had given to Cora, and Cora's all out desperation to pack and be out of the room before Red Bone returned for the night.

Cece had crouched hidden under the couch in their small hotel room. It had been her favorite hiding spot, because it was small and private, yet she could still see what was going on in the room. She'd often hidden there while Cora entertained her customers. The day Cora made up her mind to leave, Cece had been hiding there. She'd watched her mother throw her few belongings into a bag, and shove the stack of cash into her purse. She was almost ready to walk out the door; they would have been long gone in a matter of moments... but then the hotel door had sprung open and slammed against the wall, making a crack and causing drywall to fall to the floor near Cece's hiding spot.

Cora had stood frozen, with her hand suspended in midair and a panicked look on her face. That was the look that often appeared in Cece's dreams. Cora knew that Red Bone did gruesome things to girls who tried to leave, and that look on her face had summed up six years worth of fear for her life.

"What were you doin' at the bus station?" he asked her in a deceptively calm voice.

She could barely breathe through her terror, and he back handed her so hard she hit the floor. "*S'il vous plait! Je suis enceinte,*" she'd pleaded with him.

"How many times I got to tell you, you stupid bitch? Speak English!"

"Please... please. I'm pregnant," Cora sobbed.

Cece didn't know what pregnant meant back then, but she did know that it was a bad thing for her mother. Red Bone lost his façade of cool and began beating Cora with an intensity that Cece hadn't seen before. She cowered deeper under the couch, afraid that things would only get worse if he saw her. It seemed like forever until he finally turned away from Cora's limp body and left the room. Cece had tried to help her mother after Red Bone left, but by then it was too late.

The same nightmare scenario had repeated itself years later with her friend Dot, but Cece closed her mind against those memories. That time she had tried to help, she just hadn't been strong enough to be effective back then. She turned off the cold water and stepped out of the shower. She was strong enough now to help her daughter, and nothing was going to make her stand aside this time.

Chapter 17

Cece sat in her bedroom and stared at the monitors for the new camera system she'd installed on her property. Norman had decided to make a nuisance of himself by showing up at her house every night demanding to speak to Rebecca, but Cece still refused to yield. When she saw his truck appear on the monitor, she bolted for the door. He just didn't know when to quit, and Cece's patience was beginning to wane. She reached the front door just as he was rounding his truck.

"How many times do I have to tell you to get lost?" she demanded.

"I'm here to see my wife," Norman gritted out as he started up the sidewalk towards the house. "Why won't she just come out and talk to me?"

"Maybe because she doesn't want to!"

"This time I'm not leaving until she tells me that for herself."

"I've been telling you all week, you're not getting in my house unless you can get past me. Do you think I'm just going to let you walk right in?"

"Look Cece, this is real life. This isn't some kind of kickboxing death match! I'm tired of this. Just let me talk to her."

"No!" Cece shouted as she glowered down at him from the porch.

His lips thinned, and he took a couple of steps toward the porch. Cece hopped off the porch and cut off his determined advance midway. When he tried to rush past her, she sent him flying with a brutal hip toss. He landed flat on his back and grunted in pain. She watched in silence as he got up and came at her again. When he got close, she tossed him again.

"Go home, Norman," she commanded.

"Not until I talk to Rebecca," he panted.

They stared at each other for a tense moment before Norman made another move toward the porch. This time, instead of trying to rush past her as he'd done all week, he grabbed her and attempted to hoist her out of his way. Cece's feet briefly left the ground as Norman's arm clamped around her waist. She didn't know whether or not he intended to throw her somewhere, but she wasn't about to let him try. She grasped the thumb of the hand that was holding her waist and gave it a vicious twist forcing his grip to loosen. When he let her go, she maintained her hold on his thumb and wrenched his arm around at an odd angle, forcing him to his knees. She stood behind him, maintaining a painful joint lock that should have stopped him.

Norman grunted in pain, and she twisted his wrist to drive home her point. She had no sympathy for him. "Leave now!" she commanded.

"Not until I see my wife."

"There's no way you can get out of this position, unless you want me to break your damn arm off!"

"You wouldn't break my arm," he gritted out as he started a slow crawl towards her porch.

"Oh? I wouldn't?" she said as she twisted slightly.

He called out in pain and winced as she bent one of his fingers back, but he didn't halt his slow, steady advance towards her porch. "I need to talk to my wife." He advanced again, and Cece twisted again.

"I'll break all your fingers if you don't stop."

He kept moving forward. He was within two steps of the porch when one of his fingers snapped. Cece detected tears in his voice as he said, "Break them all! I don't care. I have ten fingers, but I only have one wife."

That simple statement managed to penetrate the hateful fog in Cece's brain and give her pause. Sudden shame at her own behavior came over her, and she released his hand as if it had scalded her. She looked down at his broken finger as he jumped up and sprinted up the steps. When he made it to the door, he glanced back down at her once before bounding inside and calling out for Rebecca. After a fruitless search, he returned; bewilderment was evident in every line of his body.

"She's not here," Cece admitted with a shrug. "She hasn't been here all week."

Norman clenched his teeth together, and closed his eyes for a moment before asking, "Where is she?" with quiet fury in his voice.

"Go home, Norman."

"Has she at least listened to any of the voicemails I've left her?" he demanded in the face of Cece's stony, silent glare.

"You mean the messages you left her on *this* phone?" Cece asked as she pulled Rebecca's old cell phone out of her pocket. "Funny thing... she was so upset she forgot it here, and I keep forgetting to give it back to her," she continued as she slammed the phone down on the cement and stomped it to pieces. "I guess I'll have to buy her a new one now." With that statement, she went inside and shut the door in Norman's face.

Cece waited for more than an hour after Norman left to drive to Karen's house.

"How is she?" Cece asked as soon as Karen opened the door.

"About the same as all week—really quiet—and I can tell she's still been crying."

"He came back again tonight," Cece sighed. "I can't believe he has the nerve to keep showing up after what he did."

"Are you sure you shouldn't just let the two of them work it out?" Karen asked.

"Of course I am!" Cece snapped. "Where's Rebecca?"

"Still in the guestroom. She skipped dinner again tonight."

"I'll take care of it," Cece said. She stopped by the kitchen to make a sandwich for Rebecca, and went to try again to talk some sense into her. There was no point pining her life away for a man, especially one who cheated on her. Her quiet knock went unanswered, so she opened the door to find Rebecca sitting in the chair beside the window, staring at the ground below.

"I brought you a sandwich. Karen told me you didn't eat supper."

"Thanks, Mom." Her voice still had the same subdued, defeated tone that had breaking Cece's heart all week. She placed the sandwich on the table next to Rebecca and sat on the edge of the bed.

"Do you want to talk about it?"

Rebecca glanced at her, and a single tear escaped as she shook her head.

"It hurts now, but it will get better. You might even find a better husband someday."

"But I don't want another husband. I just wish he would at least try to apologize and make up for it, but I haven't heard anything from him all week. That's what hurts the most right now."

Cece had to swallow hard to get past the guilty lump in her throat as she looked at Rebecca. She had to remind herself that she was right, and that she could never allow Norman another chance to hurt her daughter.

"I guess it was just a matter of time before they got back together. They were high school sweethearts, you know. I never understood what he saw in me anyway," Rebecca sniffed.

"What do you mean you don't know what he saw in you?" Cece sat forward and demanded.

"Haven't you ever seen his ex-wife? She's a six foot, blond bombshell. She could have any man she wants."

"Stop talking like that. It doesn't matter what this other woman looks like. You are still beautiful. I'm sure Norman thinks so, or you two wouldn't be so... happily... married..." Cece's voice trailed off when she realized what she'd said.

"What am I going to do, Mom? I'm pregnant with twins, *his* twins, and he doesn't want me anymore."

Cece frowned, and rubbed her temples. "I'll tell you what you're going to do. You're going to get a divorce and get on with your life. Don't waste another second thinking about him."

"But I love him!" Rebecca wailed as she broke down into tears again. "Sunday everything was perfect, and now this. What did I do wrong?"

"Honey, you didn't do anything wrong." Cece stood up and stroked Rebecca's head as she cried. "You didn't do anything wrong."

The sandwich sat untouched on the table as Cece and Rebecca both stared out the window. Each was reflecting on the many ways one's life can take a sudden turn. Cece grappled with her own conscience as an unwanted image of Norman looking just as miserable as Rebecca rose up before her. What if she was wrong to keep them apart?

"Are you sure I shouldn't call him, Mom? What if he's just feeling too guilty or afraid to call me first? That message I left him on Monday was pretty dramatic."

Cece couldn't maintain eye contact, so she sighed and looked back out the window. Now would be the time to tell Rebecca that Norman had called, but she just couldn't get the words out. "No, you shouldn't be the one to call first," Cece said after a long pause.

Shane drove home from the airport, and had to fight the urge to stop by Cecilia's house before going home to change. He'd taken the redeye flight from Colorado so that he could spend his two days off with Cecilia. Things had gone so well on their date that it was impossible for him to keep her off his mind. He hadn't anticipated having the weekends off, so it was a nice surprise when he'd found out that training only took place during the week. He also hadn't anticipated wanting to spend every free second he had with Cecilia.

Once he was home, he got directly in the shower. He wanted to surprise Cecilia and take her out today if she had time. He knew she'd probably be available, because her shop was still closed for renovations. He planned to stop by and drag her out with him no matter what excuses she threw at him. His mood was so light he sang in the shower, and even continued to whistle after he stepped out. It took him a minute to realize someone was banging on his front door. He grabbed his robe and hastened to see who it was.

"Where have you been all week?" Norman pushed his way in and demanded as soon as Shane opened the door.

"Up at that water rescue training facility in Colorado." Shane took in Norman's besieged appearance and asked, "Is everything alright?"

"No!" Norman shouted. "Becky left me, and her crazy mother won't let me anywhere near her. I don't even know where she's staying."

"Sit down, and try to breathe. Let me get dressed, and when I get back out here start from the beginning."

Norman sat down hard on the sofa and dropped his head into his hands. He took out his cell phone, and Shane left the room. While Shane dressed, Norman sat and listened to the angry voicemail Cece had sent him on Monday. It seemed like the millionth time he'd heard it, and it still upset him just as much as the first time.

"What's this about Rebecca leaving you?" Shane asked when he returned. "Why would she leave you?"

"Because she saw Julie attack me. It came out of nowhere. One minute I'm playing basketball, and the next she's all over me, and Becky saw the whole thing."

"Wow, she has some nerve doing that with your wife standing right there."

"Neither one of us knew Becky was watching. I pushed her off of me as soon as I got over the shock. I had no idea Becky saw, until I got a message from her crazy mother later that night. When she didn't come home, I was worried about her, and then I checked my voicemail and realized she'd taken off to her mom's house because she saw Julie jump on me. I tried calling, but she never answered or called me back. I figured she was upset, so I went straight over there to explain, and I haven't even been able to do that."

"How long did it take you to get over the shock?" Shane asked as he tried to keep a straight face.

"I don't know—a few seconds. It took even longer to get her off me. She had her legs wrapped around my waist like she was trying to squeeze the life out of me."

"And what do you expect me to do about it? Sounds like this is between you and Rebecca."

"Didn't you hear me when I said her crazy mother, AKA *your fiancée*, won't let me near her?!"

"Just call her and talk to her over the phone."

"Her mother broke it last night when I tried to get past her. She broke my damn finger too."

"Cecilia did that?" Shane queried with a raised eyebrow as he looked down at Norman's splinted finger.

"She did a heck of a lot more than that. She's nuts! You gotta talk some sense into her so she'll let me see Becky."

Shane sat forward, "You didn't hurt her, did you?"

"Hurt *her*? Haven't you ever seen what that woman does to guys she don't like? Every night this week, I've asked her nicely to let me see my wife, and she's acted like a nut. A complete nut!"

"What did she do?"

"Monday night, as soon as she opened her door and saw me, she kicked me, literally kicked me, off the porch. I didn't even get the chance to open my mouth to say anything. I'm lucky I didn't break my damn neck tumbling backward down her steps."

Shane's eyebrows shot up an inch as he listened to Norman's tirade.

"So, there I was, laying there hurt, and she comes stomping down the steps and tells me, 'The only way to get in this house is to get through me, and you don't have it in you. Go home Norman,'" he mimicked Cece in a falsetto voice.

"Well, what did you expect? You cheated on her daughter—her *only* daughter—her *pregnant* only daughter."

"I did *not* cheat on my wife! And she won't even let me explain what actually happened. Every time I tried to get past her all week, she did some crazy Kung-Foo moves, and the next thing I know I'm flying all across her yard landing on my ass. It was humiliating, and she was doing it for fun!"

Shane snorted, "What makes you think she did all that for fun?"

Norman let out a humorless chuckle and said, "Last night, after she broke my finger, she let me go inside, and Becky wasn't even there. She hadn't been there all week! Cece knew that, and she still kept up the 'you gotta get through me to get to her' crap."

Shane tried hard not to laugh in the face of his brother's anguish, but a chuckle managed to escape anyway.

"It's not funny," Norman gritted out in his best military commander voice, "not even a little bit."

"Sorry, it's just that it's not like you to make such a bonehead move."

"But I didn't do anything wrong. Julie jumped on me!"

"Oh, so I guess it was a good idea to play a game of basketball with your hot ex-wife while your current wife is probably feeling unattractive and emotional because she's pregnant with *your* twins. Smooth move ex-lax."

Norman stared at the wall for a couple of seconds, and then let his head drop down into his hands. "You're right," he mumbled, "I am a bonehead."

"I'll tell you what; I'll talk to Cecilia for you, but you need to stay away from her so she can cool down."

"That might take a few centuries," Norman mumbled through his hands.

"She's not that bad."

Norman held up his hand with the broken finger and said, "Not that bad, huh? I beg to differ. You should hear the message she left on my cell." Norman pulled out his phone, dialed his voicemail box, and handed the phone to Shane so he could hear for himself just how bad Cece could be.

Shane listened as her voice came on sounding deceptively conversational at first. "Hi, Norman. I came home this evening to find my daughter waiting for me on my front porch. Ordinarily I look forward to a visit from my daughter, but not when she's here because her idiot husband broke her heart. She told me all about your little play date with Juliana, and then she cried until she threw up. You better hope I never see you again, *ever!* Unless you want to be known as a dickless wonder for the rest of your life."

"I don't think she'd actually follow through on that," Shane reassured his brother after handing the phone back to him.

"As if I'd give her the chance," Norman snorted.

"Well, you did let her break your finger."

Norman pinned Shane with one of his more serious looks, one that he typically reserved for work situations, and said, "Domestic violence is a serious issue, Shane. I honestly don't think you should marry that woman. Do you really want to live with someone who will fight you every time you get on her bad side?"

"You don't know anything about what goes on between me and Cecilia. She'd never break my finger," Shane snorted.

"I'm telling you, she's evil. I find it hard to believe she gave birth to someone as nice and sweet as Becky. Maybe she's not even her real mother. Think about it; she's so mysterious about her life before she had kids, and she's way too young to have a fully grown daughter. They don't even look alike! When's the last time you met a mother and daughter who had absolutely no similar features? The hair, the eyes, the skin tone, even their bone structure is like night and day. What if she kidnapped

Becky? Have you ever thought of that? How much do you really know about her?"

Shane felt his good humor starting to dissipate in the face of his brother's accusations toward Cecilia. "Anything else you want to talk about? I'm tired of hearing you run her name through the mud. No one made you hang out with your ex. You know how she is."

Norman shook his head and reclined back on the couch as if he had every intention of staying for a while.

"Is there something I can do for you?"

"What?" Norman popped up. "Am I not welcome in your house now?"

"You don't really want me to answer that after you've been harassing my fiancée all week."

"I see how it is," Norman mumbled as he reclined again.

"If Cecilia stops by, you better pretend you're not here."

"Yeah, that'll work. She'll see my truck out front and assume I parked it here so I can walk home."

"You can stay," Shane relented with a sigh, "but if she happens to stop by, you'd better make yourself scarce."

"Not a problem. That woman is the last person on Earth I want to see today."

Shane slipped on his shoes and said, "I'll be back later," on his way out the door.

He drove straight to Cecilia's house, and when she didn't answer her door, he tried the bakery next. Construction workers were all over the place, and any semblance of her little shop was long gone. Shane stepped inside and noted all the changes that had taken place just in the last week. The floors had been ripped up, the center wall removed, and all the old display cases disposed of.

"May I help you?" an older man stepped forward and asked.

"Yeah, I'm here to see Cecilia Graves. She's the owner."

"I know who she is. You the architect?"

"Architect? No, I'm the fiancé."

"Oh," the old man looked delighted with that news. "Maybe she'll be happy to see you. It's been a rough week around here. She said she was going upstairs for a while."

"Thanks," Shane smiled at the man. He started toward the back, but the man stopped him.

"She's up the stairs on the other side of the building," he said, pointing into the side that Shane wasn't familiar with.

Shane picked his way past all the workers and equipment strewn about the floor. He recalled Cecilia telling him that an ice cream shop was once on the other side of the wall. He briefly looked around at the front before going to the back to find the second set of stairs. He didn't want to catch her by surprise like he did last time, so he made a little more noise than normal on his way up the stairs.

At the top, he found the door wide open, and he could smell roses wafting from the room. He expected a small apartment, much like the one at the top of her bakery, but this space was huge and completely open, except for the counters lining all of the walls. Cecilia stood in the middle of the room tinkering with something that looked like a stove, but he wasn't sure. She was wearing casual clothes instead of the white uniform she always wore to work, and not a hair on her head was out of place. She certainly didn't look like she'd been fighting all week.

"Shane!" she blurted out in surprise when she finally looked up and noticed him. "I thought you'd be gone for a month."

"I'm going back up there Sunday night. I just wanted to come back here for a couple of days since I have the weekend off," he explained.

"Oh?"

"I wanted to see you. How is everything?"

"Great," she lied.

"Norman stopped by my house this morning."

Her hands froze over the concoction she was working with.

"He said you've been giving him a hard time this week."

"Oh really? Is that all he had to say for himself?" she sneered.

Her abrupt change in demeanor almost made him back up a few steps, but he held his ground and said, "He said a lot more than that, but that was the gist of it. Look, Cecilia, I know you think this isn't any of my business, but he's my brother and he's pretty upset with you for keeping him from his wife all week."

"His wife?! He's upset with me? How dare you come in here and tell me that? That idiot cheats on my daughter and you expect me to just step aside and let it continue? She's better off without him, and first thing Monday we're going to see a divorce lawyer."

"So now you've decided they're getting divorced too?"

"Yes!"

"What does Rebecca have to say about that?"

"That's none of your business."

"Cecilia, maybe you should stand aside and let them work it out for themselves."

"She's my daughter. I'm not going to allow him the chance to hurt her again. Once a cheater, always a cheater."

"Norman says Julie jumped on him, and he pushed her off, so technically he didn't cheat," Shane pointed out.

There was a long pause before Cecilia finally responded, "Rebecca didn't mention that part."

"She probably left before it happened. Norman admits that it took him a minute to get her off of him, and I know he's being honest. I know my brother a lot better than you do, and he's no cheater. All he cares about right now is talking to his wife. Why do you think he let you abuse him all week?"

"Stop, Shane. This isn't your business."

"It's as much my business as it is yours," he countered. "Just let them work it out. You don't always have to be so fierce."

"So you're taking his side?"

"This isn't about taking sides. I'm telling you to stay out of it. It's one thing to be there for you daughter, but it's another to keep them apart when they can work through this. You're acting like he hit her or something."

"No I'm not."

"Yes you are."

"If he'd hit her, he'd be dead."

Shane ran an aggravated hand through his hair as he looked down at Cecilia. She had to be one of the most difficult women he ever met. "You want to have lunch?"

"Lunch? Why?" She looked up at him with wide eyes and a little frown, as if she weren't quite sure what to make of his invitation. She was obviously stuck in argument mode right now.

"Because I flew halfway across the country to see you, and I don't want to waste time arguing," he said.

"You came back just to see me?" The hard line of her lips almost softened into a smile.

"Yes." Shane didn't wait for her to speak again. He took her hands and pulled her close to his chest for a hug. He held on for a long time, breathing in her scent, and absorbing some of her pent up negative energy. When she relaxed and hugged him back, he smiled. "This was the longest week ever. I missed you."

"I missed you too."

"I love the way you smell. I don't think I've ever smelled soap that smells so much like roses," he said as he sniffed her hair again.

She giggled and said, "I don't use soap that smells like roses. I always smell like them because I distil rose water to use in my recipes. That's what I'm doing now."

"Rose water?"

"Yes, I make rose oil too, but that takes forever. I could show you how I make the rose water before we go to lunch."

Shane noticed that she seemed to calm down considerably when she got the chance to explain something that had to do with her work. He was more interested in getting affectionate than he was in the process of making rose water, but he listened anyway. At the end of her demonstration, he said, "I'd like to try some of the cake filling you make with the rose syrup. I can't think of another bakery that does that around here, and that gives you a competitive edge. Why haven't you ever advertised the fact that you do this?"

"I don't know. Most people wouldn't think to request a cake with rose flavored filling, even if they knew it existed."

"Why don't you try it on the one for our wedding? You could make at least one of the tiers rose flavored. The guests would love that. They are the sort of people who love anything elitist or gourmet sounding. Even if they don't love the flavor, they'll love the concept."

"I'll think about it."

"You ready to head out for lunch? I'm starving."

"Sure. Just tell me where you want to go, and I'll meet you there."

"Meet me? Why can't we just ride together?"

"Because I need to stop by Karen's to check on Rebecca. I want to make sure she's eating properly."

"Whose idea was it for her to stay there? Yours?"

231

Cecilia stiffened at his question, but he hadn't meant to sound accusing. "Why do you need to know?" she asked.

"So it was your idea."

Cecilia shrugged and looked away.

"You really need to stand aside right now and let Norman and Rebecca sort things out on their own."

Cecilia was silent again, but she looked more sad than angry as she stared down at the jugs of water she'd just finished capping. Something he'd said must have gotten to her, but he decided to let it go for the time being. "I won't say anything else about it. Let's go eat."

When Shane returned to his house later that afternoon, Norman was still sprawled on his couch.

"Did you talk to her?" Norman demanded before Shane could shut the front door.

"Some."

"Some? What is that supposed to mean? Either you talked to her or you didn't."

"She's coming over for a while this evening, and we'll talk more then. She did tell me where Rebecca is staying."

"Where?" Norman sat forward, all eagerness as he awaited Shane's reply.

"You're not going to like it," Shane warned him.

"Just tell me."

"At Karen's house."

"Who the hell is Karen?"

Shane raised his eyebrows and said, "Karen Christian Holly. K.C. Holly the MMA fighter."

"Why is she staying with a fighter? What's she got to do with anything?"

"Karen and Cecilia have been best friends since your wife was six years old."

"Great. So she has two crazy women guarding her."

"Pretty much, and Karen lives in an exclusive gated community. No one gets in there without a security pass."

"Even better," Norman muttered. "I don't even know what you see in that woman. You look up evil in the dictionary and I bet there's a picture of her."

Shane shrugged and said, "Look up stupid in the same dictionary and you'll be there playing basketball and kissing your ex."

"I was in the wrong place at the wrong time."

"However you excuse it, no one made you spend time with her. And to top it off, you know exactly how she is. I'm having company for dinner, so you can't stay."

"I was about to leave anyway."

"Look man, I'm sure things will go back to normal soon. Don't sit around looking like it's the end of the world. You two will work this out."

Norman stood up and yawned on his way out the door. He looked only slightly better than he'd looked on the way in the door. Shane gave his shoulder a squeeze as he left.

Chapter 18

He'd passed right by her, and she'd smiled at him in the park. Women never smiled at him, so he'd ducked his head down and hurried on. He was used to being invisible, and he wanted to remain that way. All month he'd been thinking about that smile. What could she have meant by it? Was it some secret mocking grin meant to ridicule him because of the debacle his life had become? Was it a show of sympathy because she too was familiar with the pain of losing a daughter? What could she have meant by that smile? Women never smiled at him.

He opened his eyes and the painful brightness that intruded on his sleep caused a sharp pain in his head. He'd dozed off last night in Sita's room again. He'd been sitting on her bed staring out the window at the stars, and now he was awake again. He didn't want to be awake again. It was such a beautiful room. The window opposite the bed took up the entire wall, and faced the hillside to the east of the house, giving his daughter a panoramic view of his secluded little property. She'd been spoiled to have such a spectacular room.

He rolled over onto his stomach, and buried his face in the pillow. All he wanted was for the morning sun to go back where it came from. All he wanted was for none of this to have ever happened. He tried to go back to sleep, but he couldn't. He hadn't had a drink in a few hours, and his hands were beginning to shake again. These days it seemed as if he functioned better when he had some liquid courage running through his veins. If he went too long without a sip he had to contend with headaches, nausea, and the shakes. Did that make him a drunk? Did he care if he was a drunk? What was a *meaningless label compared to the horrible truth? He'd rather think of himself as a drunk than a father without a daughter.*

He'd been telling himself every day since Cece smiled at him in the park that today was the day he would go and put flowers on Sita's grave. But every day he hadn't been able to get out of bed or off the couch long enough to make it beyond the bathroom. His nose twitched at the repugnant stench whenever he entered his own bedroom, so he'd started sleeping in Sita's room instead. Today, he really was going to visit her grave. He stood up on wobbly legs and padded out into the massive hall. She deserved some flowers. As he passed by the ornamental, golden hall mirror, he caught a glimpse of himself and remembered why he couldn't visit Sita's grave today. He'd sworn to bring justice with his first visit to her grave, and he still hadn't made it right yet. He still needed to talk to Cece.

He stumbled into his office and sat down at the desk. The letter was up to ten pages now. Soon it would be finished, and he could give it to her. He needed her forgiveness, but even more desperately, he needed her to understand.

He watched her step off the bus, and his old heart immediately tripled its speed. He wasn't so sure if the park at night was the best place to meet her, but he couldn't stand the idea of letting her see his face clearly. She wouldn't recognize him, but he still didn't want her to look upon him in disdain. If he were completely honest with himself, he'd admit that he couldn't stand to have anyone's eyes on him since he'd lost Sita.

As Cece neared him, he jumped off the path and hid in the shadows. He listened to her footsteps as they fell rapidly across the pavement and grew louder as she got closer to him. Just a few yards away now, she was almost there. He clutched at his chest, feeling at once for both the flask and the letter. His palpitations grew unbearable as she came within a few feet of him. He grabbed at the letter, but when he pulled it out of his pocket, the flask dropped to the pavement and startled her.

She whisked around, and then froze for a moment. He felt her eyes scanning the darkness, looking for him, but he couldn't make himself step forward. He could barely breathe, until she turned away and continued walking down the path. Her pace was much quicker now, and he cursed at himself for missing yet another opportunity to talk to her. But no! He could still catch her. He clutched the letter in one hand and sprang into action, chasing her down as he called out her name in the darkness. "Cece! Cece Graves!" he panted in strained tones.

She glanced back at him once, with a look of pure fright, and then she bolted. She ran so fast he had no chance of catching her, but still he tried. He had to make her understand, for Sita.

As soon as she heard the loud clinking of the bottle hitting the pavement, Cece got the feeling that something was terribly wrong. She quickened her pace to hurry home, all the while admonishing herself for being silly. There was nothing to fear here. She lived in a nice neighborhood. She was safe. The past needed to stay firmly behind her. She did not have to jump out of her shoes at every odd sound. Just when she'd managed to calm her racing heart, she heard a voice from the past calling her name. It was the same effeminate, heavily accented voice that had peppered more than half of her nightmares. She'd only heard it one other time in her life, and it was scorched indelibly in her memory, like a permanent scar on her brain.

"Cece! Cece Graves!"

Last time she'd heard that voice it had been threatening her.

"So your name is Cece Graves? Thank you for making it so easy to find you. If you ever tell anyone I *will* find you, and I *will* kill you," that voice had promised over and over again, and she had believed it. And now he had found her. Or was she just imagining things again? Usually that voice was restricted to her nightmares, but she knew she wasn't in one right now. She was always tied down in the nightmares, but now she was running. Even as these thoughts ricocheted through her mind, she continued to flee as fast as she could.

As the yelling behind her grew fainter, she glanced back once, but it was too dark for her to see more than a vague impression of a person's shadow. That one glance back was almost her undoing. The instant she turned back around, she ran into another shadow that had no intention of letting go. She nearly screamed as a pair of hands clamped around her shoulders, but instinct kicked in instead. She thrust her knee up with enough force to free herself from the shadow's iron grip. When it doubled over in pain, she stepped back and kicked it again. As the shadow in front of her fell, she sensed the one behind her closing in on her. She sprinted away on legs that felt shaky and clumsy as they carried her across the park.

Too afraid to go home alone, she ran straight to Shane's house to find that he wasn't home. Rather than wait for him outside, she skulked back to her own house and sneaked inside. She turned on all the lights and went through every closet and cupboard in every room. When she found nothing out of the ordinary, she also went through the security footage captured by the external cameras around her house. Nothing unusual appeared on the surveillance video, but still she had to go through the entire routine several more times before she stopped shaking enough to function.

Her throat was parched from all the deep breathing, so she went to her kitchen to drink a glass of water, and then promptly threw it up. She paced in circles, trying to settle her stomach, but nothing she told herself helped her calm down. She walked through her house in such a state of agitation and emotional pain her skin felt like bugs were literally crawling all over her. She stopped pacing after a while and sat down, but she couldn't remove that effeminate voice from her head, calling her name in the darkness. She beat her fists against both ears in a desperate attempt to banish that voice from her head, but still it was there.

"If you go to the police, you're a dead little girl!" the voice had rasped at her in the darkness. "Get in the water! I'm watching, so you better wash good. If it looks like you're trying anything funny, I'll kill you right now."

Her thirteen year old legs had been awfully unsteady as she'd stepped into the running shower. Cold water had spurted out at her, snatching her breath away and adding to the disorientation she'd felt after being blindfolded and tied down for so long.

She sank down to the floor of her empty living room, reliving both that cold shower and the fear that had almost crushed her completely. Who had grabbed her in the park? Why had he come looking for her after all these years? Despondent tears sprang from all the memories she'd stuffed down over the years, memories of things no person should ever have to endure. Every detail of that torturous event attacked her all at once, and she opened her mouth to scream out in silent agony. She felt threatened down to her very soul as she curled up into the corner and wept into her hands.

Once Shane wrapped up his month of water rescue training, his relationship with Cecilia took a sizable leap forward. Upon his return to Nashville, they started spending time together on a daily basis. Their relationship managed to progress, even with Norman and Rebecca's separation looming in the forefront of Cecilia's mind. There hadn't been anymore altercations with Norman, but her stance on keeping them apart hadn't changed. Shane didn't pressure her about it, and they managed to have some meaningful interactions despite her animosity towards his brother.

Since the details of the wedding had started taking over his life, Shane made a more conscious effort to enjoy their quieter moments together. His favorite part of the day was his short walk through the park with Cecilia when she got off the bus in the evenings. Every night for the past week, he'd met her somewhere around the fountain and took the long way back to her house. He loved the way her face lit up when she came around the bend and saw him standing there waiting for her.

For the past few days, he'd been gently nudging her to consider making the wedding they were planning into a real one. He smiled as he recalled their last conversation on the subject. They had been sitting on her front porch, enjoying the crisp evening air. Her hand had been in his and her head had rested against his shoulder.

"Do you really think you should be inviting so many people?" she yawned.

"All I'm doing is inviting everyone who calls and drops hints that they want to be included on the guest list."

"But Shane, over five hundred people? Don't you think that's excessive?"

"Not at all. They're all just more potential customers for you in the future."

"I guess when you put it that way, it makes sense."

"Everything I do makes perfect sense," he smiled.

She looked up at him with a raised eyebrow and gave him a playful punch to the arm. He caught her hand and brought it to his lips. "So, while we're on the subject, have you ever thought about what kind of wedding you'd want to have if you ever got married for real? Don't all girls fantasize about that at some point in their lives?"

He felt her grow tense beside him, but she took in a deep breath and answered anyway, "I've never fantasized about a wedding or even marriage. I did always dream about being successful and independent. I have that now, so I guess all my dreams came true years ago. Being well known and respected as a cake designer would be like the icing on top of everything else."

"Independent, huh?" Shane said. He tightened his arm around her and breathed in the rosy scent of her hair. "Do you think you'll ever want to marry a man? I understand that independence is important to you, but marriage and independence don't have to be mutually exclusive."

"Please," she scoffed. "I've seen how the average married woman acts like she can't do anything without her husband attached to her hip."

"Not all marriages are like that," Shane countered.

"Name one that isn't."

"Your daughter's marriage isn't like that. Aside from you, she's the most independent person I know, and she and Norman have a very loving relationship."

"Yeah, before he messed everything up."

"We don't have to get back on that subject again. They're going to work through it, and you know they're a good example." When she didn't say anything for a few minutes, he pressed on. "Actually, I'd say that a stable, committed relationship with the right person can reinforce someone's independence and make them stronger in the long run. What do you think about that?"

"I don't know. I don't put much thought into relationships. I guess that comes from not wanting to get my hopes up about someone. Other people can only disappoint you if you let them, and I decided long ago not to let anyone have that power over me."

"With that attitude, you're missing out on some of the best things life has to offer. If you can't open yourself up to the possibility of some disappointment along the way, how are you ever going to let love in?"

"You make it sound like it's so simple and easy, but it isn't. When I was younger, all I ever wanted was for some nice people to adopt me, so I let myself hope for years—*years*. And then when I finally did get lucky with a nice family, they gave me back to the state. They told me they would keep me, and adopt me, and love me, but they gave me back instead. Why should I open myself up to that kind of pain and disappointment again when my life is just fine the way it is?"

"What if you came across someone who wouldn't do that to you? Would you run from him because of things from your past that had nothing to do with him?"

"I guess I'll find out if I ever come across him."

"*When* you come across him, and he asks you to marry him, don't say no based on things that happened in your past. Can you promise me that?"

"That depends. Who am I having this conversation with? Shane, my friend and pretend fiancé who is doing my business a huge favor? Or, Shane, the man I'm dating?"

"Since I'm only one person, I guess it's both, but mostly it's the guy you're dating—the one who's falling for you."

A faint shout in the distance snapped Shane back to the present just in time to see Cecilia come flying around the bend. She was obviously running from someone, so he sprinted towards her to help. Someone shouted her name again, and she glanced over her shoulder just before he caught up to her. When she turned back around, she slammed into him full force, and if he hadn't reached out his hands to steady her, they both would have tumbled to the ground.

He opened his mouth to ask her what was wrong, but she looked down and grabbed at his hands in wild panic. Someone shouted her name again from the shadows beyond the bend, and the next thing Shane knew, a terrible pain had exploded in his groin. He doubled over in agony, and when he looked up again he saw Cecilia's foot coming directly at his face. He barely had time to flinch before it connected with a solid thwack to his nose. He fell to the ground, and she leapt over him, continuing her wild flight into the darkness.

"Cecilia! Wait!" he called out, but she kept running and was quickly out of sight. It took a few minutes for the pain to subside enough for him to let go of the affected area and stop rolling around on the ground. His nose bled, and felt like it was probably broken. He sat up and gingerly prodded at his nose to feel for any obvious breaks in the bone. He was about to get up when someone appeared beside him. The person was wheezing and so far out of shape they kept stopping to recover. Shane squinted into the darkness and was able to make out the figure of a very old and slender man.

"Cece!" the man wheezed several more times, but Cecilia was long gone. When the man tried to jog past him, Shane reached out and grabbed his ankle, causing him to fall to the ground.

"Why are you following her?" Shane rasped out past all the pain in his nose and his groin.

"Don't hurt me," the old man huffed as he cowered, covering his face with both hands. "I have to give her something, but I startled her and she ran from me."

"Why are you trying to give her something at night in the park with no one else around?" Shane asked with menace in his voice as his grip around the old man's ankle tightened.

"Please!" the man wailed in such a feminine tone Shane thought for a second that he might actually be a very ugly old woman and not a man at all. He squinted at the man again just to be certain. "It's because my daughter was raped, and then she killed herself. I need to talk to Cece. Please don't hurt me! I just want her to understand."

"Is this about the foundation?" Shane demanded.

"Yes! The Cece Graves Foundation, for survivors of abuse and sexual assault," the man said as he fumbled frantically in his pocket. He pulled out a crumpled brochure and thrust it at Shane.

"I didn't mean to scare her," he said with tears in his voice.

Shane felt bad for manhandling the little, old guy, so he let go of his ankle and stood up. The man stood up too, and when he looked up and noticed the height difference between them, he blanched. Even without the tears all over his face, the man was one of the most pathetic creatures Shane had ever laid eyes on. He shook like a leaf, and sadness wafted off of him in palpable waves. Shane felt like he should have offered the old man a hand, and instead he had knocked him to the ground. He was about to apologize when the man suddenly took off in the direction he came from. He ran so slowly, and with such an awkward gait, his attempt to flee was almost comical. Shane found it even more farcical that he couldn't have caught the old man even if he'd tried, because Cecilia's kick had affected him so badly.

Once he'd seen the old man, Shane didn't see the point in chasing Cecilia. She'd obviously been startled by him, but she hadn't been in any real danger. They could talk tomorrow after she'd had a chance to calm down and he'd had a chance to recover. It was difficult for him to let it go; almost everything inside him screamed for him to follow her, but he knew she liked to be left alone while working through emotional stresses like this one. He knew she still had nightmares, but for the sake of their relationship, he gave her space instead of expressing too much concern. That was what she'd told him she wanted, but sometimes it was really difficult to comply with her wishes. This was one of those times.

Shane bent down to retrieve the brochure the man had dropped, and found a sealed envelope with Cece's name lying on the ground beside it. After briefly wondering about the contents, Shane stuck the envelope in his pocket and limped home for the night. Blood stained the front of his shirt, and he had serious doubts as to whether or not his testicles would ever feel normal again.

After he made it home and took a shower, he sat for a long time on the edge of his bed and stared at the envelope. He wondered if he should even bother giving it to Cecilia. She already had enough stress in her life without adding on the woeful tale of a complete stranger. Reading about that man's daughter would likely stir up painful memories from her past, and she'd been so relaxed for the past few weeks. In fact, if the drama between Norman and Rebecca didn't exist, he could have described her mood as purely happy. He didn't want the contents of some stranger's life to ruin that for her.

He also spent a lot of time trying to figure out why Cece had been so frightened by such a small person. If she could bring a man his size down with just two swift kicks, she should have been able to laugh off the threat from that pathetic old man in the park. Yet she'd run from him as if her life had depended on it.

Eventually he fell asleep, but something about Cecilia's reaction to the old man kept niggling at the back of his mind. After a few hours of tossing and turning, he finally gave up trying to sleep and pulled the envelope out of his wastebasket. As soon as he read the first line of the letter, a sick feeling settled in the pit of his stomach. He sat on the edge of his bed and read on:

Cece Graves,

I'm sure by now you've cursed me a thousand times in your mind, maybe even a million. I've always been sorry for my part in what was done to you all those years ago. I've just never had the courage to come forward and apologize. I guess you are wondering why I suddenly have the courage to come forward now, but it isn't courage. It's just that now I have nothing to lose.

Just last year, my own daughter was raped by several young men from her university. Following a very public and humiliating trial, the men were acquitted and my daughter ended her own life.

From the first moment of this ordeal, I've known that my present circumstances are the universe's way of paying me back for what happened to you in Atlanta. I believe you Americans might call it poetic justice, but I know it as karma.

For months now, I've been trying to gather the courage to beg you for the forgiveness that I know I don't deserve. My dear daughter, Sita, would be shocked at my past actions if she were alive today. I doubt even she would forgive me, and she's loved me her entire life. I've thought a million times about what I should say and how I should say it, but nothing I've come up with seems to be enough. Nothing I can say to you will ever take it away or make it right.

The impact of those actions didn't become clear to me until I witnessed my own daughter fall apart when it happened to her. I wish with my entire heart that I could take away the pain she went through, and all the pain you must have gone through. The night I found her in her room dead, I felt as if my soul had been permanently ripped from my body. I will never be a normal, simple man again. My daughter was the only person I had, the only person I have ever loved.

I've been trying to tell you for months now how sorry I am, but I never seem to catch you at the right time. That is why I decided to write this letter instead of trying to explain in person. There is just too much to say. Last time I saw you in the park, you smiled at me. You didn't recognize me. You wouldn't of course, not after all this time, and not after being blindfolded until I set you free. Whatever you think of me, I hope you remember that I did set you free, although I didn't have to. I can't bear to imagine what that man would have done to me had he caught me.

Perhaps you will forgive me enough to tell me what happened to Sarah. I watched you visit her grave in the cemetery the day of that big thunderstorm. In all these years, I never considered the fact that a child could have resulted from my actions. Now that I know I've likely fathered two dead daughters, my pain has increased beyond measure. Only you could know for sure if Sarah was mine as I suspect, but I don't expect you to tell me. Actually, I expect that after you read this, the police will drag me off to prison any day. It is what I deserve. It is what those cowards who took my Sita away from me deserve...

The rest of the letter gave details about the last few months of his daughter's life, but Shane only skimmed over the multitude of pages. The letter grew more rambling and detached from reality as it went on. He didn't realize he'd crumpled some of the pages in his fist until he was able to tear his eyes away from the last page he read. All this time he had been right to suspect that someone was following her. Suddenly, the apologetic note left on her car the week of the fire made perfect sense. He just never suspected that it had come from the very man who had raped her all those years ago. Now he understood why Cecilia had been so panic-stricken in the park tonight. She must have recognized something about him, even after more than two decades. He threw on some clothes, gathered up all the pages to the letter, and called his brother Brent on the way to Cecilia's house.

"It's four o'clock in the morning; this had better be an emergency," Brent groused into the phone after the first ring.

"It sort of is. I really need you to pull some strings for me, Man."

"What kind of strings?"

"There's an envelope on my counter in a plastic baggie that I need you to come pick up and run a DNA test on. I can't really get into all the details right now, but I'll come by your office today and tell you everything."

"Just tell me what you can right now."

"The cretin who raped my fiancée twenty something years ago just left a letter confessing to the whole thing. He's been following her around for months, and he's seriously deranged. He needs to be taken off the streets ASAP. See if you can get a rush job on getting a DNA sample off the enveloped that he probably licked and compare it to a sample from Rebecca. If he's her father, which he is, then that's all the proof we need to put this guy away."

Brent sighed into the phone one time before saying, "Okay, I'm on it. Is your spare key still under that plant?"

"Yeah," Shane said as he disconnected.

Shane stuck his phone in his pocket as he approached Cecilia's door. He raised his fist to knock, but the door came open as soon as his knuckles connected. He stepped inside and called out for Cecilia, but there was no answer. There were no signs of a struggle and her car was still in the garage, so he started searching for her in the same manner he would search for victims in a fire. He stomped through the house and called her name repeatedly as he searched every room, including all the closets and cupboards. Eventually, he found her huddled deep in the corner of her closet under a pile of blankets clutching a kitchen knife. She hadn't heard any of the noise he'd just made, and was still sound asleep. He removed the knife from her hands and set it aside before attempting to wake her.

"Cecilia, it's Shane," he said several times as he gently shook her shoulder.

Eventually her eyes popped open, "What are you doing here? How did you get in?"

He ignored her first question for the time being, and said, "You left your door open. Are you okay?"

"No."

"Do you want to tell me what's wrong?"

She sat up and rubbed sleep out of her eyes. "I honestly think I may be losing my mind. Last night it seemed like two men tried to grab me in the park, and one of them... well one of them sounded just like someone else. Someone it couldn't have been. I thought I'd gotten over being so paranoid, but last night was so real. I actually thought someone was after me, and that one of them grabbed me when I tried to run. I've been scared out of my mind all night, but now I'm not even sure how much of it, if any, actually happened." She peeped up at him when she was done talking. The look in her eyes told him that she expected him to judge her somehow.

Even if he hadn't been there last night, and read the letter, he still wouldn't have judged her. He put his arm around her and said, "One of the men in the park last night was me. You were running from someone, and you bumped into me, but you kicked me before I could ask you what was wrong."

"That was you?"

"Yes."

"And the other man?"

Shane pulled the letter from his pocket. "He was there too. He dropped this before he ran off last night." He handed her the crumpled pages of the letter and went on, "I should warn you; he's been following you around, and he's definitely the man who raped you."

Her eyes flashed up at him and she let out a ragged sigh. "So I'm not crazy," she said, reaching for the letter.

"No, you're not crazy at all."

She didn't say anything for a while, but her hands shook as she looked down at the letter.

"Come on; let's get you out of this closet."

"I'm sorry I kicked you last night. I thought you were someone else. I even ran straight to your house to find you, but you weren't there."

"I'm here now, and that criminal can't hurt you anymore. We're going to make sure he spends the rest of his life behind bars," Shane said as he put his arm around her and pulled her against his chest. "I'm not going to let anything happen to you."

Shane didn't want to intrude on what was certainly one of the most private moments of her life, so when she pulled back, he let her go and quietly stepped out of the closet. He walked around her house and looked for something else to do. The sun hadn't come up yet, and the house was in disarray from his search for her earlier. He went around closing all the doors and cabinets. When he finished, she still hadn't come out of the closet yet, so he sat and waited patiently on her bed.

When she finally did emerge, she looked even more morose than when he'd first found her. He stood up to give her another hug. "I've already called my brother Brent. He'll get this taken care of quickly," he said as he gathered her up in his arms again.

"What do you mean?"

"I saved the envelope to turn in for DNA testing. Once we get the results and add that to his loony ten page confession, he'll go to prison for a long time for what he did to you."

She stiffened and looked up at him with accusation in her eyes. "Why did you have to involve your brother?"

"Because he can help. Don't you want this to be over? Don't you want justice after all these years?"

"But it isn't that simple, Shane."

"How much more simple could it be? The man confessed, and even he expects to go to prison. He said so himself in that letter."

"It still isn't simple. You just don't understand."

"What don't I understand? That he raped a thirteen year old? Sure, it happened years ago, but it still happened!"

"I know that! But don't you think seeing his daughter go through the same thing and then losing her is punishment enough?"

"It's sad that's what drove him to confess, but it doesn't take away what he did to you. I can't believe you, of all people, would defend him." He pulled back so he could see her face, but she kept her eyes directed at the floor. "Cecilia, he needs to go to prison. Letting him be free to go about his merry way isn't going to bring his daughter back."

"I know," she said with tears in her voice. "I know it won't bring her back, but I just don't feel right about dragging all of this out right now. I mean, I've moved past it. I don't want to have to testify at some trial and have people asking me questions about my life back then. None of that is anybody's business."

"There probably won't even be a trial, Cecilia. He confessed, and he's clearly unstable. And he's been stalking you for months now. Doesn't that concern you at all?"

"Look, Shane, I appreciate your concern, but I need some time to think about all of this."

"What is there to think about?"

"I just..." she hesitated and then walked away from him when tears started coursing down her cheeks.

"Cecilia, this is a good thing. And with the DNA results you won't even have to look at this guy again. This man hurt you so bad you won't even allow yourself to love. You've spent years living a half-life, and letting fear dictate almost every move you make, all because of him. Don't you want justice for what you went through? My God, Cecilia! You were thirteen! And you got pregnant. He may be a small person who has a sad story, but this man is still a monster."

Shane's phone rang before Cecilia could say anything else, and the only reason he took the call was because it was his brother Brent.

"I have the envelope, but I'm going to need to enter the letter as evidence too. I also need to get a sample from Rebecca, either I could go to her, or she could come to my office to submit it later today. It takes a few weeks to get DNA results back from the lab, so the sooner we get started on this the better."

"Thanks, Brent. She just finished reading the letter. I'll bring it when I come to your office later. Are you going to be able to pick this guy up for stalking her? He's been following her around for months."

Brent sighed into the phone. "That might be kind of dicey. Unless you have some proof that he broke into her house or her business, I can't. Plus I still don't know who the guy is. Does he leave a name in his letter?"

"No. There aren't any personal details about him, only things about his daughter."

"So right now all we have is a confession letter from a John Doe, and a possible DNA match. She could file a restraining order against a John Doe with a DNA profile that matches the one we generate from the letter, and we can pick him up as soon as he violates it, but I can't just assign a detail to watch her. That would be seriously overstepping my authority based on what little we have to go on at the moment. I need more, and that letter will help."

"We can talk more about all this when I come to your office. I'll give you a call before I head over. I'll try to talk her into seeing if we can get a restraining order."

"Talk her into it?"

248

"She doesn't want to cooperate."

"Well that could make things pretty difficult, and by difficult I mean damn near impossible."

"That's not what I wanted to hear."

"I'll take care of what I can on my end, and you do whatever you think is best on yours."

Shane disconnected and found Cecilia in the kitchen staring out the window. Water ran out of the faucet as she held her hands under the flow. She wasn't washing them; she just held them steady as the warm water continued over them and down the drain. She was lost in thoughts that Shane could only guess at. He stood behind her, wrapped his arms around her, and pulled her close to his chest. Every bit of the tension and sadness inside her was evident to him; he knew she wanted him to drop it, but he took in a deep breath and said, "You need to get dressed so we can go down to the courthouse and try to get a restraining order against this guy; it's a longshot, but we have to try. After that, we're going to stop by Brent's office and start the process of getting him off the streets."

"Shane..."

"I'm not taking no for an answer. Not this time, Cecilia. This is too important, and if you can't do it for yourself then at least do it for all the other women who have gone through the same thing without ever getting justice." She let her head drop back against his chest, and he bent down to kiss her forehead. "I know it's hard, but you can do this. You did a beautiful job raising your daughter all on your own, but you don't have to do this alone. I'll be there with you every step of the way. We can do this, Honey."

"Shane, I can't. I just can't."

"Why can't you? You've let this one man have so much power over you for so long. Why let it continue? What am I missing here?"

She pushed away from him and tried to walk out of the room, but Shane refused to let her go. He whisked her back around and tilted her face up. She tried to avoid his eyes, and he sensed shame in her expression. "What don't I understand?" he asked more gently.

She wrenched her face out of his grasp and tried to get free again. He kept a firm hold on her. "What don't I understand, Cecilia?" he whispered.

"Let me go!" she attempted to snarl at him but, her voice broke into a pathetic little sob.

Her pain became his at that moment, and he felt tears stinging the back of his eyes. "I care so much; just let me help you. *Talk to me.* I want to understand. Why let him go free? Why let this one man continue to have so much power over you?"

She struggled against him, and even struck him in the chest several times as she tried to get free again. Her punches lacked any real conviction, and she finally just gave up trying to get out of his arms and let her head fall to his chest in surrender.

"We have to wait until we get the DNA results before we do anything else," she whispered.

"Why?" he whispered back.

"Because..." she paused as her breath came in short gasps that sounded like a panic attack. Her entire body shook as she went on, "He wasn't the only one."

Tears escaped Shane's eyes as he closed them tight and breathed in the rosy scent of her hair. "How many were there?"

"I'm not sure, and I wouldn't be able to identify any of them even if I knew. I was blindfolded the entire time."

"How did you recognize the man from the park?"

"His voice. He's the only one who spoke to me. He's also the one who let me go. He said that, if I ever reported it, he'd find me and kill me, so I ran. I just kept running."

"Let you go? What happened? Were you kidnapped?"

"Something like that."

"Can you recall anything else about it? Like who kidnapped you? How long were you held captive?"

"Shane, please. I can't deal with all these questions right now. I just can't." She hid her face in his shirt again, and he felt her tears, warm and wet, against his skin.

"We'll get through this together. You tell me what you want me to do, and I'll do it. I'll do anything for you."

"Just drop it then. Let's forget all about that letter and move on."

Shane wanted to howl out in frustration, but he somehow contained his emotions and told her, "I'll do anything but that. I'd kill that guy before I'd just drop it." He hadn't intended to make such a strong statement when he'd opened his mouth, but now that the words were out, he didn't take them back. "We'll see what the DNA results say, and then we'll go from there," he added in a softer tone.

"Okay," she relented.

"In the meantime, you are not staying alone. I'm not taking no on that point either. If you don't want to come to my house, I'll just stay here with you until this gets resolved."

"That's not necessary."

"Yes it is."

"You didn't let me finish. I can stay with Karen. It's safer there, Rebecca is there, and she already has a full time bodyguard to keep her dad from wandering off. I'll be more comfortable there, because she lives in a gated community. The chances of him getting in are slim."

Shane gritted his teeth. "I didn't think about Karen. I'd rather have you with me, but her house sounds like the best option right now."

Cecilia straightened up and said, "You don't have to play the hero here, Shane. I can handle this on my own."

"Just because you can, doesn't mean you should. You have so much going on right now, all of it big and life changing. How about letting me carry some of the load? Trust me, I can handle it. Besides, I've already told you I'm here to stay." He sealed his words with a kiss to her forehead. He made such a loud smooch with his lips the sound echoed in the empty kitchen. When he looked down at Cecilia's face again she was smiling. It was a small smile, but it warmed his heart none-the-less.

When she wiped her eyes and yawned, Shane looked down at his watch. It wasn't yet five in the morning, and he was starting to feel the effects of his sleepless night. "I don't know about you, but I think it would be a good idea to get a little more sleep before starting the day. The courthouse won't be open for a few more hours, and Brent doesn't expect us until this afternoon."

"Will you stay here with me? I don't want to be alone right now."

"Of course I'll stay," Shane said.

She looked up at him, and then took his hand. She led him back to her bedroom, and lay down on top of the covers. When he lay down beside her, she inched closer to him until they were face to face. He reached out and drew her against his chest.

"Thank you, Shane," she whispered.

"For what?"

"For always being here when I need you."

Chapter 19

Brent sat in his car and wondered how he'd let Cece talk him into what he was about to do. He was a District Attorney for Middle Tennessee; he was not some two-bit private investigator who needed to sneak around to collect evidence. He'd felt incredibly silly when the security guard at the gate had smirked at him for showing his official badge to get into the neighborhood. Shane and Cece were the only two people, besides him, who knew about the letter. Brent had taken possession of the letter a few days ago, and the lab had been working on generating a DNA profile from saliva on the envelope and dried tears on the text of the letter. Now all he needed was a sample from Rebecca to compare it to.

Cece had been adamant about not wanting her daughter to know anything. She'd insisted on having Brent come collect the sample out of the trash tonight, and he just wanted to get it over with as soon as possible so as not to delay the lab results. Cece seemed to think sneaking around was the only way to avoid potential questions. Rebecca chewed a lot of gum, and Cece had promised to place a used gum in a plastic bag at the top of the trash can. Brent was supposed to retrieve it after all the lights went out for the night. He'd been sitting in his car for more than an hour, waiting for the last light to go out.

As he sat, trying not to feel too frustrated about how long it was taking, he thought about some of the cases he'd worked during his career as a criminal prosecutor. Cases involving sex crimes against children tended to stick in the minds and hearts of most people who worked them, and he had personally prosecuted a number of such cases. During his one interview with Cece, he'd gotten the feeling that she was holding back a heck of a lot more than she was telling them. He'd taken Shane aside and told him that, even if the DNA didn't match up, there was still a good chance of prosecuting the perpetrator if they could secure a full taped confession and Cece's testimony in front of a grand jury. He hoped it wouldn't come to that. He hoped for a swift and easy conclusion with a DNA match. If they had that, they could prosecute him for statutory rape with or without Cece's help. After the DNA hurdle was cleared, the next step was to figure out just who the hell the guy was.

Brent closed his eyes briefly as he yawned, and when he opened them again, the last light was out. He waited several more minutes before getting out of his car. Cece had placed the bag at the top of the can more than an hour ago, and the neighborhood was completely quiet now. He crept up to the trash can, opened the lid and lifted the bag out. Just as promised, there was a small wad of red gum in the bag. On the way back to his car, he paused to stick it in his pocket, and something knocked him down from behind. When he tried to get up, someone grabbed his arm and twisted it in such a way he thought it was going to break. He tried to turn his head to see who was holding his arm, but a foot came down slowly on his neck. It applied just enough pressure to make him go completely still.

"What the hell were you doing going through my trash?" a female voice demanded.

Brent almost laughed at his rotten luck. It wasn't enough for him to get caught, but he just had to get caught by the one woman he'd most like to avoid. "Still like to attack first and ask questions later, I see." His mouth was jammed against the pavement, making that statement painful to get out. It sounded much cooler in his head than it did coming out of his mouth.

"Do I know you?" she asked with some hesitation.

"Not really, but believe it or not, I had legitimate business here tonight. I'm taking care of something for Shane and Cece."

"What?"

"I'm not at liberty to say."

"Who are you?"

"Shane's brother, Brent Gregory."

"How do I know you're telling the truth?"

"Check my cell phone. It's in my back pocket. Cece just left me a message about an hour ago. Read it if you want to." When she didn't move he added, "I'm not going to try anything, Karen. Just take out the phone if you want to see the message."

"How do you know my name?"

"You introduced yourself at their engagement party a few months ago, right after you threw your drink in my face."

Those happened to be the magic words that got him released. He slowly got to his feet and looked down at her. She was just as stunning as he remembered from their first encounter. She'd been wearing a strapless dress that showed off the best shoulders and back he'd ever seen. He'd approached her in order to strike up a conversation. He'd only seen her from behind all evening as she'd flitted around from group to group like some elusive little fairy. Once he'd finally gotten close enough to say hi, he still hadn't been prepared to encounter the most gorgeous woman he'd ever seen in his life.

"This is some party," he'd said from behind her, and then she'd turned around. Her hair was a pure, platinum blond that shone like a halo on top of her perfect features. Eyes too clear light blue to be real, big wide eyes that a man could get lost in, had looked up at him in surprise. As he'd looked into her face, every single thought in his head escaped him and he'd stared like a primitive idiot with his mouth hung open and said, "Oh my God!" He'd been lucky to get that much out.

Her surprise had melted away into anger as she threw her drink at him. "Good for you, you got to stare at Karen Christian Holly, the famous MMA fighter," she'd snarled up at him. He was too shocked to do much besides wipe his face as everyone in the immediate area stared at the two of them. Karen looked around once with a horrified expression, and then zipped out of the room. He hadn't seen her since, until tonight.

He reached into his back pocket and handed the phone to her, "Check the text message log," he instructed.

"It's in the top of the trash can," she read out loud. "What's in the top of the trash can?"

"Only Cece can answer that question. I didn't mean to scare you, so I'll be on my way now."

"You didn't scare me," she snorted. "And I'm sorry about what happened at the engagement party. I don't normally treat fans that way, not even the ones who get all star struck like you did. I was having a bad month, because I'd just found out that I have to retire soon. I could give you an autographed poster to make up for it."

"You thought I was a star struck fan?" he chuckled

"Weren't you? That's how most people act right before they start with the screaming and the asking for my autograph," she explained.

"Honey, when I went home that night I had to Google you to figure out just who you were. I'd never heard of you—not that I'm not impressed now—but I wasn't star struck that night."

"Then why did you act like you were?"

"I noticed you at the party, and I wanted to talk to you and maybe ask you out, and then when you turned around and I saw your face, I kind of forgot to think for a couple of seconds."

"You wanted to ask me out?"

"I did," Brent said as he turned and walked back towards his car. He felt her eyes boring into his back almost the whole time, but despite the almost overwhelming temptation, he didn't glance back even once.

Two weeks later, Shane was in the middle of wrapping up his work for the night when Karen walked into the classroom.

"Hello," he smiled at her. She looked like she wanted to say something, but she hesitated in the doorway before entering.

"I bet you're wondering what I'm doing here," she began with a frown.

"Are you here about that thing that happened with my brother?" he asked.

"Which thing?"

"You tossed your drink on him at the engagement party. He told me all about that weeks ago; don't worry about it."

"Not that thing. I'm here about the other thing. I caught him sneaking around my trash the other week, and when I confronted him, he said he was doing something for you and Cece. What was he doing?"

Shane sat down at his desk, feeling like he was about to go into battle woefully unprepared. "That's something I can't talk to you about."

"I think you can," she sat down across from him as if she had every intention of staying for a while.

"Look, Karen, you might find out what's going on soon, but I can't talk about it right now."

"I think you *can*. Remember a few months ago when I told you all about the day Sarah died? That's something she never talks about—*ever*. I can tell something is up, and you'd better tell me what it is."

"Karen, I can't. I promised her I'd keep this to myself."

"She's my best friend, Shane. Why would she trust you with whatever is going on and not me?"

Shane sighed and ran a hand through is hair in aggravation. "Look, if it makes you feel any better, I found out by accident. If given a choice she wouldn't have told me at all."

"So, it means nothing to you that I confided in you for her benefit? You know I wouldn't do anything to upset her. I'm only asking because I care."

"I understand that, but I can't talk about any of this right now. All I can say for sure is that Cecilia is going through a difficult time in her life, maybe even one of the hardest things she's ever dealt with. Hell, even I'm having a hard time with it all."

"What could possibly be worse than the day her daughter died? I was there, and trust me, *that* was the worst time of her life. It was the worst time of my life too."

"I'm sure it was, Karen."

"It was," she stressed as she got up to leave. Shane wasn't sure, but he thought he detected the gleam of unshed tears in her eyes as she glared at him on her way out the door. He sat at his desk and tried to calm down before calling his bumbling brother.

"Hey, Shane! I was just about to call you," Brent answered on the first ring.

"How did you manage to get caught? Karen was just here asking a bunch of questions about you snooping in the trash! What the hell were you doing going through her trash? I thought we agreed that Cecilia would bring you the sample."

"Well, she texted me that day and told me she didn't feel comfortable doing that. She said she'd leave it in the top of the trash. I think she's paranoid about going out alone, so I didn't give her a hard time about it."

"Did you have to get caught though? She really wants to keep this quiet until we have the DNA results. She could barely tell me that the guy who's been following her around wasn't the only one. She's not ready to talk to her daughter about any of this, especially since we don't even know for sure if we have the proof we need."

"We know now. I have the results on my desk in front of me. That's why I called."

Shane sat forward, "And?"

"Do you want to come down here and we all find out together? Or should I just open it and tell you now?"

"Just tell me now, so we can move forward." Shane listened to the rustling of papers over the phone line as he waited.

"We got him," Brent said.

"What does that mean?"

"Means this guy dug his own grave. I was worried about prosecuting this case because the statute of limitations ran out more than ten years ago. I was hoping to get an exception based on his confession and Cece's testimony, but now we don't even need that. In the state of Georgia, the statute of limitations for prosecuting sex crimes against children doesn't apply to cases with DNA evidence. Impregnating a thirteen year old is about as strong as the evidence gets in cases like this. He is definitely the father, and Cece is definitely the mother. Now all we need to do is figure out who this guy is, and notify the Atlanta prosecutor. She'll be the one handling the sexual assault portion of this mess, but I can assist her as much as she allows."

Shane closed his eyes and said a silent prayer of thanks. At least now they could move forward with or without Cecilia's consent.

"My assistant already ran his profile through the national database, and there were no matches. There weren't any print matches either. Whoever this guy is, he's never been in any serious trouble; at least he's never been caught."

"What's the next step?" Shane asked.

"Now that we have the DNA evidence, I can file stalking charges against a John Doe with a DNA profile matching the one we generated from the letter. The Atlanta prosecutor will have to file the charges for the sexual assault using the same DNA profile. Once that's done, I can dedicate some more resources to catching this guy. I think the best chance we have of catching him now is to narrow our search down to older men who recently lost a daughter in the Atlanta area. It may sound simple, but it takes time and resources to generate a list of suspects and then to narrow it down. I'll do everything I can, but this is going to take some time."

"I understand. Can I help out with anything?"

"See if you can get her to come in and give a detailed statement about everything that happened to her. She's holding back a lot, and I can tell. Once we know all the details, we might be able to find this guy. I've worked so many cases like this one, it's second nature to me to be able to tell when victims feels shame. You need to push her to talk, but not too hard. She probably feels like she's going to be judged for what happened, so be delicate."

"I can do that. Anything else?"

"Yeah, totally off topic, but tell her friend Karen she should keep her damn hands and feet to herself," Brent said before he disconnected.

Shane gathered up his things to leave the classroom, but on his way out the door, Karen hopped in front of him. "Who's been following her around? And what do you mean he wasn't the only one? What the hell is going on?"

"Jeez, Karen! Why the hell were you listening to my conversation with my brother?" Shane demanded in outrage.

She took a couple of steps back and shrugged, "I wasn't planning on it. I was about to leave when I heard you mention my name. I had to listen to the rest after that," she explained.

"You've got a lot of nerve—"

"No, *you* have a lot of nerve!" she interrupted. "First, you come out of nowhere and steal my best friend from me, and now you're trying to shut me out. Just tell me what's going on right now."

"Good grief. You're just as bossy as my sister, Shelly. If you were a little taller and had red hair, you would be her," Shane muttered as he stepped around her and started walking from the building. Karen stayed close on his heels, nipping at him with questions and comments the entire time. When Shane reached his car, he said, "I'm on my way to talk to her right now. I have to tell her something before I talk to you or anyone else about anything. She needs to know this first, and then it's up to her whether or not she shares it with you. I'm sorry to disappoint you, Karen, but that's my final word."

Cecilia was locking the door to her bakery when Shane arrived. The construction workers and contractor were already gone for the day, and she looked relieved to see him. Brent's words about her being nervous to go out alone echoed in his mind as he looked at her.

"Brent called me about the results. It's a match. He's definitely her biological father. He's going to be prosecuted just as soon as we find him."

"What?" Cecilia squeaked in shock. "The guy from the park *is* her father?"

"Yes, it's him."

"I honestly wasn't expecting that. After all these years of wondering and imagining the worst, it seems too easy that Rebecca's father is just some harmless, sad old man who is trying to turn himself in. I actually feel sorry for him."

"Well, you shouldn't. Any man who would rape a thirteen year old *child* gets what's coming to him."

"I agree," she sighed.

"What are you thinking right now?"

"What else is there to think about?" she looked up at him with a lopsided attempt at a smile. "Actually, the wedding has been on my mind today. I was thinking we might have to call it off or postpone it now that I have this other stuff going on."

"Why would we postpone it? I thought it was what you wanted. You've already started on the renovations, and all the invitations have gone out. It's less than three months away."

"I was just thinking that you might not want to be associated with me now that this investigation is starting. Don't you remember all the attention we got after the engagement party? Imagine what they'll print in the paper about this."

"I remember, Cecilia, but I never minded. And it doesn't matter if there's an investigation going on or not, I'm proud to be by your side."

"But you don't know what details might come out and be made public."

"Whatever comes out, I'm here for you. Haven't you figured that out yet? Every time you confide in me about something like this, you act like I'm going to think less of you, but I don't. In fact, I don't know if it's possible for me to think any more highly of you."

She looked up at him for a long time, the streetlight casting shadows across her face and obscuring the expression in her eyes. "But you hardly know anything about me," she whispered.

"Yet I know more than anybody else," he whispered back.

She didn't answer. She just stared up at him, and her piercing, silver gaze searched his face for something. He wished he knew what it was, but he didn't ask because he had a feeling that even she didn't know what she was searching for.

"Listen, Cecilia, I didn't come here just to give you the news about Rebecca. I also wanted to tell you that Brent needs you to come in and give a more detailed statement about what happened to you."

"Why?"

"It'll help them narrow down the list of suspects. He's taking this very seriously, and he's already opened up a case file. You can help get this guy off the streets before he does the same thing to some other young girl. That is if he hasn't already."

She caught her breath and said, "That isn't fair, Shane. You don't know anything about what happened, so don't you dare try to guilt trip me."

She turned away from him and stalked off toward her car. Shane hesitated on the sidewalk before catching up to her. "Cecilia, wait," he said as he reached out and grasped her arm. "I didn't mean it that way."

"Then how did you mean it?" She jerked her arm away and wiped at the tears on her face.

"I just want you to cooperate so this guy can pay for what he did to you."

"But he wasn't—"

"Yes, I know!" Shane interrupted. "He wasn't the only one. But he participated! He's the one who let you go. But not before he had his way with you! I wish to God there was a way to find whoever else was responsible. Maybe after we catch this guy, he can lead us to the others."

"He probably has no idea what was going on. He can't help; no one can. It happened, it's over now, and that's all there is to it."

"That's *not* all there is."

"You're acting like it happened to you!" she shouted at him.

"And you're acting like it *didn't* happen to you!" he shouted back.

They both stared at each other for a tense moment, breathing hard. "Shane, please," she said eventually. "I don't want to fight with you, not about this."

He took a deep breath and reached out for her hands, "I don't want to fight either, but I still think it's a good idea for you to at least talk to Brent. He wants to help; heck, he *can* help. He's prosecuted a lot of cases like this one."

"Okay. I'll do it on two conditions. First, I need some time to think about it all. I've been trying to forget about all the details since it happened, and I've never told anyone about it before."

"I understand. What's the second condition?"

"I don't want you or anyone else there. I have to do it alone, or I don't do it at all."

"Why wouldn't you want me there?"

"I don't think I can talk about any of it in front of you."

"If I have to stay away to get you to cooperate, then that's what I'll do."

"Can we please drop it for now? I'll let you know when I'm ready. Okay?"

Shane squeezed her hand and then hugged her close. "Okay. Let's go get dinner before you go back to Karen's house."

Chapter 20

Norman smiled to himself, because after what seemed like forever without his wife, his luck had finally improved. Cece had blocked his attempts to talk to Rebecca at every turn, but he'd found a way around her. Trying to reach her by phone had been a lost cause. When he'd tried to see her at work, the girl at the front desk had told him she was on an extended leave due to her pregnancy. Norman didn't know if it was true or not, but they wouldn't buzz him into the facility, so he left. It seemed like his only option was to sneak into Karen's house, and that is exactly what he planned to do tonight.

His luck turned when the security guard had let him into the neighborhood, mistakenly believing that he was there to meet a real estate agent about a property that was currently on the market. His luck improved even more when the property just happened to be an older, vacant house right next door to Karen's. It didn't have an alarm system, and it had been relatively easy for him to break in through one of the back windows on the bottom floor. He sat in one of the upstairs rooms adjacent to the one his wife was staying in, and gazed at her through his binoculars.

He caught a few glimpses of her as she readied herself for bed. She sat at the window for a long time, staring out at the sky and the ground below. He wondered what she was thinking, and he tried to rehearse what he should say to her when they finally did come face to face. What could he say to get her to listen and not immediately throw him out? He was still in the process of gathering enough courage to go to her window and get her attention when Cecilia walked into the room. He definitely hadn't been expecting that. He'd assumed Cecilia was staying in her own house, and, after all of his recent dealings with her, his first instinct was to duck down and hide. He had no idea how she might react if she caught him trying to talk to Rebecca, and he didn't want any trouble tonight.

"Dammit!" he cursed as he watched them through his binoculars. Cece sat on the edge of the bed and watched Rebecca as she stared out the window. The two of them said very little, but they both looked like the weight of the universe was on their shoulders. Eventually, Cece stood up and hugged Rebecca before exiting the room. Norman glanced down at his watch. It was past ten, and he really hoped Cece was about to leave soon. She got up at the crack of dawn every day, so she should be headed home any moment.

Cece didn't leave the house before Rebecca left the window, and Norman sighed as he watched his wife get in the bed and turn off the lights. He wanted to go to her and get her attention before she fell asleep, but he didn't want to deal with her mother. All he knew was that Cece hadn't left the house; he couldn't tell what room she was in now. It took almost another hour for the rest of the lights in the house to go out. During that time, Norman debated whether or not he should just abandon his mission and go home. Going home would be the easiest course of action, but it wasn't the one he wanted to take. He didn't know when he'd get the chance to talk to Rebecca again, and he was miserable knowing that she thought the worst of him. He was even more miserable knowing that she was nearing the end of her pregnancy and he wasn't able to share this special time with her.

He thought about the last morning they'd spent together being lazy in bed. The babies had kicked his hand through the safety of Rebecca's belly, and the two of them had chuckled about it for a long time. They'd discussed baby names and debated about what color to paint the nursery. The more he thought about that day, the more he missed her. It seemed like forever since he'd had the chance to talk to his wife, and nothing was going to make him pass up this opportunity. Cece may have said she'd hired a lawyer, but he hadn't received any papers yet. Rebecca was still his wife, and she was pregnant with his daughters. There was no way he was going to run home like a coward when she was just feet away from him.

A large oak tree, with branches that spanned both properties, sat just outside the window. He surveyed the area and planned an easy way to get into the window his wife had left open. The trunk of the tree was on Karen's property, but the longest branch extended over the wall and almost to the window he was watching from. If he managed to make a good leap out of the window he could catch that branch and then climb through the tree to get onto Karen's property. Once he did that, it should be easy to get into Rebecca's window. He'd just have to be careful not to frighten her. Once he made up his mind what to do, Norman scanned the perimeter one last time and got to it.

Rebecca lay in bed that night, trying to understand her mother's cryptic remarks from earlier that evening. Cece had always been a mysterious person. All her life, Rebecca had felt like a stranger to her own mother, but tonight Cece had been trying to confide in her. Rebecca was used to asking and getting less than half of her questions answered, so Cece's attempt to open up without being questioned was far out of the ordinary.

"Rebecca," Cece had said as she stood behind her stroking her hair. "Do you remember the first time you ever asked me about your father?"

"Yes."

"I'm sorry for screaming at you just for asking me a question. You were just a child and you didn't deserve that. I'm also sorry for the way I finally did tell you."

"It's okay, Mom. I already told you I forgive you for that. You were just hurting inside, and I understand."

"How can you be so understanding? I hurt you so much when you were younger. Don't you ever get mad about that?"

"No, Mom."

"Well, you should. You deserve better. I've done a lot of things I'm not proud of. I just want you to know that I regret all of it. I deeply regret it."

"Why are you bringing this up now?"

"Rebecca, I..."

"What, Mom?"

"I found out something today."

When Cece hesitated for a long time, Rebecca prompted her again. "What did you find out?"

"Nothing really; I guess I just wanted you to know that I love you, and I want to make it up to you."

"Make what up to me?"

"I've lied to you about a lot of things," Cece admitted.

"What have you been lying about?"

"I didn't tell you the whole truth about what happened when I got pregnant with you and Sarah."

"So, you lied about being raped?"

"No!" Cece gasped. "I would never lie about something like that. It just didn't happen exactly like I told you it did, or like I thought it did."

"What do you mean, Mom?"

"The man who fathered you, he might not be the absolute monster I made him out to be."

"I don't understand, Mom. Were you lying about being raped?" Rebecca asked again.

"No! I told you I wouldn't lie about that!"

"Then how could he not be a monster? You were thirteen. He had a weapon. He forced you. How could he *not* be a monster?"

"It's a long story, Rebecca. Not everything is as black and white as your teachers would have you believe in grade school. I just wanted you to know that," Cece said as she stood up to leave the room.

"What happened, Mom? Can you just tell me now? Don't you think you've kept enough secrets in your life?"

Cece's hand paused on the doorknob and she looked back at Rebecca. "It's not a good bedtime story, and you need your sleep. We'll talk more tomorrow. Good night, Honey."

Rebecca tried to figure out possible explanations after her mother left, but eventually the exhaustion of being pregnant with twins got to her. She fell into a sound sleep, and had one of her recurring dreams about being back in her husband's arms. These days, her dreams were the only place she allowed herself to think about how much she missed him. Usually in her dreams, they were back at home, lying in bed with the stars shining on the ceiling above them. The dreams were always very idyllic, with Norman gazing deep into her eyes and smiling. She always smiled back, and reached out to touch his face. Then she would read his thoughts, and the dream would melt away because she heard a quiet thought that she didn't like from somewhere deep in his mind, a thought about his ex-wife. Every time she had that dream, she woke up with a sad feeling in her heart. How could he have cheated on her?

Tonight's dream started off differently. Instead of being transported back to her own bed, she suddenly became aware of his presence here in Karen's guest room. She felt the bed settle and she rolled involuntarily towards his weight.

"Becky, it's me, Norman," he whispered in her ear.

"I know who it is," she giggled. "I know my husband." She scooted closer to his warmth, wanting to enjoy the good part of the dream while it lasted.

"My God, you have no idea how much I've missed you," he whispered as he pulled her close and kissed her. This dream wasn't like the other dreams at all. She felt this kiss down to her toes, and it didn't end prematurely with thoughts of Juliana. This kiss deepened and blossomed into an all-consuming force of nature. When his hands began to caress her round belly and the babies reacted with furious kicking, she realized this was no dream. She froze in uncertainty.

"Norman?"

"Yes?"

"What are you doing in Karen's house?"

"I came to see you."

"Why?" She pushed him away as her hurt feelings came rushing to the surface all at once. "Things not working out with you and Juliana?"

"There's nothing to work out. She jumped on me, and I pushed her off. Rebecca, I'd never cheat on you. I know how much that kind of betrayal hurts, and you are the most perfect woman I've ever known. I'd have to be the world's biggest idiot to cheat on you."

"I haven't seen or heard from you in months, and you expect me to believe you just like that? I sat there and watched you flirt with her for almost half an hour before you two kissed. I *saw* you," she whispered furiously.

"I tried calling you. I left you about fifty messages begging you to come home or at least call me back, but your mother broke your phone."

"Don't you dare bring my mother into this. My phone is right here, and there is nothing wrong with it." She grabbed the phone off the nightstand and stuck it in his face so he couldn't possibly miss it.

Norman clenched his jaw and said, "Go get your mother right now, and ask her in front of me what she did to your phone."

"Fine. I will," Rebecca said as she struggled to get out of the bed. Her large belly combined with the tangled sheets to hamper her movements, adding to her frustration.

"On second thought, don't bother. I'd rather talk to you without your mother around for right now."

"Why? Are you worried I'll find out the truth?" she demanded.

"Becky, I am telling the truth. Ask her tomorrow if you don't believe me. But tonight could we just talk about it without involving anyone else? Please?"

She relaxed back on the bed, partly because she was embarrassed by her lack of mobility and partly because she didn't have the heart to refuse his plea. "Okay, so talk," she said.

"First of all, I love you and I miss you like crazy. I don't know what you saw that day, but I was *not* flirting with her. I was minding my own business, and she came along and invited herself to play in our game. Everyone else left because she was making things awkward, and I was about to do the same when she jumped all over me. You must have left right after she did that, because you obviously missed what happened next. If you'd seen it, you never would have thought I was cheating on you."

Norman paused to inch a little closer. When she didn't say anything, he mistook her silence for a green light and started pulling her into his arms.

She stiffened and pushed him away, asking, "What happened next?"

"I pushed her off of me, and she fell on her ass. I told her to keep her damn hands to herself, then we shouted at each other for a few minutes just like old times, and then I went home to you. But you were gone. As soon as I got your mother's message, I went straight to her house to talk to you and clear all this up, but she wouldn't let me see you. In fact, she attacked me multiple times when I asked to see you."

"You expect me to believe all of that?" She was trying hard not to let him see her cry. She wanted to believe him so badly, and it hurt to keep pushing him away. During the course of their conversation she'd pushed him away so many times, but no matter how many times she swatted at his hands they came back every time.

"I can prove it." He pulled his cell phone out of his pocket and gave it to her. "Check my saved messages. Your mother is on there several times, warning me not to come back to her house. Now, if I hadn't been there, why would she tell me not to come back?"

Rebecca listened to the messages as she allowed Norman's words to sink in. Earlier that evening, Cece had admitted to lying about things. Heaviness grew in her heart as she listened to the messages that proved her mother had been lying and deliberately keeping them apart.

"Becky, she said you wanted a divorce. Please tell me you haven't hired a lawyer. I love you too much to lose you over this nonsense."

"I don't want a divorce, but she was trying to convince me to get one. I've been so hurt, Norman, so hurt that you never even tried to call me. Now that I know you did try, I don't know what to think."

"Becky, you know me better than anyone else. I wouldn't cheat on you, especially not with her. I am guilty of thinking it was okay to hang out with her for those few minutes. And I'm not even asking you to forgive me right now. All I'm asking right now is that you let me make it up to you. Let me prove to you that you can still trust me."

She felt him reach out to her again in the darkness. His presence filled the room and electrified her emotions, but she still hadn't seen his face yet. A sudden need to look into his eyes prompted her to turn on the light. He sat on the edge of the bed, wearing dark clothing that blended in with the night. He looked tired and worried, but he also looked like he had a smile lurking somewhere just under the surface.

"It's good to see you, Becky," he said as he reached for her again.

Her eyes locked onto his, and his look of tenderness and naked longing made it impossible for her to push him away again. "It's good to see you too," she whispered as she placed her hand in his.

"Can I stay with you tonight? I just want to hold you."

When she nodded, he kicked off his shoes and stretched out in the bed, pulling her into his arms as he settled into a comfortable position.

"What happened to your finger?" Rebecca asked when she noticed his splint.

"Your mother broke it a few weeks ago when I tried to come talk to you."

Rebecca cringed and said, "I'm afraid to ask what else happened. I've seen what my mom can do to people in the ring."

"Let's not talk about your mother right now. I just want to hold you in my arms. No telling when she'll come back and try to finish me off," he joked.

"How did you get in here anyway? Everyone else is sleep right now."

"I came through the window."

"This is the second floor, Norman. How did you really get in?"

"I came from the empty house next door. I climbed through the tree and jumped the last few inches to catch the window sill. You really shouldn't sleep with the window open, by the way."

"We do it all the time at home."

"But at home, I'm there to protect you. Becky, come home with me in the morning," he whispered against her hair.

"I don't know, Norman. I really feel like there's more to discuss before things just go back to the way they were."

"So you're going to make me climb through the window every time I want to talk to you?"

"No, but—"

"Becky, please come home with me," he interrupted. "Don't you miss home? If you want me to sleep in the other room, fine, I'll do it. I'll give you whatever space you need. Please just come home so we can get through this. I already feel like I've missed out on so much."

"I need to talk to my mother before I leave." She felt Norman's arms tighten around her, but she didn't relent. She needed to give her mother the chance to tell the truth on her own before leaving.

"How is it that you can continue to forgive her for everything she's ever done to you, yet you leave me as soon as I make one mistake?"

"You can't compare what I saw with you and Juliana to my mother doing what she thinks is best for me."

"Your mother is crazy. She needs serious help. Those nights when I came to talk to you, she liked hurting me. She may have been raped, but that's no excuse to be mean, hurtful, and abusive all the time."

"My mother is not abusive."

"Maybe not to you, but she has a mean streak like you wouldn't believe."

"Norman, if you came here to get me to go home with you, trash talking my mother isn't going to help."

"Becky, I love how sweet and wonderful you are, but sometimes you're just too forgiving."

"That's the same thing my mom said when she was giving me reasons not to call you first," Rebecca sighed. "You're here now because I'm giving you the benefit of the doubt, so don't you dare ask me to do less for my own mother."

"Okay. You do whatever you feel you need to do in the morning, but when I leave this house, so do you. I can't spend another night without having you and the girls safe at home with me."

Rebecca sat up and pinned him with a fierce look of outrage. "You don't get to tell me what to do. I'm not the one who is wrong here."

Norman took a deep breath and said, "I wasn't trying to imply that this is your fault. I just really want you to come home. Please, Becky. Christmas is coming up soon."

Rebecca stared at him for a long time before she finally said, "I'll come home with you in the morning, but you need to let me talk to my mother before she sees you."

Shane walked through Brent's building and tried not to notice the stares he got from the people working there. Most of the men in the office were of the softer variety, and the tallest of them were somewhere just shy of six feet. The women looked like painted porcelain dolls, as they clicked up and down the hall in their high heeled shoes. He felt way out of place and overgrown among the office people and he often wondered how his brother could stand to work in this environment all the time. He felt much like a bull in a china shop as he tiptoed through their immaculate floor of offices.

"Hello again, Shane. Mr. Gregory is expecting you," Brent's secretary said as he approached her desk. She immediately stood and ushered him inside. He was aware of her strong perfume and the smell of hairspray as she stood too close to him on their way through the door. Shane felt uncomfortable, but he tried not to let it show as he walked into his brother's office.

Brent's office was several times larger than Shane's living room, and it had a deluxe corner view of the city. All of the furnishings were modern, streamlined, and masculine in a bold yet stylish way. Brent was still on the phone, so Shane sat on the sleek, black leather sofa near the window and gazed out at the city below as he waited.

"Did you come here to tell me the good news?" Brent asked as he joined Shane near the window.

"Yes. Cecilia said she'd answer any questions you have as long as I stay away while she does it."

"Good. When's she coming in?"

"I'm not sure. She says she needs some time to deal with it all, and maybe talk to her daughter before all of this comes out in the open."

"That's a good idea. With the foundation and all this attention from the tabloids, this case might just turn into a media nightmare."

"Yeah. I was thinking the same thing."

"Has she talked to you about any new details?"

"No, but I get the feeling she wants to. After the fire she had a lot of nightmares, so I know it still affects her. I can see how much she struggles with this, and it kills me that she won't accept more support."

"Well, we need to move on this. The sooner she comes in to give that statement, the sooner we can get this guy."

"It's a little more complicated than catching just this one guy."

Brent's hands froze over his designer tie. "You mean multiple offenders? Is that what you meant when you told me he wasn't the only one the night we got the DNA results back?"

"Yes. And she never saw any of their faces. She recognized the one who left the letter by his voice. She doesn't seem to think he's a threat anymore, but she's still scared to death of something or someone."

"This changes things. It's imperative that you get her to come in soon."

"I'm working on it," Shane assured his brother as he got up to leave.

He found Cecilia at the top floor of her building, sitting at a small desk, drawing in her sketchbook.

"What are you working on?"

"Ideas for our cake. Well, the one for the fake wedding."

"May I see them?"

"Sure." She stood up and handed him the book. "At first I was thinking something colorful and art deco might work, but it just doesn't feel right to me."

"Why don't you just design the cake you would want for your own wedding," Shane suggested.

"Because it wouldn't be extravagant or expensive enough. I think your guest list is starting to intimidate me."

"I didn't think anything could intimidate you," Shane smiled.

"Scores of rich and powerful people I don't know looking at my work is about as intimidating as it gets."

"I see."

"Enough about the cake. What brings you by?"

"Do I need a reason to see my girl? Other than the fact that I miss her?"

"You look like something is up, Shane."

"You're right," he sighed. "I just came from talking to Brent. They really need your help to catch this guy."

"I knew it had something to do with that."

"The sooner you go talk to him, the better."

"I know." She walked over to the window and gazed down at the street below. Shane stayed where he was and watched her.

"The pain is never going to stop if you keep running from it," he said softly.

"I know," she said as she shivered and rubbed her arms.

He came closer and put his arms around her from behind. They both stared down at all the people passing by on the sidewalk below. Every once in a while, a strong gust of wind blew some leaves down the street, and the people huddled even deeper into their jackets.

"What are you thinking about?" Shane whispered.

"I was just looking at all the people and wondering if he's passed by my shop today. How could the same man have been following me around for months, even figured out where I live, and I never even noticed him? You saw him that night in the park. What did he look like?"

"It was too dark for me to make out his face very well. My description wasn't any help when I told the sketch artist in Brent's office."

"Shane, please. What was he like? I need to know."

"He was very small for a man. Maybe about an inch or two taller than you when he stands up straight. Old, out of shape, skinny. He smelled like a liquor cabinet. He had a dark complexion and a bald spot. I got the impression that he was from somewhere in the Middle East. If I had to guess, I'd say he was probably Indian. Honestly, he seemed like some sad, old man with a pathetic life."

"So he looked Indian?"

"Yes, probably southern Indian based on his dark complexion."

"I guess that explains why Rebecca's skin is so much darker than mine, yet her hair texture has always been silkier than mine. I've always wondered about that."

"Cecilia, we could go talk to Brent right now if you want. I'll stay away while you do it."

"I can't. I need to talk to Rebecca first."

"When are you going to do that?"

"I don't know. She's upset with me right now."

"Why?"

"Norman. He outfoxed me, and now she knows I was keeping them apart. I found them together this morning, and she confronted me about everything. There was no point in lying about it anymore, so I told the whole truth. I think this is the most upset she's ever been at me."

"So, she's back at home now?"

"Yes, and she won't answer her phone when I call."

"Would you like for me to try to talk to her?" Shane offered as he hugged her more tightly against his chest.

"No. I'll give her space. I know I was wrong. I knew it the whole time I was lying to her, but I just couldn't stop myself. She deserves better."

"She'll come around when she finds out about everything else that's going on right now. She'll understand."

"No, Shane. I'm not going to tell her just to get her to talk to me again. I'm not going to guilt her into it. I was wrong, and she's right to stand up to me for a change. She dished it out pretty good this morning."

"Are you okay?"

"Yes, of course. Thank you for telling me what he looks like."

Chapter 21

Shane lay in bed and endured yet another sleepless night. He was torn between thoughts of the man from the park and thoughts of Cecilia. Something about the stalker had seemed very familiar, but, no matter how much he thought about it, he couldn't remember when, or if, he'd seen the man before. Perhaps part of the familiarity lay in the fact that he was Rebecca's biological father. The clock beside his bed said it was 3:30 a.m. Cecilia was probably getting out of bed to start her day. Shane wondered if today would be the day she talked to Brent. Over the past few weeks, he'd been very careful not to pressure her too much about talking, but his silence on the subject didn't mean he'd forgotten about it.

That afternoon, Cecilia went out to lunch at a restaurant near her bakery. The renovations were at a stage where it was best if she stayed out of the way, and she couldn't think of much else to do with herself. She hadn't been out alone since the night the man had frightened her in the park, and she was nervous to be doing so now. He could be anywhere, and she wouldn't recognize him unless he spoke. Ever since Shane had described him, she found herself scanning the faces of every man who looked even remotely Indian with great mistrust and suspicion. Even as she walked around fearing another confrontation with him, in the back of her mind she almost wished for it.

There was another confrontation that needed to happen, but she feared she might never be ready for that one. Red Bone, the man who had killed her mother and taken everything she'd ever cared about, lurked in the back of her mind like a disease that was slowly infecting all her thoughts. She wanted to be able to close her eyes and not see those steel, gray orbs of his boring into her with naked, merciless hatred. She wanted to remember her mother doing something other than being controlled and ultimately beaten to death by Red Bone. She wanted him to pay for all the wrongs he'd done over the years. She wanted all those things, but fear held her back.

She sat in the corner of the restaurant and stared into her drink. She'd ordered hot tea with lemon, and she watched as a curl of steam rose up from the hot liquid. The doors to the restaurant opened, and she glanced up to see who had entered. When it wasn't a small Indian man, she relaxed and looked back down at her tea.

"Cecilia? Is that you?" a female voice with a Spanish accent demanded from a few tables over.

Cecilia turned towards the voice. It was Shane's friend, but Cecilia couldn't think of her name at the moment. She just smiled and waved.

"It's me, Magda. Gus's wife," the woman continued.

"Oh, hi Magda," Cecilia replied with little enthusiasm.

Magda got up and motioned for Cecilia to join her. "Come on over here. I'm meeting my sister for lunch. We can all have lunch together."

Cecilia didn't know how to refuse such an enthusiastic invitation, so she grabbed her tea and switched tables.

"Viri should be here any minute. How have you been? I haven't seen you since the engagement party."

"Things have been great. How are you and Gus?" Cecilia replied in her polite, professional tone.

"Gus is always busy at the academy and the fire station. Just like Shane. How are the wedding plans coming along?"

Cecilia's face went blank. "Wedding plans?" she echoed.

"Yes. Where is the reception going to be? We got our save the date, but we haven't got an invitation yet. It is going to be on Valentine's Day, right?" Magda said.

Cecilia didn't know anything about the wedding, and until just now she didn't even know the date. "Umm, yeah. I'm not sure where the reception is going to be, but I'm sure it'll be great."

"Cecilia, are you okay? You look like something is on your mind."

"Yeah, just thinking about all the planning between now and the big day," Cecilia lied.

"Forgive all my nosey questions. I just love weddings so much. What does the dress look like? Can I come with you for your next fitting?"

"I don't have a dress yet," Cecilia said without thinking.

She realized she should have lied when Magda took in a deep breath and said, "*Dios mio!* How are you going to get married in less than two months and you don't even have a dress yet. You're supposed to pick the dress before you do anything else!"

Cecilia almost laughed. She thought the cake was the most important part of this wedding, but she wasn't about to tell Magda that. "Maybe I'll go dress shopping this week. With the bakery still closed down for remodeling, I've got nothing else to do."

"Don't wait. We should go now, right after lunch. I'm not doing anything else today, and I'd love to help you pick one," Magda offered.

"Okay," Cecilia agreed, partly because she didn't want to spend the rest of the afternoon alone with her thoughts and partly because she now felt a sense of urgency about the dress. How embarrassing would it be to have a substandard dress in front of the high stepping crowd that was to attend her wedding? The wrong dress could be disastrous.

Cecilia stared down into her tea again as Magda continued to go on and on about various bridal shops in the city. Magda was sure Cecilia would be seen without an appointment because of who Shane's family was. Cecilia tried hard to pretend she cared. She really didn't want to offend Shane's friend.

"I'm sure Viri could recommend someone. She works with brides all the time," Magda was wrapping up when Cecilia looked back at her.

"Recommend someone to what?" Cecilia asked, embarrassed that she'd been caught not listening.

"Someone to custom make a dress for you. She knows lots of good seamstresses and designers. She used to be a professional ballroom dancer, and she had all of her costumes custom made. She gives dance lessons now, and she's helped a few brides find the perfect dress at the last minute. I'm sure she could recommend someone to help with your dress too," Magda explained with her ever-present smile.

"Are you sure she'll want to help me out?" Cecilia asked.

Before Magda could answer, the door to the restaurant opened again, and they both turned to look at the woman who stepped in. The woman smiled and waved at Magda, and Magda waved back. The woman had the same dark hair and eyes and olive toned features as Magda, but there all similarities ended. Viridiana strode across the restaurant like she owned the place. Her dark hair fell in luxurious waves down her back, and Cecilia noticed the streaks of gray and silver in her tresses as she neared their table. The way she moved her body reminded Cecilia of the women in the glamorous old Hollywood movies. She floated across the floor in an easy, graceful way that made Cecilia want to sit up straighter and check her own appearance for flaws.

When Viri got to them, her dark eyes went directly to Cecilia's. "So I finally get to meet the famous Cece Graves," she smiled as she stuck out her hand in greeting.

Cecilia shook Viri's hand, noticing how soft and delicate it seemed inside her own grasp. "How did you know it was me?" she couldn't stop herself from asking.

Magda laughed and said, "You must not watch much TV or read any tabloids, or you'd know that your face has been all over them since you got engaged."

Cecilia didn't know how to respond to that, so she let out a nervous chuckle.

"Actually, Shane told me what you look like," Viri corrected.

Cecilia didn't know whether she should be offended or flattered that Shane had talked about her to the first woman he ever loved, and probably still loved. She resisted the temptation to say something like, 'Oh really? And what else has he told you about me?'

Magda started talking again before things got too awkward. In her effervescent way, she told Viri all about Cecilia's wedding dress predicament. Viri gazed at Cecilia with a pensive expression for a moment before agreeing that she did in fact know several good designers who would love the chance to make a dress for such an important bride.

"Now, for the more important question," Viri smiled after the dress issue had been settled. "Have you ever taken any dance lessons? Or were you planning to kick-box your way around the dance floor in front of everybody?"

By the end of the day, Cecilia had selected someone to design her dress and signed up to take dance lessons three times a week at Viri's dance studio. Standing up on a raised platform in her underwear as the seamstress measured every inch of her wasn't exactly her idea of a fun day, but it was better than spending time alone dwelling on the past. She'd tried several times to talk to Rebecca, but all she could do was leave messages on her voicemail.

The woman who would design her wedding dress was around Viri's age, and the two of them had been friends for years. Her name was Catherine Burke, and she'd designed custom wedding dresses before. Most of her design experience was in making dance and ice skating costumes for athletes who competed at the national level. The highlight of her career had been a design for a local young woman who had competed in the winter Olympics back in the 90's. Cecilia was impressed by Catherine's body of work, impressed enough to hire her on the spot without talking to the other designers on her list or even setting one foot in a bridal shop.

"If you'll trust me, I have an idea for a dress that will blow your mind," Catherine said as she sketched furiously in a notepad. "We can meet again in a few days, and I'll show you some sketches and materials you might like."

"As long as it isn't some puffy, princess dress I'm sure I'll like it," Cecilia said.

"Got it. No puffy princess fluff for you. You didn't strike me as that type of bride... How do you feel about color?"

"Whatever you think is best," Cecilia answered.

Compared to the way her first dance lesson went later that afternoon, the consultation with the designer had been a breeze. As soon as Cecilia agreed to take lessons, Viri and Magda hauled her directly to the dance studio. Viri had immediately started counseling her about her posture and the way she walked.

"I know you're a fighter," Viri said over and over again as she pranced circles around the room, "but you need to move your body like a dancer."

Cecilia followed her around the room with her shoulders back and relaxed, and her hands framing her hips as she concentrated on doing the step-ball-change move to the music playing in the background. The entire room had mirrored walls, and Cecilia was very aware of her body. She watched herself during every turn about the room; she fought the constant urge to frown at herself and stomp off to go kick something. Viri did the simple moves effortlessly, rhythmically, and even sensually. Cecilia felt like an ungraceful ox by comparison. All of her training in Judo and Muay Thai had focused on getting the moves correct and having power and flexibility. She'd never had to worry about her arms framing her hips in a way that made them look appealing, or stepping down with her toes first when she walked so that it would appear that she was floating.

Just when she was about to tell Viri she'd had enough of the prancing around, the door opened and Shane walked in. He stood in the corner and observed them for a moment before Viri acknowledged his presence with a small smile exchanged through the mirror. Cecilia tried not to let herself care that Shane was there, but she missed several steps and got off track. When Viri looked back at her and noticed, she tried to correct Cecilia's off rhythm by reminding her "Step-ball-change, step-ball-change," several times until she got it right again.

The music ended a short time later, and Viri floated over to Shane's corner to greet him. Cecilia walked to the opposite corner to put her shoes back on before facing her faux-fiancé. As she covertly watched them, she couldn't stop a small part of herself from thinking that they looked good together. Viri was obviously older than him, but she carried herself with such poise she looked better than women half her age. Cecilia wondered what Viri would think if she knew their engagement wasn't real.

"Cecilia," Shane said her name in that way she was coming to love. She'd always hated her name, and preferred Cece or even Coco as her mother had called her when she was a child, but when Shane said her name, it sounded feminine and pretty. "Viri was just telling me that we are to be here every Monday, Wednesday, and Friday when I get off work so that she can give us lessons for our reception. Was this your idea?"

"Not exactly, but I agreed to it," Cecilia confessed. "Actually, I assumed it would be just me getting the lessons. Don't you already know all the ballroom and Latin dances?"

"He does, but he is your partner, so you'll need to practice with him. I should have made that clear," Viri interjected. "He's actually the best partner I ever had when it came to lifts. Being a fireman has its advantages; he's very strong."

Cecilia looked at him in time to see a slight redness creep into his face. "Lifts? What exactly do you have in mind for this choreographed wedding routine?" he asked.

"That's what we were discussing while you were over there in the corner with your shoes," Viri explained at Cecilia's questioning look. She then turned back to Shane and continued, "Remember that swing routine we did for that competition in New York the year we met? You two could do a short version of that for the first half, and then the second half could be a romantic foxtrot to one of those jazz standards you love. Isn't that the reception theme? Didn't you just tell me that you're going to have a big band for the ballroom?"

"Ballroom?" Cecilia asked.

"Thanks, Viri. That was supposed to be a surprise," Shane sounded irritated as he looked down at the older woman.

Viri just shrugged and said, "Sorry."

"I'm not sure if Cecilia will have time to learn all those complicated moves and all that footwork before the wedding. I thought it might be best to just do something simple like a waltz," Shane said with a concerned look in Cecilia's direction.

"She can do it. And since when do you ever go for simple and uncomplicated?" Viri taunted. When Shane still looked unsure, she turned to Cecilia and said, "We'll show you the routine, and then you can decide whether or not you want to learn it." She then walked off before Shane could respond again.

"I'm sorry if Viri has been giving you a hard time today. I know you don't need this right now, with everything else going on."

Cecilia knew he was referring to the letter and the investigation, so she raised a hand to stop him before he went on. "I actually had fun with Magda and Viri today. Karen has never really been into anything other than fighting. It was nice to focus on something lighter for a while." She'd embellished the truth a bit, but it was better than talking about the investigation again. She didn't even want to think about it, much less talk about it.

He placed a hand on her shoulder, and the expression on his face was laced with concern as he opened his mouth again. Before he could speak, however, Viri returned with a CD and told him, "I have the music. I'm ready when you are." She then inserted the disc in her sound system and took up a very poised and professional looking stance in the center of the room.

"I can't wait to see this," Cecilia smiled as she backed away from Shane.

He joined Viri in the center of the room just as the opening bars of the swing classic, *Big Noise from Winnetka,* began to play. As Cecilia watched, a change came over Shane. His posture reflected Viri's, and his dance steps were just as sharp and precise as hers. As the excitement built within the music, excitement was also tangible in Shane and Viri's execution of the dance steps and powerful lifts in their routine. If Cecilia hadn't been so enthralled by their dancing, she might have found space in her head to be jealous of the obvious chemistry between the two of them.

Viri looked flushed as she walked up to Cecilia and said, "You think you can learn to do that in six weeks? If you can get through that swing routine, the foxtrot should be a breeze."

Cecilia had never been one to back down from a challenge. If she could learn everything Karen had been throwing her way for the past twenty years, then this dance routine should be simple. "Of course I can," she said as she raised her chin up a few notches.

Dancing for a few weeks gave Cecilia the chance to focus on something other than the things going wrong in her life. Before she knew it, Christmas came and went, and Rebecca still wasn't talking to her. She'd tried calling more times than she could count, but none of her messages got through to Rebecca. She thought about driving over to her daughter's house to beg her forgiveness in person, but she didn't want to cause trouble. She kept going back over her own behavior and wishing she had been able to talk some sense into herself while she'd had the chance.

Shane wasn't around as much as he had been in the fall, because work and wedding preparations were taking up nearly all of his time. She rarely ever got to see him outside their dance lessons, and during those, she had to concentrate. He never said anything about the investigation, but she knew he was thinking about it. Sometimes she caught him looking at her with an expression that reminded her of the way Miss Georgia had looked at her the day she'd been taken into state custody. It was a look that said she was a victim, a thing to be pitied, and petted, and patronized. The only thing almost as bad as having been raped in the first place was the knowledge that once everyone found out about it, the way they treated her and even thought of her as a person was completely altered. Cece didn't want to face the inevitable questions about her past, and she certainly didn't want to be judged for the decisions she'd made that night.

It was the first week of the new year, and Cecilia lay in bed, staring at the ceiling. This was the third night in a row that she'd been awake all night, thinking. Mostly her thoughts just took her around and around in circles, never really getting her anywhere. She made little lists of reasons to keep her life to herself, and then she made lists of reasons to tell everybody the truth about what really happened all those years ago. Most of the details were things she wished she could forget, but if she hadn't been able to forget in more than twenty years then perhaps she never would. Maybe Brent could work a miracle and Red Bone really would pay for everything he'd done. But then the voice of reality whispered in her ear again, telling her that he would never pay. He'd always escaped the law before, and she didn't even know his real name; he'd never pay.

Her cell phone chirped in her ear and startled her out of her thoughts. She snatched the phone off of the nightstand and looked at the display. She didn't recognize the number, but she answered anyway.

"Cece?" Norman's voice said.

"Yeah. What is it? Has something happened to Rebecca?" Cecilia demanded.

"No, she's going to be fine. I just thought you might like to know she's having the babies tonight. We're at Vanderbilt Children's Hospital right now."

"Why are you at Vanderbilt? Is something wrong?"

"Everything's going great so far. Her blood pressure was high, so the doctor decided to deliver today. She has pre-eclampsia, but like I said, she's doing okay. I just thought you might want to come though."

"I'll be right there," Cecilia said before disconnecting. She threw on her clothes and rushed out of the room, calling out to Karen on her way past her bedroom door.

Karen emerged just as Cecilia was rounding the bottom of the staircase and asked, "How long has she been in labor?"

"I don't know, but Norman said she has preeclampsia and I know that's bad. I'm leaving right now," Cecilia answered.

"Wait, I'm coming with you," Karen said as she rushed down the stairs and out the door after Cecilia.

"Karen, go back to bed. You don't need to come. She's my—"

"Cece, don't you dare say it!" Karen cut in. "I know she's your daughter, but I've known her since she was six, and I love her as if she were my daughter too."

Cecilia looked at Karen's face, and decided not to argue further, but when she glanced down and saw that Karen was standing on the step barefooted she said, "At least go put on some shoes first."

"I have some in the car in my gym bag. I'll put them on while you drive," Karen answered as she pulled the door closed behind her.

Vanderbilt Children's Hospital was a short drive from Karen's neighborhood, but Cecilia felt like it took forever to get there. All kinds of nightmare scenarios played in her head as she drove. Karen didn't talk much on the trip, other than to mumble things like, "I'm sure she's going to be okay."

By the time they found the labor and delivery section of the hospital, Cece had endured another twenty minutes of not knowing whether or not her daughter was going to be okay. She was pacing circles around Karen when Norman walked into the room.

"She's fine, they're prepping her for a C-section right now," he said before her brain had time to form a question.

"Where is she? Can I see her?"

"They won't allow more than one person to be in operating room with her, and I didn't tell her I called you," Norman said with a serious look.

"You mean she didn't ask you to call me?" Cecilia asked with a sick feeling.

"When all this stuff started earlier, I told her I'd call so you could be with her, but she wouldn't let me. She said you'd just be mean to her about it, and she didn't need the extra stress today. I can tell she wants you here though. She's been down since she came home."

"If she doesn't want me here, why did you call?"

"Because she's my wife. I love her. I know that she'll feel bad later for not wanting you here, but also because I'm afraid that if something happens and you're not here with her, she might not..." Norman's voice trailed off, but Cecilia understood his meaning.

She sat down hard in the chair behind her and said, "Just tell her I'm here, and tell her that I love her too," as a single tear fell from her eye.

Norman turned to go back to Rebecca, and Cecilia added, "Norman, I'm so sorry about everything I did to you. I don't expect you to forgive me, or even believe me, but I am. You're a really good husband for my daughter."

Norman nodded, and then he disappeared down the hall.

"She's going to be fine, Cece," Karen said as she grabbed Cecilia's hand and squeezed.

A short time later, a nurse came into the waiting room and called for Cecilia. "You'll need to go into the first room on the left, and change into the sterile clothing on the bench. You have ten minutes until the procedure starts," the nurse said as Cecilia followed her down the hall.

"So, Rebecca wants *me* in there with her instead of her husband?" Cecilia asked.

"No. You're both allowed in, hubby's on one side, and you're on the other," the nurse clarified.

Cecilia stopped asking questions and changed as quickly as she could. When she emerged, the nurse ushered her into the operating room. Norman sat on Rebecca's right side, holding her hand and looking down at her in a way that reminded Cecilia of the way Shane looked at her sometimes. Norman smiled down at Rebecca and said something that made her laugh. Cecilia couldn't see Rebecca's face from her vantage point; she saw the top of her head and the big white sterile sheet separating her into two distinct halves, the half where she and Norman would be, and the half where the doctors would perform the surgery. A sudden memory of the white sheet that had kept Sarah out of view as they moved the car the day of the accident flashed in her mind, and she had to fight back tears. *The white sheet did not mean Rebecca was going to die!* She told herself sternly.

"Go on," the nurse prompted at her back. "She knows you're coming in."

As Cecilia inched forward, Norman looked up and made eye contact with her, and then he bent down and whispered something in Rebecca's ear. When Cecilia got to Rebecca's other side, she caught a glimpse of her face and was startled by Rebecca's changed appearance. Her face was so bloated she almost looked like a completely different person. Cecilia had to make a conscious effort to keep the alarm from showing on her face.

She didn't really have time to say anything before the doctor came in and got started on the procedure. Rebecca didn't say much, but she did allow Cecilia to hold onto one of her hands. Norman held the other one to his lips and whispered encouraging things to her as he stroked her hair. Five minutes into the procedure, the first baby was born. The doctor held her up above the white sheet for them to see, and then immediately handed her off to one of the neonatal nurses. Two minutes later, the doctor held up the second baby, and Cecilia watched the look of delight that came over Norman's face when they were both pronounced healthy.

"Did you hear that?" he whispered to Rebecca. "The doctor said they're fine. You were so worried about having them a little early, and they're fine. Now let's focus on getting you better."

Cecilia turned away, and looked across the room as the nurses examined and cleaned her granddaughters. Norman's words and Rebecca's small sounds of joy floated to her ears as she watched the babies. Their little arms flailed, and their tiny fingers grasped at the air above them as they screamed loud enough to make all the nurses in the room smile. Cecilia smiled too as she thought about the night Rebecca and Sarah were born. The doctor and nurses had been amazed that they'd had so much hair, and even Mrs. Lee had cracked a smile when she looked at them. It took another forty-five minutes for the doctors to finish the surgery. During that time, Cecilia was content to sit silently holding Rebecca's hand as she observed the babies.

When they wheeled her into the recovery room, Norman said to Cecilia, "I'm going to see the babies, so you two can spend some time together."

Cecilia walked into the room after the doctor stepped out. He smiled at her as he passed, so she assumed that meant Rebecca would be fine. Rebecca was lying back with her eyes closed, but they popped open just as soon as Cecilia walked into the room.

"Thanks for letting me sit with you during your surgery," Cecilia said.

"Thanks for coming. You didn't have to."

"Of course I did. What did the doctor say about your blood pressure?"

"I'll be fine. The preeclampsia wasn't severe, but it did get worse all of a sudden after I got to the hospital. I haven't been this puffy all day. They said my kidney function should return to normal now that they got the placenta out of me. I'll probably be in the hospital for a few extra days." Rebecca's voice sounded like she was on the verge of falling asleep as she talked. It reminded Cecilia of the way she felt the night she became a mother. Tired, emotional, overwhelmed, and in awe of the power such a small being could have on a person. "How did you do it, Mom?" Rebecca asked after the long silence.

Cecilia didn't have to ask what she meant. "When I look back on it, I honestly don't know. I just knew that I had to take care of you and Sarah no matter what," she whispered. Now would be the perfect time to start a discussion about why she'd really run away, and tell Rebecca about the man who had fathered her and talk about the investigation, but Cecilia just couldn't bring herself to do it. Rebecca was tired and going through a medical crisis, the last thing she needed was an emotional upheaval. "I've always loved you, you know. It might not have been easy for me to show it all the time, but I did always feel it. Part of the reason I pushed you away is because I never really thought I deserved to have a daughter like you. You were always everything I wished I could have been when I was younger. I got into so much trouble because I was always fighting and making situations worse, and you were always so sweet and patient. I remember how you could give me one look that calmed me down when I was about to lose it over something silly. When you looked at me like that, I always felt ashamed that I couldn't be a better example for my own daughter, and then I dealt with that feeling by pushing you away. I've always thought you deserved a better mother than me." When Cecilia looked down at Rebecca again, she was sleeping. Cecilia smiled and shook her head; she wondered if Rebecca had heard any of what she'd said.

The automatic blood pressure cuff tightened to take another reading as Cecilia stared down at her daughter.

When she heard Norman out in the hall talking to the doctor, she bent down to give Rebecca a kiss on the forehead and left the room. Her husband probably wanted to spend time with her now.

The waiting room was no longer nearly empty. Cecilia walked in to find that half of Norman's family was there along with Karen. Shane, Shelly, and Brent were all sitting in the chairs with serious looks on their faces. Cecilia smiled at all of them and said, "Rebecca and the babies are going to be just fine."

"Thank God!" Karen spoke first. Her fervent voice dispelled the tension in the room and everyone else let out a collective sigh.

"When can we see the babies?" Shelly asked.

"I was about to head over to the nursery right now. I didn't get to see them for very long in the operating room."

A nurse escorted the five of them to the nursery, where they all got to see the babies. Cecilia stood closest to the glass as she looked down at them lying side by side in their miniature baby beds. They looked so tiny, but they also looked so beautiful and healthy at the same time. Both of them were sleeping, so no one got to see what color their eyes were. Cecilia listened as Shelly and Karen speculated that the most likely color would be either brown like their mother's or blue like their father's.

"I think it's safe to say they got their hair color from their grandmother," Shane observed as he clasped Cecilia's hand. The babies both had a full head of light brown hair almost the same color as Cecilia's. In the months since the fire, she hadn't used the black color rinse once, and her natural color had fully returned. At Shane's comment, she reached up one hand to touch her hair and smiled. She suddenly felt so happy looking down at the babies that she almost giggled.

"They're so cute it's hard to believe they're real," Cecilia breathed. She knew she probably sounded ridiculous, but she couldn't stop herself from gushing about her granddaughters. Everything they did was amazing. The one on the right was sucking on her fist, and that was amazing. The one on the left yawned, and that was amazing.

She stood there staring at them for so long she didn't even notice everyone else had left the nursery until Shane whispered in her ear, "How does it feel to have two beautiful, healthy granddaughters?"

"It feels... amazing," she whispered back.

"I take it you and Rebecca made up?"

"I think so."

"Good. Maybe now you can talk to her, so Brent can really get this investigation going."

And just like that, Cecilia was pulled back into the real world where not everything was so amazing.

"She has preeclampsia; she doesn't need to talk about stressful things right now."

Shane sighed and pulled away to look at her. "Somehow I knew you'd say something like that."

"Shane, please," Cecilia said as her eyes returned to the babies. They were so cute. "The wedding is in a month. For the next few weeks, I'll be focusing all my time on helping Rebecca adjust to being a new mom, finishing up the training for my new assistants, making sure the remodeling is completed on schedule, making the most important wedding cake ever, and learning that dance that Viri insists is going to wow everyone. Just let me get through that before you ask me to let everyone pry into my past."

A long, heavy silence passed. Cecilia felt his frustration, but she stood her ground. She simply was not ready to talk to Rebecca or Brent yet, and Shane would just have to accept that fact.

Finally, he sighed and said, "Okay. Not another word from me until after the wedding. There's been so many serious things going on lately, we both need a break from it all. For the next few weeks we can just focus on the lighter side of life—the dancing, the flowers, the cake, the ceremony and reception. We're supposed to be a happily engaged couple, so that's who we're going to be for the next month. I'll just think of it all as a bright, cheerful spot in the midst of so much darkness. Don't think for a minute that I'm going to forget about that guy and what he did to you, Cecilia. It keeps me up at night, and tortures me knowing that he, and whoever else was there, did something so terrible to a child and got away with it for so many years."

Shane's sobering words sank in, and Cecilia continued to stare down at her beautiful granddaughters as he wrapped his arms around her and held her for a long time. Wanting to embrace the lighter concerns in her life, even if they were only a temporary reprieve from her past, Cece said, "Viri really is a demanding ballroom instructor." At her words, Shane laughed and hugged her tighter.

Chapter 22

The day of Cecilia and Shane's wedding dawned gray and dreary. There were 30mph gusts of frigid, dry wind and a blanket of winter clouds hiding the sun. The weather forecast called for a few flurries throughout the day and more severe winter weather to come in just a few days.

It was only five o'clock in the morning when Cece opened her eyes, but she felt like she'd slept half the day away. On a normal day, she'd be at the bakery putting sheets of cakes and cookies into her walk-in oven. While the cakes baked, she'd be at the giant mixer making the buttercream frosting that served as a crumb coat for most of her special projects and the main décor for most of the simpler cakes. By the time the cakes, cookies, brownies, and frosting were done she'd begin decorating everything, starting with the cakes for the display cases and any orders that were to be picked up within a couple of days. She had her scheduling down to the minute, and she usually took her first break around 8:45, just before opening.

Today, however, she was doing none of her usual tasks. Instead, she was sitting in her window seat, staring out at the winter sky and trying to wrap her mind around the enormity of today. She hadn't seen Shane all week. He'd been doing last minute wedding preparations, and she'd been assembling the cake that would make or break her career. She wondered what his thoughts were like this morning. Was he now regretting the hasty proposal that had ballooned way out of proportion? When she'd agreed to his crazy scheme, she never imagined it would turn out like this. Almost a thousand people were expected to attend the wedding and reception, and all eyes would be on her and her cake.

Shortly after six, her entourage showed up at her door. They hurried her into the car waiting at the end of her sidewalk, and whisked her to the famous estate outside of town where the wedding and reception were to take place. Last time she talked to Shane he'd told her that his grandmother, of all people, had called to congratulate him on getting married and offer Howard Hills as the venue. The ballroom hadn't been used in decades, and the entertainment media had been buzzing about the world-renowned ballroom since the day Shane announced the wedding would take place there. People had been curious for a long time; everyone wanted to know if it was dilapidated as it was rumored to be, or if it had been kept in pristine condition for the past fifty years. Cece was just as curious as everyone else, though she would never admit it. She figured that the ballroom was probably old, but well cared for.

About twenty minutes outside of town, they turned down a private drive that seemed to go on forever. Eventually they came to a tall, ornamental wrought iron security gate. The driver identified himself, and the gate swung open, giving them access to a dignified stone path that led to the mansion. Cece glanced at the sleek looking team of people who were supposed to make her flawless for the day, and saw that they looked just as curious as she felt. She let down her window and stuck out her head to get a good view as they approached the historic mansion. Despite the cold wind ripping at her hair and the flurries chilling her face, she kept looking and enjoyed every second of the ride up the stone drive.

They rounded a bend, and the mansion came into view all at once. The impressive façade included Palladian style stone columns arranged symmetrically around the entire mansion. The two columns on either side of the main entrance were larger and more detailed than the smaller columns stretching out along the many wings of the structure. The stained glass dome above the ballroom that she'd heard so much about was clearly visible from outside. Its gentle, colorful swell above the otherwise gray edifice caught her eye and held it as the car got closer to the entrance. It was one of the most magnificent places she'd ever seen in her life. Even with the backdrop of the gray clouds and the barren winter landscape, it was beautiful. She had to remind herself to breathe normally as she craned her neck to stare up at all the intricately carved details in the stone. It was better than anything she could have imagined—better than a fairytale castle.

Cece sat down as the car came to a stop; she laughed softly when she saw the members of her entourage all hanging out the opposite window. "Impressive? Isn't it?" she grinned. At the sound of her voice, they scrambled back in so fast they bumped their heads together. Cece smiled, and so did they.

The driver came around to Cece's side and opened the door. As she stepped out, an older woman in uniform rushed out the front door and draped a coat around her shoulders. She was then whisked into the foyer where even more people were waiting for her.

"Miss Graves, I'm Agnes, the head housekeeper. We're all honored to be at your service. Anything you want, anything at all, you must not hesitate to ask," an older, gray-haired lady stepped forward and said.

"I was told the cake was delivered last night. I'd like to see it," Cece smiled.

"Certainly, Miss," Agnes said. "You'll have to forgive the kitchen today. There's a lot more going on than usual." Agnes then turned and led Cece toward the kitchen.

Cece took in everything as they left the entryway and walked down an immense corridor that eventually led to the kitchen. It felt strange to be in a place so at odds with everything she'd known growing up. Her footsteps echoed in the marble hall, and she momentarily wished she'd worn a quieter pair of shoes.

Halfway down the long corridor, Cece noticed one of the many sets of doors that led to the ballroom. Her steps slowed down as she tried to peak through the ornate glass doors, but the gloomy day made it impossible for her to see what was inside without opening them.

"Sorry, Dear," Agnes said as she gently ushered Cece on. "Mr. Gregory's orders were to keep you happy, but not to let you see the ballroom until tonight when everything's finished."

"Why?" Cece asked.

"I don't know, but he was *adamant* about it."

Cece moved on without protest. After going down a few more small hallways that branched off the main corridor, Agnes opened a very ordinary looking set of doors that led to the kitchen.

At that point, Cece glanced back at the cluster of people who had trailed her to the kitchen and said, "I'd like to go in alone, please." She ignored the strange looks they gave her, and stepped through the doors alone.

Half of the nervous tension inside her dissipated as soon as she saw the cake. It sat safely on a wheeled cart inside the walk-in fridge. She circled around it several times, examining it for damage. When she found none, she breathed a sigh of relief.

The make-up artists, hair stylist, seamstress, dress designer, and uniformed servants were still standing just outside the kitchen door when she returned. Agnes stepped forward and smiled at her. "Shall I show you to the bridal dressing suite?"

"Yes, please," Cece answered in a formal tone, because everyone else was being so formal and that seemed to be what was required of her.

They embarked on another long walk down many corridors and hallways that eventually led to the living areas of the mansion. The hallway leading to the bridal suite had a distinctly different feel from the more formal public areas of the mansion. Suddenly, there was wall-to-wall plush carpeting and the atmosphere was warmer and more inviting.

The bridal dressing suite was luxurious and expansive. Her dress had been delivered, and was on display on a manikin in the center of the room. Flower arrangements were clustered throughout the room, and a table with an assortment of snacks, breakfast items, and fresh fruit had been set up along one wall. While Cece was busy looking around, still trying to take in everything, the make-up ladies rushed to the enormous vanity and opened their cases, revealing all the beauty tools they'd brought along. Cece had never seen such an assortment of make-up in her life. She glanced at her reflection, and then back at the wedding dress. There was so much to do between now and the ceremony.

"Let's get started then," she said mostly for her own benefit, but everyone else in the room sprang into immediate action at her words.

"The photographer wants to get started on the wedding party photos in half an hour, so let's get you into the dress,"

Catherine said as Shelly, Rebecca and Karen looked on. They had all arrived shortly after Cece, and they were now all sitting around in the plush chairs in their wedding finery. Rebecca didn't look like she'd had twins just six and a half weeks ago, but she did look like a mother now. There was a fullness to her hips and breasts that hadn't been there before the pregnancy, and now that her giant belly was gone, the changes to her body were more obvious. Cece hadn't been able to fully realize that her daughter was a woman until after she'd given birth. Now she felt a poignant tenderness as she observed her daughter. She'd never have the young, innocent Rebecca back, but she was just fine with that. Actually, she looked forward to knowing the more empowered young woman who stood before her now. Time never moved back, only forward, and it pulled everyone and everything along with it.

Rebecca and Karen assisted Catherine in getting Cece into the wedding dress, all the while gushing over the unique design. Cece wasn't so sure that such a colorful dress was a good idea, but everyone who saw her in it seemed to think it was incredible. She had her back to the mirror as the women all fussed over her and made a myriad of last minute adjustments to her dress. When Cece finally looked into the mirror, even she was taken aback. This was the best she'd ever looked in her life. Everyone else surrounded her, beaming at her and assuring her that she was the most beautiful bride ever, and all Cece could feel was regret; it was all for a cake. How different would she feel right now if this really was her wedding day?

A knock sounded, and Karen said, "The photographer...he's five minutes early."

One of the uniformed servants hastened forward and opened the door, but it wasn't the photographer; it was Shane.

"You're not supposed to see the bride before the ceremony!" Karen screeched.

Shelly rushed forward with, "Whatever it is, it can wait!" as she attempted to shut the door in his face.

"It can't wait," he said as he firmly pushed the door open and stepped into the room. "Can all of you please give us a moment alone?" He looked so serious, sounded so serious, that everyone immediately cleared the room.

Cece stood rooted to the spot in the center of the room. Had he changed his mind about everything? She swallowed and asked, "What's up?"

He didn't answer right away; instead he turned and closed the door.

"Don't tell me you've changed your mind."

"No! It's not that at all," he quickly reassured her.

He stared at her for so long, she started to think he disapproved of her unconventional wedding dress.

Shane honestly couldn't think of a plausible reason to have forced his way into the bridal dressing suite, other than the fact that he just felt like he *had* to talk to Cecilia alone before the wedding events officially began. There she was, standing in the center of the room looking like a magazine cover come to life. She was so exquisite he wanted to stare at her to his heart's content; the only problem with that was that he'd probably never get enough of her.

"I just wanted to come check on you and make sure you're still okay with all of this. *Are* you okay?"

Cecilia looked up at him in obvious relief. "I'm okay," she smiled, but there was something lurking in her expression that pulled at his heart. Maybe she was thinking of the talk she needed to have with Rebecca. He'd told her he wouldn't pressure her about it until after the wedding, and he had a feeling she saw today as something of a deadline.

"Hey," he smiled as he got closer to her. "Remember that bright spot I told you about the night the babies were born? Today is that day. You don't need to worry about anything. I'm not going to turn into an ogre and drag you straight to Brent's office at midnight tonight, Cecilia. I just want you to enjoy today."

"What about you? Are you okay with all this?" she asked.

While he considered his answer, Shane thought again about the number of times he'd almost told her how much he loved her. "I've been okay with it since the beginning; it was my idea. Remember?" When she didn't say anything else, he went on, "Are you ready for this? Once we step out there, you're going to have to be on all day, pretending like this really is your wedding day. It won't work if we aren't affectionate. It has to look natural... to *be* natural."

"I know. I can do it."

"Can you?" he asked as he inched even closer to her. He didn't stop until he was close enough to cup her face in his hands.

"Of course I can," she said more quietly this time as she looked into his eyes.

"I know it's awkward, because we're still dating, but things can go back to the way they were when this is over if you want." He didn't want to pressure her about anything today, he just wanted to set her at ease and cheer her up a bit, but standing so close to her, close enough to breathe in her energy and look into her eyes, tended to sap him of his resolve and his better judgment. He felt her arms go around him to return his embrace, and all he could think about was how much he loved her and how much he wished this really was their wedding day; he wasn't thinking that she might not be ready to hear it yet. Before he could stop himself, he felt the words tumbling out of him. "Cecilia, let's just make today our real wedding. We already have a license, and all the guests, including everyone we care about, are here. Let's make it official and skip the annulment later," he whispered in her ear. "Cecilia, I love you, and I want you to be my wife for real." He still wasn't thinking as his lips sought out hers and lingered above them, savoring the moment. Just then, all he could do was feel.

She didn't say anything to his proposal, but she did kiss him. The first touch of her lips was always soft, warm, and sweeter than he remembered. Her arms wrapped around his neck as his went around her waist, and he noticed that she tasted like fresh fruit and ginger. He could have stayed like that indefinitely, but their kiss ended with a sharp knock on the door.

"Is everything okay in there?" Karen yelled.

"Yes," Shane answered. His eyes never left Cecilia's face, and he wished it wasn't so hard to tell what she was thinking sometimes. "Are you okay?" he asked.

"I hope you aren't going to ask me that every time we kiss today," she whispered with a smile.

He smiled back and said, "I promise I won't." With those words, he offered her his arm and they stepped out into the hall together.

"Is *that* what was so important?" Karen demanded as she pointed at Shane's face. Everyone else in the area chuckled and looked away as Agnes discretely handed Shane a handkerchief to clean Cecilia's lipstick off of his face.

He spent the next hour watching the photographer capture candid shots of Cecilia and the bridal party as Agnes gave them a tour of the mansion. The original plan had been for the pictures of the bride and groom to be taken after the ceremony, but since Shane was already with them, he was included in many of the pictures. As they walked up the main staircase that led up to a landing just under a small rotunda above the foyer, Cecilia reached out for his hand and smiled at him several times. The large picture windows along the length of the staircase allowed them an unimpeded view of the winter landscape outside. Flurries swirled around in the gusty wind, and the quality of the light filtering in added a sense of coziness to the day. He imagined what it would be like to spend time cuddled up by the fire with her on a day like today. All the smiles she tossed his way had to be a good sign.

The last picture they took on the stairs was by far the best. The photographer wanted to get several shots of Cecilia descending the stairs alone, so he could capture all the details of her wedding dress. The bodice of the dress was made of a shimmery, ultra-sheer mesh material that hugged her curves. It was winter white, and almost completely see-through. The detail that saved the dress from scandalous indecency was the strategically placed, colorfully embroidered flowers that covered the bust area and swirled down in a delicate little trail around the waist of the dress. Where the bodice ended, the full skirt of the dress was gathered together by a single clasp made up of more flowers. The skirt had two layers, the inner layer was a rosy red colored satin, and the outer, more voluminous skirt was white with trim that matched the inner skirt. The outer skirt reminded Shane of a dramatic opera cape his mother wore once when his parents went out to the theatre. It was an interesting detail he'd never seen on a wedding dress before, but it worked well because this dress didn't have a train. He liked watching the way the dress billowed out behind her as she walked. It was one of the most unique and fashion forward wedding dresses he'd ever seen, and it seemed to fit her personality perfectly.

He was lost in thought when the ceremony began that afternoon. His brother, Brent, nudged him and gave him a quick smile as they took their places in front of all the guests. Shane had asked Brent to be his best man partly because he was the only one in the family who had any idea about the stress that he and Cecilia were dealing with. He watched absent mindedly as multiple women and young girls came down the aisle. Most of the ten bridesmaids were relatives of Karen's, all of them were young women whom he didn't know well. Karen was the maid of honor, so once she made it to the altar and took her place, Shane straightened up his posture and waited for Cecilia to appear in the chapel entrance. When she did appear, everyone in the chapel turned to get a glimpse of her and a collective gasp went through the place at the sight of her dress. Shane smiled at her and maintained eye contact as she strode toward him. He was glad he'd seen her in the dress in private first; otherwise he might not have been able to keep his thoughts decent throughout the ceremony. She finally got to his side, and Karen's father placed her hand in his before stepping back. The old man had tears in his eyes as he looked directly at Karen and said, "You're next," prompting a laugh from everyone in the chapel.

Throughout the entire ceremony, Shane kept looking down at Cecilia's dress. The bodice was so thin most of her smooth skin was easily visible. He found it so much easier to imagine her naked after seeing her in the risqué wedding dress. While the preacher talked about what marriage meant, and delivered a little sermon to everyone, he listened with half an ear, but when it was time for them to state their vows, he focused all of his attention on the words he said. When he promised to love, honor, and cherish her in the good times and the bad, until death parted them, he meant it. His eyes stayed locked on hers, and he tried to detect some hint of what she was thinking as she spoke the same vows to him.

They were pronounced husband and wife, and everyone cheered as he resisted the urge to give her a lingering kiss. He wanted her to be at ease, so he gave her a bear hug and picked her up to plant a kiss on her cheek. She seemed to appreciate his gesture of circumspectness, and she smiled and kissed his forehead as he held her up.

They walked down the aisle hand in hand, and as soon as they stepped out of the chapel, the wedding planner was on them again, ushering them to their next scheduled place. Shane wished he'd had the foresight to include more alone time with her so they could talk, but then he hadn't planned on blurting out his feelings before the ceremony either.

Cecilia was whisked away for a quick touch up from her beauty team, and Shane went to check that everything in the ballroom was as it should be. The dining tables had been set up on the mezzanine levels along the perimeter of the dance floor. There were four mezzanines; all of them branching off of the single grand staircase he and Cecilia would walk down when they entered the ballroom from the servant doors of the top mezzanine. It would look remarkable to all the guests, but it required a lot of stair climbing for him and Cecilia before the grand appearance. After Shane checked that the cake had been placed according to his instructions, he was supposed to join Cecilia and the wedding planner at the top mezzanine off of the ballroom, where they were to spend the next forty-five minutes taking pictures with the complete wedding party and some of the guests.

The guests slowly trickled out of the chapel and meandered around the bar set up in the main corridor for cocktail hour. Shane slipped into the ballroom while no one was looking. The cake was set up behind a curtain of flowers, and it was to be unveiled with everyone looking. The wedding planner had suggested keeping it hidden to build suspense. Shane walked behind the curtain and looked up at the magnificent cake again. Cecilia hadn't let him see it at all while she'd worked on it through the week. He didn't get his first glimpse of it until last night when it was delivered. At first, Cecilia had insisted on doing it herself, but Shane managed to convince her to let him take care of it. First of all it was massive, and it took him and a professional crew of three other men to move it properly without damaging it. The other reason he'd insisted on being the one to move it was that he'd arranged a last minute surprise for her.

The editor of the most popular wedding magazine in the country had contacted him a couple of months ago for permission to cover his wedding. He'd agreed to the feature on the condition that the magazine allow an entire page of the feature to be for the cake alone. The editor had wanted to see the finished cake before signing off on the deal, and last night Shane had let the photographer into Cecilia's bakery so he could send some pictures of the cake to the editor. The results of his late night escapade had been swift and very satisfactory. The editor had been so impressed by the cake, she'd agreed to Shane's terms, and even said she wanted to put the cake on the cover. She'd sent more professionals to the Bakery, and Cecilia's cake had a photo-shoot last night before being delivered to Howard Hills. It had another photo shoot at the mansion, and she had no idea that she was about to be a new star in the cake world.

The band was tuning their instruments as Shane emerged from behind the flower curtain. He walked over and greeted the musicians with a friendly smile before making his way upstairs. Cocktail hour would be over soon, and the guests would fill up the ballroom over the next half hour. If he was lucky, he might be able to steal a few minutes alone with Cecilia.

"What am I supposed to do when we get to the bottom of the stairs?" Cece asked for the third time. The wedding planner was so busy giving out instructions to everyone else she hadn't heard her the first two times.

"You and Shane will go to the left where the receiving line will form, but first you have to pause and pose together as you are announced. That's when the photographer from the magazine will start taking reception shots of the two of you. You have to go left because that's the direction the videographer expects you to go."

Cece repeated the woman's instructions to herself and tried to calm down some. She hadn't peeked into the ballroom, but she heard the bright chatter filtering through the doors in front of her. The rest of the wedding party and attendants had already gone through the doors and descended the staircase to the applause of all the wedding guests. Even the wedding planner looked a little nervous as she smiled at Cece and Shane and said, "You're next." Then she opened the doors and said into her headset, "Cue music for the bride and groom."

Shane grasped her hand as the two of them stepped forward together. The band below them launched into the 1940 big band classic, *In the Mood,* as they started down the grand staircase. For the first few seconds of their descent, Cece was blinded by the camera flashes from below, and she held onto Shane's arm for support. She was so immediately overwhelmed she might have fallen all the way down the stairs if she hadn't been holding on to him. The stairs were a lot steeper than she thought they'd be, and between the loud cheering and the band she couldn't hear her own thoughts. When the flashes died down some, she looked up at the storied glass dome above them, and then down at all the beautiful tables and flower arrangements. Everything looked so perfect, so over the top romantic, that she couldn't help but smile again for the millionth time that day.

At the bottom of the stairs, another photographer crouched down in front of them as they posed. Another bright flash, and then they were walking off to the left, where a man with a video camera followed their movements. Most of the guests were still clustered around the entrance and sprinkled about the dance floor. Cece and Shane took their places at the receiving line with Karen and Rebecca, and a line of guests quickly formed to greet them.

Most of the people who walked by to shake their hands and wish them well were unfamiliar to Cece, but she beamed at everybody today. Numerous VIP's from other parts of the country had showed up, but after being introduced to the governor of New York, several CEO's of fortune 500 companies, and a few well known Hollywood actors, Cece stopped trying to keep track of how many important people had come to her wedding. People moved quickly, but the receiving line still took more than half an hour to complete. Just as it was wrapping up, the wedding planner appeared again to remind them that the next item on the itinerary was their first dance as husband and wife. Catherine appeared and deftly removed the outer skirt to Cece's wedding dress, converting it into an elegant dance costume in a matter of moments.

They hadn't had a moment to sit down, and already it was time for them to do their exciting, yet difficult, swing dance. As they took their place in the center of the ballroom, Cece tipped her head back and looked up at the stained glass dome above her. She'd run out of appropriate adjectives to describe everything that happened today, so she didn't even try to find one to describe the ballroom. There simply wasn't a word that could do it justice.

"What are you thinking about right now?" Shane asked.

"I was just committing this moment to memory, since I'll probably never be in such a magnificent place again in my life," she admitted.

Shane didn't get the chance to respond, because the music had started. For the next five minutes, the two of them executed the technically difficult dance flawlessly. Viri had drilled the steps and lifts into them until the routine became second nature. They didn't have to count steps and memorize anything tonight. All they had to do was feel the music and follow their instincts. When the last series of lifts happened, Cece felt excitement coming from their audience in tangible waves. The end of the swing portion of their dance came when Shane tossed her up, and then caught her after she'd executed a full split in midair. Everyone cheered so loud after that move; she barely heard the music change into the slower song that would accompany their foxtrot.

"I can't believe I just showed a ballroom full of people my wife's legs like that," Shane joked as their dance came to an end. They held each other for an extra-long moment in the middle of the dance floor. Once the applause died down some, they took their seats.

Cece slipped her feet out of her heels as soon as she sat down. Her feet were throbbing after being on them almost continuously for the past three hours. It was now just past five. The wedding planner reminded them that the toasts and dinner were up next. Cece was grateful she wouldn't have to stand again for at least another hour. The cake cutting ceremony was the reason behind the entire day, but it wasn't the moment that had been on her mind all evening. Every time Shane looked at her or touched her today, her mind meandered back to that moment when he'd told her he loved her. She wanted to hold on to that moment forever.

Shane had been waiting all evening for the perfect time to tell Cecilia that her cake had made the cover of her favorite magazine. Just before the cake cutting ceremony, he was about to tell her, but Rebecca walked up to hug her. He stepped back and let them have their moment.

Clearly the cake had touched Rebecca in some personal way that Shane didn't know about.

Rebecca asked her where she got the idea for the design, and when Cecilia said, "*The Rainbow Goblins*," Rebecca grabbed her in an emotional embrace.

After Rebecca faded back into the background, Shane and Cecilia cut the cake in front of everyone.

As soon as Shane got a moment alone with Cecilia, he asked, "What was that all about?"

"What?"

"Why was Rebecca so emotional about the cake? And what are rainbow goblins?"

Cecilia chuckled and said, "I think she's just overwhelmed right now because her body is still adjusting to motherhood. *The Rainbow Goblins* is a book by Ul De Rico. I used to read it to her when she was younger. It was her and Sarah's favorite book. The inspiration for this cake came from the last scene in the book when all the flowers and birds absorbed the color from the rainbow to help it hide from the goblins who wanted to eat it."

"The cake is so beautiful; I didn't even want to cut it," Shane said as he glanced back at it. People were still gathered around it, circling it and studying the intricate design. He'd done the same thing when he first saw it the night before. Cecilia had made flowers and miniature birds in various stages of development, and then applied them to the cake in a way that made them appear as if they were somehow morphing from the colors in the frosting. Even the photographer from the magazine had said it was one of the most artistic cakes he'd ever seen.

"I'm happy people seem to like it. I had a hard time coming up with a good idea for the cake. When you told me to make the cake I'd most want for my own wedding, I was at a loss because I never fantasized about having a wedding. But then I thought about the cake I would have made for Rebecca's wedding if I'd been there, and this was what came out. I wish I'd been there for her when she got married. I saw the pictures of her wedding cake and felt so bad. I could have given her something spectacular, something she deserved."

They had a few more quiet moments together, they danced some more, and then it was almost time for their departure. Shane watched from Cecilia's side as all the single women gathered on the dance floor for the bouquet toss. Cecilia stood next to the railing on the first mezzanine level, and looked out at the hundred or so women who were vying for a good position. She seemed to be scanning the crowd for something.

"What are you looking for?" Shane asked.

"Karen," Cecilia said with a playful smirk. Shane looked around too, and spotted Karen still seated at her table. She clearly wasn't interested in trying to catch the bouquet. He also spotted his brother Brent nearby, watching Karen. When Shane looked at Cecilia again, her eyes were on Karen, and she raised her arm as if she were about to try to launch the bouquet into space. Shane tried his best not to laugh like a maniac as the bouquet sailed clear over the crowd of now crestfallen women on the dance floor and straight into Karen's lap. Karen looked up in surprise, and Cecilia just smiled and waved on her way out of the ballroom. With that final laugh, their wedding day was officially over. He had one more surprise, but they would be alone when it happened.

The wedding planner was waiting by the back exit that led to the guesthouse. The small path to the guesthouse wound through the formal gardens and around several sculptures, so it was a picturesque and relaxing way to end such a hectic day. Before they stepped out of the door, Shane removed his jacket and draped it around Cecilia. "You need this more than I do with that see through dress you have on," he said.

She accepted his jacket without protest and preceded him out the door. He placed his hand on her waist as he followed. They were about halfway to the guest house when he heard the first crack of the fireworks. He hadn't warned her to expect them, and she flinched until he said, "Turn around and look; it's a good thing."

When she turned, he kept looking at her instead of watching the fireworks display going on behind the mansion. This moment had been worth waiting all day; the look of childish delight that came over her face filled him with joy.

"Oh!" she gasped as she watched the bright colors explode against the wintery night sky. "Those are so pretty!" She even jumped up and down and clapped her hands like an excited child.

It was a short display, lasting only five minutes, but it was enough to make her happy. By the end of it, she was looking at him like he'd just handed her the moon.

"Your daughter told me you'd never seen fireworks before, so I thought you might like to see some tonight. And before you ask about the cost, let me assure you that it was minimal. A friend and I put it together, and he's such a pyromaniac he volunteered to set it off for free," he said with a smile.

She didn't say anything to that, instead she smiled at him and reached out for his hand. The flurries had died down earlier in the evening, but the air was still very frigid as they walked the rest of the path toward the guest house. Her hand felt warm and comfortable nestled inside his.

The path meandered through a sculpture garden, and they paused for a few minutes to admire an old stone statue of the goddess Aphrodite. The statue was stretched out along a bench in a pose that could only be described as sensual. The strategic draping on her gown and her facial expression were too tastefully done to be considered scandalous, but there was no doubt that they were looking at the goddess of love.

When Cecilia shivered, Shane stood closer and wrapped his arms around her.

"I don't know why, but I really like that statue," she said.

"Me too. It reminds me of the way you look in my dreams sometimes," Shane admitted.

She drew in a sharp breath and asked, "You have dreams about me?"

"Why wouldn't I? I love you." When she shivered again, he took her hand and pulled her along. They walked the rest of the way to the guest house in silence.

As it came into view, she said, "This place is huge. I was expecting something normal."

"It's actually about five thousand square feet, but it's separated in half, like a duplex. Norman and Rebecca are staying in the other side tonight."

"Where are the babies?"

"I knew you were going to ask me that. They're with a babysitter right now. They've been there since the ceremony started. We can go see them if you want."

"It's late; I don't want to wake them."

Cece looked around the entrance to the guest house as Shane shut the door behind them. Just like the bridal suite, and the chapel, and the ballroom, there were little touches of romance all around them. Now that it was just the two of them, Cece almost didn't know how to behave. Was she supposed to just switch off all the natural affection that had been between them all day? Or was she supposed to respond to his earlier declaration by falling into his arms and agreeing to live happily ever after with him?

She turned towards Shane to find him leaning against the door with his arms crossed and one ankle over the other. He looked so relaxed she felt some of the tension leave her body.

"I'm glad you liked the ballroom." He smiled and reached out his hand toward her. It felt so natural for her to lay her hand in his and move closer.

"Everything was so perfect today, it's hard to believe that it was all for a ca—"

"Shhh..." Shane cut her off with a gentle finger over her lips. "Let's just enjoy tonight. We don't have to talk about that right now. I don't know about you, but I'm kind of curious to see what the honeymoon suite looks like."

"Me too," Cece confessed with a slight smile. She looked up to see an answering smile in Shane's eyes and her body relaxed a little more. They walked hand in hand down the hall leading to the master suite. When Cece heard they were spending the night in the guest house she'd imagined a normal sized house. This one was just as impressive as the main mansion; it was just on a smaller scale.

When they reached the double doors, they each turned a knob and pushed at the same time. The doors swung open to reveal a lovely room, complete with all the usual romantic trimmings. "Yet another perfect room. It's a shame this one will have to go to waste," she sighed. "How is it possible to have crammed so many perfect things into one day?"

"It doesn't have to go to waste. Even if you don't want me in here, you can still enjoy it."

"But I wouldn't feel right taking this room when the estate belongs to your family. I'm the outsider here."

Shane ignored her protest and pulled her into the room, where she was instantly enveloped in the fragrance of flowers. "I think you'll find a bunch of lady products just for you in the bathroom. Why don't you check it out?"

"But..."

"No buts, Cecilia. I'm sure it's filled with a bunch of stuff *I* don't need; I'm a guy. Have a nice bath, and then we can talk when you get out if you want. I'll be in the room next door."

Before she could reply, he left the room and closed the door behind him.

Cece felt deflated at his abrupt departure. He'd been so attentive all day that she'd expected a good night hug at the least.

It really was a shame for such a beautiful room to go to waste. She fingered the fine, silky coverings on the bed on her way to the bathroom. In the bathroom, she found just about everything she could imagine needing for one night. She undressed as the tub filled with warm water. Once she'd removed all of her wedding clothes, she sat on the side of the tub and poured in the scented bath salts. While she waited for the salts to dissolve, she removed her make-up and cleansed her face. During her de-glamorization, she reflected on all that had happened today. Everything from the ceremony to the fireworks had been so perfect it was like living in a fairytale. Even the part where her prince charming had confessed his love for her had been perfect. The problem with fairytales was that she didn't believe in them; she never had, and she never would.

She hadn't been able to say the words to him earlier, but her love had been in that kiss and in every look, touch, and smile she'd given him today. She'd never felt such powerful emotions in her life. There was the absolute joy that he told her he loved her, and then there was the pain of the fact that he didn't *really* love her. He didn't know enough about her to know if he could love someone like her. She wanted to be with him, not just as a friend and not just for a little while, but at the same time she was afraid to reach out to him. She wasn't about to tell him just how much she wanted him around. He came from one of the wealthiest and most powerful families in the world, and she was the orphaned daughter of a prostitute. Even if he could accept her and where she came from, how could she ask him to be with her? She had way too much baggage to subject him to a long-term relationship with her. Ever since that night in the park, he'd been going out of his way to be good to her. The concern in his eyes, the warmth of his touch, and his fierce determination to vanquish all her demons touched her deeply. But those things also served as reasons why they could never be together. She didn't want to be responsible for ruining his life the way she'd ruined her daughter's. She'd just keep her feelings to herself and get on with her sordid, dramatic life when they parted ways in the morning.

She lay back in the warm water and closed her eyes and thought about the way Shane could look at her and melt her tension away with a single smile. She imagined his arms around her, as they had been all day, and fell asleep in the tub.

A quiet knock at the door woke her. "Yes?" she called out.

"Just making sure you're okay. You've been in there almost an hour."

Cece emerged from the now tepid water and wrapped up in the oversized bathrobe. She opened the door to the room and said, "I'm out now."

He was standing next to the bed, looking impossibly handsome in a plain white t-shirt and a pair of sweats.

"I have something for you," he smiled.

Cece sighed and said, "Don't you think you've given me enough already?"

He shrugged and said, "You bring out the generosity in me. I'll let you get dressed and be back in a few minutes."

After he shut the door, Cece sat down hard on the bed. She really wished he would stop being so nice to her. Parting with him would be hard enough as it was. She opened the armoire where Agnes had assured her she would find her clothes. When she looked for the t-shirt she'd packed, she found a silk night gown with a note from Karen instead. Cece growled at her friend's well-meaning though misguided intentions. She knew she shouldn't put it on, but part of her wondered how he would react if he saw her in it.

She slipped it on and looked into the full length mirror. She ran her fingers through her hair and preened a little, noticing how much better she looked in the soft candlelight. Shane's sudden knock startled her, and she grabbed the bathrobe. She threw it on over the lingerie and opened the door.

"Come in," she said as she tucked her hair behind her ear and looked up at him.

"I thought you were going to get dressed."

"I did. Karen decided to steal my overnight bag and replace my things with a gift."

"Oh, really?"

"It's lingerie."

"Oh..." he said with a look that reminded her of Superman's ex-ray vision. "Is that why you're keeping that damp robe on?"

"Yeah, that and the fact that it's cold in here," Cece admitted.

"We can't have you cold on your wedding day," Shane said as he hastened over to the fireplace. He placed a few logs inside, and soon had a fire going.

While he was busy tending the fire, Cece opened the armoire again and removed the present she'd wrapped for him early that morning in the bridal dressing suite.

"What's this?" he asked as she handed it to him.

"It's a gift. A parting gift, I guess."

He opened the gift without speaking again. There was a framed portrait of his mother inside. She'd been working on it in her spare time over the past month; it was one of the best portraits she'd ever done.

"How did you do this? I didn't even know you could do portraits," he said eventually.

"I got the picture from Norman and Rebecca. I've been doing portraits for a long time. I took a few art classes here and there when I had time over the years. Drawing skills come in handy when it comes to sketching cakes for customers," she explained.

"I really didn't expect this. I'm speechless." He sat down on the bed and continued to admire the small portrait in his hands.

Cece sat next to him and placed her hand on his arm. "I'm glad you like it."

"Like it? I love it." He got up and put the portrait on the nightstand. "Now I have something for you."

Cece's heart leapt into her throat as he pulled a small jewelry box out of his pocket. She was reluctant to accept it, but he prodded her.

"Go on. Open it," he said.

Inside was a locket, a large heart-shaped silver locket with a single lily engraved on the front. "Thanks, Shane, it's lovely," she said.

"Open the locket, Cecilia."

She looked at him with questioning eyes, and then she opened the locket. What she found inside caused her hands to tremble and her eyes to tear. "Where did you find this?" she whispered. She couldn't keep the emotion out of her voice as she stared down at the only picture she had of Sarah and Rebecca together. She'd taken it the year Sarah died, and she'd always kept it in a small frame beside her bed. She thought she'd lost it in the fire. She thought she'd never see Sarah's little face outside her own memories again. Tears fell from her eyes onto the locket and briefly obscured Sarah's smile before she wiped them away. "I thought I'd lost everything. How did you find this?"

"It was mostly luck. When the floor of your apartment collapsed it fell down to the fourth floor to an area that only had smoke damage. The people who lived in that apartment found it when they went back to salvage their own things, and they turned it in to the fire station. I held onto it until I found someone who could do photo restoration. It was burned, but you could still see their faces."

"Thank you, Shane. You didn't have to do this for me."

"I think I did have to," he responded as he put his arm around her.

Cece turned to him to tell him he didn't have to keep being so nice, and his lips were suddenly on hers. There was a hunger and a fire in this kiss that hadn't been there before. Cece felt a shock of sheer exhilaration spark through her. Her arms somehow wound their way around his neck and pulled him closer as she returned his kiss. She felt what little control she had over her emotions slipping away in that moment, but her complete acceptance didn't last long.

The moment she felt the soft mattress against her back she had to fight back the uneasiness that always settled within her when she thought about sex. She pushed at his shoulders, and he rose up to look at her.

"Jeez, Cecilia, don't look at me like that," he said as he gave her some more space.

"Like what?" She sat up and said. The added space between them managed to break through the romantic fog that had been clouding her brain a minute ago.

"Don't look at me like you're afraid of me. How could you think for a second that I would hurt you? Or do anything against your will? When I told you I love you earlier, those weren't just pretty words to make you feel good before the ceremony. I meant it."

"But you *can't* love me." The soft whisper escaped before Cece had the chance to censor herself.

"Why can't I?"

"You don't know anything about me. You don't know where I came from." She kept telling herself that the son of a billionaire and the daughter of a prostitute did not belong together.

"I know all the important things," he countered. "I know you are the most fascinating person I've ever met in my life. I know you are strong and beautiful and graceful. I know that you are a loving and caring person. What's not to love?" he said as he reached out towards her. His eyes willed her to accept his hand and take part in this beautiful moment.

He looked so open, so tender, that she almost reached back as she had earlier. She wanted to fall into his arms and tell him all the things she loved about him, but she just couldn't reach back this time. "There are things about me and my past that would shock you," she whispered instead. "Whatever feelings you think you have for me would vanish if you knew where I really came from."

"Try me. Tell me, and see for yourself that I really do love you, all of you," he challenged her with a look that bordered on angry.

She thought about all that had happened in that hotel before her mother died, but her mind couldn't form the words to begin a sentence that would make sense of so much darkness. How could she tell anyone what she'd run away from, and then willfully run back to years later? "I can't," she whispered. Her skin was crawling again from thinking about all the things Red Bone had done. "I don't think we should see each other anymore after tonight. That portrait was a parting gift... You deserve someone better than me, someone simple and uncomplicated, someone with a lot less baggage than I've got." Tears stung the back of her eyes, but she turned toward the fire so he couldn't see them.

"Cecilia, I understand you're afraid right now. Brent told me it would be hard for you to talk about your past because it might bring up feelings of shame. Honey, I'm not going to think any less of you because bad things happened to you when you were younger. Please stop pushing me away because of what you're worried I'm going to think about you. I am not going to judge you. You have to trust me on that."

"Maybe the reason I'm pushing you away has nothing to do with the investigation, maybe I'm just not the right woman for you. Maybe I can see that, and I'm trying to do you a huge favor by letting you go on without me in your life."

"That's not why you're pushing me away. You know what your problem is, Cecilia? You don't know what it truly means to love someone. All those years, you were afraid to let your own daughter express her love to you, because you were scared you weren't capable of returning that love. Now you know she loves you no matter what, and your relationship grew stronger after you accepted it as a fact of life. It's obvious how much you love her now that you've stopped being so guarded. Maybe you're arguing with me right now because you're afraid to accept my love. It's new, and it's different, but it's still the same. The love between a man and a woman isn't exactly the same as what you have with your daughter, but it is just as powerful and just as wonderful. Maybe you think that I'll expect too much from you in return for my love, but that's not the way love works. Listen to me Cecilia...love, real love, is free from all demands and expectations. It's a free gift, and all you have to do is accept it as it is. Even if we never see each other again after tonight, you should know that wherever I am, whatever I'm doing, I'll still be loving you. Even if I move on and have other relationships, it won't diminish the love I have for you. So, if you're ever down or lonely you can take small comfort in the fact that at least one man in the world loves you the way you deserve to be loved."

"Why are you making this more difficult than it has to be?"

"Because, I'm trying to convince you to give us a shot. In an ideal world, I wouldn't have to sit here on my wedding night convincing the woman I love to give me a chance to make her happy, but this isn't an ideal world."

She opened her mouth to protest again, but Shane stopped her. "Don't say anything else right now, Cecilia. I just want you to think about it, and at least consider the possibility of staying with me. I'm not like those men who hurt you, or those foster parents who abandoned you. Don't hold what they did against me."

He ran his fingers over her knuckles as he spoke, melting her tension away. The same sense of calm that came over her every time he was near came over her now. Maybe it was the look of absolute sincerity in the midnight depths of his eyes, or the romantic atmosphere, or maybe even the afterglow of the wedding and reception; or maybe she'd never know exactly why, but Cece said, "I'll think about it," right before she reached out for his hand. They lay back in bed together, tracing the outline of each other's fingers, caressing each other's palms, and not letting go for one second during the night. Cece tried to remember all her reasons for parting in the morning, but as the night wore on, those reasons became flimsy, like a gossamer fog fading quietly in the morning sun.

Chapter 23

Cece stepped out of the car behind Shane, and the blustery February wind ripped at her hair and clothes. She wasn't wearing a winter coat, because today they were flying to Hawaii for their surprise honeymoon. That morning at breakfast, Shane's family had presented them with the unexpected two week vacation, and backing out hadn't been an option. Shane told her multiple times during the drive to the airport that he'd had no idea about the honeymoon trip. He'd also made it clear that he thought they should go together, and "see how things go." Cece could hardly believe it, but she actually agreed with him. She'd never been on a vacation, so she was excited about the trip.

"The weather really took a turn for the worst," Shane smiled at her as she took his hand. "I hope this doesn't delay our flight."

Cece barely heard him over the roar of the wind in her ears. He trudged ahead to open the door to the terminal, and a slip of paper hit her in the face. The strong wind momentarily plastered it to her chin; she blinked a few times and pried it off to look at it.

"You coming?" Shane smiled at her when she paused in front of the door.

She was about to step through the door, but a strong sense of déjà vu came over her. She looked down at the paper and froze. This moment was eerily similar to one that had happened about twenty-seven years ago. She'd been thirteen and alone, unsure and uneasy about the future, and by chance she'd found a bus ticket to Nashville blowing in the wind. The ticket that had hit her in the face just now wasn't a bus ticket though, and it wasn't to Nashville; it was to Atlanta.

Cece was transported so quickly to the past she became largely unaware of her current surroundings. Some part of her was able to recognize that she was standing in Nashville in mid-February about to embark on a trip to Hawaii, but really she was miles away. A trance came over her, and she relived the moment when she'd found the bus ticket to Nashville and made the split second decision to run away. *Red Bone*, her mind whispered at her. This time she couldn't block it out as she always did; the whisper grew stronger and more insistent, until it was the only thought in her head. For years she'd wondered if that man would ever pay for all the things he'd done, things he'd done to her, to her mother, to Dot, and to countless other women. Within the space of a second, years of paralyzing fear were replaced with the sudden, overwhelming need to confront him. If she didn't go back right now, while the courage was coursing so strong through her veins, she may never find the nerve to go back there. "I have to go back," she whispered as she turned her back on the terminal and jogged toward the line of taxis at the curb.

"Take me to the bus station," she told the driver as she shut the taxi door. During the ride, she allowed herself to think about that fateful trip from years ago. She'd made the choice to throw herself out into the unknown rather than deal with the certainty of having her baby taken away and raised by the state as she had been. She had been a scared little girl, running away from the only home she'd ever known, a place she'd hoped to never see again. And now she was on her way back.

The taxi pulled to a stop in front of the bus station, and she paid as she exited. When she'd arrived in Nashville all those years ago, this bus station hadn't been so big. It had been a mere stop next to a gas station. She looked around at all the people inside, hiding from the cold winter wind, as she approached the ticket counter. Some would call those who took the bus the dregs of society, but Cece looked around and felt kinship with them. There was a young mother with two small children and a baby in line ahead of her. The baby stared at her as drool fell from his mouth onto his mother's shoulder. A tattered little green crochet hat was perched on his head.

Cece looked away from the baby and caught sight of an old man leaning on the wall across the room. He wore frayed socks and sandals that were a few sizes too small. He made eye contact with her, and she smiled at him. She looked around at all the other people as she waited for her turn at the ticket counter. The bus station was filled with people who either didn't have a car or couldn't afford a plane ticket. Cece had grown up around people like these; she was one of them. Despite her quality clothing and shoes, and her current impeccable appearance, she would always be one of them.

"May I help you?" the young woman behind the ticket counter asked. She took a look at Cece's designer attire and asked, "Are you lost, Ma'am?"

"No. I just want purchase a ticket for the next bus to Atlanta," Cece answered.

"That's it outside boarding right now. You sure you want to take the *bus*?"

"Yes," Cece said as she presented the woman with her credit card.

"Okay," the woman said as she typed on the keyboard in front of her. She handed Cece a printed ticket and smiled kindly. "There are no transfers, so if you just stay on the bus you should be fine."

Cece took the ticket and jogged outside to the bus. All the other passengers had boarded, and the last available seat was next to a young woman in a military uniform. The young woman's pensive gaze remained fixed on something outside the window as Cece took her seat. Cece leaned her head back and closed her eyes as the bus departed. The hum of the engine drowned out the noise of quiet conversations around her. She allowed herself to access all those parts of her subconscious that she'd fought with for years. She thought about the day her mother died and even all of the miserable days both before and after that day. For the first time ever, she also allowed herself to wonder what had happened to Dot. Somewhere deep inside, she knew it was something just as terrible as what had happened to her, if not more so. She explored the dark chasms in her mind so thoroughly she hardly noticed the five hour bus ride.

Cece waited until everyone else got off the bus, and then she got out of her seat with slow deliberation. She clutched her purse close to her body and left the bus. She hadn't set foot in Atlanta since she'd left as a child. The bus station loomed in front of her, and suddenly the past seemed very much like the present again.

The Atlanta bus station was much smaller than she remembered it. As a child it had seemed like a huge labyrinth, teeming with strange people and reeking of uncertainty. Now, as she stepped inside and looked around, all she saw were weary travelers and a large building that had absolutely no hold over her anymore.

She stepped outside and wrapped her scarf around her head to protect her ears from the cold wind. She hadn't worn her heavy coat that morning because she was supposed to be on her way to a tropical paradise. Now she wished she had it. The old neighborhood was a long walk from the bus station. She stuffed her hands in her pockets and started the long trek to the first home she ever knew as a child.

Every step she took was like an eerie echo of all the steps she'd taken to get away, only now she was going back. She had to be crazy to want to confront him now; she couldn't deny that something had snapped inside her. Even the knowledge that he could hurt her again didn't halt her progress. Her feet continued to carry her forward, no matter what obstacles her mind threw at her.

She'd only gone a couple of blocks when she heard someone calling her name. "Cecilia!" Shane's voice called out from somewhere far behind her. She turned to see him running towards her from the general direction of the bus station.

"What are you doing here?" she asked when he reached her.

"I think the better question is what are *you* doing here?" he panted.

Cece knew he was referring to her abrupt departure from the airport. She'd left him standing in the door, holding their overnight bags, with a confused look on his face. "I'm sorry I left like that this morning, but I had to. There's something I need to do, and you shouldn't be here. Where I'm going isn't exactly the safest part of town."

"If you think I'm just going to leave you alone here on the street, you're about to get a serious reality check."

"How did you know where I was?" She changed the subject, because his tone suggested he was seriously displeased with her.

"I jumped in a cab right after yours took off and paid the guy to follow you. I saw the bus take off right after you got on, so then I made the cab driver follow the bus all the way to Atlanta. Cecilia why on earth did you run off like that?! Do you have any idea how worried I was? If anything happened to you..."

"Well nothing happened, so you can calm down."

"Why didn't you just tell me you wanted to come here? I would have come with you."

"Because I didn't want you to see where I came from. I'm sorry, Shane, but there's something I need to take care of. I'll give you a call when I get home."

When Cece turned to continue down the street, Shane fell into step beside her.

"What are you doing?"

"I'm coming with you. You're my wife now, and apparently you need me even if you're too stubborn to see that. I wouldn't let any woman go into a potentially dangerous situation without help, especially not the one I love."

At his words, a little jolt went through Cece, but she didn't slow down. She walked a little faster; she didn't want to lose her nerve and completely abandon her purpose. If he wanted to tag along, she would just have to deal with it. "Things might get a little scary for you," she warned,

"Oh? And not for you?"

"I grew up here, Shane. I've seen the worst this place has to offer."

They walked in silence for the next hour. Shane offered her his jacket several times, but she refused because she had her own light jacket and he had on short sleeves. Eventually, Cece saw several familiar landmarks. So much had changed it was a wonder anything had remained the same. Houses that had seemed new when she left now appeared old and dilapidated. They passed by her old school and her old group home. The school still looked the same, except that the stone façade had been weathered by the years. The group home no longer housed orphans; the sign in front said that it was now a pregnancy crisis center.

Cece turned the corner that marked the last leg of her journey and reached out for Shane's hand. She stopped and took a deep breath. In less than a mile, she would be back. If she hadn't already come so far, she would have turned and ran.

When she'd lived here before, sex trafficking and child prostitutes had been a common sight along this very street. She'd grown up in the heart of it all, in the hotel run by her mother's pimp. This street had been notorious in those days. It was no place for anyone to walk alone, especially not a woman who didn't already have the protection of a pimp.

Cece looked ahead, and kept going. The hotel was still there. After all these years, it was still standing and it looked almost the same as she remembered it in her nightmares—ramshackle, rundown, seedy, and disgusting because of everything it represented. The neon sign that used to cast an ugly orange glow over all the women on display in front of the building had lost all of its letters to vandals. Graffiti was spread across almost all of the walls, and several windows were missing from the rooms. It obviously hadn't been used by anyone other than the homeless in years. Cece slowed down and circled around to the back of the hotel. She stopped beneath the balcony of the room she'd fled that night.

She looked up at the rusty, iron railing and shuddered. The blackness on the other side of the sliding glass door reminded her again of who and what she'd run from all those years ago. "Hold my purse," she said to Shane as she tossed her bag to him. She then backed up a few steps, sprinted forward, and jumped up to grab the bottom of the second floor railing. The cold iron scratched at her hands, but she held on and managed to pull herself up enough to use her legs to help her climb over the railing. Once she made it onto the balcony, she kicked the glass out of the sliding door, reached inside to unlock it and stepped inside.

Shane watched as Cecilia pulled herself over the balcony railing and disappeared inside. It took him about half a second to decide to follow her. When he hoisted himself over the railing, it didn't feel nearly as graceful and catlike as it had looked when Cecilia did it, but he got it done and held on to the purse in the process. He entered the hotel room and looked around. The afternoon sun did nothing for his surroundings. All the furnishings were either in pieces or missing. Something resembling the remains of a mattress was in the middle of the floor. It was so stained and slashed that it looked like multiple crimes had been committed on it.

The door into the hallway was broken and hanging askew from the top hinge. Beyond the door was only darkness. He heard movement in the small bathroom, and went in to find Cecilia standing at the sink staring into what was left of the shattered mirror. His eyes met hers through the mirror, and he waited for her to speak.

"When I was on my way down here today, I actually thought that this place would be the same as it was last time I saw it," she said.

"Is this where—"

"Shhh... Shane, if you ask questions, I may never get it all out. Please, just don't ask me anything right now."

"Okay. I'll just listen to whatever you want to tell me."

She raised her fist and knocked out what was left of the mirror. The remaining pieces shattered the heavy silence as they fell into a glittering, jagged pile in the sink. She walked out of the bathroom and leaned against what was left of an armoire. Her head dropped into her hands, and for the first time since he'd met her, she sobbed. She took deep, ragged breaths and her shoulders shook with the force of her emotions, but other than that she didn't make a sound. He wanted to put his arms around her and ask her what this place was, but he kept quiet and gave her space. Eventually, she looked up and dried her face on her sleeve. He offered her his handkerchief and leaned next to her.

"Take a good look around, Shane. This is where I grew up. My first memory in life came from this room right here. Room 216. This is where I lived with my mother before the state took me away. I was six at the time, but I remember it all very well. My mother's name was Cora. I don't know much about where she was from, but I know she didn't want to go back. She didn't speak much English, and neither did I until I learned in foster care.

"My first memory happened right over here under the couch. I was hiding, because my mother had to work. I always hid under there while she worked. I didn't like hearing what all those men did to her body. She was a prostitute, and her pimp only put up with me if she kept me hidden and didn't use me as an excuse to refuse customers... And, I'm pretty sure her pimp was my father. He looks just like me. Same light reddish brown hair, same complexion, same gray eyes. I've never hated, or feared, anyone as much as I did that man. Everyone around here called him Red Bone. He owned all the girls who lived in this hotel, and even some of the ones who didn't live here. He owned my mother, and he thought he owned me too.

"I remember everyone being afraid of him, even when he wasn't angry. Everyone who knew him was afraid of him. He was always going around beating on everyone. Sometimes he said he did it just to 'keep them in line,' but I think he enjoyed inflicting as much pain as possible, especially on women.

"One day, my mother and I sneaked out to go talk to this older lady who used to live up the street. Miss Georgia B was known for helping girls leave the streets if they wanted to. She never went out in street herself, but all the girls knew where to go find her. My mother took me over to her house that day, and the two of them talked for a long time. Mom cried and told Miss Georgia that she was pregnant. Miss Georgia gave her some money and a ride down to the bus station to buy a ticket. She was going to give us a ride back to the station later that afternoon when the bus was supposed to leave, but my mom had to come back here to get our things first. She hadn't brought them with her when she first went to talk to Miss Georgia.

"When we got back to the hotel to pack, I just remember feeling so relieved. I didn't really understand all of what was going on, but I did understand that I wouldn't have to hide under the couch anymore while my mother sold her body to men. So, there I was under the couch, in my favorite hiding spot, as my mother packed. She hardly had anything, just a few clothes and some papers, some pictures, and the money Miss Georgia B had given her. She was almost done packing; maybe another two minutes and we would have left this place forever. But you know what happened? He came in and caught her. It wasn't like those scenes you see in suspense movies, where the music builds up and warns you that something terrible is about to happen. One minute we were almost free, and the next he'd kicked the door in. Someone must've told him we were at the bus station that day, and he came in to punish her. She begged him to stop, even told him she was pregnant, but he just kept kicking her.

"I was too afraid to do anything except stay hidden, even after he left the room. I laid there, expecting my mom to get up. Usually, when he knocked her to the floor she would lay there for a few minutes, and then she would slowly get up. That time, she didn't get up. After I reached out my hand and felt all the blood under the couch, I came out and tried to help her, but it was too late. I sneaked out of the hotel and ran down to Miss Georgia's house, but I didn't know the right words to say to tell her my mother needed help. I was covered in her blood though, so she called the cops. She stayed with me while the police went into the hotel to help my mother. It took them forever to come back out, and when they did, they talked to Miss Georgia. I remember her hugging me really tight, so tight it hurt, and she kept telling me that everything would be okay. A lot more people came after that. They brought her out in one of those black bags. No one told me it was her, but I knew. This was a pretty bad neighborhood back then, so I'd seen those bags before.

"They took me to the police station and asked me a bunch of questions, but I didn't say anything, because I was scared and I didn't understand what they were asking me. Eventually, some woman came to take me to the group home. My first night there was when I met Dorothy. She was a few years older than me, and she seemed to know an awful lot about the way things worked for children in the foster care system."

Cecilia stopped talking and moved away from the armoire. She walked over to the window and stared out at the dumpster below. The old man who had been sleeping when they first got there was now staring up at them. "You mentioned her before. Were you and Dorothy very close?"

"Yes," Cecilia whispered. "I loved her more than it's possible to love just one person. She was everything to me back then. She was my mother, my older sister, my best friend, my mentor." She wiped her eyes with his handkerchief again and looked up at him. "I still can't believe you followed me all the way to Atlanta, just to learn that I came from this," she said as she looked around the room.

Shane looked around the room as well. He didn't know what to say, so he stayed where he was and waited for her to continue.

"Dot may have been everything to *me*, but she didn't really matter to anyone else. I moved in with a foster family when I was ten, but she spent her entire childhood in the group home. She was big, dark, and she wasn't very pretty, so no one wanted to take her in. She understood that, and still she was nice to me. After I moved away to a different neighborhood, I'd still sneak back to this side of town to see her. My foster parents used to get on me about it though. It finally got to the point where they told me that if I ran away again, they'd give me back. As much as I loved Dot, I didn't want to go back there. It wasn't nearly as bad as living in the hotel with Red Bone beating on my mother all the time, but I didn't want to go back there.

"I sneaked out one last time to give Dot my address and phone number so she could contact me. For a few months, we talked on the phone when my foster parents weren't around, and then one day—nothing. She just stopped calling me, so I sneaked out again to find out why. Turns out she got sick of living in the group home, so she ran away. By that time I was twelve and she was fifteen. She'd always talked about how she knew she had no chance of getting adopted, and she was going to be on her own once she became an adult anyway. She just left early. I could understand that; I might even have done the same thing myself. What scared me was that she stopped calling me. I figured that if she was okay she wouldn't have stopped calling me.

"That year, me and my foster father fought all the time. He kept me involved in Karate, because he thought it would help me have more discipline over my emotions. I'm not sure how well that worked out though. I got into fights at school and got suspended a few times. I just didn't care about anything but Dot.

"Finally, out of the blue, one day I was home alone after school and she called. She came on the line sounding scared and really stressed out. She said she just wanted to check on me and see if my adoption had been finalized. I told her it hadn't, and we talked for almost an hour. I kept asking her where she was and what she was doing, but she wouldn't tell me. And then I heard someone in the background telling her to get off the pay phone. I asked when she could call again, and she said she couldn't. I was about to ask her if I'd ever see her again when I heard someone in the background again saying, 'Girl, you better get off the pay phone and go make that *money* before Red Bone comes around here,' and then the phone disconnected.

"If I hadn't heard that last part, I might have assumed she'd be okay, but that one name changed everything. I knew there couldn't be more than one pimp named Red Bone in that general area. I don't know how she got mixed up with him, but I couldn't let her get herself killed. She was going to end up just like my mother; I *had* to do something. I hid under the couch like a little coward while he killed my mother and her baby, and then

I let him get away with it because I was too afraid and too stupid to talk. I was not going to let him have the only person left in the world who I loved and who really loved me. So, I left my school books and came back here to this street to find Dot and drag her back home with me if I had to.

"I walked up and down the street looking for her all evening. When I finally found her, she'd just stepped out of some guy's car. She was still fixing her clothes as he drove off. When I looked at her it was like seeing my mother all over again. She didn't look anything like she did when we lived in the group home together. She had on high heels and her ass was crammed into a skirt so tight I could see everything. She wasn't even wearing underwear. I went running up to her to confront her, and she just kept pulling at her clothes and telling me to go home. She kept trying to walk away from me and telling me, 'Cece, you shouldn't be here!" and I just kept following her and screaming, 'Neither should you!' Everyone on the street could hear us, and I think she only stopped to talk to me so I'd be quiet.

"I swore to her that if she came home with me, my foster parents would take her in and help her the way they were trying to help me. She started crying and said, 'Cece, open your eyes and look at me! Don't nobody give a damn what happens to some little, ugly, black girl. I don't look like you, and that's why you got adopted and I didn't. Do you know how many foster families took one look at me and moved on? Even black folks don't give a damn about me.' So, I looked at her and told her that I gave a damn about her. I told her that I loved her and that she deserved better than to be some man's nut rag. That pissed her off. She looked like she wanted to spit in my face and said, 'Go home to your parents, little girl.'

"She just kept calling me little girl after that, as if she were so much more grown up at just fifteen. She tried to push me away and stomp off in her hooker shoes, but she fell. Everyone on the street could see her ass, so I took off my jacket and put it over her. She laid there for a minute and cried. She said, 'I never wanted nobody to see me like this. I never wanted *you* to see me like this. Please just go away, Cece.' I leaned down and hugged her and told her that Red Bone had killed my mother, and then I told her that I knew someone who could help. I begged her to let me take her to Miss Georgia's house. I'd never talked to her about my mother before. She looked surprised and said, 'He killed your mother? How?' I looked her in the eyes and told her the truth. I said, 'She was one of his whores. Red Bone is my father... Dot, please let's just leave this place.'

"I could see in her eyes that I was getting to her, so I stood up and pulled her to her feet. I told her to come on because Miss Georgia lived just up the street, and then she panicked and said, 'What, now? You want me to go right now? I can't go looking like this. Let me go change first. Red Bone won't be back until late, I have time.' I told her no; actually I screamed it at her. I remembered how he came out of nowhere right before my mom was almost free. I grabbed her and started yanking her down the street. I told her she could use my jacket to cover up until we got to Miss Georgia's house.

"We passed by the hotel without anyone giving us problems, so I relaxed. I stopped yanking on her arm, and we just walked normally. Then we got to this bar that used to be about half a block from the hotel... We didn't even get past the alley, and there he was. He'd been back there with some girl when he heard me and Dot talking. He stepped out right in front of us, just as calm as if he didn't have a care in the world. Dot froze, and I grabbed her and told her to come on. I swear it felt like my heart was about to explode; it was beating so hard. When we tried to go around him he grabbed her by the hair and dragged her into the alley. The other girl ran off down the street, and I stood there. I literally couldn't move, Shane. He had Dot in the alley, and I could hear him hitting her. I don't remember how I made myself go back there, but I do remember that when I saw Dot on the ground, I lost it.

"I jumped on his back and started screaming at him to get his hands off her. Dot looked up at me like she thought I was crazy and said, 'Cece, get out of here. Girl, run!' I didn't run. I tried to fight him. He got me off his back and slammed me on the ground. He got right in my face and said, 'Who the fuck do you think you are? You stupid little bitch.' I screamed at him, 'You killed my mother! You better leave my friend alone!' He looked at me and snarled, 'Your mother?' Dot kept telling me to get out of there, but by that time I was more angry than scared, and I was too stupid to realize what I was doing. I should have run and gotten some help, but I stood there and screamed at him some more. I said, 'Yes! Her name was Cora, and you *killed* her. I saw you with my own eyes!' After I said that, he laughed at me. He actually laughed in my face and said, 'Yeah, I remember that stupid bitch Cora. She didn't speak English. The customers loved that French shit. She made me a lot of money. You came here to take her place, Cora Junior?'

"I lost it, Shane. For that man to stand there and joke about killing my mother...it made me lose my temper and my common sense. I honestly don't remember how I got from the ground to him again, but I ended up in his face hitting him and trying to scratch out his eyes. I wanted him to suffer, but he was bigger and stronger. He won the fight. The last thing I remember in the alley was that he slammed my head against something hard. When I woke up, I was back here in this room tied down to the bed. He remembered killing my mom, so he put me back in here to make some kind of point. And I got the point—he could do whatever he wanted to me and get away with it."

The light outside was almost gone, and the room was almost pitch black. Shane glanced back down at the mattress. He knew it probably wasn't the same mattress from all those years ago, but that knowledge didn't stop the feelings of disgust and rage that welled up inside him. Cecilia's silhouette showed clearly in front of the darkening sky, and the full moon was visible behind her. She covered her face with her hands before speaking again.

Her voice was quieter and more distant as she went on, "When I woke here, he was sitting in the chair beside the bed. I was tied down spread eagle, completely naked, and he was sitting there laughing at me. I pulled hard and broke free for a moment, but he pulled out his gun and made me get back on the bed. Then he made one of his friends come in and tie me so tight I couldn't feel my hands and feet, and then he gagged me and blindfolded me. While he did all these things, he kept telling me all about what he was going to do to me. I'll never forget what he said; he told me he was going to make me wish I was dead, and then, when I was begging him to kill me, he might just let me pull the trigger myself.

"I can't go into all the details of what happened in here, Shane... Red Bone had a lot of customers, the kind of men who don't ask questions about why the girl they paid for is tied to the bed. After the first day, I started praying for God to take my life, and after the second day, I stopped believing there was a God. They all ran together in an endless stream of men sent here to torture me. At times it took all my concentration to keep myself calm and breathe past the nausea. No doubt Red Bone would have let me drown in my own vomit. Every once in a while, he came into the room to taunt me and say nasty things about my mother while one of his girls cleaned me up a little. It all hurt so much. I cried even more when he came in with the girl. I didn't want them touching me anywhere, especially not there after everything else that was happening to me. I just wanted it all to end, but as long as I refused to beg him to kill me, he kept it going. By the third day, I stopped responding. I don't think I had anymore tears left in me by that point. I just tried to shut it all out and make my own little world inside my head. It didn't stop the physical pain, but I believe it kept me sane.

"It finally ended when some guy came in and took the rag out of my mouth while he was on top of me. He kept trying to kiss me, and I kept turning my head. His tongue in my mouth was just as disgusting as the other thing he was doing to me. When he finally stopped trying to stick his tongue in my mouth, I started begging him to stop, quietly though, because I was afraid Red Bone would hear me. I remembered hearing somewhere that if you could make yourself seem more human to the person hurting you, it might make them stop, so I just introduced myself over and over again. I kept telling him that I was thirteen and telling him my name over and over again. It didn't make him stop, but it must have got to him in some way, or he wouldn't have let me go.

"When he untied me, I could barely stand, but he forced me into the bathroom anyway. He made me get in the shower and watched while I washed myself. I never saw his face, because he wouldn't let me take off the blindfold. I didn't even know what time of day it was... After I finished in the shower, he shoved me out onto the balcony and threw my clothes at me. He said that, if I went to the police, he would find me and kill me. By the time I took the blindfold off, he was gone. It was night, so I got dressed and jumped off the balcony into the dumpster and ran home. I didn't even stop to find Dot. I never saw her again after that night in the alley. A few days later, I saw a story on the news about a burned body found in a dumpster a few blocks from here. After what he did to me, I was pretty sure he killed her like he did my mother.

ADRIENNE D'NELLE RUVALCABA

"I got home to find that my foster parents had reported me as a runaway. We fought, and they sent me back to the group home. Those four days I was gone were the last straw. I was put in a different group home that time, and after I realized I was pregnant, I ran away for real. I had no idea what kind of baby I'd give birth to, but I did know that I didn't want it to end up in the system like me and Dot. I thought it would have a better chance with a real mother, so I made up my mind to run away before I actually thought about where I would go. I found a bus ticket to Nashville one day, and it seemed like some kind of sign, so I used it. I met Mrs. Lee my first night in town, and by the end of the week I had a full time job. She was like my fairy godmother. Out of all the men who came in there to hurt me, the one who fathered Rebecca was the only one who thought enough of my life to untie me. If he hadn't done that, I'd be dead."

Shane didn't say anything as he allowed Cecilia's story to sink in. He couldn't see her face in the darkness, but he felt her eyes on him, watching and waiting for a reaction. He crossed the room and said, "I think you've had enough of this place for a lifetime." He pulled her out into the chilly night air, and they made their way back to the ground.

He looked around and felt like he was seeing the world again for the first time after a long captivity. The oppressive darkness of the hotel still lingered in the back of his mind. When Cecilia shivered, he took off his jacket and draped it around her shoulders. He pretended like he didn't mind the cold, so she wouldn't protest again as she had earlier when he offered it to her.

"Did you really think you were just going to walk right in and confront him after all these years?" he asked as he pulled her into his arms.

"Yes."

"What if you had found him? What then?"

"I don't know."

"That's exactly the sort of confrontation I want to be around for. I'm glad you didn't come here alone and find him. That's something that we can do together. He has to pay for everything he did."

"I know."

He hugged her tighter and kissed the top of her head as he thought about the next step for them. "Are you ready to let me take you someplace warm and safe now?" he asked.

She drew in a ragged breath and said, "I'd like to walk by Miss Georgia's old house first. I just want to see if it's still there after all these years. She helped a lot of women over the years."

"Okay, Cecilia. Lead the way."

She took his hand again, and they walked down the street side by side. It was only six o'clock, but there was very little traffic on the street. There was a winter weather advisory for the entire area, and a mixture of ice and snow was supposed to be moving in sometime in the next twenty four hours. Shane knew that if they didn't get going soon, they may very well be stuck in Atlanta for a few days.

Less than five minutes away from the hotel, they came to an older house with a very small but well-kept lawn. Cecilia paused at the walk and stared silently at the front door. A porch light was on, and there was movement inside. Cecilia stood there so long Shane finally just suggested they knock on the door to ask if the current owners knew what had become of Miss Georgia.

"We can't do that. She was old back when I was a kid, she's probably not even living anymore," she protested.

When Cecilia continued to stare instead of moving on, Shane started up the walk to knock on the door.

"What are you doing?" she asked as she attempted to stop him.

"I'm just going to knock on the door and ask. We're already here, and the worst that will happen is that they'll slam the door in our face. I can handle that," he said. He ignored the yanking on his arm and kept going.

"Okay, okay, just let me do the knocking," Cecilia relented after a few more halfhearted tugs on his arm.

Cece hopped in front of Shane and crossed the small porch. Her heart was thumping in her chest for what seemed like the hundredth time that day. She didn't want to bother the people who lived here now, but she didn't want to wonder who lived here for the rest of her life either. She gave three quiet taps, and then waited.

To her surprise, the door opened almost immediately, as if whoever lived there had been waiting for them to knock.

"May I help you?" an old familiar voice asked from behind the chain lock.

Cece's heart leapt again. Could her ears be deceiving her? "Miss Georgia B?" she asked.

"Do you need some help? Are you one of those girls from up the street?"

"No, I don't need any help," Cece said with tears in her voice. "You probably don't remember me, but my name is Cece, Cece Graves. I used to live in this neighborhood years and years ago, and I just—"

Suddenly the door was thrown open, and Cece was face to face with Miss Georgia. "Of course I remember you!" she exclaimed as she gaped up at her. "Child, all these years I thought you was dead!"

The years and miles that had separated them faded into nothingness as Cece felt Miss Georgia's arms go around her. She was warm, loving, and so familiar it brought tears to Cece's eyes. She clung to Miss Georgia's delicate frame and noted the changes that time had wrought in the old woman's body. As a child, Cece hadn't spent a lot of time with her, but Miss Georgia had always seemed like a strong and capable force. Now, in her old age, she felt frail. "I'm not dead," Cece finally choked out past all the emotion and tears pouring out of her.

"All these years.... I thought you was dead," Miss Georgia said over and over again as she and Cece clung to each other on the porch. Eventually, Miss Georgia let go of Cece. She took a step back and said, "Come inside so I can look at you."

When Cece stepped forward, Miss Georgia noticed Shane for the first time. "He's with me," Cece told her.

"Who is he?" Miss Georgia asked.

"He's my..."

When Cece hesitated for a long time, Shane stepped forward and offered his hand to Miss Georgia. "I'm her husband," he said with a smile.

Miss Georgia smiled back and chided Cece, "Why didn't you just say so?"

"We're newlyweds. Our wedding was just yesterday," he explained.

"Well, congratulations! Come in and make yourself at home."

They spent the next half hour sitting on her tiny couch. Cece told her about the bakery and all the positive things that had been going on lately. Shane stayed quiet for the most part and let the two of them visit. Eventually, the lighter tone of conversation gave way to the inevitable questions about the past.

"Everything seems to be going good for you, Cece. What made you come back here?" Miss Georgia asked.

Cece struggled with that question, but opted for the simple truth in the end. "I came back to find Red Bone. He killed my mother, and he did terrible things to so many people; he doesn't deserve to be free."

Miss Georgia sat back with a deep sigh and asked, "Why in the world did you wait so long?"

"I was scared," Cece admitted.

Miss Georgia reached out for her hand. "That man has been gone for years now," she said quietly.

"Where did he go?" Cece asked.

"I don't know. He left this neighborhood after I run him off this block."

"You ran him off?"

"I sure did."

"How?" Cece and Shane asked simultaneously. Miss Georgia was small, frail, and very old; she didn't look like she was capable of thwarting a notorious pimp.

"I got the good people of this neighborhood to stand up and protest his hotel with me. It took a few years, but his customers stopped coming. They didn't want to be seen and recorded by all of us protestors."

"How did you get people to protest with you?" Cece asked, incredulous.

"I started going out on the street, asking for help. More than a year after he took off, I found out that there was a tax lien on the property. I took up a collection to help me raise enough money to pay for it."

"Pay for it? Who owns it now? You?" Cece demanded.

"I own it. I used the money I got from people in the church and the neighborhood plus the money I had saved up— every penny. It wasn't worth much, and the owner fell behind on the taxes. Red Bone never owned the hotel in the first place; he just acted like he did, because he had the owner in his pocket. When there were no more girls, there were no more customers.

The owner went out of business. After Red Bone took off, the rest was easy. All I had to do was pay the tax money they owed, and now it's mine," she answered in a very matter of fact tone of voice. Cece and Shane exchanged a look of pure disbelief as she went on. "I wanted to do something good with it, but the bank won't loan me any money. It's just been sitting vacant since he left. I can't even get it torn down right now, but I'm working on it."

"If the bank won't loan you any money, how are you going to do that?" Shane asked.

Miss Georgia looked at him with a small twinkle in her eye. "Young man, I own this house outright. I'll mortgage it if I have to. I'll go back out on the streets and take up another collection if I have to. That place has been a dark spot on this neighborhood for too many years. I can't tell you how many girls have lost their lives and their dignity in that place. I'm sick of it."

"You won't need a loan from the bank, Miss Georgia," Cece said as she reached out for her weathered hand. "I think you've done more than enough for two lifetimes, and now you can relax. You won't need a loan."

"I won't?"

"If you'll allow me to be your partner, I believe we can do something with it together. Just tell me how much you need for the demolition, and I'll write you a check right now. Of course, I'll want to be directly involved in planning for the next step. I have an idea, but we can talk about it more another time. I don't want to keep you from your dinner."

"I ate dinner two hours ago. Are you two hungry? You look hungry. I'll make you something."

Before Cece could refuse, Miss Georgia was getting up and making her way to the kitchen.

"What are you thinking of doing?" Shane whispered at her when Miss Georgia was out of earshot.

"I think I'll do what Rebecca would probably do. Maybe we could tear it down, and build some sort of community center. This neighborhood could certainly use one."

"Do you have any idea what kind of money a project like that would take?"

"I think I do, Shane. Don't worry about that though," Cece smiled. "Even if I never make another dime at the bakery, I still have enough, thanks to Mrs. Lee. I've been feeling guilty about her leaving everything to me, because I didn't need it. I think this is something that I'm supposed to do."

After Miss Georgia fed them a simple meal of chicken soup and cornbread, Cece took out her checkbook. She barely raised an eyebrow as Miss Georgia showed her one of the estimates for demolishing the hotel. She simply wrote a check out to Miss Georgia for more than the amount on the paper. At first, Miss Georgia refused to take the check, but Cece looked her in the eye and said, "I lived there for the first six years of my life. That man killed my mother, my best friend, and he almost killed me too. Think about how much you want that place torn down—enough to mortgage your house. I want it torn down just as badly as you do, if not worse. The only difference between us right now is that I can easily afford it. Please, just take the money."

Miss Georgia started crying, but she wiped her eyes and accepted the check with a solemn look. "I noticed you two walked from up the street. Where are y'all staying for the night?"

"I don't know right now. We took the bus to town, and we didn't get a room anywhere."

"Well, you're welcome to spend the night here. I have a spare room. I don't like the idea of you walking the streets at night. Red Bone may be gone, but it still isn't safe... what with all these young people traipsing around with guns nowadays."

Cece looked up at Shane, and he said, "Thank you so much for your kindness. We'd be honored to stay the night, Ma'am."

"Yeah, we'll stay," Cece agreed with a tender smile for Miss Georgia. She looked like she hadn't had any company in a while.

The next morning, Cece and Shane left with the promise to keep in touch.

# Chapter 24

"Cecilia, I hate to say it, but with this freezing rain coming down, we're not going to be able to book another flight from here for at least the next few days." Shane and Cece were sitting in the Atlanta airport, and Shane had just gotten off the phone with the airline. When they left Miss Georgia's house, he tried to salvage their honeymoon trip, but so far it wasn't working.

"I'm really sorry I caused all these problems," Cece said as she looked at the long line of stranded travelers waiting for their turn at the ticket counter. She'd run off and rudely left him standing at the Nashville airport, and now they were stuck in Atlanta without transportation. The weather outside was getting worse by the minute.

"I have a suggestion, but you may not like it, especially when Hawaii was the alternative," Shane said.

"I'll just pay for a rental car, and we can go home. I don't really feel like going on a vacation anymore; I just want to be alone right now."

"Alone?" he asked.

She suspected she'd just hurt his feelings, but he'd mistaken her meaning. Something deep inside her had undergone a monumental shift in the last 48 hours. She didn't want to be alone on her own; she wanted to be alone with him. She loved him.

Before she could speak again, he said, "I have a cabin a few hours north of here. If you really want to be alone, I could take you there. If you go back to Karen's house, you'll have to deal with a bunch of questions, and I still don't like the idea of you being alone at your place."

By the time they made it to the cabin, the freezing rain had given way to a heavy snowfall. Great big moist flakes of snow fell down and clung to every surface and every branch of every tree in sight. Shane went inside to start a fire as Cece sat on the step and watched the snowflakes fall all around her.

The temperature was frigid today, but the absence of wind made it bearable. The flakes drifted down peaceful and straight as she watched. She caught sight of one flake and followed its path until it landed, and then she looked up again to find another flake to follow. She sat on the step for nearly an hour, huddled inside Shane's large fleece-lined winter coat. When her nose and ears started getting numb, she decided it might be time to go back inside. She reached out and caught a snowflake. Its stark whiteness contrasted with her black glove, and she marveled at its shape and pattern before it melted. She reached out to catch another one when the door opened behind her.

Shane joined her on the steps. He was so large and the step was so small she had no choice but to move to the very edge to make room. He smiled and put his arm around her and pulled her close against his side. Now that he was sitting beside her, the urge to go inside rapidly diminished. She leaned her head on his shoulder and a small sigh escaped her.

She'd never seen snow outside the context of the city before. When snow fell in the city, it always started out as a nuisance. It hindered travel, and turned quickly into an ugly, brown tinged mess. Between the snowplows with the salt brine mixture and the motorists with their impatience, the streets always managed to look like a muddy, slushy nightmare. Cece had never been a fan of snow, or ice, or even winter for that matter.

The undisturbed wilderness here at Shane's cabin gave her a new appreciation for winter precipitation. Out here, it was actually serene and beautiful. Shane's quiet presence beside her contributed vastly to her enjoyment of the snow. She covertly glanced at his profile several times; he really was an exceptionally good looking man. She wondered how he could also be so nice and unassuming.

After she sniffed several times, he finally spoke. "You can see the snow just as well from inside. It's pretty cold out right now."

"What's the temperature?" she asked.

"It's 15 degrees out here. We should go in and get warm." He stood up and pulled her to her feet, not giving her the chance to protest.

She didn't realize how cold she'd been until she stepped inside the warmth of the cabin. The past two days had been hard for her. She hadn't felt so exhausted and emotionally spent since she left Atlanta the first time. She didn't realize going back and facing it all would have such a profound physical effect on her.

Shane hadn't said much since yesterday, and she refused to ask him what he thought of her now. His opinion of her was none of her business. She imagined he might now be trying to think of a way to let her down gently. He probably wanted to retract his hasty words of love now that he'd had a chance to digest all she'd told him. He now knew more about her than anyone else, and she'd never felt so exposed and vulnerable before in her life.

She was so deep in her own tremulous thoughts, she didn't even bother to look around the cabin until Shane said, "It's really rustic, but at least here no one can bother you."

She tore her eyes away from him and looked around. The cabin was extremely small, but the high ceiling saved it from feeling as tiny as it actually was. It was an A-frame cabin with exposed roof beams and a single picture window that took up the entire southeast wall, from the point where the roof came together all the way to the floor. The view facing out towards the massive hill they'd struggled to climb was breathtaking in its stark splendor. There was very little floor space, but he'd used it wisely. A small fireplace was opposite the window. On one side of the fireplace, there was an oversized cast iron tub, and on the other there was a small kitchenette with what appeared to be a wood burning stove. The only piece of furniture was a large padded chair that sat in front of the fireplace. The bed was in a loft built adjacent to the window and accessible by a ladder tucked discretely to one side.

"There's just enough room for one." Shane's words hung between them, and Cece couldn't mistake his meaning.

She blinked back the tears that stung the back of her eyes and asked the most mundane, practical thing she could think of at the moment. "Where's the bathroom?"

Shane looked surprised, and then embarrassed, before he answered, "Out back. It's an outhouse."

Cece turned and finally noticed the other door on the side of the cabin. She guessed the outhouse was somewhere beyond the door. She looked back at Shane and did her best to smile at him. He walked over to the fireplace and put another log on the fire.

"I've already heated some bathwater for you. I'll go now, so you can take a bath and relax."

"Okay. I guess you'll need this," she said as she shrugged out of his coat.

"I need to take care of a few things before the roads get too bad later tonight. You should have plenty of time to yourself. Just make yourself at home, and give me a call if you think of anything else you need other than the obvious things." He spoke quickly as he donned the coat. The moment he finished talking, he was out the door and disappearing down the steep hill.

Cece walked over to the tub and stuck her finger in the water; it scalded her. She'd have to let it cool down some before she could use it. As she waited for the water to cool, she walked around and explored the small cabin. She found a small closet that contained a few cleaning supplies, and before she knew it, she was down on her hands and knees scrubbing the floor. It was just like old times at the bakery. The cabin looked like it hadn't been used in many months, but Cece managed to make it sparkle. If she was going to be here alone for a week or more, she might as well be comfortable.

While she was down on her hands and knees scrubbing the floor, she found a hollow spot under a loose board near the chair. At first she tried her best not to wonder what was inside the hollow, but eventually her curiosity got the better of her. What she found was as unexpected as it was sad. The secret little spot contained a collection of articles that ruthlessly villainized Shane after several firefighters had died in a fire while under his command. Cece skimmed through most of them before she felt guilty enough to carefully place his mementos back as they were. She ran a finger over the rank insignia on the formal uniform before she closed Shane's box of memories. As she reset the loose floorboard, she felt slightly guilty for having been so nosey.

The tub was large enough for her to lie down and fully stretch out her legs in the water. She submerged herself in the warm water and allowed the water sounds to fill her ears. Her eyes drifted shut, and she tried to focus on the peaceful stillness around her. She tried to relax, but every other second Shane would pop into her head. Their wedding and reception had been magical, and then the very next day she'd plunged them both head first into the ugliness of her past. What had she been thinking to tell him all those things? They hadn't talked at all on the drive up to the cabin; the silence between them had a different quality than before. It had been impossible to tell what he'd been thinking, and it had been just as impossible to ask. By the time they'd parked the rental car and walked the last rugged mile up the hill to the cabin, she'd been on the verge of crying. Of course he didn't love her. She should have left Red Bone and her mother buried in the past where they belonged.

She sat up and hugged her knees to her chest as the now tepid water swirled around her. She reached for the bar of soap and bottle of shampoo on the small table beside the tub. When she opened the shampoo, she was struck by the familiar scent; it must be the same shampoo he always used. Cece lathered her hair with it. As the suds ran down her neck and back, she imagined Shane's hands on her body. Her own hands followed the path of the suds and skimmed over her breasts as she thought of Shane's warmth and strength surrounding her. She closed her eyes for a while and enjoyed the natural progression of her thoughts. By the time she emerged from the tub, the water was cold.

Once she exited the tub, she put on the blue, terrycloth bathrobe that hung on a nail beside the fire place. It was so large, the hem of it dragged across the floor as she made her way to the chair to sit in front of the fire. She didn't have a comb, but fortunately her hair was easy to manage, unlike Rebecca's. She ran her fingers through her wet tresses and worked out the tangles as she stared into the fire. The cabin was small and cozy, but she'd never felt more alone as night fell. Once her hair was mostly dry, she climbed up the ladder to the loft. She curled up on one end of the bed, tucked her feet up into the robe, and fell asleep clutching Shane's pillow.

There was a definite chill in the air when Cece woke up the next morning. The fire had long since gone out, and bright morning sunlight reflected off the snow and streamed into the cabin. Amazed, and grateful, that she'd slept through the night she stretched, yawned and wiggled her toes as she savored the early morning atmosphere. She was still wrapped up in Shane's bathrobe, but she'd managed to get under the blanket at some point during the night. She lay facing the window, and the woods beyond the cabin caught her eye. There was nothing but pristine white snow and tall trees as far as she could see. She snuggled deeper into the covers and stared outside for a long time before she finally decided to get out of bed.

She turned away from the window, and noticed Shane sitting in the chair below the loft. He looked up at her with a thoughtful expression on his face.

"How long have you been here?" she asked. Her heart skipped a beat, and she smiled. There was no way she could hide the joy she felt at seeing him sitting there. She'd spent the night nursing her hurt over her lost opportunities to show him her softer side. She'd thought she wouldn't get the chance to spend some actual quality time with him, and suddenly there he was, looking as warm and comforting as ever.

"You were sleeping when I got back last night. I didn't want to wake you," he said quietly.

"You didn't spend the night in the chair, did you?" As soon as the words left her mouth Cece wanted to take them back. He didn't need to know that she'd spent the night in emotional agony, longing for him.

"I did," he admitted.

"Oh."

At her crestfallen expression, Shane got out of the chair and climbed up the ladder toward her. "Did you want me to share the bed with you?" he asked as he softly touched her cheek. When she didn't immediately respond, he looked deep into her eyes and said, "It's okay to admit when you need someone."

"I thought you weren't coming back," she finally said.

"You thought I'd abandon you here in a winter storm with no food and no supplies?" he asked with an incredulous look. "I had to go, so I could make it back before the roads got too bad around here. I told you to call if you thought of anything you needed while I was at the store. I got all the basics covered, but sometimes women need things that boggle the male mind."

"Oh... I thought maybe you were in a hurry to be out of here because you couldn't stand to be around me after everything I told you yesterday in Atlanta," she admitted.

Shane ascended the ladder the rest of the way and stretched out beside her. He pulled her into his arms and stroked her hair and kissed her forehead before speaking again. "I told you I love you, Cecilia. I meant it."

She looked at him and almost told him she loved him too, but something inside her wouldn't let her say the words. She said the next best thing instead, "I'm glad you came back. At the airport, when I told you I wanted to be alone, I meant alone somewhere with you."

"I wouldn't have left you out here all alone. I'd never leave you, especially not because of what you shared with me yesterday. I love the fact that you trust me enough to finally just relax and let me be there for you when you need me. Yesterday was a big step for us. I apologize if I seemed distant, but I didn't know what to say... I still don't. It's appalling to imagine any young girl going through that, but it was *you*, the woman I love. I'd give anything for the power to erase that experience from your life." He threaded his fingers through her hair as he spoke

All the pain and vulnerability she'd kept hidden for so many years had risen to the surface. She felt tears in her eyes as she looked at him, but she didn't attempt to mask them or shield herself from his scrutiny.

"You don't ever have to hide who you are from me," he said as he touched her tears with the pads of his thumbs.

"I know that was a lot to take in all at once, but I survived it. That's the important thing. If I could survive what Red Bone did to me, I can survive anything. I've dealt with it all," she whispered.

"No, you haven't dealt with it," he disagreed. "You've lived with it and gotten on with your life in a big way, but you haven't dealt with it. You haven't even been able to talk about it until now, you still have nightmares... and you haven't been able to allow yourself to fall in love with a man. Honey, you haven't dealt with it."

But I'm in love with you, Cece thought to herself. Despite everything, he'd managed to entrench himself firmly in her heart.

342

"When I get back home, I'm going to start seeing a therapist. Rebecca has been suggesting that for a while now."

"Good. In the meantime we can just relax here for a couple of weeks. Or if you want, we can still try to go on what's left of that tropical vacation when the weather clears up some. No one expects us back in town until next month."

"The last thing I want right now is to be around a bunch of people I don't know. Can we just stay here?"

Shane couldn't miss the fact that she'd said "we." She knew there was only one bed. His heart picked up speed as he asked, "Together?"

She snuggled against his chest and whispered, "Yes, if you don't mind."

"And you're okay with the fact that there's only one bed?"

"It's not like we've never slept in the same bed together before."

"Yeah, only two times, and never for two straight weeks."

"If you'd rather not, then forget I said anything."

"Cecilia, it's not that I don't want to sleep with you. There's nothing I'd love better than cuddling up to you, but remember that night you attacked me?"

She lowered her gaze to the region around his chin and said, "I only did that because I didn't want to admit that I liked sharing a bed with you. I'd never shared any part of my life with a man before. I'll be honest with you, Shane; that first night you held me—after the nightmare—that was the first time in my life I've ever felt completely safe. I feel so safe with you, like nothing can hurt me when you're around. I just didn't want to start getting used to that, so I pushed you away. I want to share the bed with you."

"Good," he smiled. "Because that chair is so uncomfortable."

"You didn't get much sleep last night, did you?"

"Not really," he admitted.

"Why don't you sleep in the bed for a while? It's still early."

"Not by your standards," he chuckled.

"Today it is. We don't have anywhere to go."

Shane looked out the window at the snow covered hillside and said, "You're absolutely right, but I'll be okay until tonight. One night in the chair didn't completely exhaust me."

She didn't answer right away, instead she wrapped both arms around him and said, "I like lying here with you, and I'm not ready to get up yet."

With the combination of that simple statement and the sultry look in her eyes, she managed to turn his thoughts so rapidly it was a wonder his head wasn't spinning. "Well, if you plan on staying in the bed with me, that changes things," he whispered.

"Why don't you get under the covers with me?" she asked.

Suddenly, the space taken up by the clothes between them seemed too great. Shane wanted to feel his skin against hers and her hand in his as they enjoyed the simple joy of physical closeness. "Yeah, just let me get the fire going again, so it doesn't get too cold in here."

She pulled him towards her for a lingering kiss, and he almost forgot that he was supposed to get up to start the fire. When the kiss ended, he stared down at her and wondered at her vastly changed attitude towards him. Just two days ago, he'd still been trying to convince her to give them a chance, and now she was the one pulling him along. He liked this new side of her. He gave her one more kiss before getting out of bed.

Cece sat up and watched as he got up and stuffed his feet into his boots. He was very aware of her eyes on him as he opened the guard and put more logs into the fireplace. He went out back to the woodpile beside the cabin and collected enough wood to last them the rest of the morning and afternoon. When he got back inside, she was sitting on the edge of the bed with her bare legs hanging over the side. She smiled at him in a way that made him catch his breath.

"I'd love to know what you're thinking when you look at me like that," he said as he approached the bed.

She scrunched her toes and looked away for a moment before she answered. "I was just wondering what you look like naked." When she looked back at him, the light played with her silver gaze, making her eyes appear brighter and the color heightened.

Shane was at a complete loss for words. A moment ago he'd been cold, and now he wasn't aware of anything other than the white hot urge to satisfy Cecilia's curiosity. He straightened his posture and maintained eye contact as he removed his clothes. He took off his jacket, shirt and undershirt first, letting them fall into a pile beside him. He hesitated for a moment before he unbuttoned his pants. After everything she'd told him, he didn't know how she would react to his obvious state of arousal, and he didn't want to shock her. The look of calm encouragement on her face prompted him to unbutton his pants and slowly lower them. Her eyes never left his, but he'd never felt so exposed before in his life. Every inch of bare skin tingled in that last moment before he removed his underwear.

He wanted to say something, but the silence stretched on between them until she spoke again. "You have such a beautiful body," she whispered. Her eyes beckoned him closer. He climbed up the ladder, and before he was fully in the loft she was next to him, hugging him close. "You'd probably be shocked if I told you how many times I've imagined us holding each other like this." She was still completely wrapped up in his robe, but as they settled into a comfortable position it fell open. She didn't attempt to close it; instead she sat up slightly and shrugged out of it.

"That's the last thing I expected to hear from you, especially after everything you told me in Atlanta," he said as he skimmed his finger over her smooth shoulders.

"I just want to be close to you... like this," she said as she pressed herself against his chest. "I don't want to think about what happened to me anymore. Not here. Not with you."

"I want to be close to you too. You can't possible imagine how badly I want to make love to you. But, are you ready?"

"If I'm not ready now, with you, then I'll never be ready."

Shane pulled her away from his chest so he could see her face. She was a grown woman who could make her own choices, but when he looked down at her, all he saw was that frightened little girl she'd been all those years ago. He wanted her to realize that she had no reason to fear anything when he was around. He leaned down and kissed her neck. His lips lingered, and he felt her pulse go wild. He smiled because his was doing the same thing. She tipped her head back to welcome his affection, and he took a moment to stare down at her in appreciation. She made no attempt to push him away or cover herself, and his desire increased yet again.

He parted her lips with his thumb, so he could kiss her again. He'd only meant to kiss her gently and then back away to give her some space to think. He didn't want to overwhelm her, but somehow she ended up overwhelming him. The energy between them shifted, and suddenly they were both sucked into a vortex that was too strong for either of them to resist. As she wound her hands through his hair and opened up so completely to him, resistance was the furthest thing from Shane's mind.

His hands skimmed over all the parts of her he'd fantasized about over the past few months, her breasts, her arms, her waist, and her legs. Both of them pulled each other closer, until there was almost no space between them. They abandoned themselves to all the longing they'd felt, and spent the next half hour exploring each other with gentle touches and too many kisses to count. Shane's touch was characterized by a possessive boldness that Cecilia didn't expect from such a mild mannered man. And as fearsome as she'd been towards him in the early stages of their friendship, he didn't expect the endearing affection that poured out of her this morning. Every touch from her was so sweet, so heartfelt, tears came to his eyes.

Eventually, her hands explored that part of him that had been aching for her touch. She wrapped her fingers around him and whispered in his ear, "Make love to me, Shane."

He looked into her eyes as he grasped her hips and positioned her. "Are you sure?" he asked one last time before taking that final step.

She met his gaze with a smile in her eyes, and raised her hips up so that their bodies were intimately connected. All he had to do was push forward, and they were joined in the closest connection possible. Once he was fully inside her, he held still and kissed her deeply as her body grew accustomed to having him there. When he looked at her again, her eyes were closed and there was a single tear rolling down her cheek.

"Cecilia, look at me," he commanded gently. She opened her eyes, and he wouldn't allow her to look away. "You're with me, and I want you to see that. Please don't close your eyes and shut me out—not now. I need to see that you're here with me and not thinking about the past."

"I'm only thinking about you," she whispered back, but there was a shadowed look in her eyes. He knew where at least part of her thoughts lay, but he didn't say it.

"Come here," he said as he changed positions. He sat up on his knees in the center of the bed, and pulled her astride his lap. Their bodies seemed to fit together even better this way. He wrapped his arms around her and hugged her close. They were now face to face, and he said "Now you're the one on top. You have all the power." He then massaged her back and waist as she started to move with him. At first she was hesitant, but after a minute she relaxed and got into the rhythm of their combined motions. He hugged her close, and alternately kissed her and whispered words of love to her. "I want you to keep those beautiful eyes on me. This is the man who loves you, who would do anything for you," he whispered against her neck.

The tempo they set was relaxed and gentle, and for the most part it was like an extended and extremely intimate embrace. Her single tear dried up, and she seemed to enjoy what they were doing. Shane kept smiling at her and saying, "I want you to feel how much I love you," over and over again. Somewhere deep in his brain, he was thinking that he could heal her wounds with his love.

"Can you feel it?" he breathed in her ear again as the intensity of their lovemaking built.

"Yes!" she said as her head tipped back and her body tensed. He felt the waves of her release surround him, and that pushed him over the edge. He held her so close as his own wave of ecstasy crashed over him, that for a moment their breathing and heartbeats were nearly indistinguishable. In that moment, they were one.

Both spent and quickly returning to Earth, they now sat clinging to each other. Cece's body felt like a tingling mass of hypersensitivity. She felt like she'd shatter into a million little pieces if she moved too much, but she wanted to savor and explore everything. She clenched her inner muscles around him and shivered as another wave of intense pleasure went through her. Shane's warm breath blowing softly against her neck, his warm hands still cupping her bottom, and his scent filling her nostrils were all stirring on levels that she wasn't prepared to analyze at the moment. She was so totally unprepared for the overwhelming feelings of closeness and love that she started crying. She wanted to stay as they were indefinitely.

Shane moved her hair to the side and kissed the top of her shoulder. He then extended his legs out in front and laid back while still holding her to him. She ended up half reclined on top of him with her bare breasts pressed into his chest. The position was a little awkward, but she barely noticed. Being this close to him, even without clothes on, felt so right, so natural, that she couldn't help smiling at him through her tears. Actually, grinning like an idiot was more accurate.

"What are you thinking right now?" she asked.

"I was just thinking about how amazing it felt to be inside you." His words produced an instant flush that spread across her entire body. He touched the tip of her nose with his finger and smiled at her. "What are you thinking right now?" he tossed the question back at her.

Cece wasn't sure how to put her feelings into words, so she kissed him again. She then allowed her eyes to roam all over his face. Eventually, she reached out to touch his scruffy morning shadow.

"I hope I didn't scratch your face. Next time I'll shave first," he said.

"Next time?"

Shane blushed at his own presumptuousness, and after a long silence said, "I hope there will be a next time."

When she looked up at him again, her eyes were lit up by a teasing smile. "Me too," she whispered.

Shane and Cecilia lazed in bed most of the morning and afternoon. When the fire started dying down, Shane got up for more wood. While he was busy with the wood, Cecilia dressed and used the outhouse for the first time. He waited outside by the woodpile for her to emerge. When she came out, she wore a look of almost comically intense discomfort. She held her hands out in front of her with her fingers splayed as if she were afraid to transmit germs. When she caught him looking at her, she quickly donned her legendary mask of composure.

"Everything alright?" he asked.

"Yes," she assured him with a sweet smile. "Where am I supposed to wash my hands?"

"I always wash up at the kitchen sink," he said as he held the door open for her. He tried not to laugh at the look on her face. She looked absolutely horrified; her look reminded him why he'd never had a woman at his cabin before. It was far too rustic to be appealing for more than just a few hours.

"How did you end up with this cabin anyway?" she asked once they were safely tucked away in bed again. They'd shed their clothing, and were lying naked under the covers.

"It's kind of a long story," Shane hedged. He didn't want to think about his reasons for leaving the New York Fire Department; he didn't want to think of the firefighters who'd died under his command.

"We have all the time in the world."

"I promise it would bore you. This is where I lived right before I moved back to Nashville from New York."

"You lived here?"

"Yes."

"For how long?"

"A few years."

She sat up and looked at him in surprise. "Why?"

"I needed some time to myself." Her breast was exposed as she stared down at him, and he leaned forward to kiss it. She responded instantly, and suddenly the spark between them burst into a raging inferno again. She didn't ask any more questions for a while.

The next morning, Shane got out of bed long before Cecilia. He tended to the fire, dressed, and headed outside to think. Yesterday had been one of the best days of his life, but also one of the scariest. Admiring Cecilia from afar was a completely different experience from the all-consuming experience of loving her up close. He felt a deeper connection to her than he'd ever felt before, as if their lovemaking had been a way of communicating on a level that touched the depths of his soul. He'd always sworn to himself that he could control his emotions enough to prevent feeling that strongly about any woman. He'd always thought he could love someone, yet still keep himself from falling in as deeply as his father did with his mother. Now he had to come to terms with the fact that he'd been wrong.

As a child, he never understood why his father couldn't move on after his mother's death. He'd often looked at him with pity, and seen his refusal to marry again as a weakness. Now, he had to shake his head at his own thoughts. If abandoning oneself completely to the power of love made one weak, then he was the weakest man in the world right now.

He walked the rest of the way up the hill on which the cabin was built. He hadn't told Cecilia about his woodshop, and he was headed there now to get something. If she felt like going for a small hike later, he would bring her here. He'd never shared this part of himself with anyone before, but he wanted to share with Cecilia.

After the tragic fire that had killed the firefighters in his rescue company, he'd left New York in shame. He'd never forget the talk he'd had with the fire chief before he left. Just after the last funeral procession, he'd been walking back with the rest of the firefighters in dress uniform, and all the formalities of the ceremony had been over. Just before Shane had entered the firehouse to change, the fire chief had called him to the side and said, "Normally, when something of this magnitude happens, it's my decision whether or not to recommend administrative leave for the commander involved. Now, I don't know whether the investigation will find you at fault or not, Son. I'm not saying you did anything wrong, and I'm not saying you didn't do anything wrong. All I know is that I've got six firefighters dead, and the mayor himself told me not to put you on administrative leave. How can you look at yourself in the mirror after asking your granddaddy to step in for you? Can't you handle the consequences of your decisions like a man?" And with a sneer, the fire chief had walked off to talk to a group of somber faces in uniform.

At first, Shane had felt a nearly uncontrollable rage at his grandfather's interference. He'd never asked for it, had never even talked to the man. The only contact they'd had was the letter he'd sent to Shane before giving him a monetary reward for essentially telling off his grandmother. Shane had never asked that man for anything, and his interference in this matter was beyond infuriating. It was humiliating. In the months that followed the fire, everyone had looked at him differently, including his best friend Gus. It was Gus's disapproval that hurt the most.

By the time the official investigation had cleared him of misconduct, his reputation was in ruins. The general consensus around the fire department was that his grandfather must have used his power to have Shane cleared. In a matter of months, the career that it had taken him fifteen years to build had crumbled before his eyes.

When he'd first moved into the cabin, all he wanted was to be left alone. He didn't want any of the attention that had come with being the notorious grandson of Edgar Howard, one of the world's richest men. The press had made him into something that was so far from the truth it was almost laughable. He'd dated one famous actress, and suddenly he was a playboy. His grandfather had tried to help him one time, and suddenly he'd benefitted from nepotism his entire life. Out here in the woods, he could escape all of that negativity. He could be the man his father had raised, instead of the man everyone else thought he was. He could be himself, and he could be self-sufficient.

What began as a quest to be alone and heal had turned into a quest to prove to himself and everyone else that he didn't need or want anyone's help. He'd spent years hunting his own food, and making furniture in his woodshop. He sold the furniture at local markets, and made more than enough to live comfortably. His needs were simple, so it didn't cost him a fortune to be happy. He'd spent most of his time alone, and eventually he'd made peace with the past.

He felt the familiarity and comfort of home as soon as he stepped into his shop. His equipment was still in pristine condition, just as it had been a few months ago when he'd come here for a weekend. All of the beautiful things he'd crafted were still sitting untouched in the storage room. He walked to the wall of the large storage room and selected one of the many violins that he'd spent years perfecting.

His father had passed down the trade of woodworking to him at a young age, and Shane had never let his passion for it die. He'd learned the art of violin making during an apprenticeship with a master in New York. It had taken him his junior and senior year in college to master the craft enough to do it without supervision. During his hiatus from the world, he'd gone from intermediate violin maker, to a master luthier. He'd made more than 100 violins in his life, and they all hung on the walls of his humidity and temperature controlled storage room. He selected one of them, and tuned it before heading back to the cabin. The sun was just starting to peek over the horizon, lighting his path.

Cecilia was still sound asleep when he got back. He set the violin down, and climbed up the ladder to look at her. She was partially covered by the blanket. One leg stuck out to the side, and the gentle swell of her bosom was visible under the cover. He smiled as he thought about the reason she was so exhausted. They hadn't been able to keep their hands off each other for more than a couple of hours since yesterday. He kissed the part of her leg that was exposed, and breathed in her unique scent. When she stirred, he looked up to find her eyes on him.

"Good morning," she smiled.

"Good morning," he smiled back. She opened her arms to him, and he joined her under the covers. "How are you feeling today?"

"I don't know what to call this feeling, but it's a good one. How are you feeling?"

"I think I'm feeling the same things my father must have felt when my mother ran away with him... like I'm the luckiest man who ever lived... like I found my soul mate."

She was quiet for a long time, but she held him close to her. He felt her body tremble against his, but he didn't press her about her feelings. She hadn't said she loved him, but he felt it; he'd felt it all day yesterday. He could wait until she was ready to say the words. "I didn't think you were the type who believes in soul mates," she said eventually.

"I didn't either, until recently." He kissed her again, and when she opened up to him, he felt the same powerful feelings that took over every time they were close. "Either we're soul mates, or we've got some sort of addiction that needs serious treatment," he joked when they separated enough to catch their breath. "Stay here. I want to show you something." He got out of bed, and picked up his violin.

"Where did the violin come from?" she asked in surprise.

"I have a workshop just up the hill from here. I'll take you there today if you want, but right now I just want to play something for you."

"You want to play something for *me*?" she asked as she sat up in bed. She held the covers to her breasts and looked down at him with a big smile.

"Why do you look so surprised? Why wouldn't I want to play something for you?" he responded.

"No reason. I just wasn't expecting it. I remember last time you played for me—the day I got caught in the rainstorm while I was visiting Sarah's grave. That was very special to me," she confessed.

Shane smiled up at her as got into position and started playing. As soon as he played the first few bars of *Por Una Cabeza*, her face lit up in recognition. He'd never in his life serenaded a woman before, but for some reason the sentiment behind the melody seemed to fit his feelings for Cecilia perfectly. She lay on the edge of the bed and studied him with those magnificent eyes of hers as he played for her. There was something so sensual, and yet so innocent, in the way she stared directly at him as if she were torn between undressing him with her eyes and enjoying the music he made for her.

"That tune was so familiar, but I can't remember where I've heard it before," she said when he was done.

Shane chuckled and said, "That was actually one of the most famous melodies ever used for the Tango. When most people think of a song for the Tango, they think of that one. The original song was written in 1935, and the lyrics are about a horse track gambler who can't decide which is stronger, his fascination with horses or his love for women."

"So which do you like more? Horses or women?"

Shane's answer froze somewhere in his mouth as she abandoned the bed and climbed down the ladder, completely naked. He'd long been an admirer of the female form, and he'd been fascinated by her form in particular ever since the day he'd accidentally walked in on her doing handstands and splits. Time stood still for a moment as he watched her descent. He noted every detail, from the beautiful contrast between her waist and hips, to the way the muscles in her bottom and legs flexed as she neared the floor. Before her feet even touched the floor, his body was completely fired up again. She turned and slowly walked the last few steps toward him. She stopped when they were toe to toe, and smiled up at him. "You weren't about to say 'horses' were you?" she asked.

"What?" he said.

"I asked you which you like more, horses or women," she repeated the question.

He had no idea what he'd done with his violin or what prompted him to drop to his knees in front of her and bury his face in her midsection. He slowly ran his hands up her bare legs and cupped her firm bottom. He squeezed it and pulled her closer as he kissed her belly. "I think the more pertinent question is which do I like better, your awesome body or your amazing personality," he said as his hands continued to caress her naked bottom and thighs.

"Why does it always have to be about the way a woman looks," she chided him.

Shane tried to pull himself away from her, he really did, but he couldn't manage to do more than look up at her as he maintained his hold on her legs. "Well, what did you expect me to do? You come flouncing down here completely naked in front of me, and think I'm just going to forget that you're the hottest woman I've ever seen in my life, and that you're naked, and that we made love all day yesterday, and that I want to do it again? It's not always about how a woman looks, but that is one of the things that gives you power over us men. We find it hard to think when there's so much beauty before us."

"Shane, get up," she said gently.

"I can't," he whispered. He kissed her belly again, and started working his way lower. He pressed his lips against her thighs and breathed her in again and again. She was so warm and inviting, he didn't have the strength or the will power to pull himself away. The fact that she wasn't pushing him, and was in fact running her fingers through his hair, encouraged him to continue exploring with his lips.

"I don't have any power over you," she breathed in a husky little whisper.

"Yes you do. Look at me, all you had to do was get naked and smile at me to bring me to my knees. You have the power to make me the happiest man in the world, just by agreeing to stay with me, to be my wife."

"Shane, how can you be so sure you want me in your life?"

"Because, I love you. I've loved you since before I ever met you. These feelings I have for you started a long time ago, when I first heard about some of the great things you've done with your life. Shelly and Rebecca talk about you frequently, and I couldn't help but admire you before I even had the chance to meet you. I always thought that you were just the sort of woman I'd want to have in my life, but I never introduced myself because the timing just seemed off. Even if I'd never met you, I probably would have admired your story and been half in love with the you I imagined for the rest of my life. But I did meet you, and I did fall all the way in love with you, all of you. Even if I could have designed the perfect woman from scratch, there's no way she would compare to you. There are so many things that I admire about you—your strength, your determination, your talent. I love the way you protect those who are important to you, and the way you're always proving that you can do anything. Do you know how many other women, how many men for that matter, would have crumbled under some of the things you've endured? You are so strong and so beautiful. I love everything about you, even the fact that you didn't think twice about kicking my brother off your porch when you thought he deserved it. And now I love the way you whisper my name when I'm inside you. I want you in my life. If you won't stay with me, at least let it be because you have some objection to *me*, and not because you think I have some objection to you or where you came from."

By the time Shane finished his statement, Cecilia had tears streaming down her face. She crouched down so that they were face to face, and touched his cheek. "I don't want to hurt you. I went through so much at such a young age, I honestly don't know if I can ever love you the way you love me. You deserve a woman who loves you just as much as you love her."

"Love can grow, Cecilia. I believe we've gotten off to an excellent start. I've had feelings for you since before we met, so it's only natural that my feelings are more advanced than yours are. But that doesn't mean we can't be happy together. I've known from the beginning that you need more time, and I'm okay with that."

"But-"

"Cecilia, stop trying to talk me out of loving you. It's never going to work. I love you, so you should just get used to it," Shane said in frustration. He then softened his tone and stood up, pulling her to her feet as he did. He sat down on the chair and invited her onto his lap before continuing, "Can we just be together for the next couple of weeks, and see how things go? Stop trying to throw up obstacles, and just let whatever happens happen. While we're here, I don't want to hear another word about all the reasons you think you're going to make me so unhappy. Can we do that? When we go back to Nashville, we can decide what to do, but for now let's just enjoy this time together."

She didn't say anything else, but he could tell he was getting to her. He remained quiet and hoped his words would sink in. He wanted her to take them to heart.

They spent the rest of the morning doing routine things around the cabin. Shane showed Cecilia how to use the wood burning stove, and she attempted to make biscuits. When they came out horribly burnt, he tried to assure her that he liked his biscuits well done. She rolled her eyes at him, and then watched in amazement as he baked a perfect batch of biscuits. He hadn't meant to show her up, but the look of admiration in her eyes did make him feel good. After breakfast, they cleaned up and got ready for the trek to his woodshop.

"What made you want to spend years living alone in the woods?" She sprung the question on him almost as soon as they were outside.

"It's kind of a long story," he hedged. He wouldn't know where to begin, so he'd just as soon never tell her that he'd caused the deaths of six firefighters.

"Does it have anything to do with that newspaper story I found my first night in the cabin?" she asked.

"You saw that?"

"Yes. I found it while I was cleaning. You did tell me to make myself at home."

Shane ran is fingers through his hair in agitation. "It has everything to do with that."

"But the article said you were not found guilty of anything. It was ruled an accident."

"I know, but a lot of people in the department, the fire chief included, don't agree with those findings."

"Why not?"

"Because my grandfather took it upon himself to interfere. They all think he used his connections to keep me out of trouble."

"Is that what happened?"

"Yes," Shane admitted. "I did make a serious mistake. Maybe not something that I would have been fired or demoted for, but I definitely made a mistake that day."

"What happened?"

Shane glanced down at her. They walked side by side up the steep hill. Cecilia's breath showed in the chilly morning air as she breathed. He didn't exactly like the fact that she'd read the article, but there was no point in trying to hide anything from her. After everything she'd told him, he owed her the same honesty and candor. If anyone would understand, she would.

"I was in charge of a search and rescue company at the time. I'd been on the force for fifteen years, and, up until that day, I had a perfect record. I think I let my early success go to my head and make me cocky. A call came in about a fire in one of the industrial parks. It was an older building, supposedly uninhabited, but in New York older and uninhabited pretty much means full of homeless people. Sometimes there would be entire families of squatters shacked up in those buildings in the winter. When we arrived on the scene, the hose team was hooking up, and I sent a search and rescue team in to clear the first three floors. There were people in the windows, we all saw them, but the windows had bars over them. We couldn't use the ladders to get them out. All the victims were below the fire floor, the entire search and rescue effort was below the fire floor. It all seemed so routine. The real danger zone is always above the fire, because fire and smoke spread faster up, not down. The hose team asked my permission to start the attack on the fire floor to get it under control, and I gave them the go ahead. If I hadn't done that those firefighters and people might be alive."

"Why was that the wrong thing to do? Isn't that the same thing that happened when you got me out of my apartment? I remember seeing the hoses going when you got me out of there. What was different in that fire in New York?" Cecilia asked.

"In your building, there was no HVAC system on the roof. In older buildings, the roof supports weren't made to hold up those heavy heating ventilation and air-conditioning systems. That building in New York was an older building with an HVAC system *added* to the roof. Between the fire and the hose team suppressing the fire, the roof couldn't hold up. It wasn't made to withstand that much load, and that's why it collapsed. It was a five story building, and when the roof collapsed it took the whole thing down. Everyone inside died."

"How were you supposed to know that the building would collapse?" Cecilia asked as she reached out for his hand. Her gloved hand felt warm inside his.

"Nobody could have known that the whole thing would come down, but I could have at least checked if there was an HVAC system added to the roof. I didn't. I saw those people in the window and reacted with my emotions first, instead of my head. The hose team hadn't been there long enough to be the main cause of the collapse; it was mostly due to the weakening from the fire and the overload from the HVAC on the roof. A more experienced commander might not have sent in a search and rescue team at all."

"So, someone else would have let those homeless people die?" she demanded.

"Yes, but not out of cruelty. A more experienced rescue company commander would have realized that it's pointless to put more lives in danger when a total collapse is imminent."

"If you had known about the HVAC on the roof beforehand, would you have just left those people to die?"

"No, but I would have handled it differently," Shane sighed.

"How?"

"I would have made the hose team wait, and did whatever it took to break the bars off the windows, so we could've evacuated with the ladders instead. The reason I didn't try that first was because I didn't think we had enough time. But, had I known that was the only solution, I would have just started there."

Cecilia didn't say anything else as they walked the rest of the way to the woodshop; instead, she tried to calm her racing mind. When the large, metal building came into view over the hill, she squeezed Shane's hand and allowed the angry words in her head to escape her mouth.

"Forget all those people who think they know best when they weren't even there. It's easy to judge when you're the one on the outside, observing what the guy in the trenches is doing as the world crumbles around him. Most people *think* they can do better under pressure, but if they had to *prove* it, they'd probably keep their damned advice and opinions to themselves. *Nobody* has the right to judge you for the decision you had to make that day. You were doing everything you could to save lives. Forget everybody who thinks they have the right to judge you for that. And that goes for your grandfather too. Who cares what he thinks about *anything* you've done in your life? I mean, what kind of man disowns his only child just because she married a man who works for a living? Is everybody on Earth beneath him because we weren't born with a pile of money at our disposal? From everything I've heard about him, he sounds like the biggest coward that ever lived. All he does is hide behind his money and manipulate people. He may be known as 'The Great Edgar Howard,' but—other than cash—he has absolutely no value as a human!"

"Jeez, Cecilia," he said when she paused to take a breath.

She looked up at him with the most belligerent expression he'd ever seen on her face and said, "*What?* Was I being too harsh when I talked about your granddad? I meant every word I said about him and all those other jerks who think they can point the finger and judge you when they *know* they couldn't have done any better if they'd been there! Why do you care so much what they think? Why isolate yourself for years just because of them? You lost your career because you *let them* tear you down! You have no idea how much that bothers me—it doesn't change the fact that I love you—but it really bothers me that *you let them* have so much power over you. You let them win!

As he looked down at her, standing there with her fists balled up and her chest heaving, Shane was torn between the urge to laugh with delight and the urge to kiss her with all the burning intensity he felt at the moment. In the end, he satisfied both urges simultaneously. He picked her up and spun her around as he smiled. She clung to him and shrieked until he stopped, and then the two of them were suddenly locked in another embrace. He somehow managed open the door to his shop, and get them safely inside. Her legs were wrapped around his waist, her fingers were in his hair, and her lips were all over his face and neck as he walked toward the couch. He barely made it to the couch before their clothes were suddenly flying every which way as they undressed each other.

In the aftermath, they lay on the couch together. Shane reclined with his arms around her, and she lay sprawled across him with her face on his chest. Despite the chill in the air, they were both covered in a light sheen of perspiration. Shane chuckled when he thought again about what she'd said.

"What's so funny?" she raised her head up off his chest and asked.

"I've never had a woman dish out such a scorching lecture while telling me she loves me. Thanks for the new experience."

He detected a hint of embarrassment in her face as she dropped her gaze to his chin. "I said that?"

"Yeah, you tossed it in there among all the other stuff, but that's what made it so great. You obviously meant it."

"I don't even remember saying it. I recall just about everything else I said, but I didn't realize I said I love you," she replied.

"Well, you said it. There's no way I'm letting you take it back," he told her with a tender smile.

"Oh, I wouldn't dream of taking it back."

Shane placed a hand on her cheek and hugged her close again. He felt the same tightness in his chest that had plagued him since he first realized he was crazy about the woman in his arms. In all his previous relationships, he'd been the one to take on the role of the white knight—always willing and able to ride in and save the day. This was the first time a woman had ever stood up in his defense. He found Cecilia's anger on his behalf to be one of the sweetest things he'd ever experienced in his life.

He buried his nose in her hair and inhaled deeply. A little cocoon of peace settled around him when he thought about the building collapse. For the first time ever, he was able to think of the events without feeling like a complete and utter failure. He knew that if Cecilia had been with him during the aftermath of the collapse, she wouldn't have allowed him to slink away with his tail dragging in shame. She would have challenged him and inspired him to hang in just a little longer and prove to everyone who doubted him that he was still a good search and rescue leader. He might have still had a chance to be fire chief. He wondered how different their lives would have turned out if they'd met and fell in love when they were younger. Would they have had a few kids and been a normal family? Would they have concentrated on their respective careers and achieved success? He had a feeling they could have conquered the world together.

PART III

Chapter 25

Cece stared at Shane's back as he locked the door to the cabin. She'd taken her last look around with a nostalgic feeling in her heart. She'd always think of it as the place where she learned the greatest lesson of her life—the place where she learned to love and be loved.

Shane turned and gave her a tender smile as he reached out for her hand. "You ready to rejoin the world?" he asked.

Cece giggled, "Ready as I'll ever be." The past two weeks had seemed like a vacation from reality, and yet it had also seemed like the most real two weeks of her life. She found an entirely new part of herself while exploring the simple pleasure of physical intimacy with Shane. She was irrevocably changed, and Shane was the impetus. She took his hand, and they walked down the steep hill to the rental car.

They made small talk all the way back to Nashville. It wasn't until they'd returned the rental car and made their way back to Shane's house that Cece brought up the investigation.

She sat down on the couch next to him with a sigh and said, "I'm ready to go talk to your brother. I'll go in anytime he wants."

Shane's eyes probed her face as he said, "I'll call him right now."

Cece didn't think to protest his abruptness; he'd been right to push her. This talk was long overdue. She watched as he placed the call to Brent's office.

After a short conversation, Shane looked at her and said, "He's there right now, and he doesn't have anything else scheduled this afternoon. I can drop you off there now if you want."

"I'd like it if you stayed, at least for part of the interview."

"I can do that."

They didn't talk on the way to Brent's office. Cece gathered her thoughts and tried to plan out exactly what she wanted to say. She'd given Shane the quick, summarized version of everything, and she knew that Brent would need all the brutal details to move forward with the investigation. She shuddered as she thought again about those four days she'd spent tied to that bed.

She clutched her winter coat tighter around her body as Shane opened the door for her. The weather was mild, but she shivered as she looked up at the building that housed the state attorney's office. She and Shane took the elevator up to Brent's office, and as soon as they stepped off, his secretary was there to greet them.

"Mr. Gregory is just finishing up a phone call, but he told me to escort you two into one of the interview rooms. If you'll just follow me," the woman said with a friendly smile.

She led them to a small room with a table and several chairs. A small microphone stuck out of the center of the table. Cece tried not to stare at it, but her eyes repeatedly returned to it as she thought again about everything that must be said.

Shane put his arm around her and whispered in her ear, "You are the only woman I've ever met who I honestly think can handle anything life throws at her. You can do this, Cecilia."

She curled into his embrace and placed her head against his chest. He held her until the secretary came back into the room and offered them something to drink. Cece accepted a bottle of water from the woman and sat down to wait. Shane sat beside her and held her hand until Brent walked into the room.

"Cece, it's good to see you again," Brent greeted her with an easy smile. He wore a suit and tie, and his appearance was so flawlessly professional, Cece momentarily felt extremely out of place. "Don't mind the suit. I just got out of court not too long ago," Brent said as if reading her thoughts.

When she didn't respond, Brent smiled again and looked at Shane, "How was the honeymoon?"

"Best two weeks of my life," Shane said with a tender smile in Cece's direction.

There was another long and awkward pause before Brent cleared his throat and said, "If you're ready to get started, we can just jump right in."

"I'm ready," Cece answered as she situated herself in one of the chairs at the table.

"I apologize again about that long phone call. I actually got some good news that concerns you," Brent told Cece as he sat down across from her.

"What?"

"The person responsible for that apartment fire last April was caught. Actually, she turned herself in last week."

"*She?*" Cece and Shane demanded simultaneously.

"Yeah. The elderly gentleman who lived next to you, the one with all the oxygen tanks, his daughter did it. She confessed that she killed him for the insurance money. Said she felt guilty after seeing what she did to that little boy who suffered third degree burns all over his body," Brent informed them.

"So, it wasn't that man who was following me around..." Cece said in wonder.

"Apparently you were just in the wrong place at the wrong time," Brent smiled. He adjusted the microphone and switched on a button.

Cece took a deep breath as Brent stated her name and the purpose of the interview for the tape recorder. When he looked at her and asked the first question, she was ready, she really was, but with her answer also came a multitude of tears. She couldn't have stopped them even if she'd tried, so she didn't try. Instead, she concentrated on giving details about Red Bone, and being as accurate as possible. By the end of the interview, she'd taken several breaks, and Shane had long since been banished to a waiting room. She and Brent were in the room alone when she revealed the horrors of her four days in captivity. By the time she finished talking about it all, the sun had gone down and her voice was hoarse from talking for so many hours. When it was over, she stared at the table for a long time. Eventually, she looked up again to see Brent holding out a box of tissues.

"I guess now you're wondering where we go from here?" he said.

"Yes," Cece nodded. "I mean, I don't even know his real name, and besides my mother and Dot, I don't know the names of any of the other women he killed."

"You'll be surprised how many victims are willing to come forward with information once someone else breaks the silence. What you've done by coming forward first is a very brave thing, Cecilia. There are many paths to take from here, and they all lead to justice," Brent assured her.

"Do you think you'll be able to prosecute him if you find him?"

"When we find him, if he's still alive, he's going to be looking at spending the rest of his life behind bars," Brent insisted as he stood up and gathered his notepad and papers. He then came around the table and gave Cece a hug. "I've handled cases like this before. It may seem like a long shot right now, but give me a few months. I didn't get elected to the district attorney's office just because I look good in a suit."

As soon as Cece and Shane left, Brent rushed back to his office. "It's going to be a late night tonight," he warned his secretary as he passed her desk.

She looked up with a surprised expression, as her hands froze over her purse. She had obviously been packing up for the day. "How late? Late like I need to call my husband and tell him I won't make it for dinner? Or late like I need to call and tell him not to wait up for me tonight?" she asked.

Brent paused in the door to his office and said, "Tell him not to wait up, and get Luther Johnston on the phone. If he isn't in his office, call his cell and his home number; this is big."

Moments after Brent sat down at his desk and pulled up the search application on his computer, his phone beeped. "Mr. Johnston is on line two," Jasmine said.

"Don't tell me you're calling in another favor this soon? Didn't I just help you get elected not too long ago?" Luther joked when Brent answered.

"Actually, I am," Brent sighed. "Do you recall that cold case file down in Atlanta that you gave a lecture on during my internship with your law firm back in the 80's?"

"Which one? I give a lot of seminars and lectures on cold cases."

"The one that you like to refer to as the one that got away," Brent clarified.

"The prostitute killer?" Luther asked with obvious anticipation in his voice.

"Yes. You're never going to believe who just came into my office to give a statement regarding your main person of interest."

"Is this a joke? You wouldn't play around with my emotions, would you? You and I go way back, Brent. Obviously I was a good advisor or you wouldn't be so successful now."

"This is no joke. His daughter, Cece Graves, came in and gave all kinds of details. She described him to a T. She didn't know his name, but she did know him as Red Bone. Now, how many other pimps named Red Bone can you think of that would have a daughter named Cece Graves? I'm positive she was talking about the same Red Bone you investigated all those years ago."

"Cedric Graves is the only one I can think of," Luther said quietly.

"I already have a DNA sample from her on file, so we can compare it to his and get the familial match with his. We had to do a paternity test on some psycho who raped her and got her pregnant when she was thirteen. That's how I ended up with this case. Apparently, Cedric kept her tied down for four days and let his customers assault her repeatedly. She's willing to testify."

"Holy shit!"

"I know," Brent said. "That's the first thing I thought as soon as she said 'Red Bone.' I didn't tell her that I was already familiar with a cold case involving that guy though. Once we go through all the old case files and do another round of interviews, I'll give her an update."

"All these years, all we needed was one person to come forward to be a witness. What are the odds that Cedric is about to be brought down by his own daughter?" Luther said quietly. "The thing that always stuck with me about that case, besides the brutality, was how no one in the neighborhood dared to say a word against that guy. All those prostitutes we talked to, and not one of them would give a witness statement. And the ones who got away, I guess they were too afraid to come back."

"How soon can you have copies of those case files delivered to me?" Brent asked after a long moment of silence.

"Give me an hour. I have to talk to Alicia first. She's the new prosecutor for Atlanta, so she's in charge of all the cold case files. Do you want to be in on a conference call?"

"No need, unless you think she needs convincing."

"Not at all. She's very outspoken about victims' rights. She'll love the idea of opening this case up. We think this guy's body count could be as high as eighteen. Almost all of the victims were women who had been into prostitution. Most of them young; all found burned in dumpsters in and around the area where he operated."

"See what you can do. If she lets you send them by courier, I'll be in the office all night. If not, just give me a call and let me know what the deal is."

That night, Cece lay in bed and stared up at the ceiling for hours after Shane fell asleep beside her. She felt as if her entire life had been leading up to the moment she experienced in Brent's office. That one moment of reckless courage that had induced her to go find Dot all those years ago had repeated itself earlier as she gave Brent the details of every wrong she'd ever witnessed Red Bone do. She half expected that he would never be found, but still she hoped for the best. After so many years of seeing him as a dark omnipotent force in her life, she didn't know what category he fit into now. He hadn't had any tangible power over her since she ran away, and now she realized that the power she'd given him over her emotions for so long was finally fading.

She moved closer to Shane, and he turned towards her and put his arms around her. "Are you okay?" he asked in a sleepy murmur.

She smiled at him and replied, "Never better." It wasn't the whole truth, but she didn't want to keep him up with her emotional concerns.

He kissed her hair and went back to sleep. She glanced at the bedside clock. It was two in the morning. Her bakery wasn't scheduled to reopen until the following Monday, so she had the entire weekend off to contemplate her life. She knew Shane expected her to stay with him now, to be a wife to him. Of course, he expected that. After two weeks of them pouring out their love for each other in the cabin, how could he not expect that?

She snuggled closer and breathed in his scent. She was going to miss him so much when she left. Silent tears rolled across her cheeks as she skimmed her fingers over the outline of his face. She closed her eyes and listened to his even breathing and his heartbeat. She concentrated on the warmth and security of his arms around her, and tried not to imagine the tender way he had smiled at her the first time they made love.

The next morning, Cece opened her eyes to the sunlight streaming into the room. Shane stirred beside her and pulled her close for a hug.

"How are you this morning?" he asked with a smile.

Cece loved how he always smiled at her in the morning, as if he were so happy to be waking up next to her. She couldn't help but smile back. "I feel like I'm starting a new chapter in life, and I'm not entirely sure where to go from here."

"What do you mean?" he asked carefully.

"I mean, as much as I love you, I can't stay here and be a burden."

Shane rubbed the sleep out of his eyes and stared at her for a long time before speaking. "Haven't we been through this over and over again at the cabin? *I love you*, Cecilia. You are not a burden to me."

"Shane, I don't think you understand. I need some time on my own to heal. If a long term relationship between us is ever going to happen, I need to know that I can stand on my own two feet without you. I need to know that you aren't just propping me up emotionally every time I have a bad night. It isn't fair to you if I take up all the emotional space between us."

"You *can* get along just fine without me. Isn't that what you've been doing for the past twenty-seven years? I don't understand where this is coming from."

"I don't mean financially, I mean emotionally. After just two weeks, I'm so used to feeling safe with you I doubt if I can ever sleep alone again."

"I want to be there for you. You went through hell, and now you're finally dealing with it all. It's completely normal and understandable that you need someone. I do not feel like I'm just propping you up in this relationship. I respect you more than anyone else I've ever known."

"And that's one of the reasons I love you so much. You are so good to me. I feel like every time I stumble, you're there with your hand out, ready to help me get steady. I don't want you to have to do that anymore. I want to be a whole person on my own first, and I may never get there if I keep leaning on you."

"Cecilia, love is about helping each other through the hard times. You are having a hard time, and I love you. Of course you can lean on me when you need to."

"But that's not what I want," she said with sad finality.

The air in the room seemed painfully thin as he reached out a hand and touched her cheek. "What is it that you want then?"

"I just want some time to deal with this and actually try to heal on my own. You deserve to be with someone who is emotionally available, and right now I'm not all the way there."

"Emotionally available?" Shane whispered with a humorless chuckle. "You sound like a self-help book."

"Shane, I'm serious."

"I know," he sighed. "I had a feeling this was coming. Last night you just kept giving me this look. It was the same kind of look my mother used to give us when she knew she was definitely going to die."

"Was I that transparent?"

"Yes."

"It's just so hard for me to say goodbye to you," Cece sobbed. After yesterday she didn't think she had anymore tears left to shed, but they were suddenly flowing freely again as she looked at Shane.

He hugged her to him and kissed her forehead as he said, "This is not goodbye," in a fierce whisper. "You told me you need some time and space to heal, not that there's no chance for us."

"But it could take months, maybe even years. I can't ask you to wait around that long for me. Of course you'll see someone else."

He stroked her hair and kissed her several times before speaking again. "After my mother died, my father never married again. He dated a few women casually, but he never got into another serious relationship. When I was a teenager, and even as a younger man, I never understood why he couldn't just move on. He was a tall, strapping, good looking guy. He probably could have had any woman he wanted, but he spent the rest of his life pining away for my lanky, freckled, carrot top mother. She was the love of his life, and he lost her. I always thought that he was too weak to get over it, but now I think that maybe he was the strongest man I've ever known. He lived the rest of his life alone, because he didn't want to subject some other woman to being second best for the rest of her life. I respect him so much for that, even more now that I find myself in the same situation with you."

"What do you mean?" Cece sniffed.

"I mean, you're it for me. As long as there's a chance that we can be together and live happily ever after, I won't even be able to look at another woman. Call me a crazy, old-fashioned romantic, but that's how I feel. Some people live their entire lives and never find what my father and mother had—what you and I have. You need some time and some space right now, and when you're ready I'll be here for you."

A few days later, Cece made the short trip to her daughter's house. She had packed up her things, and talked to Karen and her new assistants the day before. Rebecca was the only one who didn't know she was leaving town for an extended time. Cece wanted to talk to Rebecca about everything, but she didn't know where to begin.

Rebecca and Norman were on their way out the front door when Cece pulled into the drive. "Is this a bad time?" Cece asked as she stepped out of her car.

Norman bent down to whisper something in Rebecca's ear, before waving at Cece and then walking around to the side of the house.

"We were just about to go for a walk," Rebecca told Cece. "What's up?"

"I just wanted to talk to you. I'm leaving town for a while, and I don't know when I'll be back."

"You're leaving? Why? Where are you going?"

"Can we go inside and talk? I'd like to see the babies."

"Sure," Rebecca said as she opened the front door. "Shelly's watching them for us, but I can go get them real quick. Have a seat in the den, and I'll be there in a few minutes."

Cece went inside and sat down. As she waited for Rebecca to come into the room, she stared out the window and gathered her thoughts. Where could she possibly begin? When Rebecca finally came into the room with her granddaughters, Cece was standing beside the window. Rebecca pushed the baby carriage over to her, and Cece looked down at the sleeping babies. "How do you tell them apart?" she asked her daughter.

Rebecca smiled and said, "Rose is the one in yellow, and Renée has on blue."

Cece bent down and kissed each of their hands before saying, "I can't believe how cute they are."

"Everyone says they look just like you—same hair, same eyes. Norman is always shaking his head about it."

"I'm sure they'll look more like you two when they get older," Cece said. They were silent again for a while. Cece continued to watch the babies and Rebecca continued to watch her.

"Where are you going, Mom?"

"Atlanta," Cece sighed. "There's something there, or *someone* I should say, that I really need to take care of."

"Your parents?" Rebecca asked with a concerned look.

"No, Honey. I don't have any parents. My mother was killed when I was young. I grew up in the foster care system."

"Why didn't you tell me about this before?"

"Because... I didn't want you to think less of me. I didn't want you to know where I really came from. I didn't want you to be ashamed of me like I was of my mother."

"Why would I be ashamed of you?"

"Rebecca, my mother was a prostitute. Before she was killed, we lived in a hotel with her pimp."

Rebecca crossed the room and wrapped her arms around Cece, "I'm not ashamed of you. I could never be ashamed of you. Why are you going back to Atlanta *now*?"

"I'm going back there to help build a community center in my old neighborhood and help the woman who tried to save my mother the day she was killed. Also, because I need some time alone to deal with everything that happened back then. Ever since the day I ran away, I've just been avoiding it all, but now I can't avoid it any more. There may be a lot of ugly things about my past coming out in public soon, and I need to be strong enough to handle it."

"What's going on?"

"One of the men who raped me has been following me around, and Shane finally convinced me to report what happened to me."

"*One* of the men?" Rebecca asked in a whisper.

"It's a long story, Honey. I don't want to talk about it all again. I just wanted to come tell you what I'll be doing for the next few months."

"Why can't we just talk about it now, Mom?"

"Because, I just can't. I've written a letter explaining everything to you. You can read it after I leave." Cece reached into her purse and removed the envelope. "Don't let this change anything. I know I haven't always acted like it, but you really are the best thing that ever happened to me. Both you and Sarah," she said as she pressed the letter into Rebecca's hands.

"When are you leaving?" Rebecca asked.

"Right now." Cece stood up and kissed Rose and Renée once more before gathering Rebecca up in a long and intense embrace. "I'll only be a few hours away, so call me if you ever want to talk. I don't know how often I'll come back here to visit, but I'm planning on at least once a month. Is that okay with you?"

"Of course. I'll visit you too, and we'll talk."

"I'd like that," Cece smiled. "You be good to my grandbabies."

Rebecca stood at the front door and waved as Cece left. She had a tear rolling down her cheek, but she looked happy. Cece held on to that look, and let it fill her with warmth. She was finally taking the proper steps to move on with her life. She was no longer going to be a slave to her past, her fears, and her nightmares.

As she drove to Atlanta, Cece thought about everything she had waiting for her in Nashville and vowed to return as a stronger and better person.

# Chapter 26

A week after Cecilia left town, Shane was sitting in his kitchen when the phone rang. The number was unfamiliar, and he answered with a racing heart, half expecting Cecilia to be on the line.

"Hey, Shane," his brother Brent's voice said instead.

"What's up?" Shane tried to keep the disappointment out of his voice.

"Is your wife around? I've been trying to get a hold of her. I need to ask her a few quick questions."

"Did you try calling her cell phone?" Shane asked.

"No. I've only tried her work number, and I keep getting her assistants. All they'll say is that Cece isn't available, but Karen is."

"Cecilia is in Atlanta. She drove down there last Monday."

"That's even better. I'm in Atlanta right now with the prosecutor. Give me her cell number."

Shane gave Brent the number and then asked, "What's this all about? Have you found out anything new?"

"I didn't mention this to you or Cece when she came in to give her statement, but that pimp she knows as Red Bone is actually a man named Cedric Graves. An old friend of mine named Luther Johnston worked a number of prostitute killings back in the 80's, and Cedric was the main person of interest linked to more than a dozen dead prostitutes. I've been in communication with Luther and the current prosecutor in Atlanta, and we all think Cece's testimony may be exactly what we need to move this case along."

"Why didn't you mention this to me sooner?"

"I didn't want to get your hopes up until I'd had a look at the case files and I knew a little more about what we were working with," Brent sighed.

"What do you know now?"

"Here's a rundown of what I did last week. Luther, Alicia, and I spent almost every waking hour going through boxes and boxes of witness statements, police reports, and autopsy reports. I also had a sample of Cece's DNA compared to a sample of Cedric's, and he's definitely her father. What I can't find is anything on her mother's death. Cece saw him beat her to death, but she isn't anywhere in any of the other files we went through. I need to ask her some questions to point us in the right direction."

"How do you have a sample of his DNA?" Shane asked.

"It's on file. He's a repeat felon, so he's had a DNA profile in the national database for years now."

"So, you know where he is right now?"

"Yes. He's serving a sentence for simple assault up at Calhoun State Prison. His release date is coming up soon though. If we can't get some information on Cece's mother, our entire case may evaporate. She's the only one we can prove Cece witnessed. Our other option is to get that guy who was following her around to testify against Cedric. We can offer him some kind of deal if he tells the truth about everything that happened while Cece was tied down."

"So if you find something about her mother, and locate that guy who was following her around, this thing can all be over soon?" Shane asked.

"I don't know about over soon, but Cedric will definitely face charges for at least one of the women he killed. It's going to be nearly impossible to dig up witnesses from prostitute killings three decades ago."

"Is there anything I can do to help?"

"It might help if you were willing to hire a private investigator to dig up more info on Cece's mother and how she got mixed up with Cedric in the first place. Alicia and I can't really focus our criminal investigation on finding out where someone who isn't even on the victim list came from. We have to be systematic and methodical; we have to re-interview people and review everything for leads that were missed. Cold cases are very difficult to solve."

"Do you have any private investigators in mind?" Shane asked.

"I can't advise you in any professional capacity, but as your brother I can tell you that I've worked with a young woman named Natalie Phillips. She's done a lot of work with finding families in closed adoptions over the last decade, and I think she might be able to work a miracle in this case."

When they disconnected, Shane called Natalie's number and left her a voicemail regarding the particulars of Cece's case. She called him back within an hour, and by the end of the week they'd set up an appointment. Shane met with her in her office after work that Friday.

When he walked in, he was completely taken aback by how young the woman looked. "Natalie?" he asked the young, raven haired woman behind the desk.

"Yes, I'm Natalie Phillips, and you must be Shane Gregory. Have a seat."

"I am," Shane smiled as he sat down.

"So, tell me more about Cece. I understand you want me to find out where her mother came from."

"Yeah, and also see if you can find out how she got mixed up with a pimp named Cedric Graves."

"What do we know about the mother?" Natalie asked as she began typing on her keyboard.

Shane sat forward and said, "Her name was Cora, and she didn't speak any English. Cece told me she spoke French, and she was afraid of going back to wherever she came from."

"Unh hunh," Natalie nodded several times as she typed furiously for a few minutes. "What's your wife's social security number?"

Shane answered, and Natalie typed some more. When she paused to stare at the screen for several moments, Shane said, "What? Did you find something?"

"What did you say your wife's name is?"

"Cecilia, but she goes by Cece."

"And her mother's name?"

"Cora."

"Now that is really interesting."

"What?" Shane asked.

"I found some court records for a Cora Graves who petitioned the Davidson County Court to become an emancipated minor at the age of fifteen. According to these documents, her employer, a Ms. Jiang Lee, testified on her behalf."

"She never told me about that," Shane said as he sat back in the chair.

"Cora Graves was listed as an endangered runaway shortly before this court case showed up. It says here in her birth record that she was born Cora Cecilia Graves to an unknown father and a mother named Corinne Nnamani-Graves."

"Does it say where her mother came from?"

"Give me a few minutes," Natalie said as she typed some more. She stared intently at the computer screen for a few minutes, and clicked through several pages of documents before speaking again. "She came from Cameroon."

"Wow, you're good," Shane smiled at her.

"That's just information from a basic background search that anyone with some time and a little info can pull off. The hard part will be finding out her association with Cedric. Lucky for you, I've just cleared my schedule to go on vacation, so I have all the time in the world— for the next month at least."

"How soon can you have some answers on how Corinne got involved with Cedric?" Shane asked.

"That depends. Right now, I think the most logical next step is to dig into Cece's childhood records. The state keeps all kinds of records on children in the system. If I don't find anything there, I'll pay a visit to Cedric and see what I can get out of him."

"Are you sure that's a good idea?" Shane asked in concern. "I don't want you doing anything to make him suspicious about the investigation. I wouldn't want him to start covering his tracks."

"I'm already ahead of you on that one. While we were sitting here, I've pulled up background searches for Cora, Corinne, and Cedric. So far, Cedric's has given me the most info. He's been in trouble with the law multiple times, mostly for assaults and pandering. He was born in Baton Rouge, Louisiana. He dropped out of school. He strikes me as the kind of guy who has some serious mommy issues. His ethnicity is listed as Louisiana Creole, and that in itself tells me a whole lot. There were some interesting conflicts between the older generation of Creoles and their children during the civil rights era, right around the time when Cedric would have been in his idealistic formative years. If I pretend I'm a young writer doing a piece on the difficulties of growing up Creole in the south during the civil rights movement, he might just open up to me a little. I'm definitely not going to come at this guy as a pushy private investigator."

"Are you sure that will work?"

"Of course. The main advantage to looking so young is that it's easier to gain someone's trust, especially if it's a man that I'm investigating. And guys like Cedric, who torment women, only do it so they can feel more significant. I'll be this guy's dream come true when I walk in there willing to listen to his side of the story and learn about all the painful reasons why he ended up hurting others."

By the end of the meeting, Shane was very impressed with the young woman. When they parted, she promised to keep him updated on her progress.

Months went by before Natalie had anything significant to report. Shane kept busy at the fire academy during the week, and on his weekends off, he spent time at his cabin. Memories of Cecilia were very strong his first night there. Long into the night, he stared out the window at the stars and wondered if she was doing something similar. He wondered what she was doing and if she ever thought of him. He thought about the few times he'd seen her wake up from a nightmare, and hoped that she was sleeping okay on her own.

Spring and summer seemed to pass in a slow motion, so he spent much of his time at the cabin crafting things in his woodshop to keep busy. When he wasn't in his wood shop, he was working on a new addition to his cabin. Next time Cecilia came, there would be a proper bathroom for her to use. Shane still smiled to himself every time he recalled the look on her face after the first time she used his outhouse. The bathroom was small and simple, but he knew Cecilia would appreciate it.

Cecilia hadn't called him since she left town, but she did send him several post cards. Each postcard was a picture of her and Miss Georgia's community center project at various stages of development. He'd received the first one when the demolition phase was completed. She'd written a short note about her progress, and signed her name with a heart next to it.

Shane didn't spend all of his days off at the cabin. He also spent a fair amount of time at Norman and Rebecca's house. Rose and Renée grew like a couple of little wildflowers, and he thought they looked more like Cecilia every day. He found great satisfaction in teasing his little brother about that fact. Part of the reason he loved spending time with the babies was because he liked to imagine that if he and Cecilia had a daughter, she would look something like Rose and Renée.

One autumn day, he got home from work to find a message from Natalie on his voicemail. "You'll never guess who I found, call me when you get this," the message said.

Shane picked up the phone and called her immediately. "What did you find out?" he asked when she answered.

"I found Cedric's mother. She's in a nursing home near Baton Rouge. I'm packing up now to fly down there. Do you want to come? Or can I just brief you when I get back?"

"No, I'll come," Shane insisted immediately. He felt like he was going stir crazy waiting to hear from Cecilia and waiting for the prosecution's case against Cedric to turn into something worth going to court with.

He and Natalie travelled to Baton Rouge that night. They discussed the details she'd uncovered over dinner, and then retired for the night. As he lay in the hotel bed, Shane thought about all the dribs and drabs of information that had come in over the past few months. The Atlanta prosecutor had re-interviewed almost a hundred witnesses, and there were now at least three other credible women who were willing to testify against Cedric. It seemed that years had softened the fear the women felt, but not the guilt they'd lived with for so long. The most frustrating missing piece of the puzzle was still Corinne's murder. The Atlanta prosecutor still couldn't even find an autopsy report on her.

The next morning, he and Natalie drove out to the nursing home where Cedric's mother had been living for the past nine years. Shane saw the family resemblance as soon as they stepped into the room.

"Isabelle Graves?" Natalie asked politely as she approached the old woman.

Faded gray eyes looked up at her, and an old voice answered, "Yes."

Shane quietly watched as Natalie introduced herself and made pleasantries to put the old woman at ease. Eventually, she got to the point of the visit and Shane listened, anticipating a plethora of new details.

"I came to ask you a few questions about your son."

"My son?" Isabelle looked confused, and then very sad before she spoke again. "My son is dead. He's been gone for more'n forty years now. Why are you asking me about him?"

Natalie and Shane looked at each other in shock. "Dead?" they asked in unison.

Isabelle lay back on her bed and pulled her shawl tighter around her frail shoulders. "Yes. Dead."

"Can you tell us anything about him?" Natalie asked.

"I can show you a picture of him and his wife," Isabelle answered before she shut her eyes and lay back again. "You're the first people who have ever come asking me about my son. Are you newspaper reporters?" she asked.

"Yes," Natalie lied. "Do you mind if we borrow the picture to use in our story? We'll bring it back of course."

Isabelle looked at them, and then reached into the drawer of the table beside her bed. Her pale, shaky hand pulled out an old, faded picture of a man and a woman standing together. She handed them the picture with a sad look. The woman in the picture wore a brightly colored dress and the man wore a suit. His arms were around her, and they were both smiling. Obviously, they were in love.

Shane flipped the picture and found a note on the back. It was in French. "What does it say on the back?" he asked Isabelle.

"It says, 'Dear Mom, I'm sending someone very special to you to take care of until I get back. She's carrying a package that I think you'll love.'"

"What did he mean?" Natalie asked gently.

"I never got the chance to ask him. She never showed up, and I never saw my son again. He died after that."

"How did he die?" Natalie asked all the questions as Shane observed in shock.

"I don't know. No one has ever come asking me about my son before," she said again as tears streamed down her weathered face. She pressed the call button, and one of the nurses came in and asked them to leave.

"What are we going to do now?" Shane asked as they left the nursing home.

"I think the best place to go from here is to Calhoun State Prison. Cedric might be the only one who can tell us why his own mother thinks he's dead."

Shane looked down at the picture again. He just couldn't reconcile the smiling, happy couple with everything he knew about Cedric and Corinne. How could they have gone from being a happily married couple to a pimp and a prostitute? It made no sense.

"Something about this just doesn't feel right to me," Shane said.

"Me too," Natalie sighed. She whipped out her cell phone and made a number of calls.

Shane paced circles around the entrance of the nursing home as Natalie spoke at length to someone. She appeared to be embroiled in a fierce argument, but after several more minutes she smiled like an angel and disconnected.

"What was that all about?" Shane asked.

"Had to call in a favor to get an interview with Cedric."

"Why?"

"Because, he's in a state prison, I can't just waltz in there and demand to see him. I needed special permission, so I had to call in a favor. His release date is in less than six months. It's now or never." She talked fast as she stomped towards the rental car, her heels clicking hard against the sidewalk.

"Are we going there now?" Shane asked as he trailed behind her. How could she walk so fast in heels?

"I'm going there now, but you can catch a plane back to Nashville if you want," Natalie tossed out over her shoulder.

"No, I'll come with you," Shane said after a moment of hesitation.

Shane sat outside an interview room with two correctional officers and watched through the two way mirror as Cedric was ushered to a metal table. The table and chairs were bolted to the floor, and Cedric was in shackles. He sat down at the table and slumped over as the guards stood on either side of him.

His reddish brown hair was cut very close to his head, and he had a multitude of prison tattoos running up the length of his bony, old arms. Shane could barely detect a trace of the happy, handsome man he had been in the photo. His face was a weathered mask of anger and menace. Deep lines marred his features and gave him a permanent look of unhappiness.

When Natalie walked into the interview room, he straightened up and looked down at her with a great deal of disdain evident in his expression.

"What the fuck you want?" he snarled as soon as Natalie sat down.

Shane and the correctional officers sat forward as Natalie's eyes grew wide. "I came here to interview you for a book I'm writing," she offered with a smile.

"You expect me to believe that shit?"

Natalie smiled, "Why else would I be here?"

"Why else..." Cedric smiled as he stared at Natalie. He licked his lips several times and said, "What's a pretty little thing like you doing sniffing around prisons? Why not 'interview' someone on the outside? Why choose me?"

"I didn't exactly choose you; someone suggested you," Natalie answered in a cool tone.

"You writin' a book about pimpin'? You need to know somethin' 'bout keepin' bitches and hoes in line?" he snarled.

"Actually, no. I'm doing some research on the Louisiana Creole community in Baton Rouge, and your mother, Isabelle, suggested I talk to you."

"You mean that old bitch is still alive?"

Natalie pulled out the photo and placed it on the table between them. Cedric's eyes went directly to the woman's face and stayed there. "She's still alive, and she seems to think you're dead. She let me have this picture of you and your wife."

"You shoulda got your facts straight before you came here," Cedric said.

"What do you mean?"

"I can't help you with your book. That's not my wife. I aint never been married. That's not me in the picture."

"If it's not you, then who is it?"

"Seems to me, if you really talked to my mother you'd already know the answer to that question," he spat out. "Stupid little bitch."

"That guy's a real piece of work," one of the correctional officers said to Shane.

"Am I allowed to go in there with her?" Shane asked on impulse.

"You could, but wouldn't that blow her cover? I thought you two wanted him to believe he's being interviewed for a book," the officer replied.

"He obviously doesn't believe that. Look at him; he's giving her a hard time because she's a woman. That's what he's good at. Why else would scores of women have refused to bear witness against him for the past thirty years?"

"I'll go in and escort her out of there, and then you can try talking to him."

When Natalie walked out of the interview room, her hands were shaking. "That wasn't as easy as I thought it was going to be," she said as she released a pent up breath.

"Are you okay?" Shane asked.

"Have you ever had the feeling you were looking at someone who was pure evil? Those eyes... he just kept staring at my chest. I swear it was like I was sitting naked in the same room as the devil."

Shane walked over to the officer in charge and said, "I'd like to go in there with him—alone."

"I can't allow that," the man said.

"I can make it worth your while."

"How?"

"This guy is the prime suspect in one of the biggest cold cases in history. He killed more than a dozen women, including my wife's mother. My brother is the DA up in Nashville, and he's working closely with the Atlanta prosecutor on this case. If I'm able to get some information that sheds more light on this case, I'll make sure to mention your helpfulness to them. It might come in handy when you're up for your next promotion."

"The guards need to be there for *your* safety."

"Look at me. Do I really look like I'm going to get beat up by some old man in chains? He needs more protection than I do, but I promise I won't lay a hand on him."

The man thought about it for a tense moment before he made eye contact with Shane and nodded his consent.

After the two guards left Cedric alone in the room, Shane and the other officers watched him through the glass. Shane didn't want to go in until Cedric started to look uncomfortable. It took about fifteen minutes for him to glance around in a worried manner, but eventually he did.

Shane waited a few more minutes and went into the room. Cedric looked up in surprise as Shane stepped in and shut the door. Faded gray eyes with a glint of malevolence stared up at him and then wavered when Shane's unrelenting gaze returned the stare.

He'd made up his mind not to speak first, and he didn't have long to wait before Cedric asked, "Who are you?" in a much nicer tone than the one he'd used with Natalie.

"Your worst nightmare," Shane answered as he sat down across from Cedric. He puffed his chest out and rested his arms on the table. He stared at Cedric as if he was itching to lay into him, but he didn't say anything else.

"What are you? Some tough guy who's gonna beat me up if I don't talk?" Cedric sneered up at Shane.

"You'd like that, wouldn't you?" Shane said in a deceptively calm voice.

"This is entrapment. You and that bitch are trying to get me to incriminate myself. I aint talkin' about shit!" the chains rattled as Cedric sat back and crossed his arms over his chest. "I been through this too many times to fall for it. I aint sayin' *shit*."

"You don't have to say shit; Cece already said it all for you," Shane said quietly. He watched in satisfaction as Cedric sat forward. There was a moment of pure panic in his eyes before he donned his nonchalant look again. "You remember a young girl named Cece Graves, don't you? You killed her mother, Cora. Or maybe you knew her as Corinne Nnamani. You killed her best friend, Dot—among others—and you tried to kill her too."

Little beads of sweat appeared on Cedric's brow, and Shane noticed that the nonchalant look was quickly melting away. "I don't know who the hell you're talking about," Cedric said with little conviction. He actually sounded a bit breathless.

"So, you don't know your own daughter?" Shane asked with a raised eyebrow. "That really is interesting."

"She's not my daughter."

"I've got a paternity test that proves otherwise."

"I don't know what you think you know, but you've got it all wrong. I didn't have nothin' to do with what happened to that stupid African bitch, Cora. She had a miscarriage and bled to death, and Cece really isn't my daughter," Cedric insisted. He sounded desperate as he went on, "Look, if you're some prosecutor with charges against me, I'll see you in court. You must not have much, or you wouldn't be here hasslin' me. I know exactly how these things work. I'm not saying shit else until I have a lawyer."

"You'd love it if I was a prosecutor, then I'd have to go by the rules, so I don't lose my job. Like I said before, I'm your worst nightmare. I don't have anything to do with the court system. Cece is my *wife*, and she told me all about everything you ever did to her."

"Your wife?" Cedric echoed.

"*My wife*. She told me everything—*everything*. You kept her tied to the bed in room 216, the same room you beat her mother to death in. She was thirteen, and you tortured her for trying to save her best friend. The prosecutor in Atlanta doesn't need my help to prosecute you. After Cece came forward with her statement, the investigators found other women who saw you commit murder, and guess what? They're all willing to testify against you now. But that's not the worst concern for you right now; I am. I come from a very powerful family, and I can make things happen to you in the blink of an eye. After everything she told me about you, everything you did to her, I don't think you deserve your day in court. The only reason you're still sitting here alive now is because she believes in justice, and I'd hate to disappoint her by having you killed before she gets the chance to put you away."

"If you have all this evidence against me, why come here looking for more?" Cedric lashed out.

"I came looking for answers about her mother. It's important to her. Obviously, you aren't going to help, so I'm wasting my time here. You might just want to confess to killing all those women, because if you get out of here, I'm going to take it as a sign that you'd rather deal with me than the justice system."

"You aint gonna do shit to me."

"After you tortured my wife, you don't really want to count on that," Shane said as he stood up and leaned across the table. He clutched the front of Cedric's shirt in his fist and dragged the smaller man halfway across the table. He stared directly into his eyes and gritted out, "I don't see anybody rushing in here to save you now, and when you get out, no one will be there to report you missing. Even your own mother thinks you're dead." He then tossed Cedric back in the chair and calmly walked out of the room.

When Shane returned to the small room on the other side of the mirror, Natalie and all the guards were hiding smiles. Cedric sat at the table alone with his head hanging down. He wiped at his eyes several times as they all watched.

"You want to try talking to him again in a few minutes when he's done crying?" one of the correctional officers asked with a snicker.

"No. I think he needs to let what I said sink in before he might be willing to talk. I'll be in town for a few days. Let him know that if he has anything useful to say I'll listen, otherwise we can leave it at what I said just now."

Natalie spent the rest of the afternoon on the phone with various assistants as she performed numerous searches on her computer. Shane just paced and tried to stay out of her way for the most part.

Long after the dinner hour passed, she finally hung up the phone and said, "We have to go back to Baton Rouge."

"What did you find out? Anything?"

"It turns out that Cedric might not be lying about not being Cece's biological father."

"There's a DNA test that says he is," Shane insisted.

"I just did a quick search of his birth record, and I could kick myself for not starting there in the first place. He has one brother born in the same hospital on the same day. He has a twin brother named Cecil. If they are identical twins, which I'd bet my Gucci sunglasses they are, it's possible for them to share the same DNA, thereby making Cedric and Cecil a match in a paternity test."

"Sounds like you have it all figured out. So, why do we need to fly back to Baton Rouge?" Shane asked.

"The man's mother doesn't acknowledge his existence, and he obviously hates her. Don't you want to know why? I think if we can answer that question we may be able to understand why Cedric would want to torture his own brother's wife."

"So, you know for a fact that Corinne was married to Cecil?" Shane asked.

Natalie glanced up at him and said, "Yes," with a solemn look and a deep sigh. "My searches on Cecil turned up a great deal. He didn't drop out of school like Cedric did. He finished, and then he spent two years in the Navy. After he got out of the Navy, he came home and got a two year degree at the community college level, and then he joined the Peace Corps. He was sent to Cameroon, and I'm guessing that's where he met and fell in love with Corinne. I haven't been able to find when or how he died, but I'm guessing his mother might be able to shed some light on that as well."

"Okay, let's go then," Shane said as he stood up to stretch.

"Hold on there, Big Guy. I've already booked our tickets for the red eye flight in the morning."

The next day, Shane and Natalie found themselves being ushered back into Isabelle's small room in the nursing home. She was sitting up in bed, watching a game show on the television when they walked in.

"Did you finish the article about Cecil?" Isabelle asked.

Natalie cleared her throat and said, "Actually, we haven't. We need a little more information about your son. We also need to know how he died."

Isabelle launched into a long speech filled with all her memories of her son. For the next half hour, she told them about every accomplishment in Cecil's life. She was most excited when telling them about the year he joined the Navy. By the time she talked of his years in the Peace Corps, her voice had taken a melancholy turn. The last thing she said was, "He sent me the picture of him and his wife, and told me that he wasn't scheduled to return home for another few months. His wife never showed up, and a week later they came and told me that he had been killed over in Africa."

"Do you have any idea why Corinne wouldn't have shown up?" Natalie asked.

Isabelle didn't answer. She pulled her shawl tighter around her delicate shoulders and stared out the window for a moment.

Natalie sat in the chair directly beside her and gently touched her hand as she asked, "Can you tell me anything about your other son, Cedric?"

387

Isabelle started and then demanded, "How do you know about him?"

"Isabelle, we're not actually reporters writing a story on Cecil. I'm a private investigator. I was hired to find information about the woman in this picture. Corinne did make it to the United States, and she was pregnant with Cecil's child. Isabelle, you have a granddaughter, and her name is Cecilia Graves. She has no idea you exist, because for some reason your other son, Cedric, chose to keep you and Corinne and Cecilia apart. Do you know why Cedric would do that?"

Isabelle looked from Natalie to Shane in astonishment. Shane came forward and took out his wallet. "Here's a picture of Cecilia on our wedding day," he said as he removed the picture from his wallet and handed it to Isabelle.

Isabelle stared down at the picture with trembling hands for a long time before she whispered, "She looks just like I did when I was young. All these years, I thought I had no family, no grandkids..." Tears fell onto the picture, and she wiped them off.

"You keep it," Shane offered when she tried to hand the photo back to him.

"Where is she? Can I see her?" Isabelle asked.

Shane felt a little piece of his heart break for her as he shook his head. "She isn't here right now, but I can bring her here to meet you soon."

"I'll tell you whatever you want to know about Cedric; just don't wait too long to bring me my granddaughter. I've been wondering about Cecil's wife and her package for the past forty years now."

Less than a month later, Shane was on his way back to Calhoun State Prison for the final confrontation with Cedric. He looked around the car at everybody. Brent and Alicia, the Atlanta prosecutor, had their heads down in quiet conversation. Natalie stared out the window with a pensive little wrinkle in her brow, but she glanced at Shane with a smile every once in a while. Brent's friend Luther kept his nose buried in a stack of papers in his lap. He reminded Shane of a more serious version of the comedian, Bill Cosby. He was quick to crack a joke to lighten the mood, but he seemed to be the most eager to see Cedric arrested for his crimes. None of them paid much attention to Shane as they neared the prison complex.

Someone's phone beeped, and Shane watched as everyone else in the car checked their cell phones.

"It's mine," Alicia said as she answered her phone.

Everyone else sat forward as she took the call. Alicia had been pacing like a caged jungle cat all morning, waiting on a call from the governor. The governor had spent the night contemplating assigning a special prosecutor to the case against Cedric, because Alicia and Brent had discovered evidence of police corruption in the case. After all the work she, Brent, and Luther had put into this case over the past nine months, she didn't want to see it fall into the hands of a special prosecutor at the last minute. She wanted to be the one to take it all the way to court. When she hung up, everyone in the vehicle watched her expectantly, but her poker face didn't give anything away.

"Well?" Brent finally asked.

She smiled and said, "No special prosecutor. I still get to handle the case, and I even get to investigate the corruption scandal that led to all the cover-ups for this guy."

"Score!" Brent exclaimed as he and Alicia high fived.

Shane stared out the window and thought about everything he and Natalie had learned about Corinne and Cecilia's life with Cedric. He honestly didn't know if he could keep from punching Cedric when he saw the man again. Everyone else in the car seemed jubilant that the case against Cedric had wrapped up so nicely. Alicia even went so far as to refer to it as a slam dunk.

Once they entered the prison, Brent and all his lawyer friends went into the room on the other side of the two way mirror. Alicia held Cedric's arrest warrant, but she'd agreed to allow Shane one last chance to get his personal questions answered before they executed it. Shane went into the interview room to talk to Cedric. He didn't waste any time with small talk when he walked into the small, drab room. "Why didn't you take Corinne to your mother after her plane landed in Atlanta? Isn't that what you were supposed to do?" he began immediately.

"I see you finally got your facts straight, Pretty Boy," Cedric said.

Shane sat down. "Between your mother's stories about you, your juvenile record as a rapist, and simple deductive reasoning, we've been able to piece together what happened all those years ago."

"Oh really?" Cedric interrupted with a sneer.

"Yes. Corinne got off the plane, expecting to meet the family of her new husband, and she got you instead. Cecil sent a letter with Corinne, asking you to escort her to your mother in Baton Rouge, hoping that the two of you would make up. But when you heard he died a couple of days later, you never took her to Baton Rouge, did you? Instead, you lied to her and threatened to have her deported back to Africa unless she started selling herself for you."

"That's all bullshit. And how would you know anything anyway?"

"Because Corinne kept the letter Cecil sent with her all those years ago. We finally located the case file for her death. The original investigator did an excellent job preserving what little evidence they had to go on at the time, but for some reason a filing clerk misplaced it. And then a series of additional clerical errors involving law enforcement officials who were involved with *you* led to the case being buried. It took us a long time to figure out that police misconduct was an issue, but once we did, we found the file. They kept all her personal effects, including a diary she kept the entire time she lived under your thumb. The whole file fits in one box—one dusty, little box that's been locked away in the evidence room for more than thirty years now. The prosecutor has *everything* she needs to put you away now."

"Then what are you doing here again?" Cedric said. There was a flat, lifeless look in his eyes. As if he knew there was no point in fighting anymore. "If she kept a fucking diary, then you know everything. Between that bitch Cora, her stupid daughter, and my mother you know it all, so why are you here?"

"I'm here for a personal reason. I could have gone the rest of my life without ever seeing you again, but I love my wife. I love her enough to realize that she deserves all the answers, especially the answer to the biggest question."

"What question is that?" Cedric asked after a lengthy silence.

"Why? Why would you go to such lengths to torture people? Especially your own family. Why would you do such a thing to your own brother's wife? Your own niece?"

Cedric didn't say anything for a long time. He just stared at Shane with a defiant look in his eyes. The look unnerved Shane, because he recognized the family resemblance in that expression. It was the same look that he'd seen on Cecilia's face a number of times.

"I don't gotta tell you shit," Cedric said with smug finality.

Without another word, Shane got up and left the room. He wasn't about to beg that man for anything.

"So, that's it then?" Brent asked when Shane stepped into the room with everyone else.

Shane nodded as he looked through the dingy glass at Cedric. He was scheduled to be released from prison today, but Alicia had an arrest warrant ready to be executed. At Shane's nod, the arresting officer stepped into the room and started reading Cedric his Miranda Rights. Cedric looked surprised for a brief moment before his face became a mask of feigned indifference.

"Cedric Graves, you are under arrest for the murder of Corinne Nnamani-Graves. You have the right to remain silent. Anything you say can and will be used against you in the court of law. You have the right to an attorney should you choose one. If you cannot afford an attorney, one will be appointed to you..."

Shane watched as the officer droned on. He was happy that Cedric was to be prosecuted for Corinne's murder, and the murders of five other women, but he still felt outrage deep inside. There wasn't enough evidence to convict Cedric for what he'd done to Cecilia, so for that crime he wouldn't have to pay.

Shane didn't hang around in Atlanta for the arraignment; instead, he flew back to Nashville almost immediately after the arrest had been made. When he got home that evening, the voicemail light on his phone was flashing. He pressed play, and Cecilia's voice filled the silence in his empty house.

"Shane, it's Cecilia. I was just calling because... well I'm not exactly sure why I called. It's just that it's been so long since I've talked to you, but I think about you every day, especially today. Most of the construction on our project is complete. In two months, there's going to be a ribbon cutting ceremony and I'll need to be here for that. I was just thinking that maybe you should be here too. If it weren't for you, this may not have happened, so I think you should be here for the ceremony. I was also thinking that I can't wait two more months to see you again.

It's been too long already. I don't know if you'll even get this message in time, but I'm on my way to your—"

The machine beeped, cutting off the rest of what she'd said. It sounded like she'd been about to say she was on her way to his house. He grabbed his phone and called her back several times, but he only got her voicemail. He gave up trying for a while, and cleaned his kitchen as quickly as he possibly could. He was about to pick up his phone and try again when a knock sounded at his door.

He rushed to answer it, his heart thumping hard, but Natalie was at the door, not Cecilia.

"Hi, Natalie," he greeted her. "What are you doing here?"

"I just came to talk to you about the rest of the investigation," Natalie said as she stepped inside.

"Now isn't the best time, I think Cecilia might be on her way over right now. I haven't seen her for so long."

"I know, but this is important."

"More important than me seeing my wife for the first time in almost a year?"

Natalie looked around at the state of Shane's house. "You're right. I'll help you clean while I talk about it."

"That works for me," Shane grunted as he got to work on the living room.

"Do you remember telling me about her friend Dorothy?"

"Yeah. Were you able to identify which victim might have been Dot?" Shane asked.

"Not exactly. I think Dorothy might have survived and moved out to California."

That statement gave Shane pause.

"You should probably light some candles," Natalie went on as Shane continued to stare.

"What? Why?"

"You haven't seen her in nearly a year, and she's on her way over right now... If it were me, I'd appreciate some candles."

"Right," Shane said as he hastened to his kitchen and raided the pantry for some scented candles. He found a few and brought them into the living room.

Natalie was standing in front of the window, and after he lit the candles he joined her. They both stood, looking out at the darkening sky. "I'll fly out to California tomorrow to follow up on a solid lead, but it's going to cost you," Natalie said as she looked up at him.

"I've already told you, I don't care how much it costs. If you can find her only childhood friend, that would be priceless to her, to me. Thank you for working so hard to find out so much so quickly."

"I actually enjoyed working for you. You kind of remind me of my dad. He was in the Marines, you know. He used to want me to be a school teacher. I wonder what he'd think about me being a private investigator instead. About ten years ago, he was murdered, and it's been unsolved ever since. Any time I can help bring closure to someone, I feel peace inside because I know what that type of closure means. I guess I could have called, but I thought a visit was better. I think I've become more emotionally involved in this case than any of the others I've worked. I'd love to meet your wife."

A tear escaped Natalie's eye, and Shane reached out to give the young woman a hug. "You know, if I had married young and had kids like my brother Ronald, I like to imagine that I'd have a daughter your age right now. If I did, and if she was anything like you, I'd be one proud papa. I know your dad would be proud of what you've done with your life, Natalie."

Shane let go of Natalie, and smiled down at her again. When he glanced out the window, he saw Cecilia standing on the sidewalk just outside his house. As their eyes met, a little spark of awareness shot through him. He thought of the way she'd looked on their last morning together in the cabin. She'd looked at him with complete trust in her eyes. "You should meet her now; just don't mention anything about the investigation yet. I want to tell her in private."

"Is she here?" Natalie asked in confusion.

"Yeah," Shane said as he pulled Natalie along and opened the front door.

They both stepped out onto the porch. "Where is she?" Natalie asked.

"She was just standing right there on the sidewalk," Shane said. "I saw her though the window."

"Well, I was standing there too, and I didn't see her. I didn't see a car either, so you're probably seeing things. Must be nice."

"Must be nice? What must be nice?" Shane asked as he looked up and down the sidewalk for Cecilia. He could have sworn he saw her standing there a moment ago.

"Must be nice to be so in love you literally see her when she's not actually there. I have to go now. I have to pack for that trip to California. I'll probably be out there for at least a couple of weeks working on some other projects; now that your case is almost complete, I have to check out a few leads on some of my routine cases."

"Okay, Natalie. Thanks for stopping by to tell me about Dot. Have a safe trip."

After Natalie left, Shane went back inside. He stared at the flickering candles for a while before trying Cecilia's cell phone again. He still didn't get an answer. He played the voicemail again. It really seemed like she'd been trying to tell him she was on her way to his house. He stretched out on the sofa and listened to the late autumn wind howling outside his house. Eventually, he fell asleep waiting for her to show up. When he woke up the next morning, the candles had completely burned down and he was still alone. He must have misunderstood the message.

Chapter 27

She'd stayed away for almost a year, but Cece was finally ready to return to Nashville, to her regular life. Only now, everything had changed. The new normal for her was still under construction at this point. When she'd told Shane she needed some time alone to heal, she couldn't possibly have imagined how rewarding the journey to find inner peace would be.

Miss Georgia was almost like the grandmother she never had, and despite her age, she'd been instrumental in the planning and execution of every stage of their community center project. The old hotel had been demolished, and construction was almost complete on the building that was to take its place. The neighborhood was already showing signs of a complete turnaround, and several community leaders had taken an interest in the project. The official ribbon cutting ceremony would take place in about a month, and the mayor was supposed to attend. Cece was excited about the ceremony. It would be a celebration of more than just the rebirth of her old neighborhood; it would be a celebration of her own rebirth.

Cece had been sitting at Miss Georgia's table, thinking about all the recent positive changes in her life. Every positive that came to mind also brought Shane to the forefront of her thoughts.

She thought about her first day back at work following their honeymoon. She'd walked into the bakery first thing in the morning, eager to prepare for her grand re-opening, and found a magazine and a note from Shane atop the otherwise pristine counter. It was the spring issue of *Modern Bride* magazine, and her cake was on the cover. She'd picked it up, and after staring dumbstruck at the cover for a few minutes, she'd flipped through the issue. Near the back, she found a three page spread featuring her and Shane's wedding, and her cake took up the entire first page of the article. The feature also included some beautiful pictures of the reception venue, and some very flattering shots of everyone in the wedding party. Cece stared at the picture of herself, smiling up at Shane in the middle of the iconic ballroom, the wedding decorations in the background, and the stained glass dome over the top of them, and realized that her wedding day had been one of the happiest days of her life. She flipped back to the cover again, and stared at her cake, her own personal creation, on the cover for everyone to see. It was one of the proudest moments of her life.

That day had definitely started out on a high note, and by the end of the day she'd made more appointments to discuss spring society wedding cakes than she ever had in the past. Before she left for Atlanta, she made detailed plans for the daily running of her bakery while she was away. She came back to Nashville to handle all of the special projects, but she left the regular tasks to her new assistant bakers and decorators. Management was Karen's new fulltime job.

In each of her trips back to Nashville, she'd visited Rebecca and the twins, but she never once contacted Shane. It had been extremely difficult for her not to contact him, because she thought about him almost all the time. Sometimes while she was in the middle of talking to the contractor about the community center project, or even a new client at the bakery, a wayward thought about their two weeks at the cabin would jump into her head and cause her to go weak in the knees. And then she would immediately wonder if he ever thought about their time at the cabin.

Keeping her distance from him had been difficult, but she was glad she did it. She needed to solidify her identity as an independently healthy person before she could be with Shane. She joined a support group and made several valuable connections with other women like her—women who had been assaulted and let entire parts of their personality remain stagnant for years. Her first priority after getting settled in Miss Georgia's house was to find a good therapist. She'd promised Rebecca she would, and nothing would make her break that promise again. Now, after more than six months of intense therapy, she felt like she was finally ready to truly engage in a meaningful relationship with a man. She'd been surprised how effective just talking about her past had been. Talking about the incident had taken away a lot of the power it had over her. During her months in therapy, that power had continued to diminish. It had dwindled to the point that she could now think about her mother and Red Bone with something other than disgust and terror. She'd never be able to forget what happened, but at least now she was on the path to healing and truly moving on with her life.

She'd been staring at the only picture she had of Shane, when a sudden need to feel his arms around her came over her. He'd always been a good friend and a constant source of comfort and strength when she was at a low point. She called Miss Georgia and told her she was going to Nashville for a few days. She called Shane's house several times before she left, but hung up on his machine when he didn't answer. After asking him to give her an extraordinary amount of space and then not talking to him for so long, she didn't know what to say. She figured it would be best to tell him how she felt in person.

Halfway to Nashville, she stopped for gas and called Shane again. She got his voicemail again, but this time she left a message. Hopefully, he would be home by the time she got there. When she turned off the interstate at the exit near Shane's neighborhood, the sun had gone down for the day. She parked her car at her house and went inside to freshen up. After being in her car for several hours, she needed to stretch her legs, so she left her car in her driveway and walked the short distance across the park to Shane's house. The late autumn wind whipped her hair into a frizzy mess, and her emotions were on edge as she neared his house. The closer she got, the more anxious she got. She hadn't talked to him in so long, she honestly didn't know what to expect. He hadn't responded to any of her postcards, and she had no indication that his love for her had remained intact during their long separation. She still loved him, but that didn't guarantee he felt the same.

As Cece started down the path, he came out from behind the bushes. After what seemed like forever, she was finally home. He reached into his pocket and felt the cold metal of his gun. He pressed it painfully into his leg and tried to stop his hands from shaking.

It was dark enough to cover his movements, and if he was lucky Cece wouldn't be gone for too long. He skulked over to her car and tried the door handle; she'd left it unlocked. He slipped inside and crouched down in the back seat.

The moon and stars were out by the time Cece reached Shane's street. She smiled and her heart lifted when his house came into view. She thought again about their two weeks at his cabin and felt foolish for worrying. Those had been the best two weeks of her life; of course he still loved her. She wondered if he missed her nearly as much as she'd missed him. She'd been the one to demand time and space to heal, yet she'd missed him so intensely at times it had felt like a piece of herself was missing.

His Jeep was parked in front of his garage, and the light from the large picture window in his living room shone out onto the sidewalk. She paused in the light of the window and glanced inside. Shane was there, but he wasn't alone.

Cece watched with a panicky, sinking feeling as he conversed with a raven haired woman whom she didn't recognize. The light from several candles was visible in the background as Shane pulled the woman close to him. Cece watched them hug, and her heart thundered with painful thuds in her chest. She was too late. He had moved on. Even after the hug ended, Shane kept his hands on the woman's shoulders as he smiled down at her and said something to her. This intimate moment between them tore at Cece's emotions, but she couldn't make herself look away. As painful as it was to watch, she couldn't move, couldn't breathe, and, no matter how much she wanted to, she couldn't look away.

While Cece stared in dismay, Shane glanced out the window. Their eyes met for an excruciating second, just long enough for her to decide that she never wanted to see him again. As soon as he looked away to say something else to the young woman, Cece sprinted home as fast as she could. She jumped in her car and left immediately. She'd been such a fool to think that he would wait for her. She'd been the one to insist that he move on and even see someone else, and apparently he had listened.

As she started the long drive back towards Atlanta, tears momentarily blurred her vision. It just wasn't meant to be, but that knowledge didn't make it hurt any less. She felt betrayed, betrayed by her own emotions for loving him so much, but most of all betrayed by Shane for giving her such hope only to be just another disappointment.

She'd been driving for more than ten minutes when she heard rustling in the back seat. She glanced in the rear view mirror and then went completely still after she heard an ominous click and felt something hard press into the back of her head.

"Just get back on the interstate and do what I say, Cece. I really don't want to have to kill you."

The man from the park! Rebecca's biological father! His voice had been such a regular fixture in her nightmares she would recognize it anywhere. She swallowed hard as the world around her spun so violently she almost swerved off the road.

"And don't you dare try anything. If you get us in a wreck you'll be sorry." She heard more movement in the back seat, followed by the click of the seat belt.

"I wasn't trying to swerve."

"Good."

"Why are you doing this?"

"Because this is the only way."

Cece didn't try talking to him again for a few minutes. She got on the interstate as he'd instructed, and tried not to imagine his plans. Whatever they were, they couldn't be good. The man had a gun, and guns had always been the one thing that could fill her with unimaginable terror. None of her skills could defend her against gunshots. Even the best doctors and medical care might not be enough to save her life if she was shot in the head. The scar on her abdomen suddenly felt fiery hot, and the back of her head felt like it was going to explode any second with him sitting behind her.

"Could you please not keep your gun pointed at my head while I drive? It's really distracting me." Her voice shook so badly it was almost unrecognizable to her own ears.

"You're just going to have to deal with it. I don't want you to try any of your black-belt moves on me."

"While I'm driving? Look, I don't want to die in a crash any more than you do."

"Okay."

Cece relaxed slightly when she heard him lower the gun. Only the shadow of his head and shoulder was visible when she glanced in the rear view mirror. "Where do you want me to go?" she asked.

"Just stay on the highway for now. I'll give you instructions."

"Why are you doing this?" she asked again.

"Because this is the only way to make it right."

"Kidnapping me isn't going to bring Sita back."

"Don't you dare use her name in my presence!" he shrieked.

Cece cringed as the gun poked her in the back of the head. She hadn't felt so trapped and helpless since the night Red Bone had tied her down. Her face crumpled into a contorted mask of horror and fear. "I'm sorry," she whispered. "I'll do whatever you say. Please, just don't shoot me."

"Tell me. Is Sarah my daughter?"

"Yes," Cece sniffed. It took all her concentration to focus on driving with a gun pointed at her head.

"How did she die at such a young age? What did you do to her?"

"*Me?* She was my daughter. I loved her. We were at a bus stop one day when a drunk driver hit her. She died instantly."

He lowered the gun again.

Cece tried to shut off her emotions and concentrate on driving. It seemed to be working until her phone rang.

The gun came up again, and he said, "Give me the phone."

"I can't reach it while I'm driving. It's in my back pocket. If you just let me pull over, I'll give it to you."

"Stay on the road."

For the next few hours, he only spoke to give her directions. They turned off the interstate and traveled down a smaller country road for a while. Eventually, he directed her down a path that was so overgrown and rutted it was barely visible from the road. They came to a stop at a large, older house that looked like it hadn't been used in decades.

"Now cut the engine and toss the keys to me," he said as he pressed the gun into her head again.

She did as he instructed, and then waited while he got out of the car. He kept the gun cocked and pointed at her the entire time. "Don't try anything, Cece," he said several times. He then opened her door and backed up several feet. "Now you get out. Keep your hands in the air, and walk towards me. That's good, keep coming nice and slow."

He flung her keys far into the overgrown weeds and shrubbery in the darkness beyond them. He then had her turn and walk backwards up the hill toward the house. He followed her at a distance of about ten feet, and kept the gun pointed at her the entire time. She stumbled over the deep holes in the yard and fell several times, and each time he shouted at her until she got up. After what seemed like a long time, he backed her all the way into an open garage.

It was too dark for her to see anything besides the shadow of the old car she backed into. He kept the gun trained on her as he felt in his breast pocket for something.

"Open the trunk," he said as he flung a key at her head.

She'd thought she couldn't possibly be any more frightened until he said that. The key was barely visible in the only sliver of moonlight that entered the garage; with shaking hands, she bent down to pick up the key.

"Open the trunk," he repeated when she hesitated.

"Please..." she sniffed.

"Open it!" he screamed.

Her hands were so unsteady she dropped the key several times before she finally accomplished the task. The latch squeaked open, and the trunk light came on to reveal a trunk filled with random items. There were water bottles, a blanket, some rope and several cheap rubber face masks. Cece felt bile rising up her throat as she looked inside. The car was an older model that had definitely seen better days. There were several oil stains on the carpet fibers. Or were those blood stains? Her stomach turned over violently at the thought.

"Get in the trunk, Cece."

"I can't," she panted.

"Get in the trunk!" his scream echoed through the silence. His gun hand was now shaking as he leveled the gun at her face. Even from almost ten feet away, the shadow of the gun filled her vision.

"Okay. Okay." She turned and climbed into the filthy trunk. "Please, don't make me get in here," she pleaded one last time before she lay all the way down.

He aimed the gun and fired off a shot at her. It whizzed past her ear and lodged itself somewhere in the car. She didn't plead again; she just flopped down in immediate compliance. He ambled up to the trunk and looked down at her once before slamming it shut.

Inky, oppressive darkness engulfed her, and she fought hard to think of a solution to the problem. She told herself not to panic, but when she heard the car door slam and the engine roar to life, breathing became increasingly more difficult. She felt the air grow thicker as her panic took over, and she spent a few minutes clawing at the trunk in dizzy dread before she finally succumbed to the darkness.

When she woke up, it was light outside. As she watched light filter in through the bullet hole in the top of the trunk, she wondered how many hours had passed. She scooted closer to the keyhole and tried to peer out. Everything was blurry through the tiny hole, but she could make out the outlines of other cars. She tried to focus on some of the road signs, but they were all too blurry. After a few hours of straining her eyes, she gave up for a while. She listened to the hum of the engine and tried not to visualize what would happen next. She'd already been through almost everything she could imagine, and the only thing she really feared now was being shot to death. Her granddaughters were nearly a year old, and she really wanted to see them grow up. She tried to think of all the reasons she wanted to live, and Rebecca, Rose and Renée were at the top of her list. Shane came in at a close second.

She chastised herself for running like a coward when he'd noticed her outside his house last night. She should have stood her ground and, at the very least, talked to him. She should have told him she still loved him; maybe he thought she didn't love him because she'd spent so many months pushing him away in the beginning. Maybe she should have called him at least a few times while in Atlanta. Maybe she should have visited him on one of her many trips back to Nashville. Maybe she should have done a lot of things differently.

Suddenly, the phone beeped in her pocket, interrupting her thoughts. She'd forgotten all about it. She grabbed it and pressed the answer button.

"Hello?" she whispered.

"Cecilia?" Shane said.

She was so relieved to hear his voice; she started crying before she could say anything else.

"Cecilia, where are you? I got part of a message from you that implied you were on your way over, and then I thought I saw you outside my house last night. I've tried calling several times... What's going on? Where are you?"

"I don't know," she sobbed.

"What's wrong?"

"He was in my car with a gun last night, and now he's taking me somewhere. I'm locked in a trunk."

"Who, Cecilia?!"

"Rebecca's father. He has a gun," she whispered again.

"How long have you been in the trunk?"

"I don't know... since sometime last night. Right after you saw me I ran home, and he was in my car with a gun!"

"Honey, you have to stay calm. Where is he now? Does he know you have your phone?"

"He's driving. He knows I have it, because it rang last night. I think he forgot to take it from me."

"Tell me everything you can about the car and where he's taking you. What color is the car?"

"I don't know. It was too dark for me to tell. I think he's been driving all night. What time is it?"

"It's nearly three in the afternoon. Can you see anything around you?"

"I tried looking out the keyhole, but it's too small. What should I do?"

"Stay calm, and don't let him know you have the phone. I think the police can use it to figure out where you are. I'm getting them on the line right now."

Cece heard another dial tone and then a 911 operator came on the line. Shane explained the situation, and then the man on the line asked Cece the same questions that Shane had just asked. Having to repeat the fact that she didn't know much got to her, and she started crying again.

"Ma'am, please try and stay calm. We'll find out where you are and the authorities will come for you."

Suddenly, the car swerved and lurched and several items slid into Cece. In the next instant, he'd thrown the trunk open. She didn't even have the sense to try hiding the phone.

"Give me the phone!" he screamed at her.

The gun was inches from her face, and his finger was on the trigger. In that instant, the darkness down the center of the barrel dominated her vision. She heard both Shane and the operator asking her if she was still there and demanding to know what was happening, but she couldn't move or speak or even breathe.

"I said give it to me!" he screamed again.

When she still didn't move, he fired several shots into the trunk. She shut her eyes against the muzzle flash and wailed, "Here take it! Please! Just don't kill me! Please!" She broke down and sobbed again as she handed over her only life line.

He snatched it and slammed the trunk down before she could move her hand out of the way.

"Open the trunk! Please!" she screamed at the top of her lungs. "My hand is caught!"

He banged on the trunk and yelled at her to keep quiet. Pain shot up her arm when he hit the trunk, but she bit down on her lip to keep from crying out again. She tried to calm her breathing as she listened to his muffled voice through the trunk.

"Who is this?" he asked. "Oh really? Well, Cece is going to be busy for a while. Don't try to find her or something really bad might happen."

He didn't say anything else, but she sensed his presence at the trunk. She tried one last appeal. "Please," she moaned. "Please, just let me get my hand out of the trunk. It's bleeding." Another moment of long, tense silence passed before she heard the key in the trunk latch again. She couldn't stop herself from calling out in pain as he lifted the trunk.

"Now you'd better keep quiet," he said. He closed the trunk more slowly that time, and they continued their journey into the unknown.

Cece ripped part of her shirt off and wrapped it around her hand to stop the bleeding. She tried not to notice the searing pain in her hand and arm when the car started moving again. Every little bump in the road seemed to magnify it, and at times it was nearly unbearable. She was pretty sure her fingers were broken, and she cried as she recalled the night she'd broken one of Norman's fingers. How could she have been so mean to another human being?

A few hours later, the trunk opened again. He tossed a bag of chips and a blanket at her and said, "Keep quiet. If you make noise, I'll kill you and anyone who tries to help you."

From her limited sighting of the outside, it seemed that they were headed north. The weather got noticeably colder and gas stations and other travelers grew fewer and farther between. After her second day in the trunk, she could make out snow all over everything when she tried to peer out. Her hand had stopped bleeding so much, but the pain had gotten so much worse she feared it might become infected. The rusty trunk had scraped off most of the skin on her fingers and left a deep gash in the top of her hand. Even if she kept it wrapped up tight and didn't move too much, the blood still seeped out very slowly.

Sometime in the middle of her third night in the trunk, the car came to a stop again. This time, when he opened the trunk, he told her to get out.

"A year of nothing, and now this?" Brent said for the hundredth time as Shane listened with half an ear. "According to that letter, he was sorry and begging for her forgiveness, so why on earth would he go into hiding for a year and then come out and snatch her like this? It makes no sense."

"Remember all those suspects you told me about before we went after Cedric? Did any of those ever pan out?" Shane asked. It seemed like he'd asked that same question at least a dozen times over the past few days.

"No. There was no such case anywhere near Atlanta. Maybe this guy was just making up the entire thing about his daughter. Criminals will say anything if they think it'll help get them off."

"What are we missing here?" Shane asked as he looked out at the room full of investigators. It had been a week since his conversation with Cecilia; a week since the screaming and the gunshots, and then that awful silence before he'd come on the line. Shane had never been so scared for anyone in his life.

His house had been transformed that week. Now there was a steady stream of police officers and federal agents plodding back and forth as they investigated. He looked around at the roomful of strangers with all their high tech equipment and listening devices. The FBI seemed to think a ransom demand was imminent, but Shane didn't agree. He didn't think his grandfather's fortune had anything to do with Cecilia's disappearance, but he still hoped the kidnapper would try to contact him. At least then he'd know *something* about how Cecilia was doing.

"They released the 911 tape to the media today. They think it might help if anyone recognizes his voice," Brent leaned over and said in Shane's ear.

Just then, one of the agents switched on his television. The midday news had just started, and Cecilia's abduction was the lead story. A hush fell over the room as the anchorwoman said, "We must warn you that the contents are very graphic and may be disturbing to some viewers." When the tape ended, the number for a tip line appeared at the bottom of the screen.

Shane hadn't heard a recording of that call. He'd been trying to focus all his energy on helping in any way he could instead of worrying. Listening to the tape just now brought forth a resurgence of his worry. The fear and pain in her voice ripped at his insides and made him weak. It was even worse than he'd remembered. He sat down and dropped his head into his hands. He cried as he said a little prayer for Cecilia. It was his millionth little prayer since her ordeal began. When he looked up again, everyone was staring at him.

"What?" he said with a broken voice, "Don't look at me like that. I know she's still alive, and we will find her."

In the middle of Cece's fifth night in the basement, the door opened and she heard a young male voice say, "Wait. No! Where are you taking me?" and then she heard a series of grunts and thumps as someone came tumbling down the basement stairs. The voice had sounded like another victim, but Cece couldn't be sure of anything in the darkness. She curled up in her corner near the furnace and stayed quiet.

"Please, don't leave me down here. I need a doctor," the voice pleaded. The basement door slammed shut, and Cece listened as the young man wept long into the night. As hard as she'd tried, she couldn't even get herself out of the basement, so how could she possibly help him?

Morning came, and a sliver of light appeared at the bottom of the basement door. Cece stood up to stretch her legs.

"Who's there?" the young, male voice called out.

Cece swallowed hard. "Cece Graves," she called out into the expansive darkness between them. "Who are you?"

"My name's Chad. Chad Wilson. Can you help me? I think my leg is broken, and I can't move it."

Cece felt her way over to the young man.

"How did you end up down here?" he asked her.

"I'm guessing the guy who pushed you down the stairs is the same guy who kidnapped me. Unless there are two of them," she answered.

"Why would he want you though? You're a woman."

"I have no idea what he's trying to do," Cece sighed.

"I know what he wants to do with me."

"What?" she breathed.

"He thinks I raped his daughter. He wants to kill me."

Cece backed away from him. "You're the one who raped Sita," she whispered.

"No! I didn't. They found me not guilty at the trial," he insisted.

"That doesn't mean you didn't do it."

"Please... I didn't do it, and I need help. Please, just help me; my leg is stuck in the stairs. It's been like this all night. Please, help me."

"No," Cece said as she shook her head repeatedly and backed into her corner by the furnace. She crouched down and did her best to ignore him for the rest of the day. When night fell again, and the little sliver of light under the door slowly faded away, she stayed where she was and tried not to cry. If he intended to kill Chad, then surely he must want to kill her too. But why? She hadn't done anything to him. In fact, she'd let him go. After Brent had decided to focus the investigation on finding Red Bone, Cece had told him she didn't want to seek prosecution for Rebecca's father. Perhaps that had been the biggest mistake of her life.

"Cece, please help me get my leg out," Chad asked again. He was obviously in great pain. Cece looked down at her hand and thought about her own pain. Tears came to her eyes. What if she hadn't been able to convince him to open the trunk so she could get her hand out?

She grabbed one of the water bottles from her niche next to the furnace and quietly picked her way back to Chad's side of the basement. She stood over him and tried to make out his features in the darkness. He breathed in small spurts, as if it hurt to breathe normally. "Did you hurt anything else when you fell?" she asked.

"Yes," he grunted. "It's hard to breathe."

"Okay. I can't see anything, but I'll do my best not to hurt you. Which leg is stuck?"

"My left leg. It's wedged between the steps and the wall," he wheezed.

Cece felt around for his leg, and he drew in a sharp breath when she found it. "Sorry," she said as she repositioned herself. She felt where his leg was stuck and assessed the situation. "Okay, Chad, I'm going to straighten you out and then pull hard to get your leg out. It's definitely going to hurt."

"Okay."

Cece grasped him under his arms and pulled him straight. "Ahh," she called out in pain as her hand started bleeding again.

"Are you okay?" Chad grunted.

"Yes. I'm going to grab your leg and pull hard now," she warned.

He stopped breathing as she gave a firm tug. His leg didn't budge, and she heard a small crunch right before he let out a piercing, high-pitched wail.

Cece let him calm down and stop crying before she asked, "Do you want me to keep trying?"

"Yes," he whispered.

She didn't waste time asking if he was ready this time; she just grasped his leg and yanked hard. She ignored his loud screams and didn't stop yanking until his leg came free. He cried for a long time as Cece sat beside him and tried to think of possible solutions.

"I don't want to die like this," he sobbed.

"Neither do I," Cece said quietly beside him as she offered him the bottle of water.

"How can you be so calm?" he asked.

"I'm not nearly as calm as I seem," she admitted. "How does your leg feel?"

"It's still throbbing, but I can take it if I keep real still. What happened to your hand?"

"He slammed it in the trunk on the way here."

"Jesus, that must have hurt."

"Did he put you in the trunk too?" Cece asked.

"Yeah. He came at me with a gun and forced me into his damn rust bucket. I don't get why he's driving around such a junk car," Chad snorted.

"Why?" Cece asked,

"Because, he's loaded. During the trial, he drove a Beamer. When his daughter pressed charges against me, I thought I was a goner for sure."

"How much do you know about him?"

"He's a musician. World class. He does a lot of piano concerts all over the world, but other than that all he does is keep to himself."

"How do you know that?"

"Because his daughter told me about it back before all this happened. We used to be good friends. I really didn't rape her," he insisted.

"Then why did she say you did?"

"Because she was drunk at the time, and so was I. We were in one of the rooms at my frat house."

"If she was incapacitated, then it wasn't consensual!" Cece snarled as she hit him in the face.

"We were both drunk, and I liked her! We liked each other."

"What about the other guys?" Cece demanded. "Did she consent to sleep with them too?"

When he didn't answer, Cece pressed on relentlessly, "Did she?"

He still didn't answer, so she hit him again and went back to her corner of the basement. "I hope you rot!" she screamed.

Chad was quiet for a long time as Cece sat in her corner and stewed, but eventually his quiet sniffles floated across the massive, dark basement to her. She covered her ears and tried to ignore him as the night wore on.

When the sliver of light appeared at the bottom of the door again, she simply stared at it for hours. Every once in a while, Chad started crying again, but Cece didn't say another word to him.

In the middle of the next night in the basement, Cece suddenly heard screams coming from upstairs. She jumped to her feet, prepared to fight, but the basement door didn't open.

The shrieks and crying continued for the remainder of the night, and Chad remained eerily silent as Cece listened. Cece wondered if this was just a prelude for worse things to come. She kept her eyes fixed on that single sliver of light for hours. When she finally saw a shadow cross over it, her heart thundered in her chest. The door opened, and she saw the shadow of a man and his gun... the same gun that had already been fired at her multiple times.

"We the people call Chad Wilson to the stand!" he called out.

"What's he doing?" Chad whispered to Cece, but she continued to ignore him.

"We the people call Chad Wilson to the stand!" he screamed again.

"I'm coming," Chad's wavering voice said. He then started a slow crawl up the stairs toward the shadow with the gun. When he got to the top, the door slammed shut behind him. A gunshot sounded, and Chad screamed.

Cece didn't hear anything else for a while, and she started crying. Even though she knew what Chad had done, it was difficult knowing that he was somewhere above her dying at the moment. She went back to her spot by the furnace and curled up against the corner. She closed her eyes tight against the darkness and imagined Shane telling her she could find a way out of this.

Shane lay awake in bed for the tenth night in a row. There had been no credible leads in the effort of find Cecilia, and the federal agents were beginning to lose hope. They'd had a quiet conversation about transitioning the search into a recovery effort, but Shane had refused to listen. His head knew that the chance of finding her alive was slim to none at this point, but his heart clung to hope. Even a small chance was still a chance.

He glanced at the bedside clock. It was almost three in the morning, the time when Cecilia would be getting out of bed to start her day if she were there with him. As he thought about the gunshots and the screaming on the phone that day, he held back tears yet again. He also thought about the night that man had dropped the letter in the park. If only he'd known then what he knew now. The man wouldn't have been able to just walk away. He'd seemed so familiar, but even after racking his mind Shane couldn't recall where he'd seen the man before. That vague sense of familiarity had stuck with Shane since the night in the park, and after Cecilia's abduction, it became an absolute obsession.

He went out to his living room and found Rebecca sitting on his couch, watching the public station. She looked exhausted and vulnerable, just as she had all week. She looked sad, but she hadn't cried once in his presence.

"How are you doing?" he asked quietly.

She shrugged and said, "I'm okay. Are you feeling any better today? I know you had a hard time yesterday."

He didn't answer right away. He just shrugged and tried to force a smile. "I really don't think she's dead," he reiterated his stance from yesterday.

"Shane," Rebecca began with a sigh.

"You know, you're acting so much like she did sometimes," he interrupted. "She acted like she could handle anything all on her own, like it was a crime to show some emotion. Rebecca, she's your mother. It really is okay to express how you feel. I can tell you're not ready to give up either."

When he looked at her again, she was crying. "I don't think she's dead. She can't be, and if she is she probably died fighting and she deserves to come home." Her voice broke, and she doubled over.

Shane started crying again too, and he reached out to hug her. "We will bring her home. One way or another, she'll come home." As he held her in his arms, he was reminded of the first few weeks after his mother passed away. He'd held Shelly every night while she cried herself to sleep. He'd taken on the role of father for her, because their dad had been too lost in his own grief to pay attention to theirs.

While he sat holding Rebecca, another program started on the public channel. An announcer came on and introduced the musician being profiled on the show that week, and when they flashed a picture of a small, bald Indian man Shane went completely still. Suddenly, that nagging familiarity came back to him and exploded into full blown recognition.

"*That's him*," he said.

Rebecca raised her head and looked at the television. "Who?" she asked.

Shane stood up and grabbed the phone, "That's the man who has your mother. I recognize him—his voice, the way he looks," he said as he dialed.

"Shane, do you have any idea who that is?" Rebecca asked with a disbelieving shake of her head. "He's one of the premier pianists in the whole world. What are the chances that he was involved with prostitution and rape of a minor?" she asked with a gentle reasoning tone. She was talking to him in the same voice she probably used on the deeply disturbed children at the mental facility where she worked.

"I've never been more certain of anything in my life," he declared. When Brent came on the line, he told him the same thing and got an almost identical reaction. "I'm not crazy," he insisted several times during the course of the conversation. One of the agents in his house had taken note, and was silently listening to Shane. After he hung up on his brother in frustration, Shane stalked over to the agent and asked, "Can you help me? I'm sure that's the guy I saw in the park that night. Please, just help me."

The agent gave him the look that said he was probably crazy, but he opened up his laptop anyway. Shane watched as he typed the musician's name into the search engine and sat down in intense relief as multiple articles about the man's daughter popped up. The agent clicked on the top article; it was about his daughter Sita's suicide. She'd been found dead the same night that he had performed in Portland after an almost year long hiatus. "Holy shit," the agent breathed as he skimmed the article. "You're right."

Within the hour, Shane's house was crawling with agents again. He listened to little snatches of their conversations as they tried to locate Cecilia.

"This guy's got properties all over the world," one of them said as she looked up from her computer.

"Run a check to see which ones he has close to here," the one in charge said.

"Already on it. I found a piece of farmland between here and Atlanta, a condo in Nashville that he just bought last year, and a couple of houses in Florida," another agent said.

"Contact the Atlanta headquarters to have them check the farmland, and we'll get on the Nashville condo. Where in Florida are the houses?"

"Already on it. One in Miami, and a small Key West beach house, and another condo in Orlando."

Shane continued to watch the rapid fire conversations, and tried to keep up with what was happening. After almost two weeks of nothing, suddenly everything was transpiring very quickly. The next few hours went by in a flurry of intense activity, and at the climax of that activity had been the simple statement from the head of the small task force. "We've located her car just outside the farmhouse near Atlanta," he said. At his words, everyone paused for a second, and then launched back into investigation mode with redoubled vigor. The small ray of hope that Shane had clung to for the past week suddenly exploded into a supernova.

A loud humming sound came out of the furnace and startled Cece. Moments later, light suddenly illuminated the basement. Cece sprang up and looked around. With the power on, she could see the basement for the first time. It was even more expansive than it had seemed in the dark, and it was furnished with luxurious, high-quality items. Her corner was littered with empty water bottles and chip bags, but everything else was pristine.

Her eyes hurt from having been in the dark for more than a week straight, and she had to keep blinking as they adjusted to the light that now flooded the basement. She looked down at her clothes; they were filthy and bloody. She tried to unwrap her hand to get a better look at it, but the piece of shirt was stuck to her wound. Pulling at it proved to be too painful, so she left it alone. She had a feeling that everything was coming to an end today, but still, she had no idea what to expect when and if he came back. She sat down in one of the brocade chairs and stared at the basement door. She took deep calming breaths as she waited for the door to open again, and when it did, she saw him clearly for the first time. He was just a small, ordinary looking, sad little man. He beckoned her forward with the gun in his hand.

"Where are we?" she asked from the bottom of the stairs.

"Save your questions," he said as he beckoned again. "Come with me."

She plodded up the stairs, and he carefully kept the gun aimed at her face as she ascended. When she neared the top, he backed up and directed her down several hallways. He followed behind her with the gun pointed at her head the entire time. The last hallway was a large corridor with expansive vaulted ceilings and gold accessories. The word gaudy came to mind as Cece looked around. This house reminded her of a miniature version of an Arabian palace. Gilded mirrors adorned every wall, and Cece saw multiple reflections of herself and the gun behind her as she walked through the corridor. It ended at a huge room with a piano sitting right in the middle.

Cece noticed Chad tied down on one side of the room, and another woman tied to a chair on the other side. Chad was bleeding and he looked miserable, but in spite of herself, Cece almost smiled. He wasn't dead. The woman on the other side of the room wore a disdainful expression. Her expensive tailored pants suit had been ripped, and her makeup was smeared all across her face.

"You're going to spend the rest of your life in prison for this, Ramesh!" she screamed at the man with the gun as soon as he walked into the room.

"No. I'm not," Ramesh answered with quiet certainty.

The woman screamed out in fury as she fought against her restraints. She didn't stop shrieking until Ramesh approached her and aimed the gun at her face. "I'm starting to think I should just kill you now, you bitch."

She shut up after that statement.

"Mr. Tibrewala, I really didn't rape Sita," Chad said.

Ramesh charged at Chad and knocked his chair to the floor as he screamed, "Don't you *ever* speak her name in my presence!" He fired a shot into Chad's foot as Cece looked on in horror.

Ramesh stood over Chad, breathing hard as the young man cried. The woman bit down on her lip and looked away.

"Now that we're all here, we're going to have another trial," Ramesh said. "This time, the one on trial won't be my daughter. I've brought someone very special to be the judge." He pointed the gun at Cece again and said, "Cece, take a seat at the piano bench."

"Me?" Cece asked. Her voice was shaking again. "Why me? I wasn't even there," she said. Everyone stared at her, but no answer was forthcoming as she sat on the bench. A small puddle of blood collected under Chad's foot as he hung his head and continued crying.

Ramesh sat down in the doorway and pressed a button. A motorized projector screen lowered over the room's only window, eclipsing the daylight that had been filtering in. Cece carefully observed Ramesh and looked for an opportunity to end this madness, but he kept one hand on his gun the entire time. Also, he was across the room, more than twenty feet away from her. If she tried anything, he could easily kill her.

Ramesh pressed another button, and a video played on the screen. A small woman with familiar facial features appeared before them. She stared wordlessly into the camera and cried for a few minutes. When she finally did speak, her voice came out in a tiny whisper.

"I don't know what to say to anybody anymore. So now I'm just going to say goodbye. But before I go, I just want you to know that I am not a whore. You hear that, Father? I am not a whore. Whatever you think of me after this, just remember that I wasn't lying about what happened to me." With that final statement, she took an entire bottle of pills, one by one, as she continued staring directly into the camera. After she took the last pill, she lay down in her bed and cried herself to sleep. She stopped moving, and then the screen went blank.

Ramesh stared at the screen as if he thought replaying it could resurrect his daughter, even if only for a few minutes. Chad wept quietly in his little corner of the room, and the woman on the other side stared at the wall beside her.

"I didn't force myself on her," Chad said at last. "Ben, Steven and Corey did, but I didn't. They came into the room after I got up to use the bathroom. When I came out, they were already on her, and they held me back as they took turns. She tried to fight them, and she kept asking me to help her, but I couldn't," Chad sobbed.

"Why couldn't you help her?" Cece asked.

"Because they were holding me back. They're stronger than I am."

"Then why didn't you testify against them when you had the chance?" Cece demanded.

"Because she accused us all, and their parents have money. They all threatened to lie and say that I raped her too if I told anyone the truth... and Sita didn't know the difference, because she was too drunk to remember everything that happened that night."

The woman across the room glared at Chad and hissed, "You stupid little shit."

Not liking the woman's attitude, Cece asked, "Who are you?"

"She's the one who told me to lie when the case went to trial," Chad admitted.

"I defended you!" the woman screamed in outrage. You got the best criminal defense lawyer in the entire state of Oregon! All you had to do was not implicate my other clients."

"But they were your real clients, because their parents had the money to pay you and mine didn't. Without me there to lie for them, they would have been convicted."

"No! Without them hiring a lawyer on your behalf, *you* would have been convicted," she sneered. "You're just as guilty as they are for not stopping it, even worse because you were supposedly her friend," she said in a voice dripping with disdain.

"And you defended all of them," Cece spoke up. "So what does that say about you?"

The woman's disdainful look briefly melted into a look of dejected confusion, but then she furrowed her brows and clenched her teeth together. "They got off, didn't they? So, I'd say it makes me a damn good defense lawyer. I'm sorry about your daughter, Ramesh, but the video and witness accounts of the way she acted that night combined to make enough reasonable doubt for my clients to go free. It's not *my* fault she killed herself. I'm sorry it happened. Nobody wanted that. Nobody expected that."

"You're not sorry," Ramesh whispered.

"What did you say?" the woman asked.

"I said you're not sorry. You're not sorry! Did you hear me that time? You! Are! Not! Sorry!"

He hadn't moved from the doorway, so he shouted at the woman from his seated position. Even from so far away, the absolute anguish in his voice blasted Cece and she had to blink away tears. She thought of the drunk driver who had killed Sarah. The day he was sentenced, he'd looked at her chin and said he was sorry. He couldn't even look her in the eyes when he said it. She'd wanted to look in his eyes and punch him in the face. Everything inside her had screamed out in fury at his pathetic little "I'm sorry," because she knew he didn't mean it.

They listened to the quiet sound of Chad's sniffles from across the room. The only other sound was the hum of the furnace and the occasional gust of wind against the side of the house. "Ramesh, why are you doing this?" Cece asked into the lengthy silence that followed his emotionally charged outburst.

"Because they deserve to suffer for what they did to my daughter, and I deserve to suffer for what I did to you." He sniffed and pointed the gun at his own head for a moment. "Sita never hurt anybody in her entire life. She was the kindest, gentlest person who ever lived. She was going to be a doctor."

"Do you think she would approve of what you're doing now?"

"I don't know," he said as he lowered the gun and stared up at a large portrait hanging on the wall.

Cece's eyes followed his to the portrait. She was struck hard by the familiarity in the young woman's features. The young woman in the portrait bore an undeniable resemblance to Rebecca. They had almost the same dark skin tone and very similar facial features. Sita's hair was long and black, but it was straighter and less voluminous than Rebecca's. Cece's breath stayed lodged somewhere in her throat as Sita's soulful brown eyes stared down at them.

"Ramesh, look at her face. I know she wouldn't want this," Cece said as she slowly slid down off the piano bench and started inching toward him.

"Sita," he whispered as he looked up at the portrait again. "Tell me what to do. How can I make it right for you?"

"Let us go," the woman across the room said.

"Ramesh!" Cece called out as he jumped up and charged across the room at the woman.

The woman raised her chin and her eyes flashed up at Ramesh as he aimed the gun at her face. "You aren't allowed to speak again. Nothing you say is of any importance. I've already decided what to do with you." The woman's lip trembled and her gaze faltered as she stared at the gun. Ramesh cocked the gun and fingered the trigger as his eyes darted from the woman to Chad and back again. Cece thought he was going to shoot, but he suddenly grabbed the woman by the hair and yanked her chair over. She slumped into unconsciousness, and he ran from the room.

Once he was out of the room, Cece didn't hesitate. She immediately set Chad's chair upright, and then she did the same for the woman. She went back to Chad to untie him and said, "So, she's a defense attorney? What's her name?"

"Madison Bentley. She's known to get people off, no matter how guilty they look, but you gotta have deep pockets to afford her."

Cece looked over at Madison. She didn't look nearly as fearsome wilted and unconscious in her chair as she did when she was yelling at Ramesh. "If I untie you, do you think you can hide somewhere until I figure out a way to escape?" Cece asked.

"Escape? Do you have any idea where we are?" Chad asked.

"No," Cece admitted.

"This is Ramesh's estate. He's known for being eccentric and reclusive. This is the middle of Oregon wilderness. The nearest town is more than twenty miles from here, and his private road is impassable once it snows. A blizzard blew through here last week. Why do you think the power has been out? It's ten below, and he has the keys to the only car."

"We're in Oregon?" Cece asked.

"Yes."

"I've never been this far from home before," she said as everything he'd told her sunk in. There had to be a way to escape without freezing to death in the cold.

"Where did you come from?"

"Nashville, Tennessee."

"Holy shit. Ramesh had you in the trunk all the way from Nashville?"

"Yes."

"Why would he kidnap you? What have you got to do with what happened to Sita?"

"Nothing." She didn't elaborate, because Ramesh had come quietly back into the room.

"It's time, Cece," he said. "You've heard what they have to say for themselves; now you be the judge."

"Judge of what?" Cece asked.

"If you find them guilty then they have to die, and if you find them innocent you will for letting them get away again. It's your decision."

"No. Ramesh, this has nothing to do with me. I'm not going to participate in your crazy game. You need help."

Ramesh walked up to the unconscious Madison and demanded, "Is she guilty of getting criminals off? Criminals she knew were monsters? Is she guilty?"

When Cece clenched her lips together and said nothing, Ramesh aimed the gun at Madison's chest and pulled the trigger. Her body jerked as the bullet entered her, and then blood started trickling from the wound.

Chad looked sick, but he didn't make a sound as Ramesh approached him. "Is he guilty of rape and of helping other rapists go free?"

Shocked out of her silence by what he'd just done to Madison, Cece screamed, "No! I find him innocent!"

"You're lying! I see in your eyes that you know he did it. Stop trying to protect his miserable life!"

"I'm not," Cece insisted. "I believe his story now!"

Chad looked back and forth from Cece to Ramesh as they stared at each other. He released a pent up breath when Ramesh lowered the gun out of his face, but then Ramesh fired a shot directly into his groin. Chad took a deep breath before dissolving into a fit of horrendous shrieks.

Ramesh then turned toward Cece. "This is the only way," he said. He took another gun out of his pocket and slid it across the floor at her. "Pick it up." Her entire body was shaking as she bent down to grab the gun. "You know what to do now," Ramesh said.

"I'm not going to kill you, Ramesh."

"Why not? I deserve it. I raped you! I kidnapped you! I shot these people! I called my own daughter a whore. Just do it!"

"I can't. You're hurting right now, and you need help. And it's not your fault I was tied down that night, but you risked your life to let me go. I can't kill you," she tried reasoning with him. Chad was crying very quietly now, like a little puppy who needed its mother. Madison's chest still rose and fell with each labored breath she took. There was still hope.

"All this time...you thought I saved you, and I was the reason you were there in the first place," he said quietly.

"What do you mean?"

"That man Red Bone and I, we had an arrangement. I traveled a lot back then, and when I was in Atlanta, he got girls for me. You were the first virgin he ever gave me, and he made me pay him more than two thousand dollars to have you first. I didn't even ask how old you were or why you were tied to the bed. All I cared was that nobody else had touched you yet."

"That was you?" Cece whispered. Tears blurred her vision as she recalled that night. Red Bone had taunted her by telling her about all the money she would make for him, and he'd described what was going to happen in explicit detail. By the time the first john had entered the room, she'd worked herself up into a near frenzy. He had turned on the bedside radio clock and tuned it to the local classical music station before he attempted to touch her for the first time. She had fought hard against her restraints as Beethoven's *Moonlight Sonata* filled the room. At first, he'd tried to shush her to get her to lie still, but then he gave up trying to calm her and angrily stripped off his own clothes. The pain that came next, juxtaposed with the beautiful piano music in the background, had never been completely banished from her memories. The knowledge that he had come back days later and raped her a second time before freeing her made her weak with revulsion.

She almost dropped the gun right then, because her hand was suddenly so shaky and sweaty. Her skin crawled as she shook her head repeatedly and looked from the gun in her hand to his face and back again. She raised the gun and placed her finger on the trigger, slowly, deliberately. He deserved to pay for everything he'd done, but when she tried to squeeze the trigger, her mother's face flashed in her mind. That look of absolute terror that Cora wore the day she died had been burned in Cece's memory forever. She also thought about Rebecca—kind, sweet and gentle Rebecca. "I can't kill you," she said as she lowered the gun. "I'm not a killer."

"Then you're going to die."

He aimed the gun at her face, and she cringed. She didn't want to kill him, but she didn't want to die either. "Wait!" she cried out. "Look at Sita's portrait. She's watching you!"

"I know, and that's why *you* have to kill me." He started walking towards her, and the barrel of the gun grew bigger as he neared her. He was less than ten feet away when he stopped again.

"This isn't right, Ramesh. Your daughter will *never* forgive you for this," she whispered.

"My daughter is dead," he whispered back.

"I'm talking about your other daughter."

"Sarah's dead too."

"Ramesh, Sarah was a twin. You still have one daughter left, and she'll never forgive you if you kill me," Cece sobbed. Her voice was shaking again, and she wasn't entirely sure he understood her.

"You're lying!" he said.

"No, I'm not. She's 28 and she looks so much like Sita you'd recognize her instantly if you ever saw her. She plays the piano like you, and she's the kindest most gentle person I ever met."

"You're lying," he said again with less conviction than before.

"Her name is Rebecca, and I can prove it."

"How?"

"I have one picture of Sarah and Rebecca together when they were small. It's in the locket I wear around my neck."

"Open it."

Cece fumbled with the locket for a few tense seconds before it came open. He squinted at it and then inched closer, still carful to keep the gun pointed at her.

"She plays the piano?" he whispered.

"Yes." Just one more step and he would be within arm's reach.

"Is she happy?" he whispered as he took that last step.

Cece's hand flashed out and grasped his gun hand. She ignored the pain that shot up her wrist, and with a quick twist she had control of his gun, his hand, and the situation. Both guns fell to the floor, and she looked him directly in the eye for the first time. "You don't get to know another damn thing about *my* daughter," she hissed.

When he attempted to jerk his arm free, she dealt him a series of swift, hard elbow blows to the head, rendering him unconscious.

In the next instant, the front door burst open and multiple people in police uniforms swarmed inside. Suddenly, there were guns everywhere and someone was shouting, "Everybody down on the floor!"

Cece raised her hands in surrender and lay down on the floor. She wept with relief as she listened to the flurry of activity around her. They checked Chad and Madison, and paramedics were called to their aid within moments.

"Cece Graves?" a kind female voice asked from above her.

"Yes?" she answered. "Can I get up off the floor now without worrying about being shot by the swat team?"

"Yes," the woman said. "That's just protocol. We have to put everyone down on the floor until we sort out the good guys from the bad ones."

Cece stood up on shaky legs and looked around at all the people who were now in the house. "Where did you guys come from so fast?" she asked.

"We've been watching the house all morning. We would have established contact to have hostage negotiations, but Ramesh hasn't had phone service for almost a year now, and there was no good way to get a line inside. You're lucky to be alive. The sniper only had one possible clear shot through that window, and you've been blocking it the entire time. We couldn't risk hitting you to get him. He had explosives wired to the doors, but the bomb squad finally diffused them just after he started shooting everybody. Good job disarming him."

Cece looked down at the guns on the floor and started crying again.

"It's over now, Cece. Let's go let the paramedics have a look at your hand."

Suddenly, it was difficult to breathe, and Cece wanted to get out of this house altogether. "I need to step outside for a minute first."

"It's pretty cold out, much colder than you're used to in Nashville," the policewoman warned.

"I was locked in a trunk for three days and then in a dark basement until this afternoon... I just want to go outside and breathe for a minute."

"Okay."

Cece ignored the wails of the ambulance sirens and the trails of blood on the floor as she made her way down the corridor. She stepped outside and looked up at the light blue, cloudless sky. The stone courtyard in front of the house held even more cops and emergency vehicles. She tried not to notice them, even after some of them stared. She kept her focus on the sky above her. It was beautiful and relaxing, and after thinking she would die in either a trunk or a dark basement, she was so glad to see it.

As she looked up at the sky, stars suddenly appeared and swirled around her, drowning out everything else as the night sky came rushing down toward her. As she passed through the stars, everything around her dissolved into nothingness, and she tumbled face first into the void. While she was lost in that dark space between worlds, she wept.

"Why are you crying, Mommy?" Sarah's voice asked from behind her.

Cece felt a warm, soft touch on her shoulder, and when she looked over, she saw her daughter. "Sarah!" she exclaimed as she wrapped her arms around the child.

"Does it hurt?" Sarah asked as she gently took Cece's injured hand in her little arms.

"Not anymore," Cece smiled. She cupped Sarah's little cheek with her other hand.

"It's going to be okay, Mommy." Sarah kissed her hand, and Cece watched in amazement as the bloody gash began to glow and heal before her eyes.

"How did you do that?" Cece asked. She flexed her hand and all the pain was gone.

"I'm so proud of you, Mommy," Sarah whispered as her little face faded slightly. When she tipped her head to the side, shimmering trails of golden particles followed her every movement and obscured her features.

"Sarah, how did you learn to do that?" Cece giggled.

"I can show you next time you come back, but right now Rebecca needs you," Sarah said.

"She does?" Cece asked as she looked around. She didn't see Rebecca, but she did see a young woman who looked a lot like her standing off to the side. Sarah giggled and skipped over to the woman, leaving glittering trails of golden light in her wake. She took the young woman by the hand and pulled her toward Cece. As her face came into focus, Cece gradually recognized her from the large portrait that had been in Ramesh's fancy music room. "Sita?" she whispered.

"She's very shy," Sarah told Cece. "She doesn't talk much."

Cece stared at Sita for a long time, mesmerized by her serene face. Peace seemed to exude from her entire being. She wore a baby pink and turquoise sari that somehow created its own light and shone bright in the darkness. The brightness wasn't painful at all; it was actually very comforting to Cece's tired eyes.

"It's almost time for you to go now, Mommy," Sarah said as she flung herself back into Cece's arms.

"Go where?" Cece asked.

"Back to my sister," Sita answered as she knelt down to hug Cece and Sarah.

The three of them stayed entwined in each other's arms for a beautiful instant that stretched on infinitely in Cece's heart and soul. "I love you so much," Cece whispered over and over again as she drifted back down to the real world and landed in a hospital bed.

Suddenly, her arms were empty, and she was very cold. "Why does my arm hurt again?" she murmured with great difficulty. "I thought Sarah fixed it."

"Mom, it's Rebecca. Can you hear me?"

"Yes." Cece struggled to open her eyes, but gave up as exhaustion won the battle.

Chapter 28

The next time Cece woke up, she was prepared for the searing pain in her arm. She opened her eyes and looked around the room, but no one else was there. She had an IV fluid needle in her arm, and her right hand was completely encased in gauze. She pushed the button on the side of the bed, and concentrated on trying to stop the spinning sensation as the bed rose. As she stared at the open door for several minutes, she thought about everything that had happened. Footsteps echoed in the hall a moment before Rebecca walked into the room with a steaming cup of coffee in her hands.

"You're awake now," Rebecca said as she set the coffee down on a table and rushed forward to hug Cece. Cece tried to hug her back, but she could barely lift her arms due to exhaustion.

"I'm so sorry about keeping you and Norman apart before you had Rose and Renée," Cece sniffed.

Rebecca pulled back and gave her a funny look. "Why are you apologizing for that again? We forgave you a long time ago."

"I know you did, but I'm so sorry. I wish I could tell you exactly how sorry I am for all of it. I've had more than enough time to think about all the things I've done; I have a lot to make up for."

"Mom, please don't worry about any of that right now. I'm just so happy you're alive. How are you feeling?"

"Honestly, I've never felt better in my life. I'm just a little tired and my hand hurts. How long have I been in the hospital?"

Rebecca glanced down at Cece's hand before she answered. "You've been here almost a week."

"A week?" Cece asked in surprise.

Before Rebecca could answer, a knock sounded at the door, and two doctors and a nurse stepped into the room.

"You look familiar," Cece said as she eyed the taller, dark-haired doctor.

"I should hope so; I'm George, one of your in-laws," he said with a smile.

"What are you doing here?" Cece wasn't trying to be rude, but she couldn't think of a single reason for him to be in her hospital room.

"He's the one who performed the surgery on your hand," the other doctor answered. "Our own orthopedic surgeon wanted to amputate it, but your husband wouldn't hear of it. He gave us hell, and then flew this guy in to save your arm."

"Amputate it?" Cece echoed.

"Yes. It was infected, and you went into shock. You've been out, because your body is weak from fighting the infection. You were a little more resistant to antibiotics due to your previous medical history, so treating this infection wasn't easy."

Cece looked down at the gauze around her arm again. She tried to wiggle her fingers and then winced as a severe pain shot up her arm.

"Don't try to move it yet," George warned. "I had to remove quite a bit of infected flesh to save your life. Your arm is never going to be exactly like it was, but with some good physical therapy you should be able to regain at least half the use of that hand."

"Can I see what it looks like?" Cece asked as she continued to stare at the gauze.

"Absolutely," the other doctor said. "Nurse Kelly was just about to change your bandages."

Cece watched as the nurse unwrapped her hand. George and the other doctor examined it, and then made a few notations in her chart. It was so shocking to Cece, she had to turn away. Seeing a severely damaged part of herself that had always been normal and healthy was too much for her at the moment. She leaned her head back and closed her eyes until the nurse finished applying the fresh bandage.

They spent a few minutes giving her a rundown of all the procedures that had been done, and telling her about her medications. When they finished, George looked at her and asked, "Do you have any questions for us?"

"No," she said quietly.

"Okay. We'll see you again this same time tomorrow when we make our rounds."

"Wait. Why can't I just leave the hospital now? I feel a little tired, but other than that, I'm fine."

The other doctor cleared his throat and said, "Mrs. Gregory, with all due respect, you are *not* completely fine yet. You nearly died from shock, because the infection spread to your blood. You're going to need to continue in-patient intravenous treatment for at least another week. Also, there's still the possibility that we might need to remove a little more flesh or even go ahead and amputate your hand. We have to make sure the infection is completely cleared up."

"It won't be so bad," George said with a smile. "You have your own private room, and your family is here with you."

Rebecca came over and placed a calming hand on Cece's shoulder. "It's going to be okay, Mom," she said in Cece's ear.

After the two doctors and the nurse left the room, Cece stared at her hand in silence for a few minutes. She should feel worse about the prospect of losing her hand, but she didn't. She still felt happier than she ever had before. She got to see her daughter again, she would see her granddaughters grow up, she would still be able to see her business grow, and she was alive. After thinking she was going to die multiple times, she was alive and safe.

"Are you okay, Mom?" Rebecca asked in a worried tone.

"I've never felt better," Cece answered honestly.

"You always say that when you're having a hard time. You can talk to me about how you feel. I know decorating cakes and martial arts is a big deal to you, and you probably won't be able to do as much as you used to."

"Rebecca, I've really never felt better in my entire life. As long as I have you, and those beautiful little grandbabies of mine, and Karen to boss me around the ring every once in a while, I'm happy."

Rebecca hugged her again, and then stood up. "I'm going to go get Shane now," she said as she turned to walk out the door.

427

"Wait! Don't go get Shane!" Cece exclaimed. She thought again about the young woman he'd been standing in the window with.

"Why not?"

"I really don't want to bother him right now," she hedged.

"Bother him?"

"Look, Rebecca, there are a lot of things that happened between us that you don't know about," Cece began. She would have said more, but she couldn't think of a good way to explain everything. Pretending to get married just to improve her business no longer made as much sense to her as it had back then.

"Shane told us everything, Mom." Rebecca said with an amused look at Cece's obvious distress.

"Everything?" Cece asked.

"Yes, everything. Even the part about the fake wedding," Rebecca grinned.

Cece sat back with a deep sigh, "I guess if you all thought I was dead, there was no point in hiding anything anymore... So if you know everything, then you also know that he's moved on. I don't really want to talk to him and make things any more awkward than they have to be."

"Moved on? Mom, what on Earth are you talking about?" Rebecca demanded.

"That night I went missing, I was on my way to Shane's house. He wasn't expecting me, and when I got there, he was already there with someone else. I saw him hugging a woman through the window. That's why I ran off in the first place."

"I'm sure there has to be another explanation besides the one you're thinking," Rebecca insisted. "I'm going to go get him and ask."

"Rebecca Graves! If you take one more step towards that door! He's already moved on, and I don't want you bringing him in here making things worse."

Rebecca whipped around with tears in her eyes and said, "You didn't see what I saw while you were missing, and after they found you and you were laying in the hospital dying. I don't know what you think you saw that night, but for the past two weeks, all I've seen is a man who obviously loves you, even if you're too stubborn to want to hear it right now."

As Rebecca turned and stomped out of the room, Cece attempted to follow. "Rebecca, get back here," she hissed as she swung her legs out of bed and stood up. The sudden pinch of the IV needle reminded her that she was tied down for the moment, but she jerked the wheeled IV cart along with her anyway. She was almost to the door when Shane appeared in the open doorway.

She hadn't been in the same room as him for almost a year, and she'd forgotten how he seemed to take up all the available space when he was around. Suddenly, the hospital room seemed tiny, and her heart felt fuller as she looked up at him. He had a tired and haunted look about his eyes, and there was more gray hair at his temples than before. His eyes scanned over her entire face, and then locked onto hers. Her hand came up involuntarily to smooth down her hair. He was neatly groomed, and she knew she must look frightful after everything that had happened.

All at once, her heart was beating too fast and the room was spinning around her. She reached out for a wall or something to steady herself and almost fell.

"What are you doing out of bed?" he asked as he rushed forward to catch her. He scooped her up and placed her back in the bed, careful not to hurt her bandaged hand. Even after she relaxed back on the pillow in obvious exhaustion, he didn't let her go, and she didn't try to push him away. Instead, she breathed him in. She reacquainted herself with all the little things that had become so familiar to her during their time in the cabin. She smelled his shampoo mingled with the masculine scent that was unique to him. She soaked in the warmth that exuded from his arms around her. She allowed herself to be calmed by his steady heartbeat... And then she thought again about that woman in the window and about how betrayed she felt.

"Have you managed to get an annulment yet?" she asked, trying to keep the bitterness and hurt out of her voice.

"You're joking right?" he murmured against her hair. "Why would I want an annulment?"

"You were with someone that night. You should get the annulment now. I understand."

He pulled back and looked at her. He ran his hands down her arms, and then skimmed his fingers over the bandages on her injured hand. "That woman's name is Natalie Philips, and she's young enough to be my daughter. She's a private investigator. Brent suggested I hire her to find out more about your mother. She stopped by that night to tell me that she found a credible lead about someone out in California. You shouldn't have run off, Cecilia."

"Did she find anything?" Cece asked. She scarcely breathed as she awaited his reply.

"After all the hell you've put me through, I shouldn't even tell you. I think you'll have to give me a kiss to make up for giving me such a hard time."

"Will you please just tell me if she found anything," Cece asked.

He leaned forward and brushed his lips against hers. "Not until I get my kiss," he said.

"I can't," she said as she turned her face. Tears gathered behind her eyes as she looked at his shoulder.

"You don't believe me about Natalie," he sighed.

"No, it's not that," she said.

"Well, what is it then? We're not back to square one again are we?"

"No, I just feel..."

When she hesitated and turned away again, he inched closer. "You feel what?" he asked.

"I haven't had a bath in two weeks. I feel icky right now."

"Cecilia, I wouldn't care if you were covered in mud and you'd just been sprayed by a skunk." He didn't give her the chance to protest again. He started kissing her, and she forgot all about her reservations. It had been far too long, and she didn't have the will to push him away again, ever.

The day of Cece's release from the hospital came sooner than the doctors had anticipated. She focused every bit of her energy on thinking positive thoughts to expedite her healing, and Shane was by her side the entire time. He supported her every step of the way, and told her about everything he and Natalie had learned over the past year. He showed her a picture of the grandmother she never knew she had, and even gave her a copy of the journal her mother had kept during her years with Red Bone. She still wasn't used to thinking of that man as her evil Uncle Cedric.

Shortly after she received her release papers, Cece was escorted to a small office on the first floor of the hospital.

"Hi, Mrs. Gregory; I'm Georgette. Your husband hired me to handle publicity while you were missing, and now I'm here to brief you about what to expect when you walk out of the hospital," an older woman with short gray hair said as Cece situated herself in one of the chairs.

"Why would I need a publicist?" Cece asked.

Shane, Rebecca, and Georgette all exchanged an uncomfortable look before Shane spoke up. "I didn't mention this before, mainly because I didn't want to stress you out while you were trying to get better. Also, I kind of thought that maybe some of the media attention would die down. Someone leaked the fact that you are being released today, and it's a circus out there. We weren't really expecting that."

Cece stood up and walked to the only window in the room. She pulled the blinds back, and took in a deep breath when she saw all the people waiting outside the main entrance. She dropped the blinds and sat back down. "Why do people even care what happens to me?" she asked.

"Well," Georgette said with a sigh. "Part of it is that your name is now synonymous with a foundation that has shined a huge spotlight on women's issues lately. There's also the fact that you recently married into one of the wealthiest families in the world, and there's been a lot of speculation surrounding your husband and his ailing grandfather's fortune. But I think most of the attention comes from the fact that people like to hear a good survival story. While you were missing, there were several candle light vigils, massive media coverage, and even a special on *20/20*. There has been a lot of interest in your safety since the night you were kidnapped. It's up to you if you want to say anything, but requests for interviews have been pouring in."

Cece sat back with a sigh.

"I support you no matter what you decide to do," Shane said as he gave her shoulder a gentle squeeze.

She smiled up at him, and then looked over at Rebecca. "What would you do?" she asked.

Rebecca looked surprised, but she answered quickly. "I would give a brief statement right now and then consent to one interview later. I think it's important to tell your side of the story, instead of letting everyone else speak for you. I also think it will be a good way to raise money for the foundation. I know we don't talk about it much, but I've always wanted you to be more involved with the work I'm doing. I've managed to start some really vital programs and I've helped to open up three shelters over the past few years. Positive attention like this will drive up donations. It's up to you, but I think you can use all this media coverage as an opportunity to come out as a valuable spokesperson for women's issues and for the foundation."

Cece allowed her daughter's words to sink in for a few minutes. She got up and peaked out the window again. There was a news crew from almost every major network. Rebecca was right, but that didn't make her any less nervous about what she knew she had to do.

She looked at Georgette and asked, "Can you go out first and let them know that I'll give a brief statement, but I won't answer any questions right now?"

"Yes," Georgette smiled.

Rebecca grasped Cece's good hand after Georgette left the room. "Thank you for doing this, Mom," she whispered with tears in her eyes.

"Does it mean that much to you?" Cece asked. She watched a single tear roll down her daughter's cheek, and felt the sting of a few tears behind her own eyes.

"It means the world to me that you are willing to speak publicly for the foundation. I've always felt that this foundation was something that we could manage together, but until today you never seemed interested. And I didn't want to push you."

"You know, when I went back to Atlanta, I never mentioned all of my reasons for going back. While Shane and I were down there with Miss Georgia, I couldn't help thinking about how much she reminds me of you. She spent her entire life savings and was willing to mortgage her house, just to make her neighborhood a better place. After everything I've been through, I knew I had to help. But you, Rebecca, you've dedicated your time and money to a cause that isn't your own. You've never been abused or assaulted, yet you take up this cause as if you've lived it. That is exactly what Miss Georgia has done. I'd assumed that she must have been a prostitute at one time; that was the only explanation I could think of for her absolute dedication to helping women like my mother... but she was never a prostitute and she was never abused by a man. She's just a hardworking woman who had it in her to change her world, even the parts of it that didn't directly affect her. I went back to help her build a community center partly because I knew it was what you would do. In fact, I've been asking myself 'What would Rebecca do?' a lot lately. I'm so proud to have you for a daughter, and I'm honored that you want me to speak on behalf of your foundation."

"Can we just call it *our* foundation from now on?" Rebecca asked as she hugged Cece again.

Cece kept her arm around her daughter's small shoulders until Georgette returned.

"They're waiting for you. We can go out whenever you're ready," Georgette said.

Cece stepped forward and instantly had a cluster of microphones shoved in her face. She took a deep breath and reached out for Shane's hand... for her husband's hand.

"A few minutes ago, my daughter told me that everyone wants me to come out here and talk about what happened to me a couple of weeks ago. For some reason, it was a big story on the news... I'm not really sure what to say about it, other than it was one of the worst things that ever happened to me. I say 'one of the worst' things, because there are things worse than being kidnapped and controlled by a complete stranger. When I was younger, a member of my own family did something similar to both me and my mother. After my father's death, my mother was a victim of domestic violence at the hands of her brother-in-law. For six years, she stayed with him, because she didn't know there was a way out of her situation.

"I'm standing here right now, not to talk to you about what I've been through; instead, I'm standing here to say something to all the women out there who are like my mother. I'm talking to women who think there is no alternative to what they're going through, women who are in the dark and isolated from friends and family, women who are afraid for their lives or for the lives of their children. Part of what abusers do is lead you to believe that life is hopeless, and that if you leave them your life will be over...but that's *not* true. You can choose not to believe those lies. You can choose a better life for yourself. If you're sitting there right now, staring at your TV and thinking about a friend you've been concerned about, then yes, I am talking about your friend. And if you're sitting there with your heart pounding wondering if I'm talking to you, then *yes*, I *am* talking to you. There is a way out; you can find help at your local women's center. You are not alone, and the first and most important step towards your freedom is for you to realize that. *You are not alone.*

"When you're trapped in the darkness, and the only door out leads to the unknown, of course you're afraid to open that door. But once you take that step and reach out for help, you'll find that what's on the other side of that door, the unknown, is what you make of it."

As Cece stepped away from the cluster of microphones, questions flew at her from every angle. Georgette stepped forward to field the reporters' questions as Shane took Cece's arm and escorted her to a car waiting at the curb. Rebecca and George climbed in after them, and they all settled in for the ride to the airport.

"How does your hand feel?" George asked.

"Feels great," Cece said as she looked down at it again. Several tears fell into her lap as she stared at the bandages. Shane's handkerchief came into view, and she accepted it with her good hand. "Thanks," she sniffed with a small smile. Cece relaxed after the car cleared the crowd at the hospital and gained speed. She rested her head against Shane's shoulder and closed her eyes.

She fought back her emotions as she thought about her mother's journal again. She hadn't been able to read beyond the record of Cora's first year with Cedric, and she honestly didn't know if she ever would read the rest. The thought of knowing everything about her mother's life was too painful at the moment. Shane looked at her with his silent, intense gaze, and then Rebecca smiled at them from across the car. Cece smiled back at her daughter.

Their plane landed in Nashville, and their few hours of quiet dissipated as soon as they stepped into the terminal. As the reporters followed them through the terminal, Shane fended them off by telling them, "It's been a long day for all of us, especially my wife; I just want to get her home."

Cece never appreciated his calm, easy presence more than she did today.

434

"Your place? Or mine?" Shane whispered in her ear after they cleared the airport crowd.

"I haven't even thought about that," Cece responded.

"Thought about what?" Rebecca asked.

"Whether we should go to my house or Shane's."

"Oh... About that," Rebecca said uneasily. "Norman and I talked about it, and we think you two might like to stay in the guestroom at our place until all this attention dies down some."

"Why? Are they at the house too?" Cece asked.

"The reporters never really left the house, Honey," Shane chuckled.

"I'll drive, so you two can relax," Rebecca said as she unlocked the car.

"What a long day," Shane sighed as he and Cecilia walked into the pale yellow guestroom in Norman and Rebecca's house. He placed their bags in the closet, and then went to use the bathroom as Cecilia lay sprawled across the bed with a sad look on her face. They hadn't been alone since he'd first walked into her hospital room to find her standing despite the doctor's orders, and now he almost didn't know how he should act. She'd been quiet and distant during her time in the hospital, and that behavior added to their year spent apart didn't leave him with much hope for their future. As much as he wanted to gather her up in his arms and never let go, he also didn't want to ask her for more than she was willing or capable of giving him. He washed his face and shaved before returning to the room. She was sitting on the edge of the bed looking down at her bandaged hand.

"Do you want me to run some bathwater for you?" he asked.

She looked up at him and nodded, her face an impassive mask. When he finished filling the tub, he sat down next to her on the edge of the bed. She glanced at him out of the corner of her eye and then tucked her hair behind her ear.

"I could help you wash your hair," he offered.

When she glanced at him and smiled, his heart picked up speed. "How did you know I wanted to wash my hair?"

"Lucky guess," he smiled back.

"Are you going to help me with my clothes too?" she asked as she stood up and faced him. She playfully struggled with the first button on her shirt as she gave him a pleading look.

"I'll help you with whatever you need, Cecilia," he whispered as he reached out and unfastened the buttons for her. When her shirt fell to the floor, she presented him with her back so he could unclasp her bra.

"Why don't we just take a bath together? That tub is certainly big enough," she looked over her shoulder and said with a small smile.

"You sure? What about your hand?"

"You'll be careful. You're always so good to me. Now get up and help me out of these pants."

"You seem to be in a better mood than you were earlier," Shane remarked as he helped her out of her pants.

"I am. I've been thinking a lot today."

"About what?"

"About where I go from here. About what I want to do with the rest of my life. All of this can't have been so I can go back to my bakery and decorate cakes for the rest of my life."

"Come on," he said as he pulled her into the bathroom. "Tell me all about it while we unwind in the tub." He settled with his arms around her, and she relaxed her head back against his chest with a sigh. "What are your plans for the future?"

"For starters, I'm going to stay more involved in my daughter's foundation. I want to be more involved in projects like the community center in Atlanta. After everything Rebecca and Miss Georgia have done, I have to do something too."

When she sat forward and didn't say anything for a while, Shane asked, "Are you ready for me to help you with your hair?"

"Yes," she answered with tears in her voice.

When they got out of the tub, Shane still hadn't thought of a response to her declarations about her future. Did she still not see a future with him? She lay down, and he sat at the edge of the bed and towel dried his hair. He willed himself not to question her about it. She'd just been through more than anyone should have to go through, and if she wanted space, he was man enough to give it to her. But then he looked down at her again. For the moment, the look in her eyes reminded him of the morning they'd first made love. The shuttered look that had been there for the past week was swiftly melting away into something that looked like trust and hope.

"Cecilia, what were you coming to my house to tell me that night?" he whispered "I know why you ran off, but why did you come in the first place?"

She looked up at him in surprise and said, "Didn't you get my message?"

"I think I got most of it. The machine cut you off right when you were in the middle of saying you were on your way to my house."

"Wow..." she said as a slow smile spread across her face. "I talked for about two more minutes after that."

"What did you say? And if you tell me you were giving me more reasons why we can't be together I might just have to call in Karen and your daughter to talk some sense into you," he half joked.

When she looked up at him with a tender smile and reached out her uninjured hand, he carefully pulled her into his arms.

"I said I was sorry for giving you such a hard time for so long. You are a good man, and you deserve better than that."

Shane gritted his teeth and prepared to argue with her one final time before dropping it forever, but then she spoke again.

"You deserve to be with someone who loves you just as much as you love them... and I think you should know that no other woman will *ever* love you and appreciate you as much as I do. You are the best friend I've ever had in my life, and you're also the best thing that's ever happened to me. You accept me without judging me or wanting me to change, and that is priceless. Your faith in me has helped me become the best version of myself. These past two years of knowing you have touched me so deeply that I can't imagine having to spend the rest of my life without you. I can't even imagine being in a relationship with another man, because I feel like *everything* I am is made better when I'm with you. When I saw you in the window that night, I was devastated. Shane, you're it for me, and I've never been more certain of anything in my entire life. I was coming here to see if you still wanted me in your life after I pushed you away so many times; I feel like I have so much to make up for."

Shane smiled at her and then kissed her until neither of them could think straight. Her eyes were smiling at him when she looked at him again. "You've known exactly how I feel about you for a while now, and you have nothing to make up for. I'm the one who kept pushing despite being warned off multiple times. The only thing that has changed for me is that now I am literally the happiest man in the world."

Some of his tears fell onto her face and mingled with hers as they smiled at each other. "Thank you for loving me so much, for loving me even when I couldn't love myself," she sniffed. "That was what got me through the week in Ramesh's basement. Every night, I would curl up in the corner and fall asleep as I imagined your arms around me. It seemed like there was no way out of that place, but I didn't lose hope, because I remembered you constantly assuring me that I can do anything."

"You *can* do anything, Cecilia," he said as he tenderly cupped her cheek.

She reached up to caress the side of his face and whispered, "*We* can do anything—together."

The next morning, Cece awoke to the gentle tapping of a toddler hand on her face. She opened her eyes to see Rose standing beside the bed, looking up at her with a smile. She reached out her hand and ruffled Rose's cinnamon curls and smiled back at her.

"What are you doing in here?" she asked quietly as she sat up and attempted to help Rose onto the bed with her good hand. Rose's little legs were too short for her to get up there alone, and even with Cece's help, she still couldn't manage to scramble onto the mattress. Cece was about to stand so she could pick her up, but before she could get her legs out from under the comforter, Rose's little face set with determination and she managed to grasp the covers and pull herself up all on her own. "Good girl!" Cece exclaimed with a great deal of pride.

"I'm sorry, Honey. I didn't realize I had an escapee," Shane said from across the room. He was lying on the plush rug near the window with Renée sprawled across his chest. "You want me to get her, so you can sleep some more?" He asked as he got up.

"No. She worked so hard to get up here. Why don't you and Renée join us?" she smiled.

"You sure? What about your hand?" Shane asked with concern in his voice.

"I haven't seen them in a while. I need some hugs from my grandbabies," Cece said as she patted the spot beside her.

Shane joined her on the bed, and he carefully guarded her arm as Rose and Renée toddled back and forth. Cece leaned against his chest and soaked in the sight of her granddaughters playing at her feet.

"I can't believe how much like you they are," Shane said. His lips were close to her ear, and a little shiver went down her spine as his deep voice caressed her.

"What makes you say that?" she asked.

"Aside from the fact that they look like a couple of mini Ceces, both of them have your independent streak. They hardly ever whine or ask for help with something new. You should have seen Rose when she tried to put on her own shoes for the first time. Norman kept trying to help her, and she got mad and threw the shoe at his head. When he left her alone, she just kept at it until she got them on—they were on the wrong foot of course, but she got it done. It was the funniest thing. I wonder how they'll take to learning martial arts," he said.

Cece laughed as she imagined Rose throwing her shoes at her father. "Poor Norman."

"Poor Norman?" Shane chuckled. "I'd say *lucky* Norman. He has the coolest daughters ever. I love watching them play together."

"Me too," Cece said with a smile.

Just then, a knock sounded at the door, and Shane got up to answer it. He had a quiet conversation with Rebecca as Cece looked on in curiosity from the bed. Rebecca collected Rose and Renée, and Shane returned to the bed.

"They're holding brunch for us. I guess we'd better get down there soon so everybody can eat," he said as he pulled her into his arms again.

"Everybody?" Cece asked as she looked up at him.

"You have a lot of people here who care about you, all of them family. There's no way we could have kept them away, so Norman and Rebecca arranged a special brunch for you."

"That was nice of them," Cece yawned.

"Come on, Sleepyhead. I'll help you get dressed. Just tell me what you want to wear," Shane said as he kissed her forehead.

"Something with big sleeves," Cece quipped as she looked down at the cumbersome bandages on her right arm.

Shane went into the closet, and then he emerged a short time later with a sleeveless dress and cardigan set. "Will this do?" he asked.

"So this is a fancy brunch?" she asked.

"I have no idea," he admitted. "I'll be wearing my nice slacks."

"Okay, I'll wear the dress."

A short time later, they descended the stairs and walked into the dining room together. Cece stepped into the room, fully expecting to see Shane's siblings along with her best friend, Karen. She fully expected the room to be filled with her and Rebecca's in-laws. What she saw instead gave her pause. There were only four people seated at the table. Rebecca smiled at her as soon as she walked into the room. The young woman who had been with Shane the night Ramesh had abducted her was there as well. Seated across from Rebecca and the young woman were two people whom Cece didn't recognize. She didn't want to stare and be rude, so she concentrated on Rebecca.

"Good morning," she smiled uncertainly.

"Good morning, Mom," Rebecca said with a special sort of smile. "I'd like to introduce you to a few people before everyone else joins us."

At Rebecca's quiet words, Cece felt a little chill run up her spine. Something made her look back at the two women she didn't recognize. There was something so familiar about both of them, especially the younger one. The younger woman was a very dark-skinned African American woman who looked to be roughly Cece's age. Her hair was well done, and her eyes had a slightly exotic slant to them. With her flawless makeup and strong features, she looked like she could have been a fashion model. Cece also noted that there were tears in those dark eyes. Cece stopped thinking about how rude it was to stare as she took in the woman's appearance. When the woman reached up to adjust her hair, Cece suddenly knew where she'd seen her before. She could never forget those dark eyes and that kind smile. "Dot?" she whispered.

Dot nodded as a single tear slid down her cheek. She and Cece stared at each other for a long time before either of them spoke. "I thought you were dead until a few weeks ago," Dot said.

"And I thought you were dead until just now," Cece sniffed.

In an instant, Dot was out of her chair and Cece was rounding the dining table. Their arms went around each other, and they stayed that way for the next few minutes as everyone else in the room looked on. Eventually, they let go long enough to look at each other again and cry some more.

"You're so beautiful," Cece said over and over again as she touched Dot's face with her left hand. "I've *always* known you were beautiful, but now everybody else knows it too," she cried.

"I know you did, and that's why I got out of there. I thought he'd killed you after he knocked you out in the alley. I left because I thought I owed it to you to make something of myself. Nobody else has *ever* loved me the way you did, Cece. Natalie told me what he did to you, Cece. I'm so sorry... I'm so sorry I left you behind. You never would have left me like that. He told me he killed you and I believed him, and then he beat me. I barely got away, and I was sick with guilt for years."

"But look at us, we're both alive... I can't believe you're here. And who is Natalie?" Cece asked.

"I'm Natalie," the young woman with dark hair spoke up at that point.

Cece turned to look at her and said, "You're the private investigator Shane mentioned while I was in the hospital."

"Yes, I am. If you two want to have a seat, there's a lot that we all need to discuss," Natalie said.

At Natalie's words, Cece remembered that there was still one person in the room whom she didn't know. She took a seat next to the older lady who had been watching her and Dot. The woman had tears streaming down her weathered face, but she looked happy. When Cece sat down, the woman reached out for her hand. Cece accepted the contact, and smiled at her.

"Cece, this is your grandmother, Isabelle Graves. She's the only living relative you have left from your father's family, besides your uncle Cedric of course," Natalie said.

Cece looked into Isabelle's faded gray eyes and smiled. "I had a feeling we were related as soon as I saw you," she said as she turned to embrace her grandmother. Isabelle's frail body trembled as Cece held her.

"How did you know?" Isabelle asked as she and Cece continued to hug each other.

"The eyes and the hair," Cece answered with a happy smile.

Shane shut the door and joined them at the table. As Cece listened to Natalie's summary of everything she'd learned, her eyes repeatedly returned to Shane's. She and Isabelle and Dot were given time and space to talk before the rest of the family joined them for brunch. The three of them didn't discuss anything heavy or emotional; instead, they made small talk as they acquainted themselves with each other. Cece knew there was plenty of time for the difficult discussions later; for now she just wanted to enjoy the happiness of this moment. She looked at Shane again and couldn't stop herself from thinking about how much she loved him. Everyone was in the middle of eating and conversing politely when Cece stood up and approached Shane. He was seated at the other end of the table, because he'd been trying to give her the space to be with her newly found grandmother and childhood friend. He scooted his chair out as she approached, but she didn't want him to get up. She just wanted to join him for a second. She sat down on his lap and wrapped her arms around his neck. Everyone looked on as she pulled him toward her for a lingering kiss. She didn't care how shocked they were at her outrageous display of affection; she loved her husband with all her heart, and she wanted him to know it.

"What was that for?" he whispered in her ear as everyone smiled at the two of them.

"For being the best thing that ever happened to me," she whispered back.

Epilogue

Six months later...

"I still can't believe you did that!" Shane chuckled again for the tenth time as he and Cece helped clean for the day. The rest of the new staff members joined in as the laughter around the bakery continued.

"Cece, you should have seen the look on Shane's face when the DA's office called," a new girl named Macey exclaimed as she wiped tables. She then went on to mimic Shane's surprised and exasperated expression as he'd taken Brent's phone call earlier that day.

Shane chuckled again and said, "Alright, Macey. You tell me what face you would make if your uptight older brother, who happens to be the DA, called to tell you that he's going to have your wife hauled off to jail if she doesn't stop causing a ruckus in his office."

"I'd probably make the same face," Macey admitted with another little grin.

Cece laughed with everybody else, but there hadn't been anything funny about the situation earlier. Karen had been avoiding her for weeks, and she'd finally forced her way into Karen's house that morning to figure out why. She'd found Karen in bed, crying and looking completely miserable. Once Karen had weakly rolled to the side and vomited on the floor, Cece had almost panicked. Karen had never been sick a day in her life. Early on in their friendship, she'd confessed to Cece that she'd never once been nauseous, even as a child. To say that the sight of her best friend in such a state caused alarm bells to go off in her head would have been the understatement of the century.

"I'll call for an ambulance," Cece had gasped as she reached for her cell phone.

Karen reached for her and moaned, "Don't you dare!" in a tone that gave Cece pause. "I'll be okay...okay? This happens every morning. By noon, I'll be ready to kick your ass in the cage," she said right before she slumped over.

"What do you mean this happens every morning? Have you seen a doctor? Does this have anything to do with the reason you had to retire? Oh my God...Karen, you don't have cancer, do you?" Cece demanded in alarm. She sat down hard at the edge of the bed, and the movement caused Karen to moan again.

"Shake this bed *one more time!*" she bit out in a nasty tone. She then fell back against her pile of pillows and held both hands up to her head. "How on Earth did you deal with this?"

"Deal with *what*, Karen? You still haven't told me what's going on..."

"I'm pregnant," Karen hissed through clenched teeth. "I went to my doctor, and told him about all this nausea I've been having. When he suggested I take a pregnancy test, I almost dropped him for being such a sexist pig. They ran a lot of tests that day, and all of them came back negative, *except* the pregnancy test."

"How long have you known?"

"Three weeks."

"Is that why you've been avoiding me?"

Karen nodded and stared at the wall with a far off look in her eyes. "I've already decided to keep it," she said quietly.

"Karen, this will be okay," Cece replied as she placed a hand on her friend's raised knees. "This baby may seem like an 'it' that's going to ruin your life right now, but you are making the choice to become someone's mother by keeping *it*."

"I know I have other options, but I've wanted this for so long. It's like a dream come true in every way except one," Karen whispered.

"If you've always wanted a child, why did you wait so many years? Did you not want to give up your career? Because if that's your reason, let me tell you right now that you could have bounced back from having five kids and still been the most

444

badass female MMA fighter around. Your training regimen still kicks my butt, and Mike and Tony wish they had half your endurance," Cece said.

"Why I waited has nothing to do with my MMA career. I would have loved an excuse to take a break from it. I waited because I never thought I had the right to have a family, not after what I did to you."

"What you did to me?" Cece asked in confusion. She then looked at Karen and found her answer in Karen's delicately crumpled features. "You mean Sarah..."

"Yes," Karen whispered as Cece carefully moved closer and wrapped her arms around her. "What right did I have to get married and start a family when you were so broken because I let my stupid, drunk, piece-of-shit boyfriend drive that day? How could I have gotten pregnant knowing it was my fault you lost Sarah? I was so afraid to tell you I'm pregnant, even now, because I just don't ever want to hurt you like that again."

Cece closed her eyes and let the tears roll down her cheeks. She knew Karen saw them, but she didn't care. Sarah was no longer the explosive topic she'd been just two years ago. "Karen, you are like a sister to me," she began, but then she struggled to find the right words. "And you are absolutely right. Back when Rebecca was younger, I would have been devastated if you'd decided to start a family. Maybe I would have distanced myself and we wouldn't have been friends anymore...I don't know. It would be easy to sit here and lie to you, and say that I would have been happy back then, but I wouldn't have. I was hurting, and I was deeply flawed because I let my pain spew out and alienate almost everyone around me. Now, when I think about those years of my life, I consider myself fortunate that you stuck by my side and put up with me for so long. Karen, you are the one true friend who has stuck with me through all of my emotional ups and downs. You and Rebecca were always like little rays of sunshine. You allowed me to be as unreasonable as I needed to be when I was hurt beyond words, and I thank the Universe every day for you. If you hadn't stuck with me, I don't know if I would have survived losing Sarah."

Karen sobbed and Cece held her and waited for her to speak. "I'm so sorry, Cece. I wish we had met under different circumstances," Karen said.

"So do I, but we had to work with what we got. Karen, I forgive you for not taking your boyfriend's keys that day when he picked you up. I cannot forgive you for Sarah's death, because you were not ultimately responsible; there's nothing to forgive you for, and I came to that conclusion years ago. You demanded that he pull over and he *hit* you; everything that happened beyond that point is on him. It's not like you could have stopped what happened next; you were only nineteen at the time. Even if you had held onto his car or jumped on top of it, a single person is no match for a two ton vehicle. Please, stop worrying yourself sick over being pregnant now. I'm happy for you. If you weren't so miserable about it, I'd be demanding to help you decorate your nursery. I'd be planning a baby shower for you. I'd be jumping up and down, screaming about how great this is... I'd be demanding to know who the father is."

As soon as Cece said the word father, Karen tensed. The atmosphere in the room changed, and Cece felt tension emanating from Karen's frame. "The father wants nothing to do with me; that's one of the reasons I'm so miserable right now," Karen said.

"Okay, so that changes things a little, but you still have family to help you. You have me and Rebecca, and you have all of our in-laws to help get you through this. Shane's family is really nice, and I know for a fact that they think of you as family."

Karen let out a mirthless little chuckle and said, "Not all of them."

"What do you mean?" Cece asked.

"The one who got me pregnant seems to think it's not possible for this baby to be his," Karen snapped.

"One of *my* in-laws?" Cece demanded.

"Yep. It was Mister High-and-Mighty, *District Attorney for the State of Tennessee*," Karen said in a pretend deep voice with an exaggerated Tennessee accent.

"Brent!" Cece hissed though clenched teeth. She immediately disengaged her arms from Karen and left the room. She was vaguely aware of Karen calling after her as she raced down the stairs. She had a thing or two to tell Brent Gregory about getting women pregnant and then tossing them off to the side as if they were used rags.

When she first arrived at his office, the staff and all of his assistant prosecutors had been all smiles. Everyone there was familiar with her because of her cooperation on the high profile cases against Ramesh Tibrewala and Cedric Graves. They lost their smiles, however, when she made a determined beeline for Brent's office.

"I'm sorry, Mrs. Gregory, but Brent's in a meeting right now. If you'll have a seat, I can—"

"Whatever meeting he's in is over, as of right now," Cece interrupted Brent's secretary, Jasmine, as she breezed past the reception desk. Several more suits tried to block her way forward, but she didn't slow down. Once they got the message that she was pissed, they backed up and called security.

Two uniformed officers entered the floor and started towards her from the far entrance to the floor. They now stood between her and Brent's door. There was also a multitude of cluttered desks in her way. She scanned the floor for the best way around them as they neared her. She didn't want any trouble with the staff, but she was going to have a word with her brother-in-law whether the staff liked it or not.

Brent's door opened just as the officers closed in on her from either side. She leapt on top of the nearest desk and sprinted across the desktops, sending loose papers flying in her wake. A collective gasp went through everyone on the floor as they watched. The uniformed officers commanded her to halt, and Brent Gregory gawked up at her as if she'd suddenly sprouted two heads. She came to an abrupt stop on top of the desk nearest him and kicked a small stack of papers at his face.

He didn't cower or flinch at all as the papers rained down on his head. Instead, he barely looked flustered as he said, "What the hell?"

"*You*, of all people! *How dare you?* You give all your high and mighty talks about victims' rights and *justice* and you speak out against criminals who abuse women and you call yourself a *feminist*, and then you have the nerve to get my friend pregnant and then abandon her and tell her it's not yours!" she screamed at him. "*You hypocrite!*"

The woman next to Brent ran for cover as the uniformed officers finally caught up to Cece. They shouted commands for her to put up her hands before they fired their Tasers at her. She complied, because she'd said her piece, and she didn't want to add any resisting arrest charges to whatever else she'd already done wrong. She knew she was way out of line, but she didn't care. The chance to confront Brent made the prospect of a night in jail more than worth it. The only problem with this confrontation was that he had an unflappable look on his face. Standing on top of the desk as she was, he had to look up at her, but it seemed more like he was looking down his nose at her as he maintained eye contact. He didn't even blink as he instructed the officers with the Tasers to stand down. He then stared at her until she obeyed the silent command in his eyes and hopped down off the desk. After he turned his back on her, she followed him into his office. He immediately called Shane, and Cece watched him yell into the phone as she sat there and seethed on Karen's behalf.

After he hung up the phone, he pinned her with a look that made her uncomfortable. Sitting there behind his enormous desk, he looked like a true authority figure. He adjusted his tie, and continued to silently stare her down. Finally, he gave his head a little shake and said, "I really would have expected better from you, Cecilia." He sounded like a school principal chastising a naughty child. "Those of us who live in the adult world believe in solving problems by using our *words*, not our hands and feet. Had you stormed in here like a normal person, I would have pushed back my next meeting and talked to you privately. But you didn't do that, did you? You had to hop over all the desks and make a spectacle of yourself. I can't tolerate that type of behavior around here—not even from family members."

Cece looked down at her hands as his calm words washed over her. "I'm sorry," she said with a sigh.

"Now that *that's* out of the way... What can I help you with?" he asked as if he hadn't heard a word of what she'd said in front of his staff. He looked so calm and professional and *uptight* she felt like an even bigger fool for her earlier behavior.

"I believe you heard every word I said out there. How dare you treat Karen like that?" was Cece's stiff reply.

"First of all, my personal life is not the business of every person who works in this office; it's not even *your* business. You, of all people, should understand that. That being said, I had no idea Karen was pregnant! About a month ago, she called me from her doctor's office and told me they wanted to make her take a pregnancy test. I told her there was no way I got her pregnant. I had a vasectomy when I was in my thirties, and years later when I married, my ex-wife wanted kids. I had the vasectomy reversed, but she never conceived. That's the main reason she divorced me. She wanted a baby, and I couldn't give her one because of a stupid decision I made in my younger years. When Karen called me, I didn't think it was possible and I told her so. She hung up on me, and she hasn't answered any of my calls since that day. If she found out she was pregnant that day—and she's positive it's mine—she damn well should have told me herself instead of sending *you* over here to humiliate me in front of the whole damn office. I've only been the DA for one term; I don't want to lose the next election over this nonsense."

Cece squelched the urge to hang her head in shame. She sat quietly until Shane arrived, and then she left with him. Everyone in the office kept their heads down and pretended to be singularly absorbed in working as she walked out.

She pulled her mind back to the present as she watched Macey clean the rest of the tables in her bakery. Today had definitely been eventful.

Shane walked over and grabbed her up in a giant bear hug. Macey and Torrence turned away from them with small smiles. "It's okay, Honey. Someday we'll all look back on this and laugh," he whispered in her ear.

"I doubt your brother will ever forgive me. He's the king of withering stares," Cece said as her husband set her back on her feet.

"I promise you, he's already forgotten about it. He's wanted to be a father for a long time, and he's probably too busy being happy about the miracle that's about to happen in his life to hold a grudge against you for embarrassing him a little."

"I hope you're right."

Shane gave her another squeeze before turning to Torrence and Macey, "Are we ready to lock up yet?" he asked them.

"Yep," Torrence answered with one of his trademark shy smiles, reminding Cece of how happy she was with her decision to hire some assistants and expand. Torrence had grown up in the foster care system, and this was his first job. Pride beamed through him every day, no matter how mundane the tasks he tackled. He was like a young male version of the kid Cece had been when Mrs. Lee had given her a chance all those years ago.

The sky was almost fully dark when Cece and Shane pulled into their driveway. As if the day hadn't been eventful enough, there was a man in a suit waiting by the front door. He looked way out of place in their neighborhood. Everything about his appearance screamed slick, big city professional. What kind of professional he was had yet to be determined.

"You want to sit tight while I deal with this guy?" Shane asked with a sigh. "I don't know how many different ways we need to tell them that Granddaddy Warbucks has no contact with us."

"You're joking about me staying in the car, right?" Cece asked with a little frown. "I can handle myself."

Shane almost choked on his sudden laughter as he replied, "I think every person in Nashville knows you can handle yourself, but maybe you've had enough action for one day, Coco. Anyway, I was more worried about letting you loose on the poor guy. He looks harmless."

Cece's answer was to exit the car without a backward glance at her still chucking husband.

"May I help you?" she said to the man on the porch.

"Mrs. Gregory, my name is Rich Whitaker, and I really need to speak to you and your husband about an urgent matter," the man said.

Cece looked at him more closely than she had the first time. She looked past his attire and noticed that there were lines of weariness in his face and there was a grim look in his eyes. "What's wrong?" she asked.

He opened his mouth to answer, but shut it when he heard the thunk of the car door closing. He watched Shane walk up to them, and then he took a deep breath and said, "Mr. Gregory, I'm Rich Whitaker, Mr. Edgar Howard's personal attorney. I've had the pleasure of working for your grandfather for the past forty years, and he sent me here to see you about an urgent matter tonight," Rich said.

Cece felt the sudden tension that started emanating from her husband. As if the day hadn't been stressful enough, now he was receiving a summons from his grandfather. Shane looked down at her, and their eyes met for a moment of silent communication.

"Would you like to come in, so we can talk?" Cece offered when she looked back at the lawyer.

"Yes, Ma'am," Rich said quietly. "I have a lot of information for you, and the front step isn't the best place to discuss such things."

Shane unlocked the door, and the three of them settled at the kitchen table. Rich opened his expensive looking briefcase as Cece poured them each a glass of water. Rich tossed down his entire glass in one gulp, took a deep breath and spoke.

"Shane, I'd like to assure you that no matter what happens going forward, I'm on your side."

"What's going to happen? What is this about?" Shane asked.

"I know you've probably been aware of the rumors and speculation that your grandfather is on his deathbed. I'm here to tell you that he is, in fact, dying, Mr. Gregory. He's not expected to last another week; he may not make it through the night. His last wish is to meet all of his grandchildren face to face before he passes."

Shane sat back and let the heavy silence permeate everyone in the room. "Where is he?" he asked eventually.

"He's at his private estate in Upstate New York. You may have heard some of the press coverage about his deteriorating health in recent years. What you probably don't know is that your grandfather never had a stroke. He's been battling cancer for the last three years. He's still fully functioning mentally, and he's been holding off on the stronger pain meds so he can be lucid when he meets you all. He has a lot to say to all of you, but especially to you, Shane."

"Did I do something to upset him? Because if he wants to confront me with anything negative about the woman I chose to marry, then I'll skip the deathbed vigil."

"It's not that at all, Shane. Over the years, your grandfather kept a close watch on all of you, but you were always the one who excited him the most. Your other siblings will receive a comfortable inheritance from his estate, but he chose you for something special. He sent me here to tell you about it; you can spend tonight making your decision and give him your answer in person if you chose to see him."

"What's this special thing he selected me for?" Shane asked quietly. He sounded like he was expecting the worst.

"Your grandfather wants you to inherit his controlling interests in two companies that you're likely already familiar with. He wants to keep them in the family, but he also wants the best man for the job to have it. He's set up provisions for you to go through an extensive five year training program. If, at the end of the program, you pass the exams that your grandfather and several other board members from his companies wrote for you, you get to call yourself the new owner of *Howard Oil* and *H&M Financial.* I don't think I need to tell you the value of those companies or the amount of capital, both cash and political, that comes with them. You are a smart man."

"And if I refuse this offer or don't pass this training program?" Shane asked through clenched teeth.

Rich looked him in the eyes and said, "You get nothing," as he pushed a document across the table. "Everything is detailed in this agreement. All the board members involved have already had their signatures witnessed. This isn't the official document; it's just a copy for you to review the terms. You'd be required to sign in front of everyone listed on the signature page, myself and your grandfather included."

"How on Earth did my grandfather get them to agree to this ridiculous idea? As soon as I sign this, I know I'm going to have to deal with lawsuits from these people. They'll challenge his will and try to take everything back by force. I'm not about to get into a legal battle over a company I'm not remotely interested in running. I'll meet him, but I'm not signing this thing. He'll just have to give it to the next guy in line for the honor," Shane said as he skimmed over the papers.

"This is what your average layperson would refer to as an ironclad agreement. Eddie was smarter than you're giving him credit for, Shane. He had this agreement drawn up more than ten years ago—way before he had any health problems. He's been watching you since your college years. Your degree in mathematics impressed him enough to make him sit up and pay attention to every decision you've made in your adult life. If he didn't think you had a shot, he never would have done this. Your grandfather is not a man who believes in celebrating or rewarding ineptitude. There's a clause in the agreement that explicitly states that if you should fail your exam, the board member or executive who was in charge of the failed aspects of your training would be ineligible to run the company. If you fail, only the person in charge of the area where you scored highest is eligible to take over in your place. Your grandfather thought of everything. There is no chance of this legal battle that you seem so sure is inevitable."

"Who takes over if I refuse?" Shane asked.

"If you refuse, the companies will be liquidated and the money will be divided among all the executives who have been loyal to your grandfather over the years. Thousands of people will lose their jobs, and a press release detailing your refusal to run the companies will go out to all the major news outlets."

"That's the most ridiculous thing I've ever heard!" Shane ground out. "Why make people suffer just because I'm not the man for the job?"

"Eddie knew you'd need something stronger than money to persuade you to try, so he put the livelihoods of thousands of people on the line. If you try, no one loses their job; that only happens if you flat out refuse," Rich said with a small smile. "I actually tried to talk him out of that aspect of this agreement, but he wouldn't hear of it."

"Does he realize that it's shit like this that makes us think he's evil?" Shane demanded.

Rich started packing up his papers as he said his final piece. "Evil or not, he has the power to change your life in the blink of an eye, and his dying wish is for you and your siblings to fly to New York and see him. If you accept his challenge, and you succeed, you'll have the power to change everything you don't like about how he runs his business. That's a powerful incentive to try. The alternative is a guaranteed firestorm of public hatred that you are ill equipped to deal with. It will be hundreds of times worse than what you dealt with last time you ran away from New York. If I were in your shoes, I'd jump through his hoops for now and accept the terms of this agreement. If you think you're a better person than he is, then spend the next five years proving it."

After Rich left, Cece and Shane spent the rest of the night trying to relax. Shane flat out refused to talk about it, but he did pack a bag and call Rich to finalize travel arrangements for the two of them. The next morning, they boarded his grandfather's private jet and flew into the unknown.

Shane took her hand and kissed it as the jet took off into the morning sky. He looked at her and said, "I swore I'd never go back there after I lost my entire career. That's the one thing in my life that I was never able to get over. When you're responsible for so much sadness, it crushes a part of your spirit that you can never get back. It wasn't until *you* that I really started believing in myself again. When you look at me, I know that I'm enough just the way I am, and that knowledge brings me such peace. I wish I'd known you when that building collapsed. I have a feeling that my entire life would have been different if I'd had you in my corner demanding that I go out there and give it all I've got. You make me want to be the best version of myself, so I'll play my grandfather's little game because I know that's what you want."

"It's not so much that I want you to play his game, Shane. All I care is that you try. You heard what his lawyer said last night. He said things could get bad for us if those companies are liquidated, and I believe him. I don't want that to happen any more than you do," she replied.

"I wouldn't be able to face myself if I were directly responsible for so many people losing their jobs, so I will try. I think this is probably some diabolical plan to humiliate me and force me to show that I'll never be as good as he is. This is all because my father was nothing more than a horse breeder who ran off with his little princess. I don't know what's going to happen once I sign the agreement, but I do know that as long as I have you on my side, I could conquer the world if it made you proud of me."

Cece raised his hand to her lips and kissed his knuckles. She then looked into his eyes and said, "No matter what happens we're in this together. We can get through anything together. Don't you forget that."

The End

The Indigo Plume Publishing Co. proudly presents

THE ENTREPRENEUR'S WIDOW

ADRIENNE D'NELLE RUVALCABA

Coming soon in paperback

Keep reading for a preview of Adrienne D'nelle Ruvalcaba's next novel. The romance continues with the story of Mariah Jones.

By Friday morning, Mariah had spent a total of six waking hours with her son. She got home just before his established bedtime every night, and made small talk with Natasha as she held him in her arms. She always half listened as Natasha gave her the rundown of everything Ty did that day. Mariah woke him up at 6:30 every morning, so she could give him his first feeding for the day before she left for work. After that first twenty minutes, he spent the next ten to eleven hours with Natasha and the four other small children whom she cared for during the day. With as much time as Natasha spent with him, she might as well have been his mother. *This is only temporary*, Mariah told herself over and over again as she stared down at Ty's innocent little face.

It had only been four days, but already Mariah had worked more than forty hours that week. "Pretty soon, it's going to be you and me again, Little Man," Mariah whispered as she watched Ty. Even at just ten weeks old, he looked like his father, so much like him it hurt.

"Don't you have to be going soon?" Natasha asked as Mariah continued to linger over Ty.

"Yes," Mariah sighed as she handed her precious bundle into Natasha's waiting arms. "You sure you don't want to come with me to that stupid charity event tonight? His Highness told me I was allowed a plus one."

Natasha released a nervous giggle as she smoothed the blanket over Ty. "I've never been to one of those fancy parties before; I didn't even go to my senior prom," she smiled nervously. "Besides, what would I wear?"

"Natasha, I have a few things that I'm sure will be suitable. Before my husband died, we used to go to quite a few of these things," Mariah said. "Just go through the closet while I'm at work today, and pick out whatever you like the most."

"Are you sure about that?" Natasha asked.

"Yes. I'll send a car from the service to get you tonight, so expect a call from me around 6:30."

"Umm, have you forgotten about Ty?" Natasha asked in a dry tone.

"No. I hired a sitter from the child care facility in the building. She's been working there for fifteen years, and everyone at work swears she's the best. For the price she asks, she better be. She'll be coming with the car that's taking you to the ball."

"You're going through an awful lot of trouble just to have me along," Natasha sighed. "I'm not so sure -"

"Well I am," Mariah cut in. "I'd really enjoy your company. Besides, when's the last time you took a night off to go have some fun? Just relax, and it will be fun." Although she'd only lived with Natasha for six days, Mariah was starting to develop genuine affection for her. Natasha was a couple of inches shorter than Mariah, and she tended to say negative things about herself. Over the past couple of days Mariah had begun to wonder why Natasha seemed to have such low self-esteem, but she wasn't ill mannered enough to actually ask. So far, Natasha had volunteered very little information about herself, but she was one of the most genuine and sweet people that Mariah had ever come across.

"Okay. As long as no one gets picked up late today, I should be ready on time."

"Great. I'll see you this evening. Keep your head up," Mariah told Natasha before she went to work. If by some miracle she got off at 5:30 tonight she'd have almost three hours with her son before she was expected to put in an appearance at the ball. Mr. Donovan had told her that he planned to arrive at 8pm. He'd assumed that she would go earlier so she could have a little fun before his arrival and the official beginning of her duties for the evening, but she'd rather stay home with Ty until the last possible minute.

By some miracle, Mariah was off by 4:30 that day. His Highness hadn't been in the office all afternoon, but he'd left a massive list of things for her to do. At tonight's ball, she wasn't going to merely trail behind him taking notes as she'd done all week in the office. Tonight she was supposed to keep notes of potential investors he wanted to schmooze, and brief him on each of them as they approached. She'd prepared a discreet stack of note cards with code names and personal details about each of them, and she was to cue him with the details at the appropriate times. She was also to act as liaison in dealing with any potential clients who approached him tonight. All in all, it was setting up to be a pretty busy evening, but there wasn't anything she couldn't handle. She'd frequently helped Tiberius recall the right tidbits to impress investors at events such as the one she was to attend tonight.

"You're home, and it's still light outside," Natasha quipped with a smile as Mariah walked in the door.

"I guess His Highness wants me to be as fresh as possible for tonight. This thing could go on until one or two o'clock."

"You need to quit with that highness stuff," Natasha said. "What if you accidentally call him 'His Highness' to his face?"

"Trust me, that won't happen. I never make mistakes like that," Mariah assured her as she bent down to pick up Ty.

He was lying in the crib, as quiet as ever, but when she picked him up she could swear she detected a smile. She hugged him close to her chest and sniffed his head. He smelled like baby powder and milk. "I've missed you so much," she whispered against his little cheek as she breathed him in. He had such a calm, reassuring presence about him, and she felt her tension melt away as she held him.

The fact that he was such a calm baby truly amazed her, because her entire pregnancy had been fraught with emotional extremes and constant anxiety about the future. For the first four months of her pregnancy, she hadn't even realized she was pregnant. She'd thought her menstruation had stopped due to the stress of losing her husband and then her home and business to his mistress. She'd never forget the day that woman had taken possession of *her* house. The police had been present to make sure there was no physical altercation as Mariah gathered up her personal belongings. She'd been physically escorted out of her own house by the local police, and that woman had stood by watching the whole time. It had been equally humiliating and heart wrenching, and incredibly infuriating.

Ty squirmed in her arms as if he felt the direction of her thoughts. Mariah looked down at the top of his head and smiled again. "I'm going to go lie down for a while," she told Natasha on her way out of the daycare room.

"You want me to keep Ty? You look tired..." Natasha offered.

"No thanks. I need some time with him. I don't want him to start thinking you're his mother," Mariah joked, but the joke fell flat. When she looked at Natasha, there was a sad, haunted look in her eyes. As Natasha turned away to tend to a toddler on the floor, Mariah opened her mouth to ask her if she were okay, but then she thought better of it and left the room.

An hour after she lay down with Ty, a soft knock sounded at Mariah's door. "Come in," she called softly. Ty waved his little fists and then smiled at her and made a quiet little gurgle.

Natasha poked her head around the cracked door and said, "I just wanted to let you know that the car is here, so I'm taking off now to go get a new pair of shoes to go with this dress. I guess I'll see you tonight at the thing."

"Yes. After your driver takes you to the store, have them swing by here to pick me up. We'll ride together. I have to be there by 8 to meet the boss."

"Sounds good," Natasha said, and then she was gone.

Mariah placed her hand over Ty's heart and marveled at how rapid his little heart beat was compared to hers. He smiled and waved his arms, and she smiled back at him. "You look just like your father," she whispered. An unwelcome tear made an appearance on her cheek, but she brushed it away quickly. Ty was a part of her future. He was her son. She needed to stop dwelling on the past, on what his father Tiberius had done.

She picked him up, and walked over to the room's only window. There was an interesting view of the street down below. Natasha's neighborhood was far less appealing than the gated community she'd lived in just last year, but there was a hominess to it that she hadn't felt in her old neighborhood. She'd lived in a house that had far more rooms than she and Tiberius could have hoped to use, and she didn't know any of the names of her former neighbors. She'd spent more time out of the country and in luxury hotels around the United States than she ever had at home. She had lived a fast paced life.

She looked down at Ty, and he stared back at her with his quiet, dark brown gaze. "Why are you so quiet?" she asked him. Heaven knew his father was far from a quiet man. Tiberius had always been boisterous almost to a fault. He'd been the self-proclaimed life of every party.

Mariah continued to ask her baby silly questions that she knew he couldn't answer, and he continued smiling and blinking at her until the babysitter arrived. Somehow, in between bouts of playing with Ty, she managed to make herself presentable for tonight's ball. She'd put her hair up into a simple twist on top of her head and secured it with several decorative combs. She applied the bare minimum of makeup, and then she slipped into her formal attire for the night. She'd selected a flattering spaghetti strapped, yellow chiffon dress. The yellow contrasted nicely with her medium brown skin tone and black hair. She allowed herself a single twirl in front of the full length mirror before she kissed Ty one final time.

"No need to worry about a thing, Miss Mariah. Little Ty is in good hands tonight," Jeanie, the woman from the daycare, assured her.

"I'm not so sure there's nothing to worry about... Mr. Donovan isn't exactly the most easy to please boss there ever was," Mariah said with a wry twist of her lips. She bent down to pick up her simple black clutch as she spoke. She checked once to make sure her notes were inside, and then she was on her way.

Mariah and Natasha arrived only minutes before Mr. Donovan and his entourage. They walked around the tables along the perimeter of the venue, and browsed the silent auction items. The party seemed to have wound down for the most part. The band played the kind of sedate music that Mariah could imagine being played in a retirement home, before bedtime. Several dozen couples slow danced on the dance floor, but other than that there were almost no signs of life at this ball. In part Mariah was relieved. The last thing she needed was a long night filled with riled up, inebriated third or fourth generation rich kids.

As she and Natasha quietly browsed and observed, Mariah took note of the general tone of the conversation. Her boss seemed to be a popular subject of discussion. There was a great deal of speculation about the future of the Donovan family name. Mariah's ears perked up at the mention of a new form of solar cell technology that His Highness's company was currently in the process of developing. The details of the new technology were cloaked in secrecy, but many speculated that it could be a game changer in the solar power industry. He was rumored to be on the cusp of some kind of breakthrough, which is why he was currently shopping around for the right investors.

Everyone whispered about his future worth, and even about the possibility of his company going public sometime in the next couple of years. Mariah also heard more than a few women whispering about how handsome her boss was. Those comments almost made her laugh outright as she pictured his neatly manicured hands.

Mariah had worked her way to the end of the silent auction tables, and was very near the entrance, when she noticed a change in the general atmosphere. Suddenly, people were pressing closer to the door and craning their necks to get a glimpse of something. The only people who didn't notice were the older couples still swaying to the elevator music on the dance floor. In spite of herself, Mariah looked up in curiosity along with everyone else. With everyone around her buzzing, Mariah expected to see a celebrity, but she saw her boss instead. She turned back to the auction table in disappointment. It was too much to hope that he'd call and tell her he'd changed his mind about this event. His arrival meant that she had to begin her duties for the night.

"Why didn't you mention that your boss was so young?" Natasha asked with a touch of awe in her voice. "The way you talk about him, I thought he'd look more like Newt Gingrich than Scott Foley."

"What does it matter that he's young? He inherited his company from his father," Mariah returned. As her boss neared, she plastered a smile on her face and prepared to greet him appropriately.

"Who is that beside him?" Natasha asked in a breathless whisper.

Mariah looked up again. On Mr. Donovan's right hand side there was a very handsome and friendly looking man whom she hadn't seen before. "I'm not sure," she told Natasha, "Probably a friend of his." On Mr. Donovan's left there was a tall, slender woman with dark blond hair. The woman glanced around at everyone watching their arrival and raised her eyebrow in a way that could only be described as supercilious. The man on the right seemed to be the only friendly face among His Highness's little group.

When Mr. Donovan and his entourage reached them, Mariah suppressed the urge to cower before him. *Did the man ever look anything other than deathly serious?* She silently wondered to herself. His eyes skimmed dispassionately over her appearance, and then alit on Natasha with a raised eyebrow.

"Miss Jones," he greeted her with a nod when his eyes returned to her.

"Mr. Donovan," she nodded back. "Allow me to introduce my friend, Natasha Washington."

"It's a pleasure to meet you, Natasha," His Highness said in a tone that implied this meeting was anything but a pleasure. He then turned to the man on his right and said, "Ben, I'd like to present Mariah Jones, my new personal assistant. Miss Jones, my best friend Benjamin Caldwell, and his sister Caroline, the current director of the marketing department."

"It's a pleasure to meet you both," Mariah said with a smile. When she glanced up at Ben, her smile felt more genuine for the first time in a long while. Ben smiled down at her with real warmth, and when he turned toward Natasha his smile widened just a bit.

"Miss Jones, I'd like a word with you," Mr. Donovan said as he distanced himself from Ben, Natasha, and Caroline.

"Yes?" she said as she followed him.

"Have you seen any of the potential investors on my list here tonight?" he asked.

"Yes, Mr. Donovan. Mr. Gonzales was over near the front of the silent auction tables about five minutes ago. Leah Donatella was in the powder room last time I saw her, and-"

"That's enough for now," he cut in. "We'll make our way toward Donatella first. Tell your friend you'll be busy."

"Yes, Mr. Donovan," she said.

Mariah turned toward Natasha, and stopped short. She saw Ben's sister, Caroline standing alone where she and Mr. Donovan had left them all together moments before. She approached Caroline and asked, "Did you see where my friend Natasha went?"

"It would seem that my eccentric brother is dragging her out to the dance floor, though why anybody would want to dance to such boring music is beyond me," Caroline said in a haughty tone.

Mariah let her eyes follow the direction of Caroline's gaze, and she saw Ben and Natasha approaching the dance floor. Natasha had a very telling little slump to her shoulders; she was obviously nervous. Ben's hand hovered near her waist for an instant without making actual contact; instead, he dropped his hand back down to his side and continued to walk without touching Natasha. "When they get back, will you let Natasha know that I had to go with Mr. Donovan?" Mariah asked, as her eyes stayed riveted to Ben and Natasha.

"Yes. And please tell John not to keep me waiting too long. I despise tepid affairs like this one."

"Certainly, Miss Caldwell," Mariah said. She was glad to be rid of the women. Caroline was obviously just as cold and prickly as her boss was.

Mariah spent the rest of the night following Mr. Donovan around, and watching him stumble his way through talking to every potential investor on her list. After the first half hour, it became obvious to her that his people skills were lacking. He didn't actually say anything offensive, but there was a general cold aloofness about him that most people seemed to find off-putting. His manner of speaking seemed to imply that he thought he was better than everyone else around him, and it was difficult to like someone with such a condescending attitude. Every investor they approached tonight asked questions about his new technology, but his single answer to all of their inquiries was that it was still in development and not open for detailed discussion with anyone who wasn't currently an investor. Mariah understood his need to be circumspect about his research, but he didn't have to deliver his answers with such terseness.

By the time they rejoined the rest of his party, Caroline looked like she was ready to slap someone, and Ben and Natasha were conversing like long lost friends.

"How did it go?" Ben asked.

"I think it went well. Better than the solar technology conference I attended in Germany a few months ago," Mr. Donovan answered.

Caroline walked up to his side and ran her manicured nails down his arm as she said, "I'm sure you were great tonight. They'll all be buzzing about you in the morning."

"Thanks," he said with an inscrutable look down at her. He then turned to Mariah and said, "Don't let me keep you any longer, Miss Jones. Feel free to dance or have a few drinks if you like. I won't need any more assistance tonight."

Mariah kept her posture straight, but on the inside she sagged in relief. The sooner she could get home to Ty the better. She would have left immediately if she hadn't happened to glance over at Natasha and Ben again. Natasha was obviously enjoying herself, and asking her to leave right now would have been cruel in Mariah's opinion. "Thanks, I think I'll just take a peek at a couple of the silent auction items I saw earlier. Have a good night, Mr. Donovan." She winked at Natasha as she walked away from them.

She pretended to be interested in random items, all the while very conscious of Caroline's eyes following her every move. Eventually, she found a quiet corner, and sat down alone. She'd been sitting for a few minutes when she heard her boss's voice near the entrance to the men's room.

"I'm telling you Ben, I'm not in the mood to listen to you go on about how much fun I should be having. Caroline is the only woman I know here, and she hates events like this."

"Well, I'm having the best time I've had in a long time. That girl Natasha is a good dancer, and she's pretty nice," Ben replied.

"What has that got to do with me? If you're having so much fun with her, why don't you go back to her and let me enjoy some peace?" His Highness grouched.

"You're making things awkward with all your damn frowning and scowling, man. Maybe if you'd ask your assistant to dance, it will come off as we're all just having fun, as opposed to I'm trying to have a one night stand with her," Ben said in a light hearted tone.

"Isn't that what you're shooting for? That's all girls like her are good for anyway," His Highness returned in a serious tone.

"Come on, you know me better than that. I like her."

"I won't tell Caroline you said that," His Highness said with a sigh.

"Tell me he said what?" Caroline suddenly became part of the conversation as she breezed right by Mariah with a stare in her direction.

Mariah fought the urge to return Caroline's stare. She looked down at her fingernails and tried to pretend she hadn't been listening to their little exchange.

"You're picking them young now," Caroline said with a snicker.

"What is that supposed to mean?" His Highness demanded.

"You should be a little more careful about who you surround yourself with. Your new personal assistant has gold digger written all over her," Caroline said in a faux whisper.

His Highness snorted and said, "I'm not even halfway temped; she's mediocre at best. It takes a lot more than a sob story and a charity case to get *my* attention."

Mariah heard a high-pitched, feminine trill of laughter, and her ears burned. She knew that Caroline and His Highness had said those things for her benefit, and she didn't know which comment had been more mortifying. Her ears burned in embarrassment, and her anger rose so quickly she actually thought about quitting right then. She didn't have to put up with insults from her boss and his associates. She rose halfway out of her chair to go confront them, but then her situation came back to the forefront of her mind. She needed this job, at least until she found something different. The only thing she had power over was her reaction to their baiting, so she did her best to laugh it off. She stood up and walked toward Natasha with her best smile armed and ready.

In the car, Mariah relaxed for the first time in hours. She melted into the seat next to Natasha. "What did you think?" she asked with a smile.

"I thought he was one of the nicest men I've ever met."

"I meant about the ball, not about Ben," Mariah teased.

Natasha giggled. "I think I only had so much fun because of Ben," she admitted. "He got the musicians to play a waltz and taught me the steps while you were with your boss. It was the best night ever. I feel like Cinderella going home from the ball."

"Then I guess that means the night was a success. Ben really seemed to like you," Mariah commented with a sly look in Natasha's direction.

Natasha smiled and shook her head. "I know he was just being nice, and I'll probably never see him again. But that doesn't matter, because I had a great time."

"What makes you think you'll never see him again?" Mariah asked.

Natasha gave her a serious look and said, "Please, I may be quiet, but I'm not naïve. If I had flirted a little more, he probably would have offered me a ride home and then suggested we continue the evening at his place. We would have had a lot of the kind of 'fun' that gets women like me in trouble. I would have gone home half in love with him, and then he would have forgotten all about me by morning. Men like him don't care about women like me. He was nice, but I would have been just another notch on his bedpost."

Mariah gave Natasha's words some thought before she replied, "He really didn't strike me as that type of guy." She couldn't bring herself to elaborate on what she'd overheard, because she had no idea about Ben's intentions. She didn't want to be the one to give Natasha false hope. They rode the rest of the way to Natasha's house in silence.

As Mariah changed into one of the "house bikinis" she silently cursed her boss and all the men out there who were just like him. She hadn't planned to attend any private parties, especially not ones where she'd have to get her hair wet. She'd spent all morning making it look perfect. It was Saturday, and she should be free to spend the day with Ty; instead she was working for His Highness.

Over the past few weeks, Mariah had started to develop a better rapport with his potential investors than he could ever hope to have, and her reward for being such a good personal assistant was more work. Why did she have to attend this nightmare of an event just because one of his potential investors was hosting it? The invitation hadn't included her, but he'd demanded that she come anyway. Life was so unfair.

Mariah looked in the mirror and wondered why there were no modest bathing suit choices in the pool house. *Because men were pigs, that's why...* she thought as she looked at her reflection. *Especially rich, successful men like her boss and her late husband.* She tried to block out everything she'd ever liked about Tiberius as she stared at her reflection. She had a three and a half month old son, and here she was at a stupid pool party, wearing a stupid bikini while her son was in another woman's arms. Mariah had tried her best to get Natasha to tag along, but she'd adamantly refused. Once Natasha had admitted that she didn't know how to swim, Mariah had dropped the matter. She didn't have time to teach Natasha to swim in just one day, so she filed it away into her 'someday when I have time' category of things to do.

Mariah gathered up as much courage as she could by posing and flexing in the mirror before going out in the open in the little black, sporty top and boy shorts bikini she chose. It was the choice with the most coverage, yet she still felt nearly naked when she stepped out into the sunlight. Instead of diving into the deep end of the pool as almost everyone else did, she sat down on the edge of the shallow end and hung her feet into the water. After about half an hour of solitude, her boss walked up beside her.

"You know, you're allowed to have at least a little fun. I won't need you in any official capacity until a little later in the afternoon," he said.

Before Mariah could reply, Caroline sashayed up beside him and raised her eyebrows in that supercilious way that Mariah had come to hate over the past few weeks of knowing her. "What's wrong, Miss Jones?" Caroline snickered. "Can't swim?"

Mariah gritted her teeth as she suppressed the initial retort that sprang to mind. "I just don't want to get my hair wet," she admitted instead.

"You black girls and your hair," Caroline laughed as she walked away.

Mr. Donovan made eye contact with Mariah for an uncomfortable moment before going after Caroline. When he caught up to her, he frowned down at her, said a few words, and then walked away. Mariah didn't know what to make of his behavior, especially after Caroline's eyes shot daggers back in her direction. A short time later, Caroline strutted out onto the diving board and posed before executing a very ordinary and amateur looking dive.

Mariah liked to think of herself as someone who didn't show off too much, but after watching Caroline's dive, and after enduring that woman's taunts and almost nonstop snide remarks, there was no way she'd forgo the opportunity to show her up on the diving board. Mariah's adoptive mother had been an Olympic medalist in the 1990's, and she'd taught Mariah how to dive early on in their mother daughter relationship. Mariah hadn't been as good as her mother was, but she had been one of the strongest members on her collegiate diving team.

She got out of the shallow end and walked calmly toward the diving boards. No one paid any attention to her until she began the long climb up to the highest diving platform. No one else had dared to use it yet, and when she stepped onto it she sensed more and more eyes on her. She was vaguely aware of Caroline hissing at her from below, "Jesus! I was kidding. Don't kill yourself!"

Mariah ignored her as she centered herself, and then prepared to execute the dive that had almost won her a national title back in her college days. She'd made a crucial mistake in competition, but in the years since, she had consistently done it right countless times in her pool at home with Tiberius watching. She closed her eyes and repeated the moves to herself as she pictured herself doing them in her head, *inward one and a half somersaults in the open pike position*, she thought just before she sprang off the dive platform. After she executed the moves, the sudden plunge into the crisp water was so exhilarating that she momentarily forgot all her animosity towards Caroline. Once her face broke the surface of the water, she heard a smattering of applause coming from everyone around the pool. When she got out, she caught a glimpse of Caroline's face; her look of complete shock made the wet hair more than worth it. Mariah quietly walked back to the shallow end and resumed her post on the boring side of the pool; she had made her point.

She ignored the fact that His Highness's eyes had been on her the entire time, at least she tried to. He was probably still trying to get over the shock of coming across a "black girl" who could swim so well, and she didn't mind at all being the one to dispel the stereotype that all African Americans were terrible swimmers. If he disapproved of her making a spectacle or herself, he could just let her stay home next time he was invited to some ridiculous party.

About The Author

My name is Adrienne D'nelle Ruvalcaba. I was born and raised in Southeast Texas. After high school, I joined the U.S. Army and served four years at Fort Campbell, KY. During my time there, I married a fellow soldier and had two children. Following my years in the service, I ended up as a single parent. After setting out on my own with my two children, I enrolled in the Engineering program at Southern Illinois University.

While at SIU, I completed my bachelor's degree in Civil Engineering with a concentration in structural analysis. Also while at SIU, I was diagnosed with Systemic Lupus Erythematosus. This diagnosis significantly changed my life. Since the onset of this disease, I have learned a lot about those around me and even more about myself. Due to some serious and sobering complications, my health has declined in recent years. I am no longer able to spend time outside with my children, or do many of the things that I used to take for granted. I'm in my early 30's, but most of the time I feel much older. After a few years of struggling to accept this illness as a part of my life, I've finally come to a more peaceful place. The most important thing I've learned while dealing with this disease is that it does not define who I am.

I've been writing since grade school, and I often take solace in the world I create in my imagination. Most of what I write is romantic fiction, meant purely for emotional fulfillment, enjoyment, and sweet escapism. Real life is difficult enough, and I believe we all need a little break from it sometimes.